HOLOGRAM

A Novel

by Jo Deniau

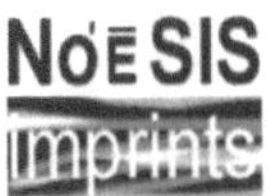

Published April 8, 2024
Printed in the United States of America

Print ISBN: 979-8-218-39261-1
Imprint: Independently published

LC Control Number: 1-13057599821

Cover Designer and Artist: Roksolana McFadden
Copy Editing, Development Editing, and Book Formatting: Jo Deniau

For information, address:
Nóēsis Imprints
P.O. Box 5723
Clearwater, FL 33758

Dedication

To all those who seek Truth, whether seen or unseen, I offer this book to bring you enjoyment, inspiration, and knowledge on your journey. I also dedicate my novel to all First Loves who were lost or abandoned, or who chose to walk the Earth with someone else at their side.

Acknowledgements

Thank you beyond measure, Catherine Alder, for being a dear friend for so many years, for boosting me up when I needed to keep believing in myself, and for being such an astute beta reader. *Merci beaucoup* to my special Aussie friend, Jeannine Bonnefin, whose invaluable support during the layers of final editing of *Hologram*—and whose "eagle eyes" after its completion—helped me keep the faith. Karen Anderson, I treasure our friendship from my many Boulder years, and I thank you for your pronouncement that *Hologram* is "an Aquarian book" while it was still in its adolescent form. And Jaymee Brandt, friend and alpha reader, I am most grateful for your recognizing *Hologram*'s worth when it was still rough around the edges.

Special thanks to teachers along the way who helped me hone my skills as a writer and editor. My seventh grade teacher, Joanne Malbone, you read passages from my essays to your unruly class of thirteen-year-olds. You assigned such topics as "Forgiveness," and you didn't flunk my piece called "Attack of the Killer Asparagus." Loving appreciation to the late Lee Dixon, copy editor at Curtis Publishing. You took me under your wing, helped me be a better editor-writer, and became my *spiritual* mother. When I visited you in Roswell, New Mexico, you didn't mention Area 51 though. I miss you. And much gratitude to the late Demia Butler Professor, Nancy Moore, who gave me a "C" on my first Advanced Freshman English essay. My crowning achievement as a senior at Butler was to earn an "A" from you in 18th Century Literature. And, Miss Moore, I know your exacting standards helped me be one of only three out of eight aspirants who passed the Master's comprehensive exams during an eight hour marathon of essay writing in the Spring of my graduation year.

Author's Preface

In many ways writing *Hologram* was an experiment for me. Writing *Hologram* stretched me as a writer, and sometimes that expansion of craft gave me literal headaches.

In contrast to wrestling with David Leone's internal and external dialog in *Hologram*, melding holography and metaphysics was a breeze. I'm a born researcher, so studying holography was fun. In addition, I lived for so many years in Boulder, perhaps the Metaphysical capital of the U.S., that even if I hadn't studied Metaphysics there I would have absorbed those vibes through osmosis.

My Marketing team calls *Hologram* "a metaphysical love story." I agree. Most readers note how interesting they find *Hologram* to be. To be simplistic, *Hologram* seems like "a head book." My first novel, *Stiff Hearts,* is decidedly "a heart book." The truth is that both novels are about becoming a heart-centered person and both of my protagonists must transcend what blocks them from enjoying heart-based relationships with others. — Jo Deniau

CHAPTER ONE

I swear, when I turned forty a rat toothed voice hissed: "David Leone's losing his virility." And a trash talking porcine tattled, "Hah! He's got that itch." In one bleak moment I noticed my arms looked like planks of cheapo poached salmon. Dammit! I'd started dumpling, too, above my belt. "Love handles." Gimme a break! Until that dismal fortieth, my sense of my own mortality was like a teenager's—nada. Now it was like all my cells cast digital death signals twenty-four-seven. I cursed my youth genes for waving their little white flags on the front lines of that fateful forty. A couple of days, weeks, and whammo! I noticed my decay suddenly. Like a toothache.

On the evening of my fortieth, my wife Jeanie (queen of the eye roll) and teenage son Eddie dragged me to the Hotel Boulderado. It wasn't my first time there. Guys from OPTIKS and I used to hang out on the second-level Mezzanine when there was a decent jazz quintet. But Jeanie squelched my partying a few years back. The beauty of the Victorian architecture in the white-pillared lobby stunned me anew. Liqueur-rich cherrywood everywhere, including the wall paneling and a cantilevered five-story staircase. Above, a long skylight canopy of stained-glass. Savvy visitors know about the special drinking fountain with the faux gold bubbler head just outside the public restrooms. There you can imbibe the sweetest, purest water you ever tasted, piped in from the Arapaho Glacier. There you can also walk on the original mosaic tile floors.

While we waited outside the hotel's restaurant for the *maître d'*, I tried conversing with my son. "I heard Calamity Jane ran a brothel in the Hotel Boulderado."

Jeanie glared at me. "That's really what you want to tell Eddie?"

"She died in 1903," Eddie said. "Before the hotel was even built."

I couldn't believe it. "How can you possibly know the date?"

"Her real name was Martha Jane Canary."

"Canary," I said. "Okay, what about the rumor there's haunted rooms on the top level?"

Jeanie shook her head. She then spooned a couple of little pink mints into her hand from a porcelain dish on top of a pulpit-like stand. Then she helped herself to a few white mints.

"Yeah," Eddie said. "They won't let people stay up there because of a rocking chair that rocks by itself."

Jeanie laughed. "Well, *I* happen to know that Benny Goodman and Louis Armstrong stayed here."

I put my arm around her. "That's because you're so musical." Over the years I had learned that a little flattery went a long way with my wife. I continued: "And there's a myth about a woman in a long gold dress standing up there by the balcony rail."

"I can confirm that," Eddie said. "A young woman jumped off the balcony to her death. The newspaper clippings said her gown was 'daffodil-yellow'."

"Daffodil."

"We should order champagne," Jeanie said.

The *maître d'* seated us by an open window on a covered porch outside the main dining area. The late-Spring air teased my skin. On Spruce Street, Yellow Cabs pulled up, and tourists heading back to Denver International defended their luggage from rowdy passersby. An occasional car snailed by, its "hangry" couple hoping for a miracle spot in the glutted parking lot across the street. Wispy chains of intermingled smoke separated above the miniature hurricane lamps on our table. Beads of condensation drizzled down our water glasses.

Eddie swabbed his fingers on the supple thigh of his dress jeans. My son had a way of turning nonchalance into a shield for whatever mischief he wished to embrace.

Jeanie noticed this little travesty. "Use your napkin, Eddie."

"Oh, let your men be Cossacks for one night," I said. But I knew that when we got home… My prime rib was superbly broiled yet gave me no joy. The fresh baked dark wheat bread and *al dente* asparagus tasted photocopied. On my tongue the champagne flattened like an un-pettable cat. Recent fantasies of my high school sweetheart Lucille Muhr had hijacked my palate. Lu was the girl I lost. She is also now a famous movie star. I never understood what Lu saw in *me*. I'm five-foot-ten, with kinky brown hair and smallish blue eyes a little too close together. True to my surname, I have a big Italian nose.

For just a few moments I let my former hometown honey steal the spotlight from my ho-hum life. While Jeanie and Eddie chatted and noshed, I wished *Lu* was sitting there. I plunged headfirst into flashbacks of Lu, which made me feel alive again. I thought only of Lu now. While in high school, Lu and I necked and kissed for hours at the drive-in movie theater just outside Circleville, Ohio, in my 1956 sky blue and white Chevrolet sedan. I didn't care that kissing Lu made my metal braces sting the insides of my lips. We barely came up for air to peek at the big outdoor screen in front of row after row of cars. On chilly autumn nights the metal heater that hung on the inside of Lu's passenger window was a joke. Everyone's car windows steamed up while we all ignored the triple features we guys paid for.

My memories of Lu were not just lusty. Her essence, her bearing, bagged me forever. I prized the way Lu coasted through a room, chin held high. She was regal yet obliging. Striking, with no hint of conceit. Alluring...and oh so vulnerable. I fell in love with *that* Lu, and I stayed in love with her. Just recalling Lu's mahogany eyes jellied my insides. I longed to see her on screen. I just knew watching her on film would ease this ache. But early on, Jeanie had threatened divorce if I saw any of Lu's films. I often wondered how my wife would even know. What a wimp I was to obey her. The love friction caused by Jeanie's jealousy was catalytic. And damned near cataclysmic. Like a juvenile delinquent, I acted out. I hid my rebellion at home but let it rip when I thought no one was looking.

My work at OPTIKS, a private research foundation in Boulder, had also grown stale. I'd been shining laser light, bending it, and bouncing it off mirrors so long that it was second nature. Mostly, I'd let holograms entertain me. And I still found it challenging to do a multiplex hologram with a full 360-degree parallax. But now I wanted out. Out of my doldrums, out of my dull marriage, out of my same ol' same ol'. I tried to deny I could ever reach some point of no return. Until a little me-voice said: *Got to do something drastic to get that asshole's attention.* (Emphasis on *asshole.*) *Tell him he better do something* weighty *before his time runs out.* I was caught in a time warp, meeting myself coming and going. I felt locked in a loop where ditched dreams might crash into events and *define my purpose.*

They say, "Be careful what you ask for." Smack in the middle of my crisis I accepted a holographic challenge. The result: a scientific discovery that would make me famous—for all the wrong reasons.

The switchboard at OPTIKS transferred the phone call from Denver millionaire Harcourt Raymond III. "I read the interview with you in last month's Sunday *Camera*," Court said. "Impressive. Do you ever freelance? I want you do a hologram of my daughter."

I panicked. All I felt like doing after work these days was drink a few Coors beers and watch Cable TV in my basement hideaway. I spluttered, "I'm sorry if I got carried away with something that just popped into my head in that interview. I'm an industrial holographer, Mr. Raymond. Not an artist." I could hear Court breathing at the other end of the phone line. He said nothing. Just breathed. It was clear that he was waiting for me to "get" something. I had no clue, so I tried to outwait him. It was no use. I said, "Okay, but to me the *project's* the most important thing."

Court finally spoke: "I wondered if you'd welcome a chance to elevate your work. You want an extraordinary life, don't you?"

This threw me for a loop! I pictured myself at the top of a rocky cliff, about to swan dive into a turquoise pool thirty feet below me. Too much to ask. Here was a king of Denver business, challenging me to transcend the banal. Hoping I'd recast myself from cliché to creator. I could feel a herd of crazy-ass chickens stalking me, staring at me with their bifocal Jurassic eyes. They cackled in my face, full-throated and full-throttle, about what a specimen of poultry *I* was.

Court spoiled my luxurious self-flagellation. "We're both busy men, Mr. Leone. If you need more time to decide—."

"Yes," I said. "I will make the hologram for you."

"You don't strike me as a man who needs a dress rehearsal. So just know you'll be making a holographic portrait of my daughter and her groom at their wedding reception. It's in two weeks, I'll have my secretary call you with directions to our home. When you get here, the logistics will be up to you."

The freedom Court had just given me to do his project scared me as much as it inspired me. It took until 3:00 a.m. the next morning for me to figure out how to pull off something I'd never tried before. After my third can of Coors beer I had it: I would use a brief film sequence to create a spectacular little moving hologram.

Two Weeks Later

I had slept only a few hours before driving to Denver in my beat up 1978 Ford Bronco. My SUV was muted green and white, with faux wood paneling on the sides. I called my truck "Woody" á la Beach Boys' surfer slang. My drive to central Denver would take about thirty-five minutes. For a change, traffic was light in the sharp curves of "the mousetrap" interchange between I-25 and I-70. A sweet, rare thing. My destination was just a few blocks from the original Victorian home of the "Unsinkable" Molly Brown on North Pennsylvania Street. During a Channel 4 news story, anchor Bob Palmer claimed Molly's own mother saw the ghost of a dead servant ascending the front stairs. People have also seen a ghost cat prowling the mansion's rooms. Though I'd read about ghosts, I didn't believe in them.

I drove up a long pale pink brick driveway past a carriage house on the left. As Court had asked, I parked behind his mansion. I surveyed the palatial main house before knocking on the door of a private entrance that was just off a huge *cordon bleu* kitchen. Harlan, Court's butler-chauffeur met me there. He smelled like freshly laundered sheets flapping on a clothesline in Rocky Mountain breezes. Harlan was less imposing and younger than I'd imagined. About fiftyish, just under six feet tall, he wore a navy blue sports jacket and gray dress slacks. With Jeanie's help, I had managed a wheaten twill blazer with a white shirt and brown-check tie but, well, my chinos…

Harlan brought me down a long hallway that was lit from above with ceiling *spots*. From a distance I could hear Melissa Manchester's fervent "Through the Eyes of Love." Harlan led me past the open doors of the mansion's vast ballroom, where guests slow-danced and drank potent (I assumed) mixed drinks and champagne. Clever lighting made the ballroom seem filled with candlelight. Some of the guests propped themselves up with their elbows on the linen tablecloths of side tables. Not as rumpled, others managed to sit upright in their ornate white wrought iron café chairs. I could smell the Sterno keeping entrees hot on the teeming buffet tables. Also: *eau de* scallops, crab cakes, bleu cheese, capers, and red onions made my passage savory.

Harlan showed me into Court's study. He then closed the French doors behind him. There I saw Court—a stately man with gray, slightly thinning hair, white at the temples. He sat in a burgundy leather overstuffed chair. He was on the near edge of portly. The large irises of his eyes left little room for the white sclera around each, making him look unnatural. During our conversation Court seldom met my eye. Rather, he often looked up and around himself as though expecting rain. He gestured toward a highly lacquered oak table and deep rose colored swivel chair about six feet away.

Court's sweeping gaze finally netted me. "Do sit down. Just to be clear, I want the hologram mostly for its novelty, though I have a keen interest in the optics side of science. When I was young, I wanted to be a research scientist. Or a classical pianist. Having aptitude for neither, I decided to make money instead." Here Court paused. "But back to the matter at hand. About my daughter Reynie. She is a champion horsewoman. She was an Olympic hopeful. Reynie still rides almost every day, but she no longer competes, thank God."

By nodding, I hoped to convey I understood. I did note the intensity of Court's "thank God."

"When Paul LaSalle—that's Reynie's groom—proposed, she quickly recovered from her disappointment at failing to qualify for the U.S. team." For the first time, Court smiled. "And Paul is not the only one who's relieved Reynie is no longer jet-setting all over the globe to compete. She's a glorious handful," Court added, "and I wouldn't change a thing about her."

I wanted Court to feel comfortable with our project. I asked him how much he knew about making holograms.

"The bare minimum."

"Do you have time for me to explain? Just the basics."

"I do have time."

"Okay then. A *gram* is writing about, or drawing a record of, something. *Holo* means that it's a whole, complete, or entire record. Making a holographic plate is in some ways like shooting with photographic film. But when you make a hologram you split a laser beam so that part of the beam reflects off a mirror and the other part off a *subject*." I asked Court to stand up. "This will help me explain."

Court stood up.

"Say you are the 'subject' of my hologram. A laser beam projects onto you. Then the hologram records what's called an 'interference pattern'. You, planted there, create that interference pattern in space. It's like standing waist deep in a still pool of water and then starting to move. Ripples form around your body and create patterns in the water. A *picture* of that wave pattern in the water shows how the movement of your body interferes with the water around you. Simply stated: A hologram reflects how a subject interferes with the movement of light.

Court grinned. "You would make a good teacher, David."

I didn't let on that teaching was my idea of hell. Stuck in a classroom with a tribe of the pimple-faced semi-literate. After all, I had been one of those students. I remembered how often I looked at the big wall clock during lectures under the glare of fluorescent lights. I sat in the back in case I fell asleep.

Court encouraged me to continue.

"So to 'play back' a true hologram, you illuminate the holographic plate from behind with the same coherent laser transmission. 'Coherent' means the laser light's frequency and wavelength don't vary. When you replay a hologram of a person with the laser beam aimed at a precise angle, the image of that person seems to hang in space."

Court looked excited. "Is that what you'll be making today?"

"I'll be making something even better. Fusing cinematography with holography to make a moving hologram."

"But How?"

"Basically with 35mm film. The result won't be a hologram in the purest sense. It'll be what's called an *integral*. A holographic 'cheat', lit from behind by plain incandescent white light. A transmission hologram. But the result won't disappoint you."

"I suppose I'll understand better when it's finished," Court said. "How will I view the hologram?"

"You'll stand three feet in front the hologram. It will seem so real you'll want to touch it. It will look like a beautiful sculpture of light. Or seem like a vivid memory. But here's the thing: if you saw a hologram of *yourself* it would freak you out. Seeing your reflection in a mirror or in a photograph is *not* the way other people see you. Looking at a hologram of *you* is like seeing a stranger across a street who reminds you of someone. It seems to call out to you, as they say some ghosts do." I shifted in my chair when I heard myself say the word "ghost."

Court got that I was anxious to start. "Shall we begin then?"

I released myself from my chair's comfy embrace. "Where do you want me to take the hologram, Mr. Raymond?"

"In the foyer. Under the skylight. And please call me 'Court'."

My excitement almost made me miss Court's invitation. Outside his study I stopped. "Could you ask your daughter and Paul to follow my instructions to the letter? Or else they'll ruin the hologram."

Court looked worried. "I'm sure they've had a lot of champagne, but who could blame them?"

We reached the expansive foyer. "Maybe start them on coffee?

"Splendid idea," Court said.

"But also have them bring two champagne glasses."

Court looked surprised. "I won't ask why. Because I figure you must have a good reason. I'll have Harlan fetch your equipment."

"Just the turntable and motor platform. I'd rather bring in the delicate instruments myself."

Court looked at me for a full fifteen seconds. It was the first time he had met my eyes directly. Now the irises of his eyes showed. "This means more to me than…" He seemed embarrassed.

"I won't disappoint you, Court" I answered.

An Hour Later

High on myriad alcoholic spirits, guests babbled softly in the ballroom. Their hammered languor was contagious. I longed to take a nap. Suddenly the Kahlúa-and-coffee voice of the DJ urged the guests to "groove" on the next song. The Cars' "Drive" began to play.

Who's gonna tell you when
It's too late?
Who's gonna tell you things
Aren't so great?

Soft blue lighting bathed the guests who were still vertical. Wrapped like wreaths around each other's bodies, they danced to their personal mystic songs. I focused on rebounding from what the lyrics to "Drive" had done to me. Made me wonder how a life with Lucille Muhr might have been. The tune made me long to hold her. But I had no right. I had betrayed her.

From inside the ballroom, Harlan watched me and waited. His entire visage inquired: "Are you okay?"

I looked away. Then Harlan whispered something to Reynie and Paul. Fancy coffee cups and saucers in hand, they followed him off the dance floor.

To me, Reynie Raymond did not resemble her father. Her strawberry blonde hair looked like it might *ignite* any second. And her tawny brown eyes reminded me of cat's eye marbles I kept in a little *chamois* cloth drawstring bag when I was a kid. Micro expressions of mischief darted across her face. The numbers of twitches at the corners of Reynie's mouth told me she had a sensitive "B.S. detector." Her groom, Paul LaSalle, looked like a cover model for *Esquire* Magazine. He was tall, attractive, clean-cut, and masculine. Unlike many Denverites who had ski goggle face tans, Paul looked to be bronzed all over. His hands and wrists, his neck. And his beautifully cut brown hair was sun-streaked. Perhaps he was a corporate lawyer? He was subtle but also sharp. I almost missed him sizing me up.

I couldn't ignore the song's lyrics, goading me.

Who's gonna hold you down
When you shake?
Who's gonna come around
When you break?
You can't go on,
Thinking Nothing's wrong,
Oh no.

All these years I hadn't been there for Lucille Muhr. Worse, I had no clue about what she had suffered without having my support. All those years of living with Jeanie and Eddie instead had turned my vague guilt into stabbing remorse. Knowing Lu must have lovers, suitors, made me jealous. But I had no right. My knees felt weak. Harlan had taken me by the arm. By the time we reached the foyer I managed to pull myself together.

To avoid as much vibration as possible, I asked everyone but Reynie and Paul to clear out. When Harlan told the DJ to stop the music, a murmur—rather, a group growl—spread among the hammered guests. I also asked Harlan to turn off the huge, multitiered crystal chandelier. I had set up my eight-foot motorized and calibrated turntable under the chandelier so natural light could shine down from above. Because the bride and groom were still half-lit when I began my work, I was afraid they'd sabotage the result. The process required me to take a 35mm movie sequence. Because I was making a 120-degree hologram, I needed to shoot 360 separate frames, with my movie camera and lights remaining stationary. Each 35mm frame recorded one third of a degree of motion.

"Please hold still," I said to the couple.

Court leaned his body just inside a doorway about twenty feet from Reynie and Paul. He peered into the foyer, his eyes aglow.

Reynie laughed. To Paul she said about me: "Who *is* this guy?"

I tried coaxing the couple. "Just try and get used to the turntable before I actually start."

Paul caught Reynie as she tilted toward him. "I've got you, Darling," he said to his bride.

Twenty-five minutes later I had shot enough 35mm frames to be ready for the denouement. I said to Reynie and her groom, "This part is a rehearsal. I want you to clink your champagne glasses together and hold that position. Not so hard! Just touch them together. That's right." I did a reading with my interferometer—an instrument that measures the limits of vibration the holographic process will tolerate. At the time, I knew it was foolish to risk the distortion that the glass clinking might cause, but something told me to go ahead with it. I began to shoot the sequence. Reynie and Paul looked dreamily into each other's eyes. I began the stop-frame sequence and I asked them to touch champagne glasses again. This time in slow-motion.

It was dusk when I headed back to Boulder. The sparse traffic felt kind of weird but made me happy. When I topped Davidson Mesa off Route 36 West, I pulled Woody off the road and parked at the overlook so I could see my city at night. This view never failed to chill me out. The view was my respite before going home. Before having to reassume the duties of being a husband and father. That night, seeing Boulder below took me back to when I moved from Circleville to attend CU. Unlike the flats of the Midwest, here were contours, hills, and mountains. Winking lights adorned my town, nestled in the valley by the Foothills of the Rockies' Front Range. No matter what the season, at night Boulder's sparkles made the burg look like Christmas.

Wee Hours of the Morning

In my basement lab I processed the holographic film and ran it through my special printer. Next I illuminated each frame with a laser beam and projected the beam through a cylindrical lens. The lens focuses an image into a vertical line. Then I holographically recorded this vertical line on Agfa Gevaert, high resolution film, twice for each 35mm frame. Finally, I mounted the result on a standard curved display—a transparent plastic cylinder. The result: a true color, three-dimensional image that seemed to hover in space. I made the display cylinder revolve so that a viewer could remain stationary and the image would move. If you lowered or raised your body, you would see the image shift through every color of the spectrum. Plus, if you reached inside the cylinder, your hand would pass right through the image. I was sure Court and his daughter would be impressed.

When I played back my work, I noticed some cloudiness that was not in the original 35mm film. What if vibration had ruined my expensive project? What if there was a glitch in the holographic conversion phase? But something about this blurry effect puzzled me: If vibration *had* caused a distortion, why did the images of the bride and groom look so sharp? Any jiggling would have left a kind of "black hole" in the hologram. I took another look at the hologram in motion. I noticed that the gauzy image gradually cleared. Then the image turned into a likeness of a little girl next to the bride!

I examined the hologram over and over. When I compared the holographic image with the film, frame by frame, I saw no fuzziness in the film version. There was only Reynie and Paul, *chinking* their champagne glasses together. This fact defied all I knew about combining cinematography with holography. I'd spent all our savings on state of the art holographic equipment, pending my commission. Dread reared its ugly head, for I had no idea what I'd do if Court reneged on his offer. Jeanie would *kill me*.

CHAPTER TWO

I called in sick the next morning. After treating myself to breakfast crêpes at Pour La France on the west end of the Mall, I took Broadway to Baseline and picked up US Route 36 to Denver. My hands relaxed on the steering wheel when I got through the Mousetrap and merged effortlessly onto I-70 to Denver. Long before, I had learned the trick of hitting the highway fifteen minutes after the hour. Lighter traffic graced my splendid, canny planning.

When I joined Court in his study to show him the hologram, he was enthusiastic—until he saw the spooky little girl standing beside his daughter. He sat down heavily in his leather chair and loosened his gray silk tie. His tie had little burgundy griffins on it. Again, the whites of his eyes barely showed. In its display, the hologram glowed.

Can I salvage my creation? Redeem myself? I wondered. "What fascinates me most," I told Court, "is the way this little girl's image starts out blurry. Then it becomes crystal clear just as the couple touches their glasses together. And see this warm glow of light shining on the couple from above? The chandelier was turned off." I let this fact sink in. Then I noted out loud how sad the child looked. Court looked stricken. I was afraid to ask him the obvious question. But I did ask him "Do you know who this might be?"

He watched the image of the little girl take form over and over. "It's incredible. How did you do this?"

"It just happened," I said. I shifted my feet. "It *is* incredible." Now I wondered if the ghost image was Reynie as a kid.

Court pulled a monogrammed handkerchief out of his pocket and dabbed at his upper lip. "But I don't understand." He looked agitated.

"Is this Reynie? Maybe something happened to her when she was a kid," I offered. "Like an accident or some other kind of trauma?"

Court looked rattled. He stood now with his hands clasped over his privates. "My daughter rarely showed unhappy feelings when she was a child. You know how children can keep things inside for years. And friends have told me they didn't hear about those things 'til *their* children were parents."

I wondered what Court was hiding. "Maybe you were reminiscing about your little girl at her reception? You know. Because you were giving up your only child in marriage?"

Court's eyes darted...everywhere. "I don't see what you mean. I am happy for Reynie. She's married a fine man who loves her very much. Who'll be a good provider."

I wanted to give Court all the reasons why this hologram was so puzzling to me. Scientifically. However being gutless by nature, I just stared at the gold torsion dome clock on Court's mantel. That moment my tension paralleled the 15-second oscillation of the pendulum—the twisting and untwisting of the spring that drove the mechanism. Tension surged in every muscle of my body.

Thank God he finally spoke: "What bothers *you* most about this?" It was the first time I noticed his uncanny way of seeing the whole picture at once.

"That this little girl *is* Reynie."

Court still had that weird look on his face. Like he was still holding something back.

I asked him if I could see some childhood photographs of Reynie to compare with what the hologram picked up. After I'd looked at three photos, I believed the image really was that of a much younger Reynie. Then I knew this was what Court hadn't admitted, but why?

At the back entrance of the Raymond mansion, Court handed me a stiff legal sized manila envelope. "Here is the commission we agreed on, You have more than fulfilled our contract." Just as he was showing me out, he stopped short. "My lovely wife Reynelda died when Reynie was seven. Neither of us has recovered. Do you believe that has anything to do—."

"I think it has *everything* to do with it!" A *eureka* feeling snapped like a launched pinball and bounced around in my brain. "I think I know how that little girl showed up. Maybe all those chandelier prisms—and the sound of the champagne glasses somehow…"

Court twisted his platinum wedding band. "I want to study that hologram. Figure how to prepare my daughter. When she gets back from her honeymoon I'll show it to her. Then we'll let *her* decide if she wants to keep it."

Later that day my best friend Josh stopped by and Jeanie sent him downstairs to my basement lab. Josh was the best person in the world to share things with. He asks only interesting questions and loves Coors beer. He noted that I looked "wrecked." When I showed him what I now call "Reynie Junior," he whistled. He took a deep swig of

Coors and ran his fingers through his Robert Redford hair. "Dave. Are you sure there was nothing wrong with your technique?"

"Trust me. I don't know. Unless it has something to do with the chandelier. And the frame where their champagne glasses meet. When I look at this hologram I get a feeling of *déjà vu*. Like in CU in my Physio and Anatomy lab the first time I saw a human fetus in a jar of formaldehyde. That fetus was dead, Josh. Yet it seemed so close to being alive that it gave me goosebumps. It was like I was looking into another dimension. Optical illusion meets the New Physics. Something science can't explain."

"Maybe the little girl is a ghost," Josh said. "I've heard of ghosts showing up in photos, but those ghosts are dead people."

"Maybe it was a dead sibling of Reynie's?"

Josh leaned forward. He'd never looked so serious. "My Grandma Peterson went through this little routine every day of her married life for fifty years. Every morning she got up, slammed her bedroom door, and went downstairs. You could hear every stair step creak. You could hear the rattling of muffin tins in the kitchen while Grandma got breakfast ready. For a month after she died, Grampa heard those same sounds every morning. After a while, he got used to it. He even found it comforting."

"Want to hear something bizarre? I think ghosts *might* be holograms. That any action repeated enough leaves traces we see as pictures. Even hear as sounds. And when someone has intense trauma at the moment of death, even stronger traces might remain."

"Then why didn't your hologram show the dead mother instead of the daughter, who's still alive?"

"I'm still working that out. I'm also trying to figure out how something non-physical can create an interference pattern."

Josh turned his green eyes toward Reynie's hologram again and said: "Getting back to your ghost theory, what about poltergeists? There's a lot of documented cases of poltergeists throwing things." He handed me another Coors.

I savored the moment, waited to pop the beer tab. "I think the energy that leaves those traces is like any kind of kinetic energy. That energy has the potential to move objects. Sometimes the propelling force even breaks things. I don't believe ghosts are *conscious* entities though. The moving of objects is just a translation of energy into kinetic force. Because the poltergeists are dead, I don't believe it's *they* who are hurting or scaring us. Their energy traces merely exist. When we sometimes happen to get in the way of a flying object, we're sure some *thing* 'threw' the object out of malice."

"If that's true," Josh said, "then how can some people *see* them?"

I'd never shared my work, or my deepest secrets, with Josh before that afternoon. It was fun hearing him echo my own thoughts of the last twenty four hours. Finally I said, "If you think about it, all kinds of energy can be translated back and forth. For example, when you make a long-distance call with fiber optics, your voice goes in one end. It gets translated into light beams that travel through thin glass wires and comes out the other end again as sound. Here's another example. Say the Russians aim a microwave beam at an American Embassy's glass window. Beside the window two American agents are discussing some top-secret, classified stuff. The microwave beam ricochets back to the Russian Embassy at just the right angle. The Ruskies intercept that as sound and tape the conversation. It's documented."

Josh stood in front of the cylinder. "Well, what will you do with your big discovery now? Is that guy, what's-his-name, still going to pay you for it?"

"Yeah. Court did pay me. But it's not as simple as that. I still have too many questions, and lots of other things are going on right now."

"Like with Jeanie."

"That's just it. I should be happy." I checked Josh's face to make sure I could trust him. "I've been thinking a lot about Lucille Muhr."

"The actress?"

"She was my hometown honey in high school," I added, hardly believing it myself.

"Are you kidding me?"

"There's more," I said.

"Hey. I saw where she's going to be on 'Showbiz Tonite'."

"When?"

Josh winked. "Afraid you're gonna have to look that up in *TV News*. Do you subscribe?"

"Yes I do." I sighed. "It's been twenty one years. Ah, Lu! None of our graduating class of two hundred ever dreamed she'd be famous."

"You grew up in Ohio, right?"

"Yeah. Circleville. We were 'the Circleville Tigers'. You know, in school, Lu was kind of a wallflower until our Junior year. Then she seemed to rise like a phoenix. She went on to Ohio State for her Bachelor's. Majored in theater. She starred in every kind of play they cast her in. Light comedies and musicals. Shakespeare even. But if she were mad or annoyed, she could *cinderize* you from across the room with her eyes. One time she kicked my orange Camaro like it was her rival. Dad bought it for me when I entered CU so I wouldn't become a hippy."

"Did that work?"

"I did wear an Afro," I said.

"What did she look like then?"

"Straight dark auburn hair, parted down the middle. Dark eyes, beautiful olive skin. Lovely body. About five-foot-six. Her last name means 'Moor'."

Josh thanked me for my "translation" and popped open another Coors for himself. "She still looks like that."

"God, it's hot down here!"

Josh ogled me. "And you never got over her."

"Eight years ago Lu called me from the West Coast. Jeanie answered the phone in our bedroom. Without a word, Jeanie handed me the receiver. Then she just stood there. I asked Lu why she was calling. Lu said she didn't mean to intrude. I was bitter, so I said: 'And you still called?' When Jeanie left the room I blurted to Lu that I wasn't surprised she called. 'There are other ways to communicate', I said. 'My wife's father died two weeks ago. It was a time of remembering, if you know what I mean'."

Josh asked me what "other ways to communicate" meant.

"I guess I sort of *sent myself out* to her in a way. You know—when a memory's so clear that you relive it *and* you're there. I admit I was trying to escape all the bad vibes in our house."

"Were you close to your father-in-law?"

"He wasn't the warmest guy," I said.

"What happened *then*? Didn't you *want* to talk to her?"

"I did, and I didn't. It hurt to hear her voice. It brought back all kinds of confusing memories. I was afraid I wouldn't want to be *me*, here in Boulder, anymore. Lu said she wanted to tell me a couple of things so she 'could move forward emotionally'. At the time, I told myself I should be more worried about *Jeanie's* feelings than Lu's. Instead of listening to Lu, I reminded her of all the vicious things we said to one another in the past. When Jeanie came back to the room I stressed, three times, that Jeanie and I are committed to staying in Boulder. Lu said her first movie would premiere soon. I gave her some lame best wishes. I guess Jeanie told my parents about the call because Mom wrote Lu a letter. After that I never heard from Lu again. Mom did tell me that Lu wrote back to her. And Mom told me was that Lu said I was the only man she'd ever loved."

"Dave! A film goddess in love with you after all these years."

"A lot of good that does me. I still wonder what made Lu the way she was in high school. I mean, apart from what I knew about her screwed up parents. She never seemed happy. Yet, her intensity attracted me. You know: the fire inside her."

"Would this have anything to do with the 'ideas' you mentioned?"

I nodded. I'd been thinking of going back to Circleville and somehow capturing Lu *in movement*. Maybe then I could *see* what happened to her in the past. Just to watch Lu move again… But I knew, for now, that I should tell no one else about my brainstorming. To escape my longing, I *had* to run that single-minded, ego driven obstacle course to make my awesome *scientific* discovery. I had to run and run and run that track, letting in little else—not even my wife and son. With what I'd seen in Reynie Raymond's portrait, I knew my plan could work. I just had to figure out the specifics.

CHAPTER THREE

I had dawdled over the Reynie Junior hologram for more than a month before Court sent Harlan up from Denver to retrieve the holographic display for his daughter. I was afraid that by being out of touch for so long I had blown any referrals this generous man might give me. I knew I hadn't achieved what I wanted. I also didn't *know* what I wanted. I can't say I resented Jeanie or Eddie. But my dark night of the soul had begun to affect them too.

Even Eddie noticed. He came home from basketball practice one night and said, "Hey, Dad. If you ever need to talk, I'm here for you."

"If I ever need to confide in you, I'll know I'm beyond hope." I immediately regretted saying this.

"Wow Dad," my son said, and disappeared.

Jeanie also had no idea where my head was these days. I guess I needed to blame *her* for it. The *it* was guilt, the great alienator. The feeling we always blame on others. Okay, so I read Ayn Rand in college. The bitch of it was that though I knew it wasn't really Jeanie's fault, I couldn't keep from resenting her. As hard as I tried to forget, that resentment had lingered since we had to get married. Our talks usually went like this:

Jeanie: "Don't you love me anymore?"
David: "Yes, dammit!"
Jeanie: "Then why are you acting like this?"
David: "You know I'm obsessed with the hologram."
Jeanie: "That's what's turned you into 'Mr. Hyde'?"
David: "Come on. I'm Italian. I have strong feelings."
Jeanie: "You're not yourself anymore, and you're Italian in name only."
David: "That's a low blow. Just because I'm not fluent in Italian and I don't go to mass."
Jeanie: "At least I didn't have to convert to marry you."
David: "What did you mean when you said I'm not myself anymore. People do change."
Jeanie: "Nobody's keeping you from changing."
David: "Then, for Chrissake, whatta you want from me?"
Jeanie: "I give up."
David: "Good!"
Eddie: "Could I just go through here quick and get some milk?"
Jeanie (to Eddie): "Don't you dare drink out of that carton!"
David: "Get back to your room, young man!"
Eddie: "Jeez!"

It took "Showbiz Tonite" on TV to bring my ignoble secret to light. Of *course* I knew Lucille Muhr would be in the show. Of course I looked it up in *TV News*. Because Jeanie had also read *TV News*, she talked up a storm during the show's theme song and the host's opening remarks. After the opening segments, the visuals cut to Lu's expansive living room in Connecticut. Lu sat back on a long white leather couch surrounded by a long array of decorative pillows.

"I would be happy to answer any questions about my work," Lu said to talk show host Sara Hope. Tossing her sleek "bob," as she did now, made Lu's hair lift and turn out like a blackbird's wing.

"I'm sure our viewers would love to know how you do it. Portray the kinds of characters you're famous for. Like the abused child in 'Faces of Fear'. And your Oscar winning role as Celia in 'Journeys Home'. Even an actress of your caliber couldn't make up emotions like that. You must have lived them. What about the rumors of your unhappy childhood?"

Lu's dusky eyes shot out darts of displeasure. "As the host of 'Showbiz Tonite', Sara, what makes you so good at probing the psyches of your guests? Imagination? Guts? Woman's intuition? Did you come from a broken home? Did you become ambitious rather than break?" A medallion Lu wore shimmered in the studio lights. When she spoke, she fingered the pendant as though it could talk for her. "We are more than collections of our past," Lu continued, "and what we are includes what we create. So, you see, Sara, if the so-called 'rumors' are true, how much do they have to do with my work?"

"I'm afraid you got me on that one," Sara Hope said. "Obviously, you're also quite a philosopher!"

"Come and sit down," I said to Jeanie. "I can't believe I just tuned in to this interview with Lucille Muhr? Eddie doing his homework?"

Jeanie hovered, buzzard-like, behind my chair.

Eddie bounded down the stairs. He almost flattened Swanky, our ginger tabby, and gathered the fiery feline in his arms. "What's going on down here?"

"That's Lucille Muhr," Jeanie said. "David. Please." She scratched the top of my chair with her fingernails. "You promised."

"I said I wouldn't see her films. Aren't you even a little curious?"

"No."

"Wow," Eddie said. "I know who *that* is!"

Lucille Muhr evaded several more personal questions.

Sara Hope sighed. "Well, could you at least tell us about your beautiful pendant? What it's made of? Where you got it?"

"It was delivered to my studio anonymously," Lu said. "It's an art hologram. Not of an object but of assorted colors. Light fractured through a prism or maybe through glass slivers. Made with lasers. I never wear it on-screen, as you probably know. I feel it's magical, though I don't know exactly why."

Jeanie now clenched the back of my neck. Her hard breaths blew on me like ill winds. "A holographic medallion? And she doesn't know who sent it to her?" Jeanie accused.

I confessed nothing. I shrugged off Jeanie's grip. "Ow!"

"Might your pendant have something to do with your new film?" Sara Hope inquired.

Lucille looked nervous. "I'm not at liberty to comment on that."

Not at liberty, I thought. *How like Lu.* She loved the Classics and Latinate words. She loved serving up pure reason. That's how she could debate like a prosecuting attorney.

Jeanie still hung over my chair. Maybe she needed to get a good, up-to-date look at the woman she perceived as her only rival. At that moment Jeanie reminded me of the character Shelley Winters played in "A Place in the Sun." The one whom the Montgomery Clift character made pregnant and then killed because he wanted to marry the Elizabeth Taylor character.

"Before we go," the host of 'Showbiz Tonite' said, "will you admit how old you'll be on your upcoming birthday?"

"That's no secret. I'll be forty."

"And still looking thirty! Thank you, Lucille Muhr. This is Sara Hope, saying 'good evening' from all of us at 'Showbiz Tonite'!"

A grand idea began to take shape. What popped into my head was wordless. Maybe Lu's laser medallion was the catalyst for my inspiration. Maybe I could somehow *reassemble* shards of memories and bits of physical movement through space holographically.

Jeanie pressed me again about the medallion. "What about the pendant?" She slid her Valley Girl blonde bangs out of her ice blue eyes.

"What?"

"The thing around her neck," Eddie offered. "Awesome!"

Jeanie frowned at our son. "Don't you have to study?"

Eddie uncoiled his lanky body. "Uh, I guess so."

"Good idea," Jeanie said. "Night, Eddie."

Eddie looked afraid all hell was about to break loose. "I'm never getting married!" he announced. He gathered Swanky up and ascended each stair with clunking, slow-motion steps. "See you in the mornin', then." He gave one final, forlorn look back at us before trudging up to his bedroom.

Jeanie clenched my elbow. "It was pure coincidence she was wearing that? You work with lasers all the time."

"Do you really believe that bauble has anything to do with me?"

Jeanie seemed embarrassed by her own obsession with Lu. She turned away from me. "She said someone mailed it to her."

I pulled Jeanie close and kissed her. "You know how much I love you." And I do love my wife. "You're intelligent and accomplished. You're a good wife and lover. And a great mother to our boy."

"Then what is it?" Jeanie pursued. "I've tried to be patient with your moods, David. But if you don't tell me what's bothering you, I'm afraid our marriage will go down the tubes." She started crying.

I couldn't admit how much I'd been thinking about Lucille Muhr, even before tonight. I was trying to find the words to explain it delicately when Jeanie pushed away from me and planted herself in the doorway of the bathroom. I wanted to be alone and think. But I resigned myself to going to bed early. Feeling oddly modest right then, I undressed. Jeanie climbed into bed. I could feel her watching me. It made me twitch. I turned my back to her. My breath tightened. I did not want my wife to touch me.

Jeanie squirmed under the covers. "You're still in good shape, Honey." She ran her finger across my collarbone.

I turned to lie on my back beside her. "So are you."

Jeanie put her head on my chest. "Not really. Not as good as at first. I guess I'm…maybe too 'vanilla' for you."

"But you had Eddie. Childbirth's hard on a woman's body."

Jeanie looked dangerously serious. "Lucille Muhr hasn't got children, right? They say she never married. I'm sure I could look like that if I had my own hair stylist and makeup artist." Jeanie must have realized she was protesting too much. "You love me?"

I rolled over and wrapped one leg around her. "Stop it. You know I do. I wouldn't trade you for all the movie actresses in the world. And, just to prove it—." I kissed her just below her ear, then on her neck. And then I laughed. "You know what? I bet Lucille Muhr has had half a dozen facelifts already!"

"Yeah, I know." Jeanie pulled me on top of her. "You are *my* David. Mine alone."

As hard as I tried, I still couldn't get Lu's face out of my mind. While I touched my wife, I let myself see Lu in a guest's chair on the set of "Showbiz Tonite." I imagined the show signing off and Sara Hope going to Lu. This didn't make sense, but I was really into it. I fantasized Sara reaching down Lu's shell-pink satin blouse and caressing one of Lu's breasts. Then Lu drew Sara down to her knees and deeply kissed her.

Cameramen and other production people looked on without emotion. Kneeling at Lu's feet, Sara pushed Lu's skirt up above the black garters of Lu's garter belt. Lu wore no panties. Next Lu unbuttoned Sara Hope's blouse while Sara started kissing the inside of Lu's thighs.

With a full hard-on, I walked up to the stage from my seat in the studio audience while Sara kissed Lu passionately at the top of Lu's inner thigh. I unzipped my trousers, pulled myself out and stood so that I almost touched Sara. This made Sara mad. She clenched her blouse closed and left the set in a huff.

Now I fantasized Lu lying on the stage in a red spotlight.

I easily slipped myself into Lu. We both moaned and pressed together again and again, like waves slapping ocean pilings. Our skin glistened.

Lucille lightly bit my shoulder and squeezed my hips with her hands while I repeatedly pushed. Then I erupted into her.

"Oh, David!" Jeanie cried. "Yes! Yes!"

To my horror, it sounded like Jeanie had shouted my name from the back of the studio. I fumbled for my clothes. Lu hung on to my legs. The production crew applauded when I tenderly kissed Lu.

"My God, David!" Jeanie lay under me, glowing with the lavish product of my fantasy.

A wave of shame hit me. Jeanie clung to me and stroked my chest. I lay beside her with titillating guilt. *I must be a sick man*, I thought. "Sorry," I said. "I think I'm done."

"It's okay if you're sleepy."

I wanted to scream. I said, "Sorry, but I'm *spent*."

"Relax," Jeanie said. "I can still have some fun."

When I finally fell asleep I dreamed I was doing holographic work in a movie studio. Lucille Muhr was giving an Oscar-level performance as a woman scorned. Tears slipped down her cheeks. She looked at me right through the camera. Her laser medallion lit up with blinding intensity. "Davie," she said, "I have waited so long to tell you that you are the only man I have ever loved." Eclipsing all else, her ebony eyes pulsed with every imaginable color and sliced into my brain.

I could feel that pulsing as if it were a drum beating in every cell of my body. I started to speak, to affirm my love for her.

Suddenly the dream changed. I saw myself skiing in bright sunshine, down a grassy slope. I wore a candy-striped neck scarf about fifteen feet long. It flew out behind me in the wind.

Though I must have been asleep, I remember laughing out loud.

CHAPTER FOUR

Juanita's restaurant served up Boulder's cheapest authentic Mexican food. On the West end of the Pearl Street Mall, the restaurant had no atmosphere to speak of. High backed wooden booths, rustic and tattered from decades of neglectful use. Some faded sarapes and discolored, droopy Mexican hats on two catty-corner walls. Cheesy Mexican music, not too loud, accompanied with scents of chopped yellow onions and deep-fried tortillas—and green chili sauce and gooey cheddar, Monterey Jack, and *queso blanco*. These rib-sticking recipes more than made up for Juanita's tacky ambience.

After our gluttonous two-for-one-Margaritas dinner at Juanita's, Jeanie offered to drive us home. I was "a cheap drunk," but Jeanie could out-swig a lumberjack. The odd thing was that she rarely drank, so I couldn't fathom her high tolerance for the stuff. "It's all in the genes," she often said.

We headed on foot to the heart of Boulder's Pearl Street pedestrian Mall. Diners had queued up in front of the Cheesecake Factory. I had stopped eating there with Jeanie and Eddie because they always took too long to order from the boundless menu. The usual evening crowd milled around the shops and other restaurants and listened to street musicians. Two acrobats queued up to do mid-air somersaults and launched their bodies from a petite trampoline. Some teenagers with hair-gelled Woody Woodpecker hairdos strolled arm-in-arm. I could almost tell where the many tourists were from—and why they were here—based on their outfits. Here and there a Hawaiian shirt. Women wearing "fanny packs" above their privates or strapped over one shoulder. Flip flops, leather sandals, or the local favorites— Birkenstocks. "Mall crawlers" wore faded jeans or tailored slacks. We passed an all-night convenience store that sported single-hose mini-hookah sets in its main window. On the bowl of a black glass and ceramic hookah a camel stretched its long neck forward.

When Jeanie caught me admiring the little hookah, she frowned. "Remember the time you made me share a joint with you?"

"Yeah. You giggled for twenty minutes and fell asleep."

"Not what you intended I'm sure."

"I don't know what you mean," I lied.

"We hadn't slept together yet. You thought it might prime the pump. You had that silly grin that means you're up to no good."

I felt annoyed. "You were plenty eager the night you seduced me. I asked you if it was safe and you said yes. But you lied, didn't you? Hence: Eddie."

Jeanie looked like she was going to cry. I hated that. "I forgot to pick up my refill," she said. It was just bad timing."

But I believed Jeanie went off birth control on purpose. To trap me. She knew I hadn't forgiven her.

Jeanie changed the subject. "Eddie misses you. You know he's a laid-back kid, but even *he* has his limits. There's our car." Actually it was *Jeanie's* car—a gold colored 1982 Volvo 240 beast of a wagon. It had V8 engine with a 6-speed manual transmission. She could kick anyone's ass in highway traffic. Also great for driving hairpin mountain curves in Colorado winters. Stinky, smoky diesel fuel, though. She said the fortified chassis made her feel safe. Tabu, the unctuous cologne she bought for herself had become one with the thick buff colored upholstery. Her "fragrance" was older than her car. Jeanie described Tabu as "a light floral fragrance," but I smelled only the sticky-sweet jasmine. I hoped I could shower when we got home.

Jeanie drove us around to the back side of the Mall to Broadway. Then she turned North.

I yawned grotesquely. To keep peace at home, I had conceived a brilliant idea. "I need your help with a secret experiment," I said to Jeanie. "It's vitally important. I hope Eddie will help too." I looked at my wife and let her see I was fond of her. "I'm sorry about the way I've been acting. Something strange is going on inside me. It's like I have too much to do and too little time. Oh, I don't mean that the way it sounds. But now my work is more vital than I can explain."

The farther north on Broadway Jeanie drove, the thinner traffic became. Still, we hit every stoplight and waited for the final green light to change. There was literally no cross-traffic. Jeanie needed to turn left, but you can't turn left on red. She even tried inching her Volvo up to the crosswalk to make the light change. I drum rolled my fingers on the dashboard until the tyrannic stoplight freed us.

Jeanie pulled into the driveway of our North Boulder home. "It couldn't be about you turning forty? I've been reading about what happens to men when they turn forty."

"Honey, I appreciate your concern. But it's much bigger than turning forty." While exiting the Volvo, I bumped my head on the door frame. "Thanks for driving," I mumbled. "Here. I'll use my key." I weaved through the kitchen and sat down on our living room couch. "Do we have any Pepto Bismol left?"

"If you haven't drunk it all." Jeanie disappeared into the bathroom and came back with an almost empty bottle of the lurid pink liquid.

"You and I have a lot to talk about," she said. She handed me a spoon from the kitchen.

"Save the spoon. I'll just chug the rest." I hoped there would be enough Pepto Bismol to tame my nausea. "Sit with me on the couch for a minute. Remember when you were in college chorus?"

"Yes, but—."

"You were solo soprano because you have perfect pitch and never needed a music queue."

Jeanie pulled away from me. "I'm not in the mood—."

"Please bear with me. Hum an F above Middle-C for me."

"Really! Time escape 'the People's Republic of Boulder'."

"Please. Over my stomach. I got a new idea while I was at work today. Hum that F over my stomach, Jeanie."

"I just have to ask: Why your stomach?"

I kissed my wife gently, then said: "Because the solar plexus is a major energy center. That's only the beginning, *if* you let me have my way. You know how people cross their arms over their stomach when they're self-conscious? They're protecting that energy center."

"What *have* you been reading?"

"That F please. Go on. It's just an experiment."

She bent over my stomach. "This is silly." But she hummed a perfect F above middle-C.

"That's not it."

"What *is* it?"

"Try an A but *up* an octave. Sustain it longer this time."

"Anything to be near you." She hummed the higher A.

My solar plexus lit up. "Keep going! That's it! Do it again!"

Jeanie let her lips hover just above my stomach.

Just at that moment Eddie came downstairs. He rubbed his eyes. "I dreamed killer hummingbirds were attacking Boulder. For cripe sake. Can't a guy get some sleep? You'll yell at me if I ask what you're doing. Been reading Tantric sex manuals?"

"Eddie," I said.

"Our family is falling apart," Eddie continued. "Every day it's something else. Every night—."

"Eddie," Jeanie said.

"I don't matter around here anymore. I'm just a fixture."

I gestured. "Eddie! Come here!"

"Don't hit me."

"Oh Eddie," Jeanie said. "When has your father ever hit you? Come here. We want to try something."

Eddie lay down on the floor in mock exhaustion. "Why can't I have normal parents?"

To Jeanie I said, "That's perfect. Go over and hum an A over Eddie. His stomach."

Eddie stiffened. "Don't touch me, you perverts!"

"Don't you want to help your dear old Dad with a holographic experiment that may be radical? Don't you?"

That got Eddie's attention. "Maybe. If you tell me what that has to do with doing *that* over me."

"We haven't worked it out yet," Jeanie said. "But if you want us to be a happy family again—."

"I know," Eddie said. "I have to obey you."

"Good boy. Now hum that 'A' over Eddie, Jeanie."

Eddie squirmed. "That tickles!"

"It works on him too," I said. "Must be genetic. Eddie. Name your favorite song."

"'Born in the USA'."

"No. Something that has a real melody."

"Dad. Puhl-eeze tell me that this means something. I'm not used to you doing new things. I like you to be predictable. The big thing is that I got to get up pretty early tomorrow to take an Algebra quiz. Is this gonna be worth the bags under my eyes in the morning?"

"Let me explain," I offered. Say that each person finds certain tunes attractive not just because of the words but also because of the song's harmonic." Both Jeanie and Eddie looked *vacant*. "Every kind of organic life has an identifiable frequency," I said. "Like rutabaga, I suppose. You could measure a specific energy frequency for rutabaga, but each rutabaga would be slightly different. Each person, then, has a definite, measurable frequency too."

"I don't know how to prepare rutabaga," Jeanie said.

Eddie rotated to lie on his stomach. "Frequency?"

I feared my son was about to drive me nuts. "Just before you fall asleep, do you ever hear a sort of 'zinging' or ringing in your head?"

"Yeah. But I thought it was my ears."

"What if you're detecting bioelectric processes going on in your brain? You know how, when you're near big electrical wires, you can hear high-pitched humming?"

"I like it," Eddie said.

"More to the point, I'll bet if you wrote a list of your favorite songs, most of them would be in the same key."

This got Jeanie's attention. "That *is* interesting, David. I know your songs. A lot of mellow folk music and some jazz. I could play the tapes and tell you what key they're in."

"Yes! Exactly what I had in mind. And if the majority are in A, I'll be crazy excited. Could you go down to Logan's Music Store tomorrow while I'm at work and buy me an 'A' tuning fork?"

"You're probably an A-minor," Jeanie quipped, "but that's a chord." She seemed pleased with herself.

I just looked at her. After all, *she* was the expert on affairs musical.

"It takes the law to make a minor," Eddie quipped. He yawned and lay back on his side. "Sometimes you guys are so weird," he said before he moved to the couch. "Be sure *not* to wake me when you figure it out. I just don't get enough sleep anymore."

Jeanie smiled at our boy. "I'm excited to be part of your Dad's work. You should be too."

"Tomorrow, my love," I said to Jeanie. "I want to sleep on it."

Eddie groaned. "Thank God."

I'd have gotten a speeding ticket if I'd driven home the next afternoon as fast as I wanted. You would think Boulder during rush hour was Midtown Manhattan. After an endless day at work, there was an unusual ninety-degree heat. Unless we're playing tennis we Boulderites don't break a sweat until it's in the upper eighties because of the low humidity. My green-light karma wasn't working that day either. I'd stopped at another of what seemed a dozen red lights. The bumper sticker on the white compact car in front of me said: "Honk If You Love Jesus." Bored, and feeling generous, I honked." The female driver turned around and gave me the finger! The woman's gesture reinforced my lifelong suspicion that most Christians live a double life. But I smiled at her like a beatific angel.

When I got home Jeanie said she'd ordered Chinese food. "I know you want to get started. I got your tuning fork. Oh, and by the way, I listened to your favorite music. I was right. You're an A-minor. Can't wait to see what you'll do with your new tuning fork."

"What *we* are going to do with it. Eddie home yet?"

"Eddie called at four. Said he was going to ask a band member what key some Bruce Springsteen tune is in. He'll get a burger on the way home. Says he has not acquired a taste for 'the Yellow Man's food'."

"Remind me to tell him that's not *PC*," I said.

Jeanie's arms encircled my neck. "Honey, I got myself a tuning fork too. In G. I've been playing with it since two. There's a special technique. It's all in the wrist. Here's the little rubber thing they sold me at Logan's to tap it on."

"It looks like a raspberry hockey puck."

Jeanie nodded. "Striking it on this rubber thing keeps you from damaging the tines. I made the tuning fork resonate really loud and held it just above my navel. And you know what? I felt it from my teeth down to my toes."

"How did you know which tuning fork is for you?"

"I didn't have time to figure out *my* songs. So at Logan's I tested seven of them in the range of the classic C-scale."

"How ingenious!"

"The one my solar plexus liked the best was the G," Jeanie added

"Let's eat."

Jeanie looked out the kitchen window. "The way to a man's heart. Oh. Mr. Harcourt Raymond called."

"Shit! I was supposed to call him today!"

"That's what he said. He thinks you're a genius, Davie." She turned and smiled at me.

I put my arms around her. "Well, I bet no genius ever worked on an empty stomach. What did you tell Court?"

"He figured his genius boy forgot. I told him you are going to be eyeballs deep in your special project tonight and that I'd remind you to call him tomorrow morning."

"You are terrific."

It took me fifteen minutes to get my wife and son to stop playing with their tuning forks in my basement lab so we could get started on my experiment. "Eddie, you get to turn the laser on. Here's the timer. It's silent, so you must keep watching the digital readout. You're going to keep the laser on for only thirty seconds. You got that?"

Stationed behind the laser, Eddie looked like a trigger-happy outlaw. "When do I do it?"

"Not 'til I tell you. When I say '*Now*', rap the tuning fork tines hard against the heel of your hand, not the rubber puck. And at the same time Eddie's going to turn on the laser beam. *Do not look directly into the beam*. We must do this like a family—together. And please don't bump the table or move your body at that moment. Okay?"

Eddie twitched in anticipation. "Dad?"

"Mmm hmm?"

"How will we know when you're ready?"

"When I say 'Now'. I'm counting on both of you to help me pull this off. If it works we'll be sitting pretty for the rest of our lives."

"Wow!" Eddie said.

I started the process. "Jeanie, stand a couple of feet away. No matter what happens, I want you to strike that tuning fork on cue! I'll be trying to focus on a terrible memory in as much detail as possible. I've got to re-live it with all my senses."

Jeanie let the hand holding the tuning fork drop to her side. "You're going to do the car wreck."

"I've got to. There's nothing to worry about if you two do your part. Okay. I'm ready to start my part." I tried to place myself back in that college weekend. Even though Lu and I had severed for good the previous weekend, we had agreed to go ahead and go to a Dionne Warwick concert at Ohio State. I'd bought the tickets months before. It was after the Old Oaken Bucket game with Indiana University. People had consumed a lot of beer. I was driving my hot new orange Camaro'. I had come to a complete stop. Something in me sensed the initial nanosecond of impact from behind me. In my peripheral vision, even before I heard that car hitting mine, I saw my books flying from the back seat toward me in slow motion. I watched the steering wheel come toward my face. *I'm going to die*, I thought. As in a montage, I saw images of Lu and my parents, my favorite dog, the faces of friends. Then everything went black. I knew I was dead.

"Now!" I said to Jeanie and Eddie. Then my head snapped back. I felt blood pouring down my forehead, into my eyes. Someone opened the car door. I passed out in a stranger's grasp.

"David!" Jeanie whispered. "Eddie, keep the laser on for the full time. Remember?"

Someone was helping me out of my wrecked Camaro when I felt Jeanie put her face next to mine. "Did you get it?" I asked Eddie.

Eddie shook all over. "You bet, Dad! I was *zinging* with energy the whole time the laser was on."

With her fingers Jeanie wiped the moisture from my upper lip.

Sweat drenched my whole body. Even the soles of my feet. "I'm sure it worked this time," I said.

"You gonna finish this up tonight?" Eddie asked. "Can I watch?"

"I am going to bed," Jeanie said to me. To Eddie: "You have some homework?"

"Nothing that can't wait 'til study hall. Please, Dad?"

"Yeah. Yeah, Eddie."

The five minutes it took for the negative to dry felt like hours. I set the precise angle of the reconstruction beam and turned it on. My throat closed. There was a beautiful, clear image of my head and upper torso. Superimposed on that, there was a fuzzy holographic likeness of my field of vision from the driver's perspective! I could see dashboard indicators behind the steering wheel. Most uncanny of all, there was a wispy bluish blur coming out the top of my head.

"Dad. What *is* that?" Eddie asked. He pointed at the bluish blur. "Did I blow it?"

I was still wondering how my dashboard indicators showed up so clearly in a small hologram that shouldn't contain them. "No," I said. "If *we* had blown it, the entire hologram would be a blur. "Hand me my magnifying lens." Trying to get a better look would be tricky because you can't get up close to a hologram the way you can with a newspaper. The image separates into colors of the spectrum. Standing a few feet from the hologram I tried tilting the magnifying lens at various angles. From my final vantage point the bluish blur looked like a little puff of amorphous blue-white smoke being *pulled* upward.

Eddie was kneeling at my left and viewing the hologram from below and to the side. "Look at it from *this* angle, Dad!"

I took Eddie's place. When I peered up through the magnifying lens, the smoky blur took shape. It was a little *me*! I could see my own head and features like I was looking at myself through a slight mist. Because "my" little arms were almost flush with my body, it was hard to tell they *were* arms. "Eddie, look here and tell me what you see."

"I see a head, chest, and arms. Why, it's a bitty you! Fuck!" Dismayed that he'd said 'fuck' in front of me, he added, "Sorry…"

"Fuck, yes!" I shouted back. "It *is* another me coming out the top of my own head." It would be hard to explain how I'd captured *myself* inside a car I'd sold more than fifteen years ago. This little me unlike the Reynie Junior image. Hers was an actual real body image of herself as a child. Mine was apparently a sort of astral body. Eddie's attention was fixed on that bluish white torso. I was amazed that the image was clear only when viewed from my son's chosen angle. I would have to figure out *why*, and this filled me with as much dread as excitement.

I also thought, *What a cliché it is that you see your whole life flash before your eyes when you believe you're about to die.* "I want to tell you what I was feeling during that wreck. Just before everything went black," I said to my son. "The moment when I knew my forehead was about to hit the steering wheel, I literally saw my whole life pass before me. In that moment I said to myself: 'I'm going to die'."

"But Dad. You didn't die," Eddie noted.

"The important thing is, I *thought* I was going to die. Maybe that intense feeling was like a flash of energy that made a bioelectric or biochemical impression in the air. That, my son, exactly parallels light exposing photographic film."

Eddie handed me the magnifying glass so I could look at the image again. "But your accident was what—before you turned twenty one? A while back in the past."

I took a good look at my little astral body's young, bluish face again. "Yes, but I just relived that experience. This means a memory is *not* stuck in the past. Memories must be alive, even when you're not calling them up in your imagination."

"Dad, if that's true, it means the past is still alive too!" Eddie was apparently surprised at how far his own mind had reached.

"That's exactly what it means, Sport."

After Eddie went to bed I stared at the hologram long enough to drink three Coors beers. I pondered this business of the past being alive. However open I was to ideas of the supranormal, I felt obliged to document this process scientifically. But I could see no way to explain what I'd just created, short of polling all of Boulder's metaphysical practitioners. And I realized that even if I did figure out how the past might be accessible in the present, the hardest thing to explain would be how I had captured it in a hologram. Hell, the only way I knew how to do it then was that you had to be thinking about *yourself*. What if I wanted to make a hologram that recorded someone else. Like Lucille Muhr in the past?

So far I had captured peoples' memories of themselves or themselves *in the past*. How could I score specific traces of someone else's life? Suppose I set up holographic equipment in the yard of the people who owned the Muhrs' old house in Circleville? How would I know what to focus my laser beam on? Just hope the traces would somehow magically appear? No device I knew of could help me tune in to the correct frequency except my mind. No. That might bring up an image from my own memory. Couldn't trust it...shouldn't let myself interfere. But wouldn't that prove I could really capture the past? I asked myself what I should do in a controlled scientific experiment to insure my objectivity. The answer: Establish a subject—Lucille Muhr—in the past. Oh, great. Lucille Muhr in the summer of 1963? June 23rd, 1963? Damn! That would be impossible.

During the four hours I slept I dreamed about Lu: We were back in Circleville, and I was walking toward her house on Tenth Street. It was about eleven o'clock on a night lit by a full moon. I could see Lu climbing out her bedroom window at the far side of the house and down her father's huge ham radio antenna. The antenna was triangular and had aluminum rungs on it. She looked to be about sixteen. I could see that when she reached the ground her expression was fixed and her eyes were glazed. There was a wooden resolve in them. Lu moved zombie-like to the front walk. I called out to her but she didn't hear me. She was heading toward the nearest busy street, which was about three blocks straight forward. Was she about to kill herself? Though I tried to run to her it was like I was on a treadmill going nowhere. Lu kept walking, her head lifted in determination to meet traffic head-on. Suddenly I saw her older sister Carla dash across the front yard.

"Lu, no!" Carla shouted. She pulled her sister's arm so hard it could have dislocated Lu's shoulder.

But it worked. Lu stopped walking in that wooden way. She began to cry like a child. Silently her tears streamed straight down her face. She sobbed: "He has a whore in there...after he wrote all those nice things to Mama in the institution. I want to die."

Something at the front door of the Muhr house caught my attention. On the porch stood their father, looming ten feet tall. His eyes glowed reddish orange, like demons in exorcist movies. Then he opened his mouth about one foot wide and emitted a subhuman roar.

I'm sure no sound technician could ever duplicate that shriek. I felt it in my scalp, in the raised hairs of my neck, in my teeth, in the pit of my stomach. In the bones of my feet.

I watched in horror while Lu and Carla got smaller and smaller. Their father grew larger and larger above them. The sisters held each other and wailed when he reached for them with his huge hands. I shouted, "Lu!" but my feet stuck. I fell forward on the ground.

My beating up on my pillow woke me. My entire body was clammy and my eyes seemed to be popping out of my face. I felt like hell. I figured I looked like hell.

Jeanie turned to me and spooned along the back of my body. "What's wrong, Honey?"

"A nightmare," I explained.

"My lion," Jeanie said, with only a touch of sarcasm.

As we lay there I wondered if my dream about Lu and Carla was sign of what I would have to endure to carry out this holographic brainstorm. I wanted to exorcise these feelings and to vent the frustration of having so many unanswered questions. One thing was for sure: this holographic trek wasn't for sissies. I knew I might need help, but I had no idea where to turn.

CHAPTER FIVE

It was the day before "Harmonic Convergence." Because I'm a holographer I loved the sound of that phrase when I heard it on the 9NEWS. I didn't need to do research, for out on the Pearl Street Mall on my lunch hour, I found a group assembled at a table in front of the stately, four-story Boulder Courthouse. Yellowish flagstones and concrete flanked middle, layered structures that reminded me of the ascending ranges of the Rockies. There, in the center of Boulder, I sat down on a bench and looked at some of the Harmonic Convergence people's printed materials.

I read that Harmonic Convergence had to do with calculations made by the ancient Mayans. According to a local writer the date Cortez landed in Mexico (Good Friday 1519) began a period of nine hellish fifty-two-year cycles. These would culminate on August sixteenth. Now we were supposedly entering a five-year period of purification. The concept of "harmonic convergence" meant that the Earth's vibrational frequency had changed on that date. "Mother Earth is an organic, resonating field of energy, and it is up to the enlightened and attuned all over the world to help form a field of resonance in harmony with hers."

I also learned that these concepts parallel those of ancient Mexicans. The Hopi Indians also believed that the Earth has chakras, just like the energy centers in the human body. And the Hopis prophesied that these Earth chakras would be awakened on the same date, beginning a purification process. This interval would culminate in a new world, where what we've considered paranormal activities will be everyday events. It meant destabilization—of governments, institutions, technology, the earth's tectonic plates—to this new kind of global relationship. I found these beliefs exciting *and* daunting.

Since mounting the hologram of me and my car wreck, I wanted to take a new approach to my work. This intense energy of change inspired me to act. Knowing there could be no better place than Boulder to help me carry out the first part of my experiment, I felt my nerves settle. I would ask Court to stake me for finding out how to pre-view holographic images created by people's thoughts and memories. It had been nearly two months since Court paid me for my original work. I was hoping he'd gotten over the shock of the Reynie Junior image and had come to feel tingling curiosity.

On the evening of August twenty fifth Court answered his private phone on the first ring. "Reynie wants to see you. When can you come down and show her the hologram? I'll pay you for your time."

I had had a speech ready to convince him to let me talk to him about my research idea. Now I was stopped dead.

"Are you there, David? Are you working tomorrow?"

"It's Sunday, so I can be there around eleven."

"Eleven," Court repeated. "Good. Then we'll have brunch on the veranda. Reynie will probably want to tell you about her honeymoon too though. And David? Could you please explain the hologram to us in *layman's* terms?"

The phone receiver clicked. *Oh, great!* I thought. *How can I describe to Reynie a process as intricate as making a hologram?* Then I got a terrific idea: I'd take Court and Reynie through the entire process by shooting a new hologram. But this time we wouldn't use *sound* as a catalyst.

To transport my equipment to the Raymond mansion I rented a closed Home Depot van with a padded interior. I had stayed up until 2:00 a.m. packing my pulsing industrial ruby laser, lenses, mirrors, and beam splitter. And I disassembled my table, sand and all. Speeding on caffeine, I wondered if, slowly and quietly, I was sinking into insanity.

So did Jeanie. "I'm worried about the money. I'm worried about your health. Why can't you just let it be? That hologram is just some freaky thing. Why don't you have it professionally examined?"

"I *am* a professional. And it wasn't an accident."

For the time being, Jeanie stopped speaking to me.

"My goodness," Court said. He, himself, let me into his foyer. Harlan was nowhere in sight. "The box with Reynie's hologram is in my drawing room. But let's have brunch first. It's *nouvelle cuisine.* You know: microscopic portions. My daughter wants me to trim down. But I'm so famished that it will be a relief to eat *anything.*"

"Please pardon me, but I had a burger on the way down. Why don't I set Reynie's hologram up in the drawing room while you two have lunch. Then I'll assemble my equipment in the foyer to do a demonstration for you. It'll also be an experiment."

"Sounds great!"

I liked this new spirit in him. "By the way, this one's on the house."

French doors led to the mansion's expansive terrace. When Court reached the doors to greet me after his lunch he said, "I have a feeling you want to ask me something later. And that it's going to cost me a lot of money." But he smiled. "No problem though," he added.

In return I smiled like the Mona Lisa.

Later Court joined me in the adjacent drawing room and Reynie sat down in a rose colored velveteen chair. In the middle of the room, lit from behind, the Reynie Junior hologram hovered in its cylinder.

"I never knew a hologram could be so beautiful! And so real." Regarding the child image of herself Reynie said, "It *is* spooky. What do you think caused this?"

I looked at Reynie's "ghost" image again. "Can you remember what you were thinking about when we made the hologram?"

"Yes. I was thinking about Mother. How does that explain—?"

"I believe you re-created a thought form of you. You were remembering your mother from a long time ago, and that created a projected image of you as a child."

With her eyes Reynie explored the room's rich burgundy Persian rug as if she'd never seen it before. "I've never had any of what people call psychic experiences. I can't say that I even believe in them."

Court leaned down and put his arm around her shoulders. "Darling, when you were little you could practically read your mother's mind. She and I often spoke of this."

"Oh, come on, Daddy. You know how close Mother and I were. It probably just *seemed* as if that's what was going on."

"I don't think so. If Reynelda was depressed in the morning, you would come into our bedroom. Practically before you got to the door you'd say, 'What's wrong, Mother?' Reynelda used to say, 'That child is uncanny'. I agree."

Here's my big chance, I thought. "I've been designing an experiment. Mr. Raymond, and would love to have your help?"

"Just tell me what to do. And please call me 'Court'."

"Follow me." I led Court and Reynie back to the very place in the foyer where I had shot the bridal hologram. "Those chandelier prisms look amazing! All gleaming in the middle of the day. This time we're gonna leave the chandelier lit. We'll need to close all those drapes."

Court looked confused. "You're not using the 35mm film process you did before? Wouldn't it be better to try to replicate that?"

"Since a 'ghost' image showed up when I used 35mm film, it will also show up when I use the pulsing ruby laser. Using this laser instead of film creates only a tiny chance of distortion. In other words, if we do get something it'll be harder to prove it was an error."

"Well," Reynie demurred. "At least I don't have to stand on that lazy-Susan thing again. Do we get to play in your sandbox?"

She had referred to my table. The big amount of sand keeps the table perfectly still. As I mentioned earlier, any vibration ruins a hologram. "You should both sit at the far end, *in the sand*. When I turn on this laser you must remain perfectly still."

Reynie looked at the table like it was a rattlesnake. "Well, in the name of science. But I did have two Mimosas at lunch."

"The better to relax you," Court said. "Okay. Up you go." Court took his daughter's hand and helped her up, as if into a horse-drawn carriage. "The effect has something to do with the chandelier's prisms, eh? They're fashioned from the finest glass."

I smiled. "I assumed so."

"Going to explain it to me, David?"

"Only if I'm right! I might only get your heads and shoulders."

Court asked me where all my ideas come from.

"I live in Boulder, remember?" I answered. "Now for this hologram I want you both to focus only on your *feelings* for the late Mrs. Raymond. You can close your eyes if it helps. Try to feel Mrs. Raymond here in this room. Ready?"

Reynie took a deep breath. "I hope we won't disappoint you."

I clamped the film holder in front of the laser and adjusted the angle of the beam splitter. Then I reset the large mirrors at the sides of the table. "Remember: I've never seen Mrs. Raymond. If she shows up, it'll be entirely *your* doing. I won't start until you both say you're ready.

Sense Mrs. Raymond. Feel your love for her. Feel how much you miss her. But please don't move. When you both agree you're ready, say 'Okay', and I'll start rolling."

Father and daughter sat in my "sandbox" under the lovely glow of the chandelier. I watched them try to tune into their late beloved and realized I'd been wrong about Reynie not resembling her father. Their faces were similar and their eyes showed the same intensity.

"Anytime you're ready," Court said to his daughter.

"Keep holding on to your feelings about her," I said.

As if by silent cue, both Court and Reynie said, "Okay."

"Keep the feeling. Just a little longer." I let the laser pulse for almost a minute. "That's it. Good!"

Court helped his daughter down from the table and smiled. "Where do we go from here?"

"Well, after I load this equipment back in the van," I said, "I'll go to OPTIKS and develop the hologram."

Court called his groundskeeper, who helped me re-pack my table and other equipment. "I'd like to come with you to your lab."

"Me too, please.," Reynie said. "My husband's playing rugby with the guys. After the game they'll be hanging out at some LoDo pub."

I wasn't so sure I wanted other people around while I went through the exacting process of developing this hologram.

"We'll follow you in our limo," Court said.

How could I say no? "I'd better tell my wife I'll be late," I said. *Oh, shit!* I thought.

CHAPTER SIX

By the time we got to OPTIKS it was 4:00 p.m. Calvin, the security guard at the entrance, was dumbstruck when Court's enormous gray limo pull up behind me. I hefted my tan leather field kit bag onto my shoulder. It contained the unprocessed holographic plate. I inserted my magnetic card in the security slot and Calvin asked me to sign my guests in. I'm sure when he saw the name Harcourt Raymond III, he almost wet his pants.

I led Court and Reynie through the vaulted lobby and down the first corridor. OPTIKS had installed full-spectrum lighting in halls and offices to avoid the toxic glow of fluorescent lights. "They hired an architect who knows about the positive effects of full-spectrum lighting on human physiology," I said. "There's also an industrial strength ionizer in the central heating and air conditioning units to clean the air."

We headed down the second corridor. "Research shows," I added, "that ionizers make employees feel better and neutralize viruses and bacteria. OPTIKS does experience rare absenteeism and a generally upbeat attitude among its personnel."

Court stopped me. "Aren't they worried about generating too much ozone? *That* is toxic!"

I felt even more respect for Court when I heard him say this. "How do you know that?"

"I wanted to install a central air cleaner in my home," he said, but the ozone thing stopped me."

"They have filters for that now."

Court sat down on a bench by my main work table. "That is very good news," he said.

Reynie laughed. "Only in Boulder," she said. In my lab she put her handbag by the metallic sink on the only clear spot. She examined every square inch of my OPTIKS lab. "This is fascinating," she said. Then she walked up to me and tapped me on my shoulder. "Does the boss mind your working here on your own projects?"

"I'd rather they didn't know for the time-being. This could be a major discovery. Before we start I want to show you one of the classic holograms of our generation. It's a copy of the hologram made by Lloyd Cross in 1974 called 'The Kiss'. I made the hologram of Reynie and Paul using the same process Cross did.

I turned on the fixture to display "The Kiss" hologram. "It's a 120-degree multiplex integral. Like the Reynie Junior hologram each 35mm frame I took contained a different view to make a single hologram. It's illuminated from the same direction as the original reference beam that was projected. See the woman wink, then blow a kiss with her right hand? Her holographic image projects from the same place she was standing when Cross made the hologram."

Court looked at "The Kiss" from several vantage points. He grinned like a kid on Christmas morning. "Why, I can see around and above her!"

"That's because each part of the hologram contains information about the entire subject. It means you could 'cut' the hologram into, say, four pieces. Each piece would show that entire subject but each would be from a different angle. You know that wouldn't happen if you cut a *photograph* in half. A hologram is like a memory in that way."

"When you see it in your mind it's three-dimensional," Court said.

I was relieved that Court understood. "This hologram is famous because it was the first of its kind. Since then holography has advanced a lot." I turned off "The Kiss" hologram.

"This blows my mind," Reynie said. "It's much more exciting than trying out for the Olympics." She blushed. "But not quite as exciting as marrying Paul LaSalle Esquire!"

"In a way, I hope to take my experiment to Olympic heights. If I can find what made Reynie Junior show up it will make me famous."

Court winked. "And probably very rich. I am getting the picture." He looked directly into my eyes and held his gaze. "How much financing from me will you need?"

I was stunned. My head swam with the possibility of being funded for my dream project.

"I've a pretty good idea where you're heading," Court said. "You're going to extend that idea of holographic memory and synthesize it with whatever turns up in the hologram we did today."

"Yes. In fact, I have a proposition to make. But I want to be fair. I don't know how many 'takes' I'll need. It might be a while before I'm successful. While I'm working out the kinks in my theories, you might not hear from me for weeks. And the next time you see me, I might be burnt out."

"Daddy, this is so thrilling! Will you help David? I'm partly responsible for his idea, you know."

"You're totally responsible," Court answered. To me he said: "You've made history already."

"First let me tell you what I think we're up against. If Mrs. Raymond does not show up in this hologram, we'll have to try again. I still feel something key is missing. Until I figure out what it is, my supplies could get expensive, even if I waste nothing. I'll gladly work evenings —and weekends too."

Reynie looked like a happy little kid. "I'd bet on you at the racetrack, David, and I always win. You'd be surprised how exactly you can pick the winners down at the paddock, or when they're posting, just by their conformation. If their muscles are too tight it means they're using up too much energy before the race has even started. They tend to clutch early. And if their muscles too relaxed they don't win either. I picked five straight winners on Derby Day at Churchill Downs one year just by checking out their conformation before race time. You can bet the thoroughbreds until two minutes before they reach the gate. So I always take advantage of that."

"That's the spirit, Darling," Court said to Reynie.

"Wait," I said. "How can there be more than one winner at the Kentucky Derby?"

Reynie measured her words: "Because the Kentucky Derby is only one of the races on Derby Day."

Court patted my shoulder. "Never mind that," he said to me. "The important thing is that now I have a worthwhile purpose in life—financing your quest. I knew I had picked a winner."

I couldn't believe Court agreed with my plan so easily. Not only was I hob knobbing with a millionaire but I was also about to realize a dream. "Let's get started. This hologram I shot today isn't going to move. Because I used a laser instead of 35mm film we have only one plate to deal with."

I explained to Court and Reynie how I made that day's hologram. "This plate uses ferro-electric crystals to record the interference pattern the laser light made when it bounced off you two. That interference pattern contained the totality of information about the outside of your bodies. Now we can reconstruct your three-dimensional images from this interference pattern."

They watched me go through the whole process. "Kodak makes these holographic plates. I use a complex developer." Here I will share the developer "recipe." It's a secret. I don't share with anyone the exact amounts:

starting with between 600 and 700 milliliters of water

less than 28 grams of disodium hydrogen phosphate (Na_2HPO_4)

more than 10 grams of sodium hydroxide

less than 20 grams of l-ascorbic acid

around 1 gram of ammonium thiocyanate

I lowered the holographic plate in the developer and set the timer. "The developing time takes two to five minutes. I'll order a pizza. My treat. Court, is Harlan waiting outside?"

Court seemed to test the *thought* of pizza on his tongue.

"Don't spare the anchovies," Reynie said.

I ordered a Mammoth Pizza Deluxe with anchovies on only a third. I couldn't bring myself to tell Reynie that just the smell of anchovies nauseated me. I gave her a twenty-dollar bill and asked her to run it down to the security guard. I told her not to get lost. "Follow the yellow-brick road. One right turn and then one left."

After Reynie left, Court put a firm arm around my shoulder. "About your proposition——. I want to open a checking account for you. But I won't tell you how much or how little is in it. In other words, you can write checks, but you won't be able to see the balance. Let's call this an incentive for you to be thrifty until you hit pay dirt. After that I'll let *you* name the figure."

At that moment I was so adrenalined-up that my appetite took a flight to Pango Pango. I sputtered my thanks.

"You know, David. This may sound like a cliché, but I always wished I'd had a son. I want to take you to lunch at the Brown Palace one of these days soon. We'll call it a business lunch...to discuss your future." Hope deepened the blue of his eyes.

I wanted to say I'd admire him even if he wasn't about to give me a lot of money. Until I could say such a thing without fawning I thought I'd better keep my mouth shut. Reynie burst through the door. Gratefully the timer dinged.

Reynie panted. "Did I miss anything? I promised Calvin he could have a piece without anchovies."

"We're ready to put the plate in the fixer. For about three minutes. It's Kodak Rapid Fixer diluted to about 1:3." After *fixing* the master hologram I let it wash for about ten minutes under running tap water. Then I added a couple drops of wetting agent and hung the film up to dry. I tried to hide my anxiety from my lab guests.

"What happens next?" Court asked. Both he and Reynie were standing so close to me the entire time that I was afraid they'd steam up the film with their breath. I calmed down by reminding myself of Court's generosity.

"Now we bleach the film. It's a cosmetic process that brightens the image and cancels out any unfiltered properties there might have been in the laser beam. It's a mixture of potassium dichromate, potassium bromide, water, sulphuric acid, and phenosafranine."

Reynie stepped back a few paces. "This won't blow up, right?"

I laughed. "No, but irritants like the bromine make it smell pretty awful so you better step back." I put on my thick rubber gloves to protect myself against sulfuric acid and put the film in its bleach bath. "Now we wait exactly one minute." After that minute I washed the negative for five minutes and hung it up to dry.

"Pizza break?" Calvin called from the door. Pizza grease and to-mato sauce already stained his mouth.

Reynie grabbed the box of pizza from Calvin. "You ate your piece on the way down here! And I notice you took the biggest slice. Get thee hence! We're doing important work here."

I washed my hands and we dove into the pizza. "We'll be able to look at the hologram later."

The big moment came. I set up a reconstruction beam—the exact opposite of the reference beam I used for shooting the hologram. "This illuminates our transmission hologram. The hologram will act like a lens. Its focal length is equal to the distance between the original laser beam and where you two were playing in the 'sandbox'. So far so good. Here goes nothing."

The hologram was a beautiful portrait of Court and Reynie. With their eyes closed and love in their hearts they looked like angels. Rainbows refracted from the chandelier prisms had projected onto their faces and upper torsos. Also a single, larger refraction of light hovered between father and daughter. I brought my magnifier up closer. I saw in the center of that refraction a full-figure image of a woman dressed in a long blue gown. She looked to be in her early thirties and even though she was a bit blurry I could see that she was quite beautiful.

Reynie, who was crying, said, "It worked." Her comment was simple, her voice vulnerable. To her father Reynie said, "Do you see that? She's wearing her blue satin dress."

"Reynelda's favorite, yes."

I felt sick with excitement. I knew that if Mrs. Raymond's image had been spawned by only the emotion both felt when I shot the hologram, Mrs. Raymond's image might have looked more like a photographic double exposure. Their emotions could not have been identical, could not have produced that single image. In contrast to clinking champagne glasses in the Reynie Junior hologram, when I took the Mrs. Raymond hologram, there was no sound. And so for me it was back to the drawing board to determine whether sound had been a catalyst in the holographic bridal portrait.

Something else about the *sound* thing bothered me: All that tuning fork rigmarole my family and I went through to capture my car accident image might not have been necessary either. Perhaps Jeanie's sounding the tuning fork had merely *focused* my memory, my intention, in that moment, like a laser beam. I pondered my next step. I decided to show Court the hologram of *me* as soon as possible, thinking maybe he could help me.

Court walked back and forth in front of the projected hologram. "There's some blurring."

"Court, you're standing too close. It makes *spectra* of the colors."

Court obediently stepped back. "May we keep this?"

"For a while. But may I please have it back when I need it?" I then beamed down from the U.S.S. Enterprise to the surface of the alien planet and was searching for intelligent life. I was just high enough that I was free-associating. Angelic, though alien, voices kept repeating the words "Harmonic Convergence," arranged in a sort of fugue. It was so lovely that I drifted into my own *contrapuntal* state.

Court interrupted. "David!" In mock panic he said, "Come back to us, David. David?"

I came around. Pizza crust dangled from one side of my mouth. "Um…" I tried to come back from…wherever.

Like a mother, Reynie removed the pizza crust and dabbed at the red sauce stains with a coarse paper napkin. "Feelings," she said.

"Yes. The harmonics of light and feelings," I mumbled.

"I'll call for our limousine." Court said. "You have a lot of work to do. *We* are going home now."

I started floating again.

Court shook my hand. "Edison went through hundreds of substances before he found the one that made the light bulb glow."

I answered, "Yeah, but he could see right away if something worked or not. I won't know until, for each attempt, I've gone through this ordeal for an entire day!"

"Don't give up, ol' boy," Reynie said. "I've a feeling you and I are going to be great friends. Ciao!"

"Phone me in the morning," Court said. "I'll give you your personal checks at lunch. Can you remember to call me?"

Captain James T. Kirk tapped his communicator and said: "Scotty: Three to beam up from these coordinates."

I needed to clean up my lab and so Court and Reynie left in their limo at 11:00 p.m. On my way out Calvin bid me adieu with a fond, "Don't hold the anchovies!" By the time I'd loaded the rental van and dragged myself into it, I was afraid I'd fall asleep before I reached downtown Boulder. But I chugged along just fine...until in the rearview mirror I saw milky black smoke spewing from the van's exhaust pipe. Then the engine light popped on. "Dammit!" I thanked God when I saw a Sunoco station up ahead.

When I pulled in, an attendant came out right away. Waving the smoky exhaust away from his face he shouted, "Turn it off!"

After I cut the engine the exhaust pipe emitted a last retort of soot, and a "chunk" sound punctuated the night.

"You can't leave that thing here overnight," the Sunoco attendant said. "I don't want to be responsible for it."

"Come on! Aren't you a mechanic?"

The attendant stood like a Doric marble column.

"I'll pay you to keep it here until Home Depot can pick it up in the morning," I offered.

"That'll be seventy-five bucks."

I felt like strangling the jerk.

"That's our price for overnight tow-ins," the attendant said, "so that's the charge for that smoker you just brought in."

Jeanie would have to rescue me in my Bronco. I cursed before asking to use the station's pay phone. What other choice did I have?

Bags under her eyes, Jeanie pulled up to the Sunoco in my SUV. Neither of us spoke while I put the back seats down and packed my equipment in the wagon. I had barely closed the passenger door when Jeanie pressed on the accelerator too abruptly. This hurled my body back and then whipped my head forward almost to the windshield. She offered no apology. Instead she asked me if I'd been drinking

In a way, she had something there. I was punch-drunk. It's what happens when I get a tad ahead of myself. "Honey, I'll make it up to you. I promise." I curled up against the passenger door.

Jeanie yawned, then blinked at oncoming headlights. "Starting when?" She stepped on the gas, making me career toward her.

I needed time. "Maybe tomorrow night," I said.

"You always say 'tomorrow'."

CHAPTER SEVEN

The next morning I checked in by phone with Court. He said he "owned" a dining table at the Brown Palace in Denver and that it was always open for him. We would meet for lunch at Noon.

I hoped I would wake up early. Jeanie was out for the morning already. I called in sick to OPTIKS, vowing to myself I'd never do so again. A voice in my head said, *You can't go on living two lives, Davie old boy. They're gonna* can *you, pal.* But I cared only about my new venture.

I was still beat from the night before. Getting ready to meet Court turned into a saga. The results of shaving were pitiful. Little pieces of blood stained toilet paper dotted my face. I prayed that I'd remember to remove them before I left the house. For some reason blow drying my hair that morning made me look like Elvis Presley on a bad day. I tried to use Jeanie's hair styling gel to puff my hair up a little. It made me look like David Bowie on a good day. Putting on underarm deodorant should have been easy, but the stick was low. The container's plastic rim scraped the hell out of my underarms and made me wonder if any deodorant had really touched my armpits.

The only good news was that I had exactly one clean, pressed shirt in the drawer. But I was driven by some masochistic whim to put on my power suit. It was expensive black wool with thin gray stripes. So far I had used it for weddings, funerals, and the Denver Symphony Orchestra. The coat was double-breasted and fit perfectly. It made me look like a prosperous businessman who also worked out in the gym four days a week. But it was eighty degrees in Boulder already. I'd already started to sweat like a pig roasting on a spit.

I looked at myself in the mirror. I couldn't picture myself *telling* Court about the hologram of me. I wanted to show it to him. Changing my mind had already become a habit. I phoned Court again and broke our lunch appointment. I asked him to come up to Boulder instead. I hoped my cancelling wouldn't make Court lose respect for me.

He said: "No problem, Son."

When Jeanie got home I braced myself for civil war. "Why are you so dressed up? You look unseasonably great, except for this." She picked a shred of bloodied toilet paper off my chin.

When I told her Court would be there soon her expression changed from shock to anger. "If you keep this up, OPTIKS is going to fire you. The richest man in Denver is coming and the place looks like a dump."

"Court won't care."

Jeanie's chin and lower lip quivered. "I care! I care that you played hooky from work today like a juvenile delinquent. You can't just take off work any time you feel like it. You need to get some perspective."

A half hour later Court's long, gray limo pulled all the way up the driveway and stopped just outside our back door. The Katourians next door peeped through the curtains of their big dining room window.

Court wore a red-and-blue-plaid cotton shirt and a cowboy string tie, denim pants, a belt with a huge Western buckle on it, and lizard skin boots. He also carried a bouquet of flowers.

"Jeanie! I have to change before he sees me!"

Harlan came with Court to our back door. He carried a humongous covered platter and knocked briskly three times.

Court burst in and laid the flowers in Jeanie's arms. "You fortunate *lady*. Do you realize your husband's going to be famous? I'm thrilled to be a part of it. Oh, this is Harlan, my driver. May he put this tray on your kitchen table? It's cold cuts, cheeses, bread, and fruit. If that's not okay, I'll send for something else." Now breathless from this little marathon of talking, Court asked if he could sit down for a minute.

I was overwhelmed with pleasure and relief—and charmed by Court's immense charisma.

Jeanie suddenly became a Grande Dame. Her voice silky and pitched lower than usual, she said, "Mr. Raymond, thank you for these beautiful flowers. We would like you to feel this is your home too, so please make yourself comfortable. Is there anything you need? A cool drink? We have lemonade *and* iced tea."

Court sat down in a kitchen chair. "Thank you, no, dear lady. Please call me Court."

I had a sudden epiphany about why Court had such a magical effect on people. He was both Old World and New World. He had a grace that showed no prejudice about social station or educational background. He made everyone feel like an equal.

"The food looks great," I said. "Forgive me for not introducing my wife. Court, Harlan, this is Jeanie."

Harlan bowed a bit. I half-expected him to click his heels together.

Court stood. "A pleasure to meet you." I half-expected him to kiss Jeanie's hand. "Now that I can see you're satisfied with the food, I'll just send Harlan on his way. I'm anxious to see the hologram you told me about. Harlan, I'll ring the car phone when I need you."

Jeanie hadn't seen the hologram of Mrs. Raymond so her right eyebrow conveyed a question mark. Gratefully she held her tongue in front of Court. She saw Harlan out and began to arrange the flowers in a tall crystal vase. She hummed to herself. The vibrato of her lovely soprano voice was like a finch's dulcet song.

Court nodded toward the kitchen. "You're a lucky man."

I sighed. "Would it be rude of me to get down to business? I mean, I want to show you a hologram of mine that you haven't seen."

Court clapped me on the shoulder. "That's what I wanted to hear, but wouldn't you like to change first?"

Jeanie peeked around the kitchen doorway and gave me a look that said, *I'll leave you two alone for now, but you and I will have a talk later.*

Upstairs in our bedroom I draped my suit, tie, and newly starched shirt over the back of a chair. It felt great to toss my socks and shoes across the room and into the corner. I put on jeans and my orange-and-dark-blue Broncos T-shirt and slipped into my favorite flip flops.

I literally bounced to the bottom of the stairs. I heard Court telling Jeanie how lovely her voice was. I knew she'd be his slave from then on. "If you keep that up," I said to Court, "Jeanie will leave me to go into the movies." *Oops. Wrong thing to say.*

But Jeanie just smiled, thank God. "You two run along now and let me do my chores."

I gave her a special *I love you* look before I led Court down to my basement lab. The hologram of me was already set up because I'd been looking at the hologram for half the night. I drew the black, light blocking curtains across my garden-level basement windows. I only had to turn on the reconstruction beam and the hologram illuminated.

Court gulped. "It's incredible! How did you do this?"

"Don't you think it's weird? You see that little figure coming out the top of my head? Have any idea what it might be?"

Court studied the hologram for several minutes. "Your spirit," he said, like it was nothing unusual. "That's your soul isn't it?"

I felt a ton of tension leave my body. "Afraid so."

"My Boy! What do you mean...'afraid'? This is a masterpiece. I don't care if it *is* your spirit. I want to know if you can do this again. If you can, I want you to start working for *me*."

"What?"

"I want you to quit your job. At least take a leave of absence. Devote yourself full-time to this work. Don't you see? It's a chance to scientifically prove the existence of something only religious people believe in!" Court nudged my shoulder to get me to sit down on my bench. "You look awful, David. Would it help if I told you that you can live easily on the financing I'll give you? I don't even need you to share the royalties you'll get from this in the future. Do you understand? I've got maybe ten or fifteen years left to contribute something meaningful to the world. Here's the checkbook I promised you. And a charge card in your name for large purchases."

I looked at Court with gratitude. What I felt at that moment made me know I was ready to say those sincere words to him that I couldn't before. "Court, I promise I won't disappoint you. I promise you'll be proud to be associated with my work. I promise I won't waste a penny. I—." I was so overwhelmed I was afraid I'd lose it. I buried my face in my hands and shook until the anxiety took a hike.

Court cupped the back of my head. "My boy, I can see how important this is to you. Don't worry. I won't interfere. You'll have total freedom. But I want you to share with me every breakthrough. As far as I'm concerned I'll be paying for your discoveries."

I felt meagre confidence Court that could get his money's worth.

He seemed to guess my thoughts. "Sharing this work with you is the most fulfilling thing I will ever do in my life. How do you put a price on something that valuable? This venture is something I never dreamed I could 'buy', if you know what I mean. In fact, it shouldn't be this easy. Think of these funds as a sort of grant, only you happen to know the grantee well."

I wanted to tell Court I'd be his son for free! That just knowing him was payment enough. That he was giving me back my youth, my very life. Instead I confessed that he might not agree morally with part of my plan. *Well, here goes nothing*, I thought. *How fast should I get to the point?* "I want to go back to my hometown for a month or so. Try to capture some things from the past through holography."

"Why would that be immoral?"

I figured I might as well fess up. "Have you heard of Lucille Muhr?"

"The film actress?"

"Yes. She and I are from the same hometown. We were sweethearts, on and off, starting with our sophomore year in high school. We ended it in the Fall of my senior year at CU."

"And you want to go back and retrieve your past with her?"

I stood up so I could pace. Pacing normally helped me think. While Court followed me around my lab with his eyes, I told him about how troubled Lu was when we went together. How nobody, not even me, seemed to know what lay back there in her life that was so upsetting.

Court leaned back against my worktable. "Then I'm sure you saw her on television a few weeks ago. Tell me—even if your plan is successful, what will it accomplish? Couldn't you just get in touch with Ms. Muhr and ask her yourself? Surely your relationship with her would get you through the door. Or just on the telephone line."

I told Court that Lu *had* called me a few years ago. That I treated her coldly. "Going back would accomplish several things. I have unfinished business with Lu. I'm stuck back in my *emotional* past. I believe inventing the right equipment is key to capturing impressions of Lu's ordeals. Then hopefully I can 'exorcise' her from my heart."

"I see. But aren't there other ways to resolve this 'itch', David? Therapy? Hypnosis? What if going back to your hometown makes Ms. Muhr even more real to you right *now*? After all, she's not only beautiful and brilliant but she's also a star."

Though I knew Court would hit every nail on the head, I wasn't ready to deal with his questions. I sensed he was about to drop another bomb on me. The kind of truth only a good friend dares to speak.

He stopped my pacing behind him by gripping my forearm. "Does your wife know about this? Your leaving to go back to Ohio would be asking a lot of Jeanie. Even the most secure woman might wonder."

I felt I'd affronted Court. I disliked how worried he looked. "I guess that's what I meant when I said you might not morally agree with my plan. It's not that I'd be having an *affair* with Lucille Muhr."

"Remember when Jimmy Carter said in *Playboy* Magazine that he had 'sinned in his heart'? Don't you think that if you relived your relationship with her it would be like having an affair with her? And that the holograms you'd make to record the past would be like 'evidence' of that 'affair'?"

"Don't other people have snapshots of past loves stashed in their attics? What's the difference between that and the holograms I hope to make?" I still hadn't convinced myself I'd triumph, so I feared Court wouldn't be persuaded either.

Indeed, Court's wan smile showed concern. He pointed to the hologram, still lit and hovering in my lab. "This hologram and a photograph are galaxies apart, and you know it. Now I agree that the *material* you want to use would probably lend itself perfectly to your process. You do need intense memories. And they must be your own. But if you're going to use your own memories, how will you discover anything about Ms. Muhr that you don't know already?"

Now I smiled back at Court. "But I won't be using my own memories. I want to capture energetic artifacts that exist in the house Lucille Muhr grew up in. To do that I need to invent some device that can detect traces from the past just sort of *floating around*."

"And you have an idea of what this device would be?"

I sat down with Court. "Well, in a way. Look at the difference between the Reynie Junior hologram and this one of me. Hers is a simple physical, single-image holographic trace. Mine has a couple of extra dimensions, a *remembered* background environment *and* a spiritual body. As near as I can tell, the extra dimensions of this hologram came about via some psychic process I went through that Reynie didn't when we captured 'Reynie Junior'. If I can grasp that process I'll have it!"

"You think you can do this alone?" Court asked.

"I have to. For obvious reasons. It's very personal. And I need this to be confidential."

"Yes," I said. "Perhaps a psychic thing." Even while rebuking *myself*. I now believed the missing link in my work was something *woo-woo*. Being a scientist I was still torn. I laughed and said, "Yeah. I guess I'm going to have to check out some unscientific stuff. You know how Boulder is. What better place to begin, as they say, to 'evolve'? Maybe I'll learn to meditate so I can be more receptive to 'the unseen'."

Court pretended to be rattled. "You expect me to pay for you to see New Age charlatans? What would they know about holography?"

"I'm asking you to remember what we shared when we were in my lab at OPTIKS: discovery and breakthrough. Holograms *are* like memories. A hologram 'remembers' an entire subject, whether that is a pattern, an object, or a person. I'm counting on that fact to get me through. Think of psychic aspects as facilitators or enhancing agents. I feel in my gut that this is pivotal. I hope you will trust me. There must be some unseen relationship between light and matter. Also remember that every kind of energy can change to another kind of energy. I'm beginning to believe that *frequency* determines what kind of energy is created. For example, energy expressed in the highest frequency might be light. The next level lower might be sound; the next, odor. Now, mind you, I've arrived at this intuitively."

Court looked brain tired. "Well," he sighed, "I guess that's what separates you geniuses from the rest of us. Suppose Jeanie resists your leaving her for the work you just mentioned? It's clear you'll need a surrogate *here* while you're gone. She'll need moral support and a feeling of family. Since your trip seems to be a necessary part of our bargain, I guess I'll need to trust you and also be your surrogate." He laughed pleasantly. "I should deduct that from your salary!"

The seesawing of adrenalin rushes and the venting of tension had drained me. "I promise to find the best 'charlatans' in Boulder."

"Maybe Reynie can help you there. Friends in her circle deal only with the finest. The ones who don't advertise. She doesn't take them seriously. But I know if she showed any interest her friends would be glad to recommend those people. In fact, I could ask her to go with you. Kind of as a backup."

"Great! You see? You are my benefactor. Not just financially."

"I'm famished. Let's go upstairs. We'll have a calm lunch and a glass of wine with your pretty wife." He paused in the middle of the stairs. "David," he said. "You continue to brighten my days. I awaken every morning feeling hopeful and happy."

"I know one thing. I'm gonna have to read up on crystals."

"You can be sure I'll be asking *why* later."

I decided not to tell Jeanie and Eddie for now about the *being away* part of my plans. I knew I must do some metaphysical research in Boulder first. Get in tune with my subconscious or whatever. If I could find techniques to make my plan work the way I hoped, there'd be no turning back. Soon enough I'd have to tell Jeanie about going to Ohio—but not *why*.

After Court left I finally did show Jeanie the hologram of me. She was as blown away as Eddie and Court. But when I told her that Court had set me up with a lot of money and that I was going to take time off from my job she freaked out.

"What if you *don't* invent anything?" Jeanie asked. "We can't have Court support us for the rest of our lives! After all, there's nowhere else in Colorado but OPTIKS who'll pay you to do holography."

"Have a little faith in your husband." What I didn't say is that I'm going to tell my boss I'm taking 'a leave of absence'."

Jeanie was only a little relieved. "On what grounds?" she asked. "Your mental health?"

"Very funny," I retorted. "There are such things as sabbaticals you know. Something OPTIKS will think might benefit them. But if I accomplish what I'm hoping, they ain't gonna get one bit of benefit from old Davie. No siree. This here's my very own baby!"

Jeanie had to jab me one more time: "I can put up with your little fits and your exhaustion from working. But I'm not sure I can stand your becoming, like, 'totally tubular'."

"You love me, Jeanie?"

"I must."

CHAPTER EIGHT

Boulder is nestled in a valley along the Front Range of the Rockies. The land itself often seems to hum with energy. I'm convinced that only someone who has actually lived in Boulder can understand how unique the area is. How powerfully the town attracts its visitors and sustains its residents. Scientists thrive here. There's the University of Colorado's Laboratory for Atmospheric and Space Physics, the National Center for Atmospheric Research, and the National Institute of Standards and Technology, which houses the NIST-F1 atomic clock. This is the U.S. national standard for time and frequency.

Arapaho Indians fought to preserve an ancient medicine wheel on land that the Feds wanted NIST to acquire. Unfortunately, the tribal people lost that battle. But they still tie colorful ribbons on the tips of tree branches and leave offerings of tobacco and corn meal near the medicine wheel. Pioneers or neighbors removed many of the black volcanic rocks not native to the area and other stones that may have formed the ring and "spokes" of the medicine wheel.

Arapaho tribal elders say Boulder is sitting on a vast bed of quartz. They claim no white man knows where the mouth of the tunnel is that leads from north of town to under downtown Boulder. The tunnel filled with a powerful pulsing storehouse of quartz. From East to West by the Fortieth Parallel, South Boulder is one of the high-energy spots along the vast ley lines of quartz that reach across planet Earth. This interests me because highly refined crystals help me make holograms.

Boulder is politically progressive and also one of the world's New Age hot spots, nurturing myriad esoteric ideas. In fact, Denverites like Reynie say: "Only in Boulder" and "Oh, you live in Boulder. You *do it* on a Ouija board." Naropa Institute, west of the Pearl Street Mall, is supported by the largest Tibetan Buddhist population in the world. Boulder offers every kind of *alternative healing* practitioner you can name. Reichians, Rolfers, re-birthers, reflexologists, acupuncturists, kinesiologists and Neuro-Linguistic Programming practitioners. Chromotherapists (who use color therapy) and toners (who help you find your own internal sounds, rhythms, and harmonics). Regressive and progressive hypnotherapists. Tarot, palm, and aura readers. Astrologers and phrenologists. Crystal healers, herbalists, and acupuncturists. Spirit channelers of all kinds, including a Lakota Sioux called Spotted Eagle, who does a three hour, getting in touch with the Great Spirit session and ending in a genuine tribal dance.

Residents of Boulder have the highest per capita income and education in the state. PhDs who long to live in Boulder are driving UPS trucks because there's too much competition for other high-paying jobs. Boulder's financial elite keep a rather low profile, except when they're shopping downtown. When you stroll the Mall, you see everything from mohawk haircuts to Western elegance. Transients and the otherwise flaky have become local personalities. For example, one night I was out with Jeanie and my friend Josh at a downtown bar where they play music from the Fifties and Sixties. Behind us sat a youngish, barefoot man wearing a tan terry cloth bathrobe. And a white towel tied around his neck like an ascot. Maybe the guy had watched too many William Powell "Thin Man" movies. Alone, the turbaned transient gestured and carried on a conversation interesting only to him. No one bothered the man until he got out on the dance floor and began doing violent karate chops, complete with Bruce Lee sound effects. The police perp-walked him away.

Even though Reynie and I became good friends, she remains a cipher to me. "You're crazy," she said over lunch at the Golden Lotus in Boulder. "*Me* go with *you* to that woo-woo workshop in Boulder? Was this Daddy's idea? If so, he and I are going to have a talk."

"Well, he said you know some people. Besides, this class should be fun. And it'll be a great overview, don't you think?"

"I don't want an overview, and I don't think it's fair that you are pressuring me to go with you."

I sensed Reynie felt more intimidated than reluctant. "You'll be safe with me," I said. I didn't want to go to the workshop alone, but I was flailing at getting Reynie to come with me.

"Scared, David?"

"What? Well, that's rich!"

"Why don't you make Jeanie go? Then you can practice on each other. I'm sure she'd like it."

It had been so long since I'd eaten with chopsticks that sticky clumps of sesame chicken kept dropping back on my plate.

"I'm thinking that it's not fair to ask your father to pay for this, uh, rather unscientific part of my research. He said you do have friends in the more woo-woo community. And I already asked Jeanie."

"Maybe Jeanie can teach you how to use chopsticks," Reynie said. she suppressed a smile and seized a morsel of egg fu young with her chopsticks.

"Can you give me a break for once?"

"I *might* go. But only if it's all right with—."

"It's all right."

Reynie had almost finished eating. "Don't you think Jeanie would mind my going to the workshop with you?"

"She knows you're just a friend."

"Friendship is not a mere thing," she argued. "Have I wasted my time by spending it with you?"

I suppressed my irritation. "You know what I mean."

"Have you no other friends? Someone you've known a long time? Someone who wouldn't mind indulging you in this?"

"My best buddy Josh, but he's been out of town for a while now. He's on his yearly fishing trip in Estes Park's Rocky Mountain National Forest. Listening to elks bugle, tying flies or something. Besides, I need a woman. I mean, I need a woman's sensibilities. I mean, I need to know how to *tune in* to a woman's psyche."

"You do need to tune into your own psyche," Reynie said. "That way you'll be more self-aware. You should get in touch with your own emotions too. I've watched you interact with Eddie. And I know how you interact with me.…In short, I keep seeing that you have little compassion for others."

Reynie had now offended me. "I'd like to know where you get all that. Sure, I don't wear my heart on my sleeve, but—."

"I keep looking for 'redeeming social value' in you," she said. "But what I keep finding is that in your body, besides an enormous brain, is a heart about the size of a walnut."

"I'm trying to find out who I am! Apart from the David married to Jeanie The David who has a teenage son."

"You could learn a lot from Eddie. He's still open and fresh."

I resented Reynie for knowing this. "We *all* were at seventeen."

"We can stay that way or become that way again." she riposted.

"For Chrissake, Reynie! Did you take *Buddha* lessons or something? For your information, I'm doing all this shit to nail what you said—to get in touch with who I am."

Reynie peered into my face. "But you're leaving everybody else out of the equation, David. And I don't understand how studying metaphysics will enhance your work."

"Number one: I don't have a full grip on how I got all that stuff in the hologram of myself. It opened a Pandora's box of questions that I can't answer by making more holograms. Number two—." I took a deep breath and asked Reynie if I could confide in her. "I already spoke to your Dad about this, and he had the same reaction. You're wondering why just inventing some new device wouldn't be enough for me?" Then I told Reynie about Lucille Muhr. "Don't you see? This whole thing is tied up with the past!"

"Why do you have to go to Circleville, Oho? Why can't you just take holograms of yourself while *you* are remembering Lucille Muhr in the past?"

"Because memory distorts. And because I need answers to questions I still have about Lu. That means I have to go back to Circleville. Right to the scene."

"That seems rather self-indulgent," Reynie said. "And you can't guarantee that going back to Ohio will turn out the way you want."

"I can't explain how I know it'll work. It's just something I must do. And I'm going to need you to help keep things running smoothly with Jeanie. Could you just do that, please?"

Reynie got so upset that she talked with her mouth full: "Now wait a minute! I'm very busy living my own life!"

"All I ask is that you remind my wife from time to time that I'm taking a sort of leave of absence. That I'll return to her with something to make her proud of me," I added, only half-believing what I said.

"You have some sadistic need to torture the poor woman? You have some kind of marriage death wish?"

"I have not asked you for anything before. Now I'm asking for your help. It's not like I'd be having an affair!"

Reynie placed her chopsticks neatly across her plate. "Oh yeah? Well, let me run this by you. You're having a passionate affair with your work. And obviously no one, especially Jeanie, is any competition for the way you feel about that. As excited as I am about your holography, I feel you're being selfish. And you're asking a lot from people who care about you. You want me to keep your marriage together while you're gone. How can I do that? By being a goodwill ambassador with your wife? She'll wonder who the hell I am to be defending her absent husband, who just happens to be pursuing a famous actress by making holograms of her from the past. David, I do know how important this is to you. Maybe it's even important to the world. Oh, hell! I can see in your eyes that you're going to let nothing stop you."

"You'll go to class with me?" I entreated.

"You should be in sales. There's no reason why I should buy *any* of this. Yet I'll admit you've reeled me in. Okay, then. But if I don't like it, I'm going to stop going. Deal?"

I picked up my *fork* so I could finish my noodles. "Deal."

I arrived inside an old dance studio on the West side of Pearl Street Mall to attend the "Grow Your Intuition" workshop. The building smelled of dancers' sweat and oil paints. In an open classroom, Aikido students performed their circular movements with partners. One petite brunette was about to take down a six-foot Yeti, who put her in a gentle hammer lock. Taking itsy-bitsy steps in a circle, she threw his center of gravity off and he went down like a felled tree. The moment Sasquatch pulled his hands away from her to catch his fall, she slipped easily away from him. Aromas of white sage and Nag Champa incense drifted through the hallways. The old stairs creaked and squeaked.

A group of New Age healers and artists shared the rooms upstairs. Several people hovered around the doorway of our room while we all waited for our instructor to arrive. The assembled group looked as anxious and excited as I felt. I couldn't see what the inside was like because the door was locked.

I got all worked up, thinking Reynie would stand me up. Maybe I *was* a chicken shit. Maybe I *was* asking too much of the people close to me. I believed I had stopped thinking and had started to act from my gut. Call it animal instinct. Call it intuition. I sensed a little door was about to open into a reality I used to ridicule. I believed it was some other level of perception that was, for now, only a glimmer. I knew that glimmer would have to grow much bigger or I would wind up only making interesting holograms that critics would say were tricks of the developing process. Without *understanding* how I got those results, I wouldn't be able to prove what those outcomes suggested: that all events—past, present and future—are alive simultaneously. That they are all accessible *now*.

I barely grasped that you could tune in to varied paths you *might* have taken. Maybe the "future" contained infinite potential for the self. And one of my own possibilities was to be with Lucille Muhr. Maybe another part of David Leone and Lucille Muhr did stay madly in love, marry, and were enjoying an exciting life together. And maybe with this other kind of training I could capture that life in holograms.

A person I thought was the instructor unlocked the door to the classroom. The group flocked in and each of us picked one of the chairs that lined the long, rectangular table. From where I sat, the instructor would be to my right, on a diagonal. We all looked each other over while we waited for the workshop facilitator. A perky young woman at the far end of the table introduced herself as Karen and asked for our names.

Then the real instructor came in. Her frowsy blonde hair had purple highlights. Her outfit seemed to correspond with what an astute local anthropologist described as "Paleo-Hippie Boulderite." The peasant skirt and shawl, the violet puffy sleaved blouse, the mixed bag of jewelry, the ankh pendant, and tribal earrings with large beads. She also wore a variety of bracelets, some silver with turquoise and red coral, and gold shaped bracelets shaped into cobras and sea creatures. The perfect New Age gypsy garb! But she did look centered and energetic. "Hi. I'm Fleur, your instructor, and—."

Reynie burst into the room. She panted. "Sorry. I got tied up in traffic on the Turnpike."

"Welcome," Fleur said to Reynie.

Reynie looked embarrassed. There was no empty seat beside me, so she sat across from me. Her look said, *Only for you, David.* And, possibly, *Never again.*

"My ad for this workshop emphasized that this is an *intermediate* class," Fleur said. "This means that none of you consider yourselves beginners. And so, instead of introducing ourselves, we'll do our first experiment. This should show us how in-tune we are."

Being a direct person, Reynie just had to comment: "But we don't know each other." Under her breath, Reynie said to me: "Give me a break. *You're* not a beginner?"

Fleur was cool. "Because most of us don't know each other, you'll have to work on sheer observation, which some people call intuition. And it should build trust, which we need to do quickly if we're going to meet the objectives of this class." Fleur pulled a high stool over and set it at the room's center-front. "Here's what we're gonna do. One at a time, we're gonna come up here and sit in this chair. Then the rest of the class will check that person out and get a 'feeling' for their personality. And anything deeper that comes through."

Judging from their faces, I could see that everyone had the same *ishy* feeling about this experiment. Reynie caught my attention. She rolled her eyes. I gave her a warning look that said: *If you leave now I'll never speak to you again.*

Though Reynie stayed, she looked like she was levitating. Her eyes conveyed *Don't mess with me, David. You know when I get tired of this, I'm outta here!* I laughed when I realized we were carrying on a "telepathic" conversation.

"To make it fair," Fleur continued, "I'll go first." She sat on the high stool and looked at each of us for a moment. Even under this raw scrutiny of the class, she seemed confident, unflappable.

I volunteered first. "I don't know where I got the information, but I feel you have...anger issues."

The class and Fleur looked shocked at my boldness.

Uh, oh, I thought. *I'm in trouble already.*

Though Fleur looked guarded now, she said, "I'm working on that." Then she laughed.

A guy named Matt, who looked like he rode in on a Harley-Davidson, raised his hand. "What's so psychic about that?" he asked, shaking his mane of dishwater blond hair. "Maybe he just read your body language."

Fleur's mouth curved ever so slightly down. "I don't believe my body language gave away what he...what's your name?"

I told Fleur my name.

"...what David picked up. The point is, even if it was just body language, most people couldn't consciously pinpoint how they knew." She turned to me again. "What else do you see?"

Obviously I'd been singled out and was now going to have to come up with something even more insightful to prove my previous perception hadn't been an accident. I checked out Fleur's eyes and what the muscles around her mouth were doing. I was seeking any discrepancies there. I'll never know what I said next had to do with that: "I think you believe you've sort of raised yourself. Like your parents didn't understand why you were so different, even when you were a child."

Fleur's eyes riveted to mine. "You're right. I can see why you came to this workshop tonight."

Then the young woman named Karen broke in with, "I sense you're having some emotional problems right now. Like you're in conflict about your love life and your spiritual work."

I saw Reynie's mouth tighten. I couldn't tell if her eyes were glazed because of apprehension or if she was going to take off because she was bored.

"Enough about me," Fleur said. "Will another volunteer please come up here?"

"I will," a pale, bookish looking male said. He had scraggly, unfashionably long sideburns and wore a black leather vest over his wrinkled gray shirt. The cuffs of his bell bottom jeans were threadbare, as if they had dragged across floors and sidewalks for decades. I figured he'd left home as a teenager because of his neglectful mother. He got up on the stool and peered out at the rest of us with a shy, but inquisitive, expression. He said his name was Keith.

I got the oddest notion about Keith, but it didn't come from thinking. I was only looking at him, taking him in. Surprising even myself, I said: "I sense you've read all of A. Conan Doyle's Sherlock Holmes books and that you've seen every Sherlock Holmes movie ever made." *Wow!* I thought. *That's specific.* And by the way he looked at me, I figured this time my credibility was about to take a nosedive.

"Do you get cable TV?" Keith finally asked. "Last night some of my friends came over to watch a Sherlock Holmes movie. And yes: I *have* read all the Sherlock Holmes books and have seen all the Sherlock Holmes movies."

At that, I began to feel so proud of myself that I almost crowed.

Reynie's eyes enlarged.

Karen came up next. Her benign expression looked phony. She told the class she was a volunteer nurse and that she was taking this class so she might become a better healer.

All at once I saw the most beautiful, translucent blue light form a corona around Karen's head and torso. I gasped. I heard Reynie gasp at the same time. Then I saw the blue aura change to a brilliant, pure white light. Involuntarily, I shouted at Karen: "What are you doing!"

"Why, nothing. What did you see?"

Reynie was both agitated and excited. "You did that on purpose!" she said to Karen.

I placed my hand on the table pointing toward Reynie, as if to reach out and take her hand to calm her. "I saw it too," I said. "Tell me what *you* saw."

Reynie described exactly what I'd noticed. Even the bit about the color turning from blue to white.

"This is a gifted class," Fleur said. "We're gonna have a lot of fun doing experiments. Looking at Reynie, Fleur asked, "Who'd like to be the next subject?"

"Oh, no," Renie said. "Make David go up now. Then *I* will."

It had been easy to sit around the table and stare at whoever was on that stool. Being up there alone, under the scrutiny of those other people and the instructor, was a different story! I took my cue from what Karen had just apparently done and told myself: *Imagine lying by the ocean. Imagine how the waves sound and the warm wind feels.*

But these attempts at blocking fear didn't work on Karen. Obviously, we had a spiritual pro here. "I feel you have psychic gifts but you're afraid of them," she said to me. "I also feel you're looking for someone, but that person is not here today. It's an intense love that cannot *be* in this lifetime."

In this process of having my soul stripped bare I got no consolation from Reynie. She looked obnoxiously smug. Her expression said, *You're getting exactly what you deserve.*

Keith, the "Sherlock Holmes" guy, said: "You showed you're sensitive to colors. Light. I'm picking up that you use light in your work. You have some question about your work and your life. You didn't say you were looking for *someone*, but I feel that you are. It has something to do with your work. This might sound strange, but—."

Fleur then jumped into the fray, probably out of revenge for what I'd said about her. "You and Reynie obviously know each other. I don't have to be psychic to figure that out."

The class laughed. I laughed nervously with them.

Fleur continued: "I feel Karen and Keith are both right. You are looking for someone, and that person is a woman."

Reynie now focused completely on what was happening in the workshop. "Now this is choice," she whispered to me.

It seemed a good time to go back to my chair. "Reynie's next," I said. I knew I was going to catch it from her, but good, after class.

Reynie moved gracefully toward the stool, her aristocratic breeding glowing like neon. Knowing her, I realized what a clever front her aristocratic façade really was. And she had accused *me* of having no heart. Inside she was probably all-jelly. But why should she be? She had everything: wealth, intelligence, charisma, a husband with whom she was very happy…

The ever quick Karen piped up. "I feel that you're a very giving person who keeps her feelings mostly to herself."

"Not her *opinions* though," I retorted.

Everyone except Reynie laughed.

Karen continued: "You're also keeping a big secret, Reynie."

Naturally, I believed Karen was talking about what Reynie knew of *my* plans. Karen's spot-on comments had made me paranoid. Though I was pleased with both my own and my classmates' powers of perception, I wondered if it would blow the lid off my own secret.

Reynie smiled. "I do have a secret." She looked at me. "But it has nothing to do with you, David."

I must have looked so deflated that everyone laughed.

"I'm afraid we're running out of time," Fleur said. "Matt, you're up last. Please let us *read* you"

Matt perched on the stool. He was beefy but pale, with big bones and broad shoulders. He was clearly trying to seem calm. His eyes begged: "Please go easy on me. I'm really a good guy."

I spotted Matt's clenched right hand. In contrast, his left hand was flat and open. I'll admit I picked up the following by way of logic, not intuition. I ventured out loud that Matt had a conflict between his brain and his emotions. That he was a sensitive person who was afraid of the intensity of his feelings.

Reynie even came out of her shell to tell Matt that he should trust himself more. "The fact that you came to this class says you're open to resolving your conflict," she said gently.

The omniscient Karen turned her milk chocolate eyes on Matt and said, "Your girlfriend's not good for you. She makes you feel bad about yourself. You should dump her."

I wondered why Karen wasn't teaching the class instead of Fleur.

Fleur apparently needed to take control again. "Time's up for today. Here's your homework for next week. I want you to bring in a photograph that has special meaning to you. Place it in a white envelope and seal it. When we get to class next week, I'll tell you what the experiment will be. See you then."

I asked Reynie to get coffee with me, but she said she had to get back to her husband. "When can we get together to talk about this?"

"I'll be too busy. But I'll see you next week in for sure." She hugged me. "I promise." Then she sailed like a swallow out of the room.

Fleur stopped me. "Can I speak to you a minute. You may be the most psychically gifted person in this class."

"Please don't use the word *psychic*."

Fleur looked surprised. "Why?"

"Because I'm a scientist."

Fleur said nothing.

"What do you think about Karen's 'mystic powers'? She's got a lot of confidence in them."

"She is pretty good, but she's got a *motive*, if you know what I mean. She's obviously read enough to know that blue is a primary healing color. And that if your aura is pure white, you're practically a saint. Her gift is projecting those colors to camouflage other things."

"Like what?" I asked. I was beginning to see Fleur knew what she was talking about. What she had picked up about Karen also answered *my* question about Karen.

"Karen's experimenting with her personal power," Fleur said. "Right now her motive is to hide things from people. To impress them with an image of her that she can control. And she's gotten very good at it. That's why you and your friend were able to see those colors. When she masters this, you won't see that sudden change in the colors. She'll be able to sustain a blue aura for longer than a few seconds. However, that won't change whatever she's afraid others will see: whatever she doesn't like about herself."

"What makes you believe *I'm* so gifted?" I asked. "And don't you think I'm hiding something too?"

"You *are* hiding something," Fleur observed, "but what you're hiding is more like a plan or a goal. Something you must do alone. You're not hiding your goal from anyone. In fact, your goal is the reason you'll find the answers you seek."

I asked Fleur if she knew what Karen meant when she said Reynie was keeping a big secret.

"I feel I do know, but since Reynie's your friend, don't you think you should let her tell you when she's ready?"

"Damn. I guess so."

Fleur smiled. "But you're not one to stand by with questions unanswered. Afraid I gotta stick to my principles on this one. Oh. Before you leave, I want to suggest something. You know when everyone was getting that you're looking for someone? Even if you already know who that person is, I'd recommend you go through hypnotic regression. Then maybe you could find out *why* you need to find her again." Fleur followed this with an explanation of past life readings and that she thought she, herself, was the best regressive hypnotist in town.

"But wait until we explore some other possibilities. One of *those* may be a better way to go. See you next week."

I had no intention of being hypnotically regressed by Fleur or anyone else. Timewise, I had to draw the line somewhere. Instead, I said to Fleur: "I just got an idea. You have all our phone numbers, right? Would you mind letting me have Karen's phone number? In case I want to talk to her before next class?"

"I would feel more comfortable asking Karen if she wants to call *you*, if you don't mind."

Two Days Later

Okay, so I gave in to being hypnotized. But my publisher warned me about what I'm about to describe. He said some idiot might try to hypnotize someone else using this process and that we could be sued. So here's the disclaimer: Do NOT, under any circumstances, try the following procedures—on yourself or on anyone else! Neither my publisher nor I may be held legally responsible for the results. I'll be leaving out a lot of the hypnotic takedown for the sake of brevity, though these parts are critical to the process. I hope my story will be read as I intend.

When you descend the stairs of the Lighthouse New Age Bookstore on the Pearl Street Mall, you feel like you're in another realm. It's Boulder's most popular metaphysical shop for locals and tourists. Lighthouse has the most up to date materials any metaphysician could desire. Shelf after shelf of esoteric books. Beautifully crafted statuettes imported from Egypt, Greece, and India. Arrays of incense, jewelry, pendulums, and wands. And a back room reserved for channelers, tarot readers, astrologers, and healers. This back room used to be a basement vault for the bank upstairs.

Oceania greeted me at the Lighthouse bookstore. She looked serene and collected—in other words, *normal*. When she saw that I had brought a cassette tape recorder, she nodded. "Your name shows great strength of character and potential for leadership," she said. She led me down a row of bookshelves and into the dimly lit back room of the bookstore. She asked me to lie back in a sort of bean bag chair. I could hear a metronome ticking in the background. No, it was tocking.

Oceania told me the metronome was set to an alpha-wave rhythm to help me relax. "I feel that you're not only looking into your past for yourself. You're also looking for someone else or trying to *re*capture someone *live* instead of in memory. I don't feel you'll be disappointed. Edgar Cayce, 'the sleeping prophet', recorded a lot about reincarnation. He said any person we know who's more than an acquaintance is someone we've worked with before. That means someone we've been closely related to, by blood or other kind of relationships, in past lives. In a past life your current wife might have been your mother. Or you might have been her brother."

I found both wacky and intriguing.

For the first ten minutes, I shared my reasons for wanting to be hypnotically regressed. I told Oceania that I was skeptical about reincarnation but I thought I'd give hypnotic regression a try. Then I noticed my hypnotist had begun matching the rhythm of her spoken questions to the beat of the metronome.

Oceania asked me to think of a symbol, some image I'd like to focus on. I chose a white, full moon in a black sky. I focused on the moon in my mind. I noticed that it was beginning to turn counterclockwise—not smoothly but in sweeps, each motion completing at each tock of the metronome. I could hear the voices of people in the bookstore and the noises of traffic outside. All sounded far away. My intellect gauged and judged what was going on while my imagination soared undisturbed—free to roam in this hypnotic adventure.

What follows is an abridged transcription of our taped session.

Oceania: "Now breathe deeply, in through your nose, as though you can feel the air passing just below the roof of your mouth. Now hold. One, two, three, four. Now slowly let your breath all the way out. (*Tock...tock...tock...tock.*) "Again. Breathe deeply. Now hold. One, two, three, four. Now slowly let your breath out. Again. Now I want you to use your imagination...And as I snap my fingers...I want you to bring...this light...into your body. Do it [snap!]...now!"

I gasped when I felt a massive kinetic force hit my body.

Oceania paused for a moment so my feelings could sink in. Then she asked me what color I chose.

"Blue," I answered.

"Did you feel any sensation when that was happening? At all?"

"Not sharp." I sounded to myself like I was drugged. "Not smooth but real fast."

Oceania asked me in what part of my body I was feeling odd.

"The top of my head."

"Great. Oh, it's a good session. Okay."

"The feeling's going down the front of my body. I feel it in my hands too." I listened to the metronome's relentless, though comforting, ticks and tocks.

"Now that you've finished your deep breathing," Oceania said, "and you have your symbol in your mind, I want you to use your imagination now...to create...in your mind...a very...very soft place. A very comfortable...soft place. And I want you to see yourself...in this place...that is so comfortable...so safe. You are very relaxed...and very much...at peace and...in a moment...I'm going to take you...to an altered state...of consciousness. To a place...in your conscious mind...where past-life...memories...are stored. To a place...in your mind...of super...consciousness, reality. We're going, to go, to a time, and a place, that your mind, has chosen, for you, to perceive. Concentrate on your symbol. Use...the beat...of the metronome...to take you deeper...and deeper...and deeper to altered...states of reality.

You're descending…levels…very quickly now…to a place…in your mind…where past-life memories… are stored. In a moment…I'm going to take you even deeper. But before I do…I'm going to give you…two…suggestions…that you…will carry out. The first…suggestion… is…that each…and every time…you're hypnotized…or relaxed…you're going to go far deeper…far faster…than you've ever… gone…before. The second…suggestion…is…that if…at any time…during this this entire…session…you feel uncomfortable…in any way…simply raise your right hand…and this will bring you… quickly awake.

CHAPTER NINE

Making another hologram was exactly what I needed. And I believed Karen could help me. The challenge with Karen was how to get her to help me without telling her why. I counted on Karen's vanity to outweigh her curiosity. She didn't disappoint me. When I told her I wanted to take a holographic "picture" of her and explained what a hologram was, she rose to the occasion. And when I asked Karen to tell me some of her favorite songs, she grasped the situation immediately. She advised me that she responded best to Middle-C. I didn't ask how Karen knew her note. Only in Boulder.

I asked Jeanie to join us in doing this project. That was so she wouldn't get upset about my inviting into our home another stranger, this time a woman she'd never met.

"I'm starting to get used to it," Jeanie said. Why did she sound so whiny? Why couldn't she say yes without spoiling her assent with her tone of longtime suffering? Oh, yes. Jeanie knew how to use her voice to great effect. I called it 'THE VOICE."

Eddie was staying overnight at a friend's house. Funny. I had no idea how many friends he had or what their names were. In times like these, I wished I lived alone. Like a bachelor, hiding out and doing nothing in his man cave.

Karen arrived wearing a sort of "guru" outfit with shades of mauve and violet. Even her little crepe shoes were purple. She wore pierced earrings that curled up and into her ears, neo-barbarian-style. And somewhere within the honeycomb of her saffron colored turban was plastered down, maybe un-shampooed hair?

Downstairs in my lab, I gave Karen instructions. "Remember what you did in class the other night?" When Karen hesitated, I verbally nudged her. "You know what I mean, Karen. I want you to project your aura as that same sky blue that you did in class. Just sit here on this stool, remain very still. Think about what you felt at that moment in class. Remember what you did while you sat up there. I don't know if *I* will be able to see the color again, but I'm hoping it'll turn up in the hologram. Okay?"

I could tell Jeanie didn't like Karen, but Karen didn't seem to notice. "Okay," Karen said.

"In case I don't see it this time, will you please say 'Now' when you feel you've got it?"

"I'll only know I've got it when I *feel* it," Karen said.

Jeanie gave me *a look*.

As Karen mounted the stool in my lab, she asked what Jeanie was going to do with the tuning fork.

"It's a middle-C turning fork. My wife's going to resonate it when you say 'Now'."

"Oh, I get it," Karen said. "You're combining energy forms to soup-up the holographic image."

I smiled at Jeanie, who looked detached. "You ready with that tuning fork, Honey?" I turned to Karen and said, "You must stay perfectly still. Throughout the process. I'll tell you when you can move."

"Righto," she responded.

I went to my spot at the other end of the table and set up the holographic plate. "Now, the laser beam won't hurt you at all. It's very low frequency. But don't look right at it. Think blue. That lovely cerulean blue. Then tell me when you have it."

Karen looked like she was going into a trance. With her eyes closed, and her fingers steepled together, she did some very noisy breathing exercises. Her breathing got slower and slower. Then she said "Now!"

The C tuning fork, which Jeanie struck, hummed like a high-tension wire. The ruby laser beamed. When its flash hit Karen's face and upper torso, she looked transfixed. When the shot was over, I had to tell her softly to "come back."

"Do I get to see the hologram now?" Karen asked.

I told her I'd develop the film later to construct the hologram. That my wife and I hadn't been together much lately and that I'd let her see it some other time.

Karen was cool with my response. "That's okay by me. Well, it's been *real*. See you in class on Monday."

After Karen left I gave Jeanie a passionate kiss. "You're a real sport. And I love you. When we get through here, I'll prove it to you."

Her eyes opened like crocuses in the Spring. A little tear glistened at the corner of her eye. "I'm so glad you're sharing this with me."

The hologram of Karen turned out to be provocative. Fleur was right. Karen had not perfected her aura trick. In class, she'd projected blue around her entire body. However, in the hologram of her, there was a halo of deep blue only around her head, which, Jeanie agreed, was still pretty good stuff.

"Tell me why you need this."

I looked again at the circle of blue light around Karen's head in the hologram. "It shows holograms can record people's *energy fields*."

"But that happened in the Reynie hologram *and* your wreck."

I shut off the hologram. "But those holograms were of memories. This happened in the *now*. One more thing, Jeanie. I must find a way to do this without using sound." I knew I shouldn't let myself get excited before going to the next step. "It's time to go to bed. I hope you don't have a headache."

"Even if I did," Jeanie replied, "I wouldn't tell you."

"But you don't, do you?"

"In a little while, I know I'm going to feel great."

CHAPTER TEN

Reynie and I arrived first for class the next Monday night. I told her about Karen's blue halo showing up in a hologram.

"My, but we've been busy."

"You're like the sister I never had," I said.

"Oh, that's sweet. And I'm happy for you. But what are you going to do with this info?"

"Show that past, present and future exist at the same time."

Reynie shook her head.

"Weren't you impressed with what happened in class last week?" I asked. "You saw that blue light too. Remember?"

"Yes, but I'm trying *not* to figure it out. I have a lot on my plate."

"What's on your plate is the secret Karen mentioned in class?"

"You'll just have to wait for a change. And if I'm not enthralled with class tonight, I won't be coming back."

"But why—."

"I have a wonderful life with my husband," Reynie said. "I can't be your sister, or your pal, any time you snap your fingers."

"You a little strung out?" I asked.

"Sometimes you act downright unhinged. I told you I'd try to keep Jeanie together while you're gone, but you haven't gone."

Man, that made me feel bad. She seemed worried, and I was being selfish. I told her I was sorry I had been such a callous jerk.

Right then, Fleur started the class. "Today I'd like you all to sit in a different chair than last time. To change the point of reference to each other. I call it 'expanding your perceptual options'."

I exchanged places with Reynie. We all had our enveloped photos in hand, including Fleur. Karen looked at me like she'd never seen me before. Keith gave me a friendly smile. Matt looked withdrawn.

"Now," Fleur said. "Starting with you, Karen, number your envelope with a '1', and on your notepad, write what's in the photograph you brought. The rest of you will number your envelope respectively. Then, you'll give your description of your photo the same number that's on the envelope. Understood? Here's our experiment: We'll pass the envelope containing each photo around the table. We'll try to feel or visualize what the photograph is. Some of you will see colors or images. Others might feel an emotion or sense some kind of movement. When you get the next envelope, write down the number and what you think is in the photo. When you're done, I'll ask you to pass your envelopes and descriptions forward. I'll add mine. When you come to your own envelope, just pass it on. Any questions?"

Reynie raised her hand. "We're going to feel what's in the envelope with our fingers, right?"

"That's one way."

Reynie gave me *a look*.

Fleur saw the look. "You might be surprised what your fingers can sense," she said. "Now when someone passes you an envelope, on your own piece of paper write down the number and your impressions of what's in the photo inside the envelope. Okay. Let's start."

To make a long story short, I couldn't get a damned thing from any of the envelopes except one: Reynie's. When I first felt the envelope, I knew it was *someone's* mother. Then I somehow got that it was a photo of Reynie's late mother. Keith was masterful at doing this exercise. His list included colors and images that seemed to fit the subjects of most of our photos. He was wrong, though, about Fleur's picture. He said the picture was of a school room. It was actually Fleur at age three. It was Christmas time. Her parents were sitting far in the background.

Karen's impressions came in emotions. She was right-on about my photo. I had rummaged through old mementos from high school and selected a photo of Lu and myself at Senior Prom. Karen got that this photo was of me and the person I was "looking for." Then we all revealed which photo we brought. When Reynie saw mine, she gave me a warning look. Karen had been way off about Keith's picture, which was a shot of him and his friends sailing. All his friends were male. With great conviction, Karen had pronounced that Keith's was a photo of flowers. Her impressions of everyone else's photos were so vague that they could have applied to anyone.

Matt had taken a primitive approach: gut feelings and gut images. Because of this, he was the most accurate about Karen's photo, which was of a terminal patient in the hospital where Karen worked. Matt said that the photo made him feel fear, pain, and sadness.

"Next Monday's our final class," Fleur said, "so I've saved the best for last. We're going to work with crystals. I'll bring some in. If you don't have any, you can use mine. And if you'd like to *buy* a few, you can do that too. Your homework assignment is to read this literature on crystals before you come next week. These handouts should give you a good overview of crystals' piezoelectric properties as well as their more esoteric uses."

"Huh?" Karen grunted.

I walked Reynie to her car. I told her I'd felt blasé about our class.

"Maybe you don't like what you're not good at," Reynie replied.

"Are you calling me a poor sport?"

"We'll see," she said. I sense you will love using crystals, though."

I opened her car door for her. "You know me well, Pal."

Reynie cranked down her window. "Now, don't worry about me. It's not an *awful* secret. In fact, it's rather exciting."

"Thanks for not telling me what your secret is."

"What are friends for? Now, I want to do something for you," Reynie said. "I want to give you a riding lesson."

"Seriously?"

"You ever ride before?"

"You must be cold sitting here with your window open."

"David!"

"Yeah. I've ridden Western a little."

"I'd like to teach you to ride English."

"What's the difference?"

"Form, mostly. And discipline. Meet me this Saturday morning promptly at 8:00 a.m. at LaGrange Stables. That's between Westminster and Boulder, off 287."

"On Saturdays I don't get up before nine."

"You'll be there on time or die." Reynie's smile was pleasant. "Oh, and David. I'd like you to bring Jeanie and Eddie with you."

Perplexed, I asked Reynie what she was up to.

"Just playing a hunch."

"Okay. I'll ask them. I'll enjoy seeing an equestrienne in action."

"You bet your sweet...cheeks," Reynie said.

CHAPTER ELEVEN

Eddie chewed with his mouth open. His tongue was whitish beige with chive cream cheese and onion bagel. As usual, he ate standing up. He leaned against the kitchen counter and glanced here, there, and everywhere like a lizard looking for insects to devour. My son was protein-mad. I was the same at his age—wanting more beef, grabbing an extra burger after dinner with Lucille in my convertible, its top down, driving through the parking lot of Big Boy in Circleville. We did not think it was stupid to drive through, over and over, while checking out the other teenage couples parked at the order consoles.

"Reynie invited us to LaGrange Stables on Saturday," I said to Eddie. "I don't really want to go, but—."

"Wow, Dad! That's great!" Eddie said. He looked like he was about to leap into my arms.

"You don't already have other plans?" Actually I hoped my son had other plans.

"I was gonna go up to Nederland with the guys," Eddie said. "We're gonna get a bite to eat at the Pioneer Inn and walk around."

I asked my son if he was dating anyone at Fairview High. I hadn't a clue about what went on in his life. It made me feel like a jerk. "When I was your age I had a girlfriend," I said.

"I know. You were in love with Lucille Muhr. And you're still thinking about her because you're getting old."

"Ouch!"

Eddie made chewing seem like an afterthought. "No. I mean you two split up after college. You married Ma, and after all these years you're still hung up on that chick. If first love does that to a guy, well...but I still have time to try. It's just that there's not any girls at Fairview I'm interested in. And I have studying and football games and eating pizza and—. We got any milk?" He opened the fridge like a man craving a beer after a sweaty day's work.

Jeanie came into the kitchen just in time to see Eddie guzzle milk right out of the carton. "I'm sick of living with barbarians," she said. "For once, can I get both of you to do two things? Drink out of a glass and put down the toilet seat when you're finished peeing!"

I thought Jeanie's use of the word 'peeing' comically undercut the fervor of her plea. "We *are* barbarians," I admitted to placate her. A new distance I sensed alarmed me. I asked her what was wrong.

"It's nothing new, David. You're just too busy to notice." She snatched the milk carton from Eddie's mouth, closed it, and put it back in the fridge. "I'm getting used to living alone."

Eddie put his arm around his mother's shoulders. "Aw, Ma. You on your period?"

"I just want to strangle both of you!"

I thought Jeanie would jump at the chance to go to LaGrange Stables. After all her complaints that we I was more focused on my work than on her. "Wanna go with us to watch Reynie ride on Saturday?"

"I can't. Remember? I have choir practice."

Since none of us went to church, I asked her what choir.

"The First Presbyterian Church of Boulder is doing excerpts from 'The Messiah' for Christmas. They advertised for a lead soprano in the *Daily Camera*, I auditioned with three other sopranos and I prevailed. And I'm proud of myself."

Eddie sat on a kitchen chair and pulled his petite mother onto his lap. "Are they paying you?"

Jeanie peeled Eddie's arms from around her waist and stood up. "Of course not! I'm doing it for the joy of singing in public again. You think you can do 'The Messiah' after a few days of practice? Christmas is only six weeks away. They want to do it right, and so do I. Don't you two have something better to do?" she shouted. Then she stormed out of the kitchen.

Eddie got the milk out again. "I still think she's got her period," he said, satisfied that he wasn't the cause of her sulk.

Eddie and I showed up at LaGrange stables just in time to see Reynie go over a five-foot jump like it was a piece of yarn on the ground. She came around to us at a posting trot.

"She's on Alsatian Prince," Eddie said.

I tried to hide how surprised I was that my son knew this.

Reynie, astride "Alsatian Prince," walked up to us.

"Gawd, you look spiffy," I said.

Reynie wasn't even out of breath. "Where's your wife?"

When I told her about Jeanie's choir practice, she said, "Maybe that's good. You wouldn't want to humiliate yourself in front of her."

Under his breath, Eddie offered: "Every woman in the Denver Metro area must be on the rag today."

Reynie smiled at Eddie and said, "Woman's job is to *civilize* Man." She dismounted and pulled a leather strap up through the slot at the top of each stirrup. Next she pulled both stirrups up to the top of the straps. Then a stable boy brought two saddled horses up and left them standing along the rail in front of us. He led Alsatian Prince out of the riding arena. "These are push-button horses," Reynie said. "If you communicate with your hands and feet correctly, they'll perform like well-oiled machines."

I checked out the two horses before me. One had pale tan splotches on it. The other was the color of cream sherry. Neither had any-thing...hanging below. "Can't I ride a stallion too? Like the one you were riding?"

Reynie broke into a smile and said, "No one rides Alsatian Prince but *moi*. And his trainer. Then she pointed at the spotted horse.

Eddie stroked the nose of the large chestnut colored horse that had come up to sniff his coat. "Luke's a gelding," he informed me.

"A gelding?"

Reynie scrutinized my face. "He's castrated."

I shifted my legs. "Oh."

Reynie brought the spotted horse up to me. "And since I prefer that you *not* break your neck, you'll be riding 'Freckles'." Reynie stared at my feet. "What's with the sneakers?!"

I was insulted. "You didn't say I should wear some fancy riding boots just to take one lousy lesson with you."

"To sit a horse well, you need shoes with heels. Okay, boys. Up into the saddle. Eddie, go ahead and take Luke. David, your horse is a cross-bred strawberry roan. 'Freckles' is her stable name."

"I have to ride a girl horse?"

Reynie looked at me with pity. "She'll take you on a rocket ride to Andromeda—*if* you can ride."

I was sure Reynie had meant to put me down. My face got hot. "I place myself in your hands."

"Good. Because if you don't, you'll take a fast trip to nowhere. Now mount your horses."

Right, I thought. I hung there with my left foot in the stirrup because I couldn't hoist myself up. In mocking contrast, Eddie mounted like a pro. I knew this was Reynie's way of getting even with me.

Reynie fought a smile. The corners of her mouth literally twitched. "Place all your weight into that left stirrup and spring up from your right foot."

When I tried to mount, I lost my balance and fell backward with my left foot stuck in the stirrup. "Stop laughing, Eddie!" *Okay*, I thought. *One. Two. Three.* "Hup!" Gratefully it worked. I slid my leg over Freckles' back and pushed my foot into the right stirrup. I felt ready to conquer the world.

Eddie had become *one* with his horse, Luke. Supremely confidant, my boy sat tall in his saddle. "Can I ride now?" he asked Reynie.

"Is Luke warmed up?" Reynie asked.

"Yep," Eddie said.

I was jealous. "Eddie's never had a riding lesson in his life!"

Reynie watched Eddie go counterclockwise around the ring. Then Eddie took Luke smoothly from a walk to a trot and then to a gallop—or "canter," as Reynie corrected me later. Eddie's body moved rhythmically with Luke's. Reynie smiled. "All I can say is, if Eddie's never had a riding lesson in *this* life, he must have been a cavalryman in some other lifetime."

I felt relieved to change the subject. I was not anxious for Reynie, or Freckles, to make me look bad. "Why, Reynie. I had no idea you believe in reincarnation."

It seemed Eddie had learned to *post* in the few seconds he'd seen Reynie do it. Now he had Luke back in a contained trot. The boy posted beautifully.

"I think I am getting the message, Reynie."

Mischief darted in Reynie's eyes. "Press your heels down, David. Don't lean back."

"When I press my heels down, it *makes* me lean back."

Reynie laughed. "That's because you have a lousy seat."

"My seat is perfect!"

Reynie persisted: "Imagine there's a straight line from your ear, down through your shoulders and torso. Down through your buttocks and down through your heels."

I *did* try to imagine that, but Reynie's instructions didn't work for me. I watched Eddie press his calves into Luke's flanks.

"You're on the wrong lead," Reynie shouted to Eddie.

Like magic, Luke had broken into a canter.

Eddie's grin was enormous. "What?" he shouted back.

"You want Luke to lead with his inside leg when you're going counterclockwise."

"Oh. I see!" Eddie shouted. He went so fast from a canter to a trot to a walk that I couldn't believe both Eddie and Luke hadn't bellied up on the arena's dirt floor. Then Luke went from a walk to a trot to a canter again. Luke's *lead* apparently had changed, and Eddie kept riding in a triumphant circle.

"Good, Eddie!" Reynie exclaimed.

It all suddenly became clear to me. "This is a joke on me, right? You've been working with Eddie!"

Reynie burst into laughter. "Serves you right, David. You can be such a pompous ass. Always in your own precious world."

I felt like "The Incredible Shrinking Man." I asked Reynie how long she'd been working with my son.

"Oh, I just started him out. He's seeing a young rider from Westminster High. She's the reason he's advancing so quickly." She smiled back at a beaming Eddie, who slowed Luke and walked up to me.

"Yeah, Dad," Eddie said. "You can meet my girlfriend soon."

I was surly. "You said you didn't have a girlfriend—."

"I said there is no one at *my* high school. Come on, Dad. Riding's easy, once you have the basics down."

I felt grossly uncomfortable. "I think I've had enough," I said to Reynie. "I told you I got the message. Can we stop now?"

Reynie smiled with affection. "What is the message, David?"

"That I've been a jerk. But a man can change, can't he?"

"Yes. What else?"

I tried, but I couldn't think of anything else.

Reynie exchanged looks with Eddie. Then her eyes landed back on mine. "I don't think he's ready yet. Do you, Eddie? I'd better take him a little farther along before we quit today."

"If you think I'm going to go on with this riding lesson——."

"Then I guess I won't be going to our last 'Grow Your Intuition' class on Monday," Reynie said.

Debased and tired, I retorted, "Blackmail doesn't become you." I started to get off my equine betrayer.

"Sit *into* your saddle, David. Now squeeze just a little with your calves. That will urge Freckles forward."

Freckles jumped, then stopped.

"Too hard, David," Reynie said. She came up to me and pressed her palm against Freckles' neck.

"Well, isn't she supposed to obey me?"

"How'd you like some 150-pound guy on your back, kicking you in the ribs? Remember: She's doing you a favor. You're a guest on her back. You've no right to demand anything of her. When you want your horse to do something, it's called 'asking'. Just squeeze with your legs until you can feel the warmth of her flanks. That's it. Now keep your heels pressed down and relax your back."

I told Reynie I was trying to "sit tall."

"Yes, but you don't want to be a freaking ramrod," Reynie replied. "Freckles can feel that you're tense, and that makes *her* nervous."

"Gosh, Freckles. I'm sorry."

Reynie perched herself atop the round pen rail. "That's better."

After half an hour of Reynie telling me everything I did was wrong, she threw in the towel. "You must be one with your horse. When you're on her back, you must be a team."

"Well, it's obvious *this* part of the team ain't doing his half yet," I admitted. I knew Eddie and Reynie had set me up. At least for a moment I felt duly humbled.

"Okay," Reynie finally relented. "Because you've been such a good sport, I'll show some mercy. Eddie, why don't you take Luke back, get his tack put away, and rub him down. And would you have the stable boy set up a vertical and an Oxer beyond the rail here in front of David. And, by the way, Eddie. I think Laurie will be here about Eleven, and she's always prompt."

Eddie blushed. "Oh, Dad? What did you think of my riding?"

"You were terrific, Son. But you have no right to be that good!"

"Thanks, Pop!"

Eddie held Freckles while I dismounted. As soon as my feet touched the ground, my knees turned to rubber. My legs ached from the top of my head down to China. "Tell Laurie I said hello."

Eddie blushed again. "Yeah, sure. You want Freckles here?" he asked Reynie. "I'll take Luke back." He took Luke by the halter and said, "See you later."

Reynie led Freckles, and helped me, over to the rail. "Imagine that. Eddie blushing. So refreshing. What makes adults lose that?"

"I guess we hide our emotions after a while."

"Speak for yourself."

"Well, you do it too!"

Reynie got serious. "I want you to feel my secret. I want you to get your brain back from Planet-X. Then, and here's the hard part, I want you to open up and try to feel my secret with your heart."

When I looked at Reynie now, I saw a most vulnerable, pleading look in her eyes. "This means a lot to you."

"You're my friend. I want you to be the most alive, caring person you can be. Because you must. Your family is going to need this from you even more. I don't want you to become one of those solipsistic guys who shine at the expense of the people who love them."

"What's solipsistic?"

"Look it up, dummy," Reynie said with an affection that surprised me. "Because I'm going to ride Freckles now. And I want you to pay close attention." She set her foot in the left stirrup and floated up into the saddle. Seeing the expression on my face, she said, "You have not had enough!"

I looked warily at the horse I'd just been riding. "Freckles jumps?"

"Just because *you* can't ride her doesn't mean *she* doesn't know how! Most people judge her by her 'quarter pounder' appearance. That's horse world slang for quarter horse. But she's deceptive. A jumper is a jumper is a jumper. Like all good show horses, she feels pride in doing well. And she depends on her rider to help her perform. Watch!"

I did watch. Reynie rode like a song. She and Freckles transitioned from a walk to a canter so smoothly that I didn't even see Reynie's legs signal her horse. Reynie accelerated the canter and circled the arena three more times. Reynie and Freckles headed for the first jump, which was standing several yards away. It had one horizontal bar. Freckles' legs sort of barrel rolled at an even pace. Horse and rider approached the jump. Right at the jump, they both shifted. After an extended moment aloft, Freckles jackknifed over the top of the jump. At that moment Reynie was leaning forward, her torso almost touching Freckles' neck. Reynie stayed in that position when Freckles' front hooves touched the ground until after the mare landed with four-footed, almost-feline grace.

Freckles took a stride forward, her momentum on her hind legs, and churned into that barreling leg motion again. They headed for the second jump. This one had two horizontal bars raised a little higher than those of the first jump. Seeing horse and rider approach the jump felt like that moment when you're getting ready for a jet to lift off the runway. You feel the thrust of the engines as the nose of the plane lifts. You're sure the tail of the plane will hit the runway and bounce. But Reynie and Freckles flew over like one large bird.

Horse and rider circled the arena again while the stable boy increased the height of both jumps. I could see Reynie and Freckles coming toward me. They took the first jump. They went over the second jump again as if in slow motion. If I'd been standing four feet closer, Freckles would have left hoof marks on me. When Freckles rolled in that flowing motion, I knew that if I let my brain interfere, it would stop what I was seeing: rainbow colors surrounded both horse and rider. Above the rainbow shone a brilliant white halo. Reynie and her mare hovered in a perfect arc over the jump for what seemed an eternity. Colors of the spectrum expanded and pulsed. Radiant joy spread across Reynie's face. A glow of achievement reflected in Freckles' eyes. Horse and rider then landed with a thud beyond the jump.

My eyes blurred. I could hear Freckles' hooves continue to pound the floor of the arena. Then there was the softness of Freckles walking and leather tack squeaking from the movement of horse and rider together. From a great distance, I heard Reynie say, "Now we're done."

I realized my face was wet with tears.

The arena had suddenly emptied, except for Reynie. She had appeared at my side. "David."

My face in my hands, I used every ounce of restraint left in me. "I'm still in love with Lucille Muhr."

"I know." From her pocket she took out a tissue and gave it to me. "That's a start. We'll just have to take it from here."

My throat ached when I tried to talk. "We?"

"Daddy and I want to help you through this. If you had kept denying it, you'd have destroyed your chance for happiness with your family. With us. Weren't you about Eddie's age when you fell in love with Lucille Muhr?"

I blew my nose loudly, unashamedly, and nodded. "When you remember someone like her, you think she's the same and you're the same. Only everything's different. You can't go back."

"And yet, you're still planning to try."

"I have to."

Reynie unzipped the legs of her leather riding chaps from the top-down. "You've been grabbing all the glory. I wanted to strut *my* stuff for a change." She draped her chaps over the rail. "I feel it's time to share my secret with you." She took my hand and placed it on her chest, just above her heart. "Can you feel it? I trust you, David. Share this with me."

I closed my eyes, felt her warmth. I let my mind go blank. I saw the sun peeking out from behind some puffy cumulus clouds. I floated along with them. Somewhere in my gut I felt something moving, pulsing like a heartbeat. When my mind tried to force an image, I let go of that need and let myself go back to feeling the pulse. It became stronger, throbbed. Then I knew. I opened my eyes and said: "You're pregnant." I let Reynie's joy fill me.

She pulled me to my feet, threw her arms around me, and hugged the breath out of me. And I held her gently, innocently. "Does your Dad know?"

She nodded.

Memories of when Jeanie told me she was pregnant with Eddie rippled through me. It was not happy news at the time. But now, love for my wife and my son flooded my whole body. I held Reynie away from me so I could look at her and wondered if all women have that same look on their faces when they tell a friend that they're having a child. "I'll never take you for granted again, Reynie."

Eddie came running to me with his girlfriend in tow. His Laurie was wholesomely pretty. They were both too young to be so obviously in love. My first thought was: *How can they know what love is?* Then I realized what a hypocrite I was. I'd been just about Eddie's age when I fell in love with Lu. I was sorry for giving my son such a hard time that morning. And I felt ashamed by Reynie's trust in me. But I felt even worse about still wanting to go through with my selfish plan. And yet, a great revelation came to me in that moment. If I did meet Lu again, she might hate who I'd become.

Perceptive Reynie told me the situation would take care of itself.

Eddie and Laurie sat in the back seat of my SUV. I was their chauffeur. Though I tried not to look in the rearview mirror, every now and then I glimpsed the young lovers holding hands, gazing into each other's eyes. Seeing my son in love made me look at myself honestly for the first time. It made me wonder what had happened to young David Leone, the still innocent one. The one who could be awed by something other than the workings of his own mind.

I dropped the lovebirds off at the Boulder Theater for a Saturday matinee of the latest Barbarian movie. You know: the kind where a Neanderthal with the build of Arnold Schwarzenegger conquers a lot of bad guys and black magic to save the heroine, who loves some other Neanderthal.

"We'll probably go out for pizza afterwards, Eddie said, "and get some videos to watch at Laurie's place. See you tonight, Dad."

I pulled away from the curb. Shook my head. I felt great affection for two kids who could go to a grade-C feature film and then spend the rest of the evening looking at videos. All the way home that day I thought about the first time Lu and I made love. We'd never gone "all the way" until she was nineteen. In my teenage desperation, I took her to see "Romeo and Juliet." It worked. We went back to my house and found that my parents had gone discreetly to bed. They did not appear for the rest of the evening. What a setup! For some reason, they'd told me in advance that I could sleep up in my sister's old bed in the attic. Lu could sleep in my old bed in the adjoining attic room. We did settle in our respective beds with all good intentions. However, I couldn't stay on my side of the attic for long!

My intense longing had been mushrooming for years. I began to tiptoe across the endless expanse of twenty feet that separated us. My bare feet found every creaking floorboard.

"Ssh!" Lu whispered. "You'll wake up your parents." And then, music to my ears: "I'll come to *you*."

I counted the quiet creaks Lu's feet made when she came to me. I drew the covers back for her, and she slipped in bed beside me. She turned and wrapped her whole body around mine. I remember thinking that as trim and athletic as she was, I had never felt such softness. And it wasn't just because of the homey flannel nightgown she wore. I could feel the heat of her breath when she pressed her face close to mine and gave me the most thrilling kiss ever!

I was still a virgin. I was afraid to ask her what to do. But I didn't have to ask her. She sat up and pulled her nightgown off, over her head. Because the attic room was so dark, I made my eyes do the impossible: I willed them to penetrate the darkness so I could see Lu's body entirely naked for the first time. I saw that she was still wearing panties. I held my breath so I wouldn't touch her breasts too soon. Then *she* pushed her panties down and pulled my body toward her. I was already hard. Most gently, I entered her. The pleasure of being inside her made me stay still, not move. It was the longest erection I would ever hold. Then Lu started moving her hips up and down and quietly moaned, making pleasurable sounds. Though I'd held out so long that it was becoming painful, I kept pushing into her. Finally her body went limp and she sighed deeply. I could feel the contents of my joy spilling out and out and into her body. My organ kept throbbing and giving her all the juices of my love. We lay awake, exhausted, together until dawn. I had only one tiny thought: *She isn't a virgin.*

"I better go back now," Lu said.

I had a funny feeling my parents not only knew what we'd been doing but wanted it to happen. Maybe they hoped we'd marry. They loved Lu and wanted to help us decide what to do.

Whenever Lu and I made love after that, it was the same. Such was our chemistry that all we had to do was look at each other. I always asked: "Is it safe?"

"Yes."

"Are you sure?"

"Yes."

By the time we broke up, there wasn't a room in my parents' house in which we *hadn't* made love—except their bedroom.

CHAPTER TWELVE

I'd lounged on the old sofa in my basement lab since after dinner, pondering whether to just chuck my grandiose plans. Whether I could do half the things I'd imagined. Especially taking a holographic trip down memory lane with Lucille Muhr. Time had slipped by so fast that when I looked at my watch it was 11:00 p.m. Jeanie would probably be asleep. When I went upstairs to make a sandwich, I found this letter from her:

Saturday, November 14   8PM

David, Honey:

You're downstairs working in your lab as usual, so I thought I'd set some things down in writing. Other than a few "I love you" and "Don't forget" notes, I guess I haven't written you a letter since we were in college. So if I'm a little rusty, please forgive me.

I've been sitting in the kitchen, trying to decide how to tell you why I feel so far away from you. The only way I can express it is to compare the David I used to know with the you of the past several months. I made a list to help me.

Former David	*Recent David*
A giver	*A taker*
A tease	*Distracted*
Communicative	*Secretive*
A sweet clown	*Hamlet, Prince of Denmark*
A helpful housemate	*A non-participant*
An attentive lover	*An infrequent lover*
A loving father	*An absentee*
A man of varied interests	*A man with one obsession*

By the way, I do realize these are my *perceptions, and that they're colored by my own selfish need to have you with me like you have been for the past 19 ½ years. I've also read enough books to know that a floundering marriage isn't usually the fault of just one partner. I can't just sit by anymore and wait for you to get over this thing. So I'm inviting you to be as honest with me as I'm being with you. For Eddie's sake, and for our marriage, please tell me what's going on. If there's something I'm doing that's upset you, now is your chance to tell me so I can try to change it. All I know is that it's making me unhappy.*

Up until last summer I feel we had a wonderful marriage. You and Eddie and I used to play "Trivial Pursuit" and miniature golf and go to movies. I wouldn't mind us just being couch potatoes, because even watching TV together would be a treat nowadays. And I don't mean watching Lucille Muhr on TV together! That about made me lose it.

You forget how well I know you. You're obviously keeping something from me, and you're keeping things from yourself. At least, the real reason why you've been going through this bizarre male change of life. In the beginning I thought it was just some tick that you would get over, some stupid "7 year itch" that would end as suddenly as it began. Now I have to admit that what's bothering you must not be just an itch, because it's somehow crucial to your work.

I understand you want to achieve some kind of greatness, but I also believe there's got to be a price for you to pay somewhere, David. Surely you can do this work and belong to us too, like you did before. At least tell me you're willing to try, and I will too. I'll even read the same books you do, so we can talk about them. I'll try to keep an open mind!

I'll probably be asleep when you read this. No matter how late it is, you can wake me up to tell me what you think about what I've said here. Or if you want to sleep on it, that's okay too. But let's talk about <u>us</u> real soon, my love. Let's do something together, no matter how trivial.
Your loving wife, always, Jeanie

After thinking about Jeanie's letter I wrote my reply and left it on the kitchen table. I could do no less for the woman I'd shared my life with for almost two decades. And yet, finally having said the thing I dreaded telling her, I somehow knew our lives would never be the same again unless I got lucky.

Dear Jeanie,

As you know, this morning Reynie gave me a riding lesson, and I was awful at it. Not only did I learn I've been out of touch with what's going on in Eddie's life, but I learned I can't ride a horse for shit! What I am afraid of is that I can't do any other things as well as I imagined either. Believe me, that riding lesson shattered any delusions of grandeur I had before. What's more, Reynie showed me how dishonest I've been with myself and you in other ways.

It's like when I turned forty, I went back in time and got stuck there, not only mentally but emotionally. Worse than that, I don't think I can move forward (out of this thing) until I get answers to some questions I still have about Lucille. Believe me, Jeanie, it's not that I want to be with her now, or even <u>see</u> her. I only need to get finished with what's been bugging me.

I don't know if you're going to understand this, but this "quest," I guess you could call it, is pivotal to the work I'm doing with Court's help. I want to succeed so you, Eddie and I can go on with the life of our beautiful family. And I'm going to need you to trust me like you have never had to (and never will have to again, I'm sure you're hoping). And, yes. Court knows. But he isn't pleased about it, Jeanie. I know <u>he</u> trusts me, but then you'll say he doesn't know me well enough. All I can do is try to show you how much you mean to me and how much I want you to be part of any discoveries I hope to make in my work.

I'm not putting this in a letter because I'm afraid to tell you face to face. I'm giving you a letter so you'll have my thoughts in writing. My word that this project won't interfere with us, except in the time I'll be spending on it.

One last thing. I need to go to Ohio after Christmas to see my folks and do some work there for awhile. I have no idea how long it will take. Please don't be angry or hurt. Please understand I'm afraid if I don't do this, I'll burst.

Your loving husband, David

I did get lucky. The next morning when I went down to breakfast, Jeanie had already read my letter. She looked more determined than upset. To my great surprise, she wrapped her arms around me and held me very tightly. But she said nothing.

CHAPTER THIRTEEN

I went to class the next Monday excited about the piezoelectric properties of quartz crystals. If you compress a quartz crystal from top to bottom you get one kind of electrical energy. If you compress it from side to side you get another. The silicate properties of quartz let it reproduce itself by literally *growing*, to be used in timepieces, to be a fine conveyor of light and sound, and to be a storer of digital information. In short: quartz crystals are both practical and beautiful.

Reynie didn't show up. A vein of chauvinism in me excused her because she was pregnant. Most of us men know that women are flaky when they are *with child*. Fleur came in and closed the door behind her. She started by telling us to lie down on the floor. We moved the chairs to the far end of the room and "lay down" on either side of the rectangular table. Then Fleur took us on a guided fantasy trip that I enjoyed very much. It began with our imagining we were walking through the woods on a beautiful sunny day. "See the blue sky through the trees," Fleur said. "Feel a gentle breeze blowing against your face. Smell the damp earth, fresh with rain. Pick a handful of wild raspberries and taste them. Feel refreshed." Then Fleur said each of us would come upon a wood "deva," or spirit, who would present us with a special gift.

I truly did see a *light fairy*, a sort of New Age "Tinker Bell" with little fluttery wings. She had golden hair. With a radiant smile, she held out a gold box to me. The box had something to do with my work.

Before I could open the box, Fleur hurried us to the next phase of our journey. She told us to proceed to a clearing, where we would find a house sized crystal. To get inside the crystal we had to imagine going up seven steps. Each step was a different color, beginning with red, then orange, yellow, green. Then blue, then indigo, and violet. Fleur asked us to imagine a door at the top of these steps. Then we pictured ourselves going inside the crystal structure, which glowed with pure white light. The exercise made me happy—and sleepy.

Abruptly, however, Fleur suggested we get ready to open our eyes. *Dammit*, I thought. *Why can't we do more with the crystal stairs?*

"Now we're going to focus the power we received from the giant crystal on each other," Fleur said. "I want each of you to come up here and select a crystal that feels right to you."

"How can I tell?" Matt asked. He might have been high on reefers.

"It will be different for each of you," Fleur said. "Your fingers might tingle. Or your hands might start throbbing. Some of you might just feel more comfortable with a certain crystal."

We examined the crystals in Fleur's collection. They were mounted with little elastic bands on blue velvet cushions. I admit I did feel energy emanating from many of them—one in particular. It was two crystals in one. When I held it in my left hand it pulsed mightily.

"That's called a twin," Fleur said to me with a look of approval. "They're both double terminated," allowing energy to flow freely in either direction." She faced the rest of the class. "Now that you've chosen your crystal, I want you to take turns laying on the floor. The person laying down will hold their crystal in their *left* hand. The person sitting next to them will hold their crystal in their *right* hand." For a change, I didn't ask why. "Now I want the one sitting on the floor to pass their quartz crystal over the other person's body. Start at the crown of the head and move slowly down to the center of their body. But don't let the crystal touch the person. Okay?"

Karen chose me as her partner for the experiment. She lay on her back beside me. I then passed the crystal over her head, face, chest, and waist before I felt anything. To my surprise, apparently through the cluster of two crystals I felt a heaviness, a darkness in Karen's abdomen. The cluster seemed to be physically pulling downward, toward her body. I asked her if there was something wrong in that area.

Karen looked pleased with me. And embarrassed. "I have awful cramps," she said. Then she got up and changed places with me.

"I feel you should turn over," Karen said. When she passed her crystal down the back of my head, she stopped at the top of my spine. "I feel little stabbing pains here."

"*I* don't feel anything," I told her honestly. Then I remembered the automobile accident of so many years ago. How I'd had chronic misalignment of my Atlas Bone since then. But usually only stress made the pain intensify. "Oh, yeah," I said to Karen. "You're right."

"Gonna let me see the hologram of me?" Karen whispered.

I responded, "One of these days."

Fleur asked us to review what happened during our experiments with crystals. Matt, Keith, and Karen asked a lot of questions. I just held my crystal in my hand and felt it vibrate. There was something in there all right. It felt alive, intelligent even. I thought, *Maybe old Dave is finally losing it.* I had to find out what made the cluster do those things.

At the end of class, we congratulated each other on how gifted we were, how much fun this last class had been, and how much we'd learned. Then Fleur hawked her crystal wares with thinly veiled hopefulness. It worked though. Keith bought two crystals, Matt bought one, and Karen bought four. I paid Fleur twenty-five dollars for the twin crystal I had been using, said goodbye to everyone, drove home, and got into bed with Jeanie.

I woke up the next morning with that quartz cluster still in my hand.

Jeanie examined the cluster. "What good is this thing to you?"

I told her I meant to "grow." I knew it was a lame comeback, but I had to defend myself somehow.

Jeanie's eyes skewered mine. "I just wanted to know if you were pulling my leg. Last night I counted the number of books on crystals by your side of the bed. There are five! And that doesn't include the ones in the living room! I looked through one of the books. It says that crystals are like your friends. It says that they *want* to help people heal and help us learn things. It says that scientists in Atlantis used them to generate power for the whole continent. Really, David! Nobody can even prove Atlantis existed, much less that they used giant crystals and finally blew themselves up with them!"

"We know about Atlantis from a pretty reliable source," I offered.

"Yeah. I read that in the book too. Plato, by way of his uncle Solon, by way of an Egyptian priest. Only Plato reported a *legend* about Atlantis that sounds a lot like Greek mythology."

"Well, what about Edgar Cayce?"

"'The Sleeping Prophet?' The guy who would go into a trance and tell people about other lives they'd lived. Including in Atlantis?"

"Gosh you're well-read, Jeanie!"

"I happen to have a house full of such books now, thanks to your temporary insanity. Naturally, I'd like to explore any possibility of finding out where you might be going, even if it's away from me."

"If you want some really good stuff, read the book about how properties of quartz parallel those of DNA."

"Which?"

"The book that says DNA and quartz are ideal templates for life. One, they can reproduce themselves. Two, they can store information. Three, they can use that information in their environment."

Jeanie looked at me with a sudden comprehension that stunned me and asked: "Does that mean quartz crystals are *alive*?"

"Even if they're not alive, every quartz crystal is literally a computer. They're made of silicates, like computer microchips."

"But computers can't reproduce themselves."

I took Jeanie in my arms. "That's right, my Honey."

"Then just answer one question please." She cupped my cheek. "Why are you reading the books?"

"Because I believe there's something in them that's *key* to a new method I'm hoping to develop."

"When will you know?"

"I'll let you know when I know," I said.

With six beers to keep me company, I was ready to spend my entire day in my basement. I snapped open my first beer and set my quartz crystal on my worktable. This would be the first of a series of adventures that would complete my long journey. At this point I feel it would be helpful to describe my twin crystal in more detail. First, the matrix (or base) crystal is tabular. A smaller one rides piggyback, like NASA's space shuttle on takeoff. In full sunlight, when you look at the place where these two crystals abut, you see what's called a "rainbow window." The books say this is rare—that this kind of crystal *chooses* a person to bestow itself on. What's more unusual about the top crystal is that it has several tiny crystals jutting out like baby rockets on one side. It's like they grew there overnight. When light shines into them, you see rainbows in these as well. On the non-terminated end of the matrix crystal are irregular jags where the crystal had broken off but is now, as they say, healing itself. There, myriad rainbow windows illuminate, vie with each other in angle and in beauty.

For now, I held back from shining a laser beam through those rainbow windows because I wanted to think more about the best method to use. Anyone watching me would think I was doing nothing. However, I entered a phase of creative thinking some call daydreaming or spacing out. I call it "spacing in," because it feels like you're slowly sinking into layers of yourself. It's like putting your toe in the ocean. Then your feet and legs. Then your waist, hands, arms, chest and neck. Finally you let yourself dog paddle a bit while you feel waves pushing and pulling you in the most pleasant ways.

Floating around inside my own mind in this manner, I let those waves of thought take me wherever they would. I got that the information in the crystal books was fine as a starting point. What *I* would do with that information was up to me. I had to be able to translate that info to holography, and instinct told me crystals would take me there. Something about using all dimensions of light in my work. Something about *remembered* light.

While popping my second Coors, I pondered the relationship between what an interference pattern registers on a holographic plate and the structure of quartz crystals—their multidimensional grids of lattice lines that record so many octaves of light. Like DNA, these spirals of molecular latticework store, process, and emit information according to their structure. In fact, I'd read that quartz crystals are virtual *tuning forks* of light. Amazingly, their structure is said to respond to a whole range of additional kinds of energy: sound, pressure, heat, electricity, microwaves, gamma rays, X-rays, and even a person's thoughts!

Naturally, I was most interested in retrieving and storing *sound* holographically. I read that a company in the recording industry was working on storing visual and digital information, data, and music in crystals. What rocked my world was reading that techies were retrieving that information and playing it back with laser beams. (CDs were first made in 1982.) I assumed that the company was really storing the information in crystals holographically. The article didn't say if they used laser beams like scanners.

Some metaphysicians claim that sound is merely *audible light*. This would mean that what distinguishes one from the other is its *form* of expression. In fact, all types of energy, even motion, can be defined by how the energies express. Thus, just like motion describes energy and the result of that motion delimits it, so sound describes energy and the result of that sound defines it.

When a pitcher throws a ball, the movement of his arm and the ball's flight through space *describe* what kind of energy he's expended. When the ball reaches the catcher's mitt, its energy is defined. Sound is the tipoff, though almost at the same time you have seen the batter swing, seen/heard the ball zip into the catcher's mitt, and heard the umpire yell "Stee-rike!" The ball's destination is amplified by the sound it makes when it gets there. In short, the entire purpose of throwing the ball is realized when you hear it smack into that mitt—or hear the crack of a bat when it starts to launch a ball deep into the outfield.

I thought I heard bells ringing. Jeanie interrupted my reverie by yelling from the top of the stairs: "David. Court's on the phone."

I told Jeanie I'd take his call downstairs. I was breathless when I picked up the receiver. "Court! My God. How are you?"

Court told me he had a feeling he should come up to Boulder to see me that day and he had something important to tell me. "You probably skipped breakfast *and* lunch."

I told Court I was eating beer. When I hung up, I felt warmth from the top of my head to my stomach. Just knowing I would see my benefactor made my project feel even more urgent and exciting.

Held securely in a small table clamp and lit by a laser, my quartz cluster became a projector of rainbows. Color swatches of full *spectra* shone all over my worktable, on the walls of my lab, and on Court and me. We both looked like the Tattooed Man of circus fame.

"That's the most beautiful thing I've ever seen!" Court said. "There are colors inside the crystal too."

"I'll get some mirrors into the act," I said. "See if I can compound the effect." I directed the laser beam through a beam splitter and reflected the resulting two beams back at the crystal. I had expected this to multiply the number of rainbows, both within the crystal and outside it. Instead, the beam splitter made the crystal glow with the purest, whitest light I'd ever seen. This whiteness was about ten feet in diameter. The darned thing looked like a hovering mother ship! I yelled upstairs to Jeanie and asked her to bring down the tuning forks.

Accustomed to the strange requests emanating from my la-bor-a-tory, Jeanie didn't even ask why. What she asked was "Which one?"

"The whole set!" I responded.

Court stayed riveted the crystal. "I don't know which is more perfect. All the colors or this intense white light."

"If my theory is correct, we'll be able to project them both almost simultaneously."

Court gave me one of those *here we go again* looks. "What do you mean, 'almost'?" he asked.

"I believe it'll be pulsing *between* the two."

"Ah. Modulation of light by sound."

"That's how the Egyptians built the Great Pyramid at Giza," I said. I had just revealed an arcane detail reaped from my metaphysical research. "Supposedly they used sonics to move those immense blocks. Not a chip or crack in any of them. They fit so precisely that you can't even fit a razor blade between them."

"That's impossible. Otherwise, when you play your stereo too loud, your incandescent lamplight would waver." Court had completely ignored the stuff about the Great Pyramid.

"We have here a special variable—a twin crystal we're using like a prism, a laser beam, beam splitter, mirrors, and tuning forks. I don't have this combo set up between my stereo and my incandescent light."

Court thought for a moment. "But where are you going with it? Will you try to make a hologram of the crystal with rainbows in it?"

"Not with just the laser beam shining through it," I said. "Jeanie!"

"Coming. I'm trying to carry all these tuning forks without letting them touch each other. Figured it might ruin your experiment. Gee! That reminds me of the movie 'Poltergeist'. 'They're *here*'," she said in a cartoony child's voice. She laid the tuning forks out one at a time on the counter by my lab sink. "We have all seven now."

"Why don't you want a full octave?" Court asked.

"Because the eighth," Jeanie said, "duplicates the first."

"Stick around, professor," I said. "You're gonna like this."

I removed the beam splitter and mirrors to show Jeanie the rainbows Court and I had seen before I split the laser beam.

"Holy cow, David! You think you can sell this?"

"This ain't no laser light show. It's much cooler. Now, I'm going to split the beam into two beams again and reflect them back into the crystal. This is the way it was when you came down here."

"I have an idea," Jeanie said. "Let's start with C and move up one note at a time. Then let's try harmonics. Musical thirds and fifths."

Court's eyes ignited. "How about a fifth of scotch?"

Jeanie told Court she could drink him under the table.

Court drew in an uncomfortable breath but said, "That's the spirit, lovely lady. David, let's do what Jeanie proposed."

"Righto. Jeanie, stand down there about two feet from the crystal. Good. Now tap C gently."

When Jeanie struck the C tuning fork on the heel of her hand, the crystal reflected with red tones, alternating with the white light like the throb and then halt of a heartbeat.

My knees quivered. "Do D!"

"Wait until it stops resonating?" Court offered.

When Jeanie struck the D tuning fork, we saw the orange band of the spectrum reflect both inside and outside of the crystal.

"Now E!"

"Take it easy, Darling," Jeanie said. "By the way, I love this."

We went through E and yellow, F and green, G and blue, A and indigo, and B and violet.

"My God," I said. "I read about this but I didn't believe it until now. People have been using colors and pitches of sound to heal for a long time. Red is at the lowest vibrational end of the spectrum. The sound of Middle C has a lower rate of vibration than the notes above it on a scale. Each color *does* correspond with a sound frequency."

Court asked: "Does this mean if we played all of them at once we'd get all the colors at once?"

"I don't think so," Jeanie shared.

I was intrigued that my musical wife had a theory about this. My gut told me she was right. "I agree, but I don't know why."

"Because the universe *wants* to be harmonic," Jeanie said, like her answer was self-evident. In a way, it was.

But I wanted Jeanie to try to articulate it, both for myself and for Court. I asked her to explain.

"I think it would turn into a muddy blur."

I decided we should test her theory. "Can you strike three tuning forks at a time, Jeanie? I'll do two and we'll have Court also do two." I counted to three, and we all struck the total of seven tuning forks at the same time.

Jeanie had been right. This atonal result made both a nauseating sound and a sickening, muddy color.

"Cleaned your aura lately?" Jeanie asked. Then she laughed from somewhere so deep inside herself that she couldn't stop.

Realizing that she had been reading more of my books, following right along with my spiritual growth, and that she had both a seriousness and a sense of humor about it made me "lose it." I laughed until I cried. Then I laughed some more.

Court was unable to resist the delicious catharsis of our laughter. "I thought we were only losing David," he said.

My friend Josh appeared in my lab out of nowhere. "Hey! Whatta you guys smokin'?"

I laughed even harder when I saw Josh. "I thought...you...were fishing!" I shouted. That, too, seemed so funny I couldn't stand it.

"Looks like you had to be there." Josh said. Then he pointed at me and said, "I think I know you." Then he pointed at Jeanie. "And I think I know this female. But I don't know this gentleman," he said, referring to Court, who had sat down laughing.

"It's like being at the dentist," Court finally said. "Laughing gas."

Josh observed the glowing white crystal on the table, the tuning forks in our hands, and the three lonely cans of Coors beer on the counter. "One beer apiece doesn't explain this."

I couldn't stop laughing. "Hell! I drank those by myself! We have some serious...Ha! Ha! Ha! Oh, God! Tests left to do. In fact, we have only begun, my lad, so there's no time for questions."

"Aren't you glad to see me? Your best friend?" Josh said, getting into the spirit of our revelry. "Don't you wanna know how many fish I caught and how big they are?"

"Only if you've filleted them for my freezer," Jeanie said.

Court extended his hand to Josh. "I'm Harcourt Raymond III."

"I'm Josh the first, I think," Josh said. "Only maybe I'll use an alias when the Boulder police come to raid this zooey place." He tapped a Coors. "I've known Dave here for about twelve years now. This man *invented* the word 'intense'. But I've never seen him laugh like this, and" (with mock tearfulness) "it does my poor heart good."

I laughed again. "Stop it!"

Like Court, Jeanie had recovered. "What time is it, Josh?"

"About four."

"We have to pick my husband up off the floor so he can get on with the rest of his experiment. Christmas is coming, and David knows he'll be in the doghouse if he forgets to shop for his family."

Josh smiled. "Maybe we'll find out what's been making such a weirdo out of your husband, Jeanie."

"Yeah," Jeanie said. "And maybe we'll also find out *how* he's become such a weirdo."

"All I want to know is *what*," Court added.

We broke out another six pack and the four of us toasted to "Grandaddy to be, Harcourt Raymond III. The crystal-laser play would just have to wait.

CHAPTER FOURTEEN

Court led me through his mansion's finished basement to his private movie screening room. Versatile Harlan served as Court's projectionist. On a movie screen about six feet high by ten feet long was a stop-frame image of Lucille Muhr. Her lustrous dark hair was done up high at the sides with ornate tortoise shell combs. She wore simple but large pearl-and-diamond earrings. One of her hands clutched a matching pearl necklace. The other hand gripped one of the "paws" of her throne-like, red velvet upholstered chair. A white cloak lay at her feet. Her face projected bare emotional agony.

The setting was an English manor house with tall windows and an empty ballroom. There she sat alone. The parquet floors were highly polished. In the middle of the outside wall was a huge fireplace with an ornate mantel. Above her dangled a many tiered chandelier almost as fine as Court's. Outside, snow lay piled in the eaves and windowsills.

"My God, Court! Where did you get this?"

"I've been a fan of Miss Muhr's for a long time. And I have collected all her movies over the years. This is from 'Journeys Home', and her character name is Celia. Have you seen this one? When Celia is six years old, her parents are killed in a car accident. Though Celia wasn't with them when the accident happened, her father's brother convinces the authorities that Celia was killed in the accident too so that he will get her inheritance. Her uncle ships her off to England, where she is raised by a childless barrister and his wife. And when Celia reaches the age of eighteen, she discovers letters from her uncle to her adoptive father. But when she confronts her adoptive father with the evidence, he snatches the letter from her and burns it along with the rest of the uncle's letters. All Celia has left to prove her identity is knowing about the letters, her resemblance to her late mother, and some rather hazy memories. It's kind of like the movie 'Anastasia', with Ingrid Bergman. Celia goes to America and begins the process of proving that she's the rightful heir to her parents' estate."

"The film was shot inside an old manor house outside of Philadelphia. I picked this scene for a special reason. The scene takes place after a banquet Celia's aunt and uncle have given for prominent Philadelphians. Disguised as the distant English cousin of a certain family (who happened to have sent their regrets that they couldn't attend), Celia slips away before coffee and dessert to be alone in the great ballroom where she used to play when she was a child."

I reeled from seeing my former beloved on screen for the first time. A glimmer of what Court had in mind made my neck hairs stand up.

Court continued: "Here, so that she can avoid making her uncle suspicious, Celia's trying to repress the hatred she feels for him. And she's remembering her parents and being put aboard the Queen Elizabeth II for England and arriving at the home of the barrister and his wife, and so forth. She won an Oscar for her work in this film."

While my eyes bore through Lu's image on the screen, I told Court only that during the years Jeanie and I had married, I had never seen one of Lu's movies because Jeanie begged me not to. But I had burned inside with a longing to do so. "Why didn't you tell me before that you had these?" I asked. "Surely you knew how much this would mean to me all these past months." I was shocked. "Court—."

"I didn't trust your state of mind until now. You know I am a moral man. If I had shown this to you before now, I would have felt like a loathsome panderer." My eyes must have seemed cemented to his, for he followed with: "Because of where you are in your work, I would be guilty of neglect by not showing you her film. My idea for this frame of Lucille Muhr is so simple that when you hear it, you'll wonder why you didn't think of it before. My only hesitation is that I might be helping you break your promise to Jeanie. On the other hand, I believe my idea could ultimately save your marriage."

I looked at Lu the actress again while she sat in the middle of that empty ballroom. "Why *this* scene?" I asked. "It makes me cringe."

Court reexamined Lucille Muhr's image too. "Because for almost three minutes, she sits perfectly still. The only movements are the play of emotions across her lovely face."

"I don't understand."

"David! Don't you see? You could make a hologram from this frame. No, you won't be able to put her on a turntable and take so many frames per degree of its turning. But look at this. Harlan, roll it, please. See how long she's sitting still? How many dozen frames of film must be going by before the tiniest change of expression shows in her eyes? Before the tiniest change takes place in her facial muscles? Oh. Look at this part. Just a slight flicker of pain in her eyes. See? It's so subtle that it couldn't distort a hologram, could it?"

When I watched, I did understand what Court meant. Not having seen Lu's work, I also felt my emotions knotting at the sight of her expressing a pain so terrible, yet so repressed. "I will have to project it without sound," I said I was trying to get back some objectivity. "I'll need a release quality duplicate of this to cut up and work with."

"You could work here. We'll set up another, more spacious lab for you. It will be my Christmas present to you. If you're wondering what's in it for me, well, it's a chance to keep my eye on you. And a chance to be nearby while you're working. That's fair."

I felt like I was going to pass out. "If you think so."

"Anyway," Court continued, "Jeanie might be happy to get you out of her hair for a while."

"You're obviously ahead of me. Tell me: if I did make a hologram using this scene, what do you think would show up? I'll have to work around these flashback sequences the film editors have inserted."

Court lifted his shoulders and straightened his sports'jacket like a man who had just scored a juicy business deal. "From what you've taught me, and from what little I know about acting, I think this. Actors draw upon past experiences to evoke the emotions of the characters they portray. If the script calls for a character to be angry, an actor recalls a time of intense anger from his or her past. In this scene, Miss Muhr must have been remembering dozens of past experiences. You've already proven that these can show up in a hologram."

While Court talked I jumped in my mind to the task at hand. "I'll need to do a 360-degree hologram to capture any such images."

"And I expect this will keep you busy far beyond Christmas, *which* I hope your family will spend here with us."

"Court? I want to watch the whole movie."

"All right."

CHAPTER FIFTEEN

"One more choir practice before the big show!" Jeanie said.

"Christmas Eve's in six days," I said.

"You know the Presbyterians. They have enough greenery for their holiday services to refoliate the Amazon jungle. You think Court will come? We won't be going to Denver until Christmas Day. I've got to be in good voice for that lullaby. The flu's going around and I'm *willing* myself not to get it."

Eddie chewed thoughtfully on an English muffin slathered with butter and orange marmalade. "Yeah. Before Christmas Break, kids at school were dropping like flies. At the last basketball game, the stands were as empty as they are for concert band shows."

Jeanie shot Eddie a look about talking with his mouth full.

"Come, come, Eddie," I said. "Half of Boulder comes to those concerts, including us."

"Well," Eddie said, "I believe like Mom that you can tell yourself you're not going to get sick and then you don't. Speaking of sick, what's the absent minded professor Dad working on these days?"

I patted my son on the cheek. "Thanks for the vote of confidence."

"Yes," Jeanie said. "What's been going on with you down in Denver?" She looked so sincere that I didn't put my guard up.

"Court and I have been Christmas shopping," I retorted.

Jeanie smiled. She slapped half an English muffin down on her plate. "My prayers have been answered. The Leone family *phantom* has been Christmas shopping."

"I like that," Eddie said. "'Family phantom'. Cool, Mom."

With my fingers I twiddled a slice of cantaloupe like a cigar. "It's all in the wrist."

"Seriously, David, what has been going on at Court's?"

I settled on telling only part of the truth. "With the work I plan to do, my lab here is inadequate. Court's setting up a bigger, finer lab at his mansion. I've given him lists of what I need, and he's supervising construction work on the inside of the carriage house on his property. I'll be able to make much larger and more detailed holograms there. He's also setting me up with film editing equipment."

Jeanie slid a plate of fruit toward Eddie. "Is it like a penthouse? Will you stay there until you've finished your project?"

"Sometimes I might stay overnight."

"It beats commuting to Ohio," Eddie said.

"Please wipe that marmalade off your chin, Eddie," Jeanie said.

I felt myself go pale. I asked Eddie how he knew about Ohio.

"Mom tells me *everything*," Eddie said. "It's no use trying to keep anything from your old son." He pretended to wipe his chin on his shirt cuff. "How's *that*, Ma?"

"I give up. You're both uncouth. Did you know that Eleanor of Aquitaine helped civilize Western Europe?"

"I didn't know. How'd she do it?"

"By bringing window glass from the Orient and putting up tapestries to keep out cold drafts."

As bored as he looked, Eddie asked: "Where'd you learn that?"

"I always beat you two at 'Trivial Pursuit', don't I?"

"That's because you're a Baby Boomer," Eddie said. "Most of the questions have nothing to do with *my* generation."

I was happy for a change of subject. "Oh, yeah? What about the science and nature questions? And the sports questions?"

"That's fine until you get one like: 'Name three ingredients in a White Russian," Eddie said.

"I see what you mean," I said. "Will you be bringing Laurie with you to your mom's performance?"

Innocent Eddie blushed. "She wants her parents to meet you."

"I think it's about time we met them," Jeanie said.

"Me too," I said.

On Christmas Eve, Boulder's First Presbyterian Church looked like a Norse landscape. King-sized wreaths, bunches of holly, and huge poinsettias overran the sanctuary. Garlands of spruce decorated with huge red velvet bows hung along the walls beside rows of pews. Music from the huge pipe organ shook the rafters of the packed church, and you could palpably feel excitement in the air. I was flanked on my right by Eddie and Laurie and on my left by Court, Reynie, and Paul LaSalle. It was the first time I acknowledged to myself how crazy it was that I hadn't seen Paul since the wedding reception. Far from being the Preppie I had imagined him to be, Paul LaSalle looked down to earth and still very much in love with Reynie. Reynie had that "pregnant lady" glow, and a pixie-like mischief flickered in her eyes.

Laurie's parents appeared in a seat behind us. Brad Hughes was a house contractor and his wife Nadine did part-time bookkeeping for a Boulder chiropractor. Brad was about my height, balding, and had a beer belly. Nadine wore too much makeup. Otherwise she looked pretty good. Though they both seemed pleasant enough, I had a feeling it would be tough to talk to them for any length of time. I hoped that, now we'd all met, Brad and Nadine wouldn't want to socialize with us much. Then a sort of "Ghost of Christmas Past" feeling pierced my heart. And, for the moment anyway, and for Eddie's sake, I pledged to be more gracious towards Laurie's parents.

The choir filed into the sanctuary. Reynie reached across her father and poked my arm to get my attention. In the sanctuary, Jeanie held a beautiful maroon, leather bound music folder. She was searching for us. I saw Court nod and smile at her. Then, with a special look, Jeanie showed me she appreciated that we *all* got there on time. From what I could see, musicians included first, second, and third violinists and violists, two *bassi profundi*, two cornets, the usual woodwinds, and a partridge in a pear tree…

I thanked God they weren't doing the entire "Messiah." By the time they got to the thrilling Tenor, singing "Comfort ye, my people," I was remembering what it was like to be an altar boy, dressed in my long black gown and white scalloped surplice. I recalled what most altar boys my age would have. Holding the bowl in which my priest, Father Duffy, washed his hands before presenting the Host. Father Duffy lifted the Host to bless it, and I held the little paddle under the chin of each mass celebrant while Father Duffy placed a holy wafer on the tongue of each. In my mind I skipped over the more tedious, rest of the mass and went right to the acolyte part. The snuffing out of the candle flames. Lowering that bell at the end of a long shaft to quench each candle flame. It was my most dramatic memory of *finishing* something. You could go through a process that had some meaning. You could come to the end of that process feeling fulfilled, resolved. It was the same as coming home from school at the end of a day. Every night you knew the work of that day was done.

By the time the tenor started the triumphant

Every va-hah-ley, every va-hah-ley / Shall be exalted...

I was reliving an autumn afternoon when I walked home from school, scuffling leaves under my brown shoes. The smell of those leaves when I buried myself in a leaf pile and wondered if there were any biting bugs in there. The smell of leaves burning while my mother and my neighbors raked them toward the smoldering center of leaf piles. That was before they outlawed burning leaves.

Noticing I was *out there*, Court nudged me with his elbow a couple of times. He gave me an extra hard nudge when Jeanie came forward to begin her first solo. He pointed at the program: *No. 12 PIFA (Pastoral Symphony), Recitative (Soprano), No. 13 Recitative (accompanied Soprano).* Though Jeanie sang this magnificently, even while I tried to look directly at her, my mind started to wander again.

I thought, *Maybe God made men and women fall in love so men would be trapped into marrying and having children. When a man looks at a woman through the eyes of love, he sees what he wants to see—a responsive, smitten, gorgeous angel of a person. Otherwise, men would probably remain polygamous and women would be stuck with bearing the seed of those philanders. But God's trap didn't work unless a man and woman were enough in love with each other. And unless they had no such obstacles to marriage as inability to communicate well, incompatible value systems, inappropriate social differences, or diverse levels of maturity. That,* I thought, *about covers it, except for the day to day drudgery of keeping a household together. Buying food and writing out checks to pay utilities, credit card balances, and various kinds of insurance. Fixing the toilet. Vacuuming and dusting, changing bed sheets, cooking, doing dirty dishes, and washing and drying the laundry. In courtship, all those Sisyphean tasks are done behind the scenes by someone's mother, leaving untouched the Neverland of romance.*

The opening musical phrases of the *No. 17 Duet (Alto, Soprano)* were completing their slow three-quarter-time, boat rocking motion when I heard Birgitta Maximillian, Alto, begin:

He shah-hal feed his flock / Like a sheh-eh-eh-eh-eh-pherd...

I couldn't help imagining Birgitta Maximillian in a horned helmet and shining breast plate, brandishing a spear. In my mind I heard her sing "Yo-ho! Yo-ho!" and saw her galloping frantically with the other Valkyries to reunite with her lover Siegfried.

As though Jeanie knew what I was thinking, she looked at me and smiled. Then she took a deep breath before she began her part of the duet: "Come uh-uhn too-oo Him / All ye that lay-hay-hay-bor..." The lilting, rising second line about made me fly out of the pew. At the very moment I noticed I was feeling it in my muscles, Eddie clung to my arm. When I looked at him, I could see tears of joy and pride in his young eyes.

When Eddie noticed, he whispered through clenched teeth: "Don't look at me!"

Without looking at the score, Jeanie gave a performance that blew me away. It was so good I had to keep reminding myself that not only did I know this woman, but she was my wife too. She was radiant, and I flashed back to when, as a boy, I stared up at the statue of the Virgin Mary. I used to kiss the statue's foot if no one else was around. When the orchestra began to play the next musical bridge, I saw Jeanie as that statue, her soulful eyes peering down at me with compassion and forgiveness. Jeanie sang "How beautiful are the feet / Of them that preach the gospel of peace, / And bring glad tidings of good things."

God supposedly made people from clay. How did he do that? And we return to dust when we're dead. What was there before dust? Oceans? First, the Word: Clay. In that clay were suspended silicates, forming a template for life. Where am I getting that? Colloidal suspension of quartz particles...silicate plates gathering organic molecules between them. Clay lumps breaking away in a storm and washing downstream to become new clay beds. Silicates within the clay reproducing themselves, cradling the organic matter that was too fragile to keep itself together. A symbiosis of life and non-life. Clay, holding what were perhaps latent polymers that in time developed genetically controlled components. What made organic life develop? Light. Light! Maybe it was light energy that moved in a spiral up through the gridwork of quartz crystals and formed the structures that would in some later millennium be DNA! Strong enough now to exist on its own, life broke free and began to create its own cell walls! I lost track of time until Court lifted me to my feet for the Hallelujah Chorus. My thoughts had made me reconsider my long-time evasion re: the G-word. He must be a cool scientist, a New Age sort of guy. A cosmic holographer!

For... the...Lord God Ohm-nip-o-tent reign-eth. / Hallelujah!
Hallelujah! Hallelujah! Hallelujah!

How could those Stone Age barbarians of the Old Testament have understood how God created them out of clay? How could those superstitious, animal sacrificing, nature fearing *roughs* have conceived that matter is *motivated* by, created out of, and perceived through light? How could those sheep-tending vision misinterpreters have realized that God was a genius of holography!

King of Kings (for-ever and ever)
And Lord of Lords
(For-ever and ever, Hallelujah! Hallelujah!)

I suddenly knew what medium to use for storing the holograms I would make from Lucille Muhr's movie footage: a quartz crystal. I imagined successive angles at which a laser beam enters a crystal, like the way I arrange sections of images on the holographic plate. Imprinting layers of the recorded images within the gridwork structure of the quartz while gauging a *resonance* specific to that crystal. There was also something about acceleration of light, and sound, making a difference in the results. A quartz crystal as a tuning fork of light! But how on earth could I calculate those angles, layers, and resonance levels?

In my mind I saw angels with seraphic wings, halos, auras of white light. Huge, puffy clouds gathering, dispersing, zooming at high speeds. Sunrises and sunsets, lightning and rainbows, oceans and mountains, deserts and plains, rivers and forests strobed uncontrollably through my brain. Finally, the angels sang ecstatically.

For-ever … and ever /
Hallelujah! Hallelujah!
Hallei … lu-jaaaaaaah!

I burned with excited fever. And years of remorse haunted me.

It was almost midnight when we pulled up in front of Boulder's Sacred Heart of Jesus Church. Jeanie sighed. She waited in the car while I tried the door. To my surprise, it opened. I was even more shocked to find that the church still contained a confessional booth because now you usually just visit your priest's office. When I sat down, the little door slid open. Hoarsely I whispered: "Bless me, father, for I have sinned."

"What is your sin, my son?"

"It is twenty one years since my last confession…and I lust for a woman who's not my wife."

CHAPTER SIXTEEN

Christmas festivities at the Raymond mansion were pure Currier & Ives. Here, just outside the Mile High City, two new inches of powder lay on the packed snow from earlier in December. Only a light wind made the air seem cold, for out here the humidity's so low that you don't feel chilled when the sun is shining. Here we have passive solar road ice melting.

Court and his family came out to the driveway to greet us.

"We have a surprise for you," Reynie said with that look in her eyes that meant only one thing. She had planned some adventure for us. "It requires you to leave your coats on."

I thought we were at last going to see my new lab, so I began to walk toward the carriage house. Unsteady on my feet with anticipation, I began weaved. I thought I heard sleigh bells and the soft *plah-plah-plah* sounds of horses hoofs in soft snow. Laughter spilled from

Court's family and mine. Then there was the glide of metal runners as a sleigh pulled by a team of stout gray horses bore down through powder and into the crusted snow.

Court kept laughing. "David! Stand still or they will run over you!"

The multi-talented Harlan pulled the reins up hard and the team of twin dappled grays came to a see-sawing halt.

I felt my face turn scarlet. "Harlan can drive a sleigh," I said.

Jeanie addressed Reynie. "You're sure tiny. When are you due?"

"Mid-April, and I plan to be as big as a watermelon." Reynie spied Eddie's regard for the dappled grays, asked what he thought of them.

"They're epic. Are they trained just to pull?" He ran his hand along the neck and flanks of the nearest steed.

"That's Kaspar. The other one's Matilda."

"Like 'Your Aunt Matilda?'"

In unison Jeanie, Reynie and Eddie said: "Because she's so gray!"

Reynie told Eddie that Kaspar was trained to harness too. "They're stouter than most pull-horses. And older. But we're not racing them professionally. Still, driving a sulky takes great discipline for both horse and driver. But there's no feeling like it. It's like skimming across a lake on a sailboard."

Paul LaSalle came over to shake my hand. "Ms. Reynelda told me she gets a special thrill out of taking you by surprise."

Reynie smiled. "That's because David's lives *ahead* of himself."

Paul put his arm around his wife's waist. "It's great to have the chance to see a legend in person."

Reynie gave me another special smile. "As the expression goes, 'a legend in his own mind'. Well, why don't you all get in now. Those goose down throws will keep you warm enough."

Eddie got in front with Harlan. "I hope you drive real fast!"

Jeanie and I got in back and covered our legs with the throws.

"Good idea," Jeanie said. "Let's race the wind!"

I felt anxiety about this adventure. "Keep on, Harlan, if you guys want me to throw up all over you."

"You'll be downwind," Eddie said. "You'll upchuck on yourself."

With his eyes straight ahead, Harlan cracked his long whip right above the horses. Kaspar and Matilda trotted until Harlan shook the reins and whistled a sharp *The-weet!* Then the coursers cranked into locomotive power. Though I couldn't see Harlan's face, something told me his mouth was twisted in a sadistic smirk.

Jeanie and Eddie shouted such obnoxious *exuberances* as "Whee!" "Yeah!" and "Woo hoo!"

The stark whiteness of the snow whizzing by blinded me. Sleigh bells jangled spitefully in my ears. The wind made the bells and the sleigh runners sound like a sawmill. When we hit a bump, my stomach lurched. "Stop!" I shouted. "Harlan!"

"This is like taking the moguls at Copper Mountain," Eddie said.

Harlan must have thought I was joking because he continued his hell-bent flight path.

I rallied for a moment. "Eddie skis?"

The sky had cleared and the sun was intense. It sliced through the atmosphere and bent my vision. The trees' zooming by made me dizzy. My stomach slogged and I leaned over the side of the sleigh to retch.

"Harlan!" Jeanie shouted. "Stop!"

I'm sure Harlan only had my best interests in mind when he abruptly pulled up the reins. But because of my posture I fell over the side and landed face down five yards behind the sleigh, where I continued to puke my guts out. I tell you it wasn't pretty. Mercifully I had avoided hurling on my holiday garb. *Un*mercifully my mouth tasted like…never mind. They delivered me in a semi-upright position to the front of Court's mansion. Eddie and Harlan walked me in cowboy style. The first pleasant thing I remembered was Court offering me brandy. I murmured, "Trauma is intensely focused negative energy."

"I'll make a note of that," Court said.

Dinner was pretty much a blur. So was the opening of presents. Trying to transmute from looking pasty to looking vital took all my energy. Every now and then I heard things like "Why, thank you!" and "How thoughtful." Reynie and Court gave Eddie a beautiful hand tooled Western saddle for pleasure riding. It was even inlaid with silver like Roy Rogers' saddle. I was aware of this only when sunlight fell upon it. I felt bad that I had never given Eddie anything this splendid, or meaningful, for Christmas.

Court had donned a thick gray overcoat. "Put on warm clothes. The drive to the carriage house is plowed and we're heading down."

I hoped we were bound for the carriage house to see Court's Christmas present to me: my new lab. Still brain dead, I began to put my boots on. They had old-fashioned latches on the front.

"Let's take David to the carriage house in the sleigh," said Reynie, the Marchioness de Sade. "Just kidding."

I was the first to reach the French doors leading out to the veranda. I pretended I wasn't desperate to see my new lab. I needn't have bothered. Everyone else seemed to be stalling.

"Just a minute. I forgot my pipe tobacco," Court said.

I wondered when Court took up pipe smoking.

Jeanie spoke in phrases as if she were about to OD on Quaaludes. "Reynie? Did. You see. My scarf. When you. Hung up. My coat?"

"Are you going upstairs, Paul?" Reynie asked her husband.

"Oh, never mind," Jeanie said. "It's here in my coat sleeve."

Eddie filched walnuts and stuffed them in his pockets under Court's approving gaze. "The shells will be good for the grounds," Eddie said.

Court nodded. "A little peppering of mulch couldn't hurt."

I stood at the door. "Uh, guys. Are *we* about ready?"

Reynie made one more pass at the buffet table. "Hold on a second. I'm scavenging for whatever white meat you all might've left."

This was a moment I wanted to let out the full range of *obnoxia* I was capable of. "It has to be white meat?!" I faced the dining room table. I wanted to scream: "I've been so sporting today that I want to strangle all of you! I've been waiting more than a month to see my new lab! *My* Christmas present. You've all had your presents! Do you have to keep torturing me when you know there's nothing else in the world I want? How much can a man—."

Reynie pointed at the vertical window aligned with the front door.

Everyone else stood outside waiting for me. "Hey, Dad!" Eddie yelled. "Don't you want to see your present from Mr. Raymond?"

Court put his arm around Eddie's shoulders. "You can call me Court," he said.

Our walk down the long drive took millions and billions of hours. All of a sudden I thought of items I'd omitted from the list I gave Court. Would I have my lab, only to stall out because I was missing a collimated mirror for the laser reference beam or a loupe for viewing single frames of film? *This must be what stage fright feels like*, I thought.

Court opened the low back door of his carriage house. "Please leave your wet boots on that rubber mat," he said. The entrance looked like it was constructed to block the view of any interloper who might enter my lab unannounced. A smile kept trying to creep into the corners of Court's mouth. "David, come up to the front of the line."

With a pleasure I couldn't hide, I sprang forward like Denver Broncos tight end Mike Barber bulldozing through the LA Raiders' front line. What awaited me would reveal a plan Court designed and carried out with intuitive brilliance. On the immediate right of the hallway was a small bathroom with a walk-in shower. Next we came to my film editing lab. It had beautiful four-paned windows that conveyed light in from the North and South. Directly in front of us a rack and trim barrel sat on either side of a long editing table on which there was a film cutter. To our right was a small work bench on which lay a large, unmarked film can. Above the work bench towered a supply cabinet.

"Go ahead, David," Court said. "Open it."

Arranged inside were film takeup reels, spring clamps, a photography loupe, cotton swabs, rolls of splicing tape, grease pencils for marking the film, rulers, trim tabs, editing gloves, and acetone for cleaning the film. Positioned diagonally across the room was a flatbed film editing machine! I had modestly asked for a Moviola, but Court obtained something even better. The viewing screen on it was large, and I noticed that there was also a squawk box for listening to the movie soundtrack. Of course there was also a film splicer.

Court noted my delight. "I found out that film doesn't get damaged on a flatbed editor. I called the head of the Film Department at CU and he told me all kinds of other things you forgot to put on your list. Oh, and David. If you ever need help with this film editing stuff, here's the number of a Graduate Film student who'd be glad to share his knowledge for a nominal fee."

Eddie responded with his usual teenage panache: "Wow, Dad!"

"Your work is way grander than I thought" Jeanie said. "Looks like I should take up a new hobby."

Reynie and Paul stayed in back. They kissed like newlyweds.

Court patted Jeanie's arm. "I want to show David his lab alone. Afterwards Harlan will give you and your very bright son a tour."

I followed Court to the far corner of my film editing lab to a double door. I mean there were two doors in a row. They were arranged so that if someone came inside the first door, not only would no light get in through the main door but also the main door would have to be opened from the *inside*.

"When Harlan brings your lunch or when I need to see you," Court said, "this green safelight will flash."

"But there's a phone out in the film editing lab," I said.

"No one will call you on that phone. If you need anything, that phone is for you to call *out* on. Your lab may be as soundproof as a recording studio but I don't want you to be disturbed from the outside in any way. Except for lunch, which Harlan will bring to you every day at Noon. That's the only contingency to this gift. You must eat! Now look around and see if your Christmas present suits you."

The floor was concrete. Behind black polyethylene drop cloths were the doors that once slid open to let carriages drive through. These doors had been caulked tightly to cover any cracks that might let in light or bad weather. The optical table in the center of the lab was even better than the one I used when I worked at OPTIKS. It had its own *reticle*, with six inch square segments numbered one to sixteen on the sides and A to H on the ends. Within each segment were crosswire lines that a holographer uses to focus the eyepieces for various optical instruments. The table's construction made it vibration-free. I figured this table alone must have cost Court at least twenty thousand dollars. The laser mounted at the end of the table was very large: fifteen-power. With the intensity of the laser light being so great, I would need only very short exposure times. This meant there would be no distortion in the results. Against the east side of the holographic lab sat a cabinet in which there was a Jodon VBA-200 variable beam splitter. There were also spatial filters, lenses, collimating mirrors, and a Spectra Candela foot candle meter. My holographic sink was on the south side of the lab. In a large cabinet adjacent to the sink there was an apparent life-time supply of film, plates, chemicals, trays, storage bottles, and plate holders. Beside this, in the west wall, was another set of double doors that led to concrete stairs.

"Please come this way," Court said.

At the top of the stairs we emerged into a room with a breathtaking view of the Rockies. There were windows everywhere! Solid glass on the south and west sides. Pull-shades decorated with delicate Southwestern colors and motifs lent privacy. There were even skylights in the ceiling. Exotic plants surrounded this space furnished like a family room. Facing the mountains in the West was a huge couch, in front of which was a low square glass-topped coffee table. On the south was a tan leather recliner. On the north wall was a home entertainment center, complete with color TV, AM/FM radio receiver, tape deck, and turntable. There was even a kitchenette with a mini-fridge, microwave, and bar sink.

"For when you need inspiration or to relax," Court said.

My throat was so clenched with emotion that when I tried to say Court's name, it sounded like: "Gghrd…"

CHAPTER SEVENTEEN

January 22, 1988

It was 11:00 p.m. Contrary to what I believed before working in my new lab, I had achieved very little. "Journeys Home" had lain in its film can since Christmas Day, except for the two or three times I viewed the scene of Lucille Muhr as Celia, sitting in that empty ballroom. When I viewed this on the flatbed editor's viewing screen, again I wondered what traumatic memories she drew on to convey what her character felt in that scene. A couple of times, through the loupe, I had even viewed the sequence of Lucille Muhr sitting motionless in her chair. The loupe magnified only what was already there. Knowing that I could waste months making holograms blind, not knowing if any ghost images would turn up, I had spent these weeks accumulating meditative music, quartz points and clusters of all sizes and complexities. And consuming lots of beer and takeout *nachos supremos* while admiring the Rockies in my upstairs "inspiration room." To escape feeling like an idle loser I had also checked out several books on film editing from CU's Graduate library but had glanced through only one or two and paid overdue book fines on all of them.

Except for my twin quartz crystal my entire collection of tools for experimenting lay neatly arranged before me on a low table in front of the main panoramic window. All seven tuning forks were wrapped in a green flannel segmented pouch like fine silver flatware. I also packed my 35-mm Nikon F-501 autofocus camera, rolls of infrared film, and my Zenith night vision scope.

Arms chicken-winged behind my head, I lay back on the couch upstairs. Light shone through the quartz twin, which I hid on top of my bookcase. The crystals created rainbows around the room. When I looked at the wall behind me I saw colors that weren't quite right. The low band of colors contained the usual red, orange, and yellow. In the high color range and coming inward: violet, indigo and blue. Green is supposed to be at the center of the spectrum. Instead I saw turquoise and rose pink! I moved the cluster slightly to see which part might be making this effect and discovered it was the bottom crystal.

When I peered into the ice clear matrix crystal and turned it in the sunlight, I saw inside a rainbow window. In the piggy-back crystal there was a smaller rainbow window. There were also little rainbows in the tiny crystals that jutted from it. I figured the reflection of two or more rainbow windows upon each other within the twins must be causing the turquoise and rose pink colors in the middle of the spectrum to be cast on my wall. So I turned the twin crystal sideways and observed the spread of colors change to very thin, quicksilver colored layers where the rainbow windows were before. The layers resembled holographic plates! When I turned the cluster a little more in either direction the metallic layers looked like etched glass.

I grabbed another beer out of the mini-fridge and headed downstairs to my optics table. I set the crystal pair on a little platform covered with black velvet at the end of the optics table opposite my fifteen-power laser. This setup would make the holographic image appear to float in space. I wanted to make a transmission hologram of the variant spectrum that the cluster had just created on the upstairs wall. To do this I would have to duplicate the specific angle of the light that was previously directed through the cluster upstairs by the sun. I added an overhead mirror in front of the crystal. Then I played with my laser angle, beam splitter, and other mirrors to make the image fall on the middle of what would become the master plate.

I adjusted and readjusted the collimating mirror and the transfer mirror. Then I aimed an expanded beam at the middle of the collimating mirror and set the beam splitter so it would aim the reflected laser beam to the correct mirror. Next I changed the collimating mirror's position so it would reflect the beam from the overhead mirror's middle to the part of the table behind it. Then I pictured an imaginary line stretching between the dot of light on the overhead mirror and the light on my optics table. This line of light had to look completely vertical when I stood behind the collimating mirror and looked at the line. That way, when I used the reconstruction beam later, I could center it directly over the plate I would use for copying. Now I determined the correct reconstruction beam angle with a protractor and set up the spatial filter and beam splitter. Next I positioned my object mirrors and object lens. Finally I adjusted the beam splitter for a one to one ratio between the reference beam and object beam and exposed the holographic plate with the laser beam.

I made this master hologram so I could get the separate colors of the spectrum in the copy. Instead of completely covering the master plate with light when I made the copy, I lit only the narrow, horizontal band which that twin crystal's reflected spectrum made. My doing this illuminated an area only a fraction of an inch high on the plate.

The results were much better than I hoped. I phoned Court.

Court joined me an hour later. "It's wonderful of course" he said.

"That's because I'm asking you to look around and up through the image. But the tradeoff is that in doing this we lose vertical parallax. You can't look over this image like you did with the other holograms."

"I see that the *layers* of color are important. They're uniformly stacked. But turquoise and pink in the middle? Isn't that unusual?"

"It's a reflection of some rainbow windows in the structure." I grinned bigger than a raccoon with stolen peanut butter crackers.

Court set the crystal back down. "It feels hot!"

"It does?"

Court looked through the twin crystal until he saw the rainbow in the matrix crystal. Then he held up the cluster until the holographic spectrum showed up. "It's like looking through a dragonfly's eye. Am I looking through the rainbow *window* at the hologram?"

I told Court to turn the crystals sideways and see what would happen with the larger rainbow window. "It's just like the slit of light I made on the master plate. From that slit you use the beam of light to expand the color. See? When you look at the matrix crystal from the side there's just this slit, not the spectrum. That's because the light's not going through it to illuminate it."

"David! Come here and stand exactly where I am now and look through this crystal."

"Don't hand it to me yet, Court. First tell me what you see."

"It's the navel of someone who's either very sunburned or it's an American Indian." Sweat broke out on Court's upper lip. "You don't understand. There's an *image* within the colors of the hologram. I can see the bottom of a sort of breastplate ribbed with, maybe, porcupine quills. And I can see the top of what looks like buckskin trousers."

"You mean it's like someone is standing at the end of the optics table?" I asked.

Court pulled me over to stand in his place. "No. It's like someone *was* standing there when you made your master hologram." He tried to place the cluster in front of my eye at the exact angle he'd been holding it. "You're taller than I am. Try stooping down a little."

"I don't see anything but a blurring of the spectrum."

"Look sideways *through* the silver slit."

I did see what Court described, so I told him I would try to look *around* the image to see if there was more. I noticed an extended image showing the stomach area of what did look like a Native American. But I also saw just enough of a beaded pouch to notice it was tied to a loop in the buckskin trousers with a piece of rawhide. "How long ago was this property developed, Court?"

"The mansion is relatively new but the carriage house is more than a hundred years old. Are you thinking what *I'm* thinking?"

"This place is haunted?"

Court looked through the twin crystal again. "If this place *is* haunted you'll think I brought in a ghost just for you." When he finally got the angle right he whistled. "Whew! Did you notice the pouch?"

Suddenly I had the best idea. If I was right it would solve the problem I was having with screening the Lucille Muhr film. "You know I don't believe in ghosts, but I do believe in holographic traces. That's how 'Reynie Junior' showed up. The trouble I've been having in working with the frames from Lu's film is that I know recording any of such traces would be as hit-or-miss as trying to get the late Mrs. Raymond's image originally. Remember?"

"But *sound* was the key then."

"I'm sure sound is still essential somehow," I said. "We just don't know how to duplicate the results. I'm not sure how to translate light and sound back and forth in the holographic process yet. What I'm really getting at is that the image we see here means there might be a way to preview those 35mm frames of Lu."

Court sat down. "You mean something about the rainbow slits might help you see any image traces created by Lucille Muhr's emotions in that scene? Of course! But what about our Indian? Wouldn't you like to take a portrait of him, including his face?"

"Yes but his most important legacy will be to help us create our *viewer mechanism*."

Court's smile faded. "What if the Indian doesn't show up again?"

"Yeah. I know. If we can't relocate our Indian how will we know we've got our previewing mechanism? Even though I don't believe in ghosts I *have* read about a few habits they share."

"I think they usually show up at the same place at the same time."

"Right! Actions or sequences of movements repeated during the lifetime of a person leave holographic ghost traces."

"So you're going to flush him out," Court said.

"I sure am."

"I hope he's a friendly ghost."

I looked through the crystal at the belly of our ghost's attire again. "Like, he won't throw things? When I see him I'll offer him a beer."

Gone for the moment was my ambition to encode holographic data *within* a crystal. Never mind that I knew a company was already trying that. I was on a metaphysical, not a technological, trail here. I realized my destination was darned far away. That what lay between where I was and where I needed to go included a hell of a lot of *process*. I resigned myself to doing some sightseeing along the way because it was clear that I needed to learn more to attain this vision.

I figured the first step wasn't just to see our tribal ghost again. I also had to find out if his image had appeared behind or in front of the crystal when I made the master. Several problems sprang from that question. First, the only way I could see the tribal fellow's image in this way wouldn't help me determine *where* the image was created, relative to the holographic plate. Second, I needed the twin crystal both as an object from which to *produce* his image and as a viewing device to *see* his image. Obviously the cluster couldn't be in two places at once.

Finally, the most suggestive problem: what if the image of the Indian was *in* the cluster instead of being ghost traces?

I looked with doubt at the "X" I'd made with masking tape. It marked the spot where Court had first stood and from which I also saw our buckskin clad friend. With the quartz cluster in my hand I turned on the laser reconstruction beam and moved to the "X". After adjusting and readjusting the angle of the cluster I could see my portrait of this tribal guy's belly. The image had to be a horizontal slice of a larger image. But did this mean that only part of the image appeared in the hologram because of the limited size and shape of the hologram? Or that the refraction of the light determined what part of the Native American's image would appear through the holographic image?

Neither Court nor I had questioned whether this sunburned belly was three-dimensional. I wanted to try to look *around* the image, so I leaned closer to the hologram and a little to the right. Though doing this helped me see a little more separation in the colors of the spectrum, I couldn't see around the Indian's belly. It was like it was a still photograph. Flat, one-dimensional. I thought, *If only I could put this cluster to my eye and move my head up and down, maybe I could see an entire image.* I squatted down and looked up *through* the image and voila! I could now see the rest of the porcupine-quill and beaded vest and a cape of what looked like wolf's fur flying back from his well-muscled shoulders. Around his neck dangled a large, worked silver amulet with a cat's eye agate in its middle. A craggy face with a razor-hawk nose and piercing ebony eyes above jutting cheekbones glared at me. My new friend had a high, narrow forehead below salt-and-pepper, very straight hair stuck through in back with two crossed eagle feathers. I was looking through the matrix crystal and up at the hologram. Now I hoped that an image of the entire Indian was encoded in the cluster.

A tangerine sunset radiated through the West window upstairs in the carriage house. The rust colored light soothed me. I lay stretched out on the couch with the rainbow crystal in my left hand. I hadn't intended to take a nap. I planned only to rest my eyes before heading back up to Boulder. I slowed my breathing and I began to play a game with myself. I breathed in gradually through my nose and breathed out noisily through my mouth. The air whistled a little in my nostrils as I drew in each breath. As I blew each breath out again I exaggerated the process by aspirating the air as it passed through my lips. At first, hearing the sounds made me laugh. Letting myself get more and more involved in the process brought me nearly into meditation. When I stopped focusing on the sounds of my in-breaths and began to pay attention to *how* my breathing felt, I relaxed even more and sank into tranquility.

My curiosity about this process and my relaxation increased. So I let myself drop deeper into the experience. Now I could feel the twin crystals pulse and grow warmer. Their energy radiated throughout my body. Behind my closed eyes I could see shimmering swatches of rainbow colors. The *spectra* showed the texture and transparency of glass. The next thing I knew, I was on the bottom step of a big spiral staircase that ascended through clear glass-like walls. It was like Fleur's guided trip up to the huge crystal structure. When my foot pressed each next step a new tone rang like successively pitched bells. Dizziness and nausea overtook me. The frequencies of light, sound, and kinetic energy harmonized to create a vibration so intense that it sounded like a huge Chinese gong in my head. It was like hundreds of little soldiers marched in step across my brain. And if my brain had been a bridge it would have collapsed.

At the top of the staircase I found myself in a quartz cathedral. Now the twin crystals in my hand were piping hot. I gasped like a fish dying in the bottom of a fishing boat when the clearest, most intense color of violet I had ever seen flooded the quartz cathedral and reflected off its sparkling planes. A perception of movement made me turn just in time to see a figure trying to sneak away. "Wait!" I pleaded.

She looked so startled that I felt a wave of compassion for her. My eyes said: "I didn't mean to intrude. I won't hurt you."

The *Being*'s eyes said: "You know you don't belong here."

"Who are you?" I asked.

"I am the Elemental of your rainbow crystal."

"Elemental?"

She stepped back, moved away from me. "I am taking the form in which you prefer to see me."

To keep from scaring her I stayed put. "Please tell me," I said with my eyes, "what an 'elemental' is."

"I am the *soul* of this crystal, at least of the rainbow parts. Don't you know what you are working with here?"

I had no idea why I deserved such a peevish response. But I didn't want to alienate this Elemental so I tried to send her calm thoughts. "I know I'm a klutz about these things, so could you teach me?"

She liked that. "You are wondering about the Shaman. And you are right about one thing: He *is* a hologram. But because he also was a great medicine man he 'impresses' me with very powerful energies. And so, though he is no longer living on your earthly plane, he is very much here now too. Do you understand?"

"But if *you* are the Elemental of this cluster, and the Indian died, how can he be here too?"

"You *are* dense, aren't you? I hope you can fathom that it's like love. When you feel real love for someone, that person becomes so much a part of you that you are one. You create a whole entity *together*. Sometimes you even find yourself doing something or saying something that is what your beloved would do or say. Now you wonder how I know these things. I would not even have taken on this form if you had not come barging in here like you did. You might have had the decency to warn me ahead of time. I am aware of these things because of the great medicine man I told you about. He knows of the heavens, and the seas, and the animals, and the people you get to see every day. Out of his imagination he also gives me pictures and feelings of all these. Out of his energy he gives me the quality of people's feelings. And he gives me knowledge of how my crystal shell looks from the outside, and I give him knowledge of how your world looks to me from the inside. That is how humans and elementals are supposed to work together."

She took one step toward me. "I told you, ignorant human, that I am the Elemental of the rainbow crystal. That is the top one in your terms. I am the one who showed you the form of the medicine man. Now in case you don't know it, you should not be attracted to this crystal unless you have enough knowledge, or enough desire, to help me do my work. In turn I could help you in your work. Now I see that you are just a dilettante."

"Okay. I admit it. I can be dense about such things. But I do have a desire to learn."

"Yes, but you want only to recapture your lost love."

"How did you know that?!"

"Oh, really. You are quite transparent." Like the other women in my life, the Elemental seemed to enjoy putting me down. "If I am going to teach you, you must turn your obsession into inspiration."

I told her I didn't understand.

She then emitted such a deep sigh that I felt I might get sucked into the crystal through the space between us. "I will give you a little view of your future. But you must promise something in return."

I said I'd try.

Here inside the crystal cathedral, the Elemental motioned for me to come over to where she stood. I saw what looked like a big mirror, only I could see neither her nor my reflection in it. "Imagine this mirror is filled with light. Imagine that it is a hologram on which you are shining that magical laser beam you play with like it is a toy."

I pictured a reconstruction beam striking the mirror, which suddenly emitted a light so dazzling I thought my eyeballs would blow. When my sight cleared I saw infinite rainbows that filled my field of vision. Their reflected spectra multiplied into countless other rainbows, some vast and others minute, covering the space in the mirror.

"You can go inside—that is, if you are unafraid," There was just a hint of a dare in her telepathic voice.

The dizziness I had experienced at the top of the spiral staircase had been nothing compared with the vertigo I felt when I walked forward, into those colors! If colors can sing, these colors did so. If one can palpably feel the vibrations of colors, I felt them. If a person can see the raw energies of those colors, I saw them.

"Now look with your *inner* vision," the Elemental said.

I felt helpless. "How?" I asked.

"Close your eyes. Focus inside the middle of your forehead. That's right. See yourself a few weeks from now. You are in your lab. You are looking at the medicine man through my rainbow crystal. You want to see all of him. You don't know how to do that. Suddenly you think of your old girlfriend's film. The one you want to make holograms from. The project you have been putting off because you are lazy, ignorant, and fearful. These are among the worst human traits."

"I see myself. I'm looking through the matrix crystal at the Indian. I suddenly realize that if I can understand how the cluster works to display his image I can probably create a device to screen specific frames of the Lucille Muhr film. With said device I would save months, even years, of random holographic printing."

"You have already thought of that," the Elemental said. "You keep forgetting so you will not have to go through with it. With my help you *will* invent something new—a way to holographically record images and their corresponding sounds and feeling tones. But you must do your part first."

I sighed. "Figure out how to make the device."

"Bingo!"

I asked the elemental of the crystal if she had a name and if I could come and see her again.

Again a deep sigh. "I don't want you to call me by a name. You got here this time on your own did you not?"

"David," I heard from far away.

"Just a minute!" I shouted back at the unseen voice. "What about the medicine man?" I asked the elusive Elemental.

"He does not speak English," she said, "so it wouldn't do you any good to call him by a name either. Besides, you will not see him in person until you have enough inner knowledge to create that viewing device. If you do not do your part and *grow*, you see, I will not be willing to help you further."

"I'm sorry to bother you." I heard the faraway voice say again.

I felt the Elemental sort of push me toward the top of the spiral staircase. Before starting back down I looked at her one more time. I only saw a wisp of violet fading in the air.

"Come on, David. Wake up!" It was Reynie.

I was in a total fog. "What time is it?"

"Your wife's on the line at the house. She says you're an hour late."

"Give me a break, Reynie. I was just going to take a little nap, and I had this terrific dream."

"Well, your dream's gonna be a nightmare if you don't get your buns back to Boulder. Pronto."

I tried to get off the couch. "But you don't understand."

"I'm sure it can wait 'til tomorrow, despite what you think. You think your own projects must be done *now*."

"Oh yeah?" I retorted. "I just dreamed about a crystal elemental who told me I should get to work. What are you doing over here?"

"I seem to be one of your keepers. And I'm sure your wife doesn't give a fig about whatever you mean by an 'elemental'. I have to go now, so will you get out of here and go back to your wife without falling asleep again?"

"Yes, Mommy."

Reynie flashed me the back of her hand. "So long, Mr. Weirdo."

"For Auld Lang Syne, can't you come back and help me with an experiment this week? I miss your cute, though caustic, support."

"I *would* like to see that Indian Daddy told me about." Then she gave me one of the sincerest smiles I'd seen from her in a couple of months. "I'll admit I've missed your wacky talk."

I hugged her. "And I know. 'Don't call us. We'll call you'."

CHAPTER EIGHTEEN

"So why *did* you and Lucille Muhr break up?" Reynie asked out of the blue. She had invited me to breakfast on the Raymond mansion veranda. Court was at some board meeting.

"Why the hell are you asking me that?"

Reynie set her yellow coffee mug down on the white wrought iron table. "Because I've been trying to figure out what's taking you so long. Your excuse used to be that you didn't have the equipment, the privacy. Well, Daddy gave that to you. Face it. You've been piddling around, David. There must be another reason."

"Come on, Reynie! If you had an inkling of the complexity—."

"You have had the answer right in your hand, haven't you?"

I ached in the pit of my stomach. "How do you know so much? You have no idea what I've been doing."

"Call it a pregnant lady's intuition. Nobody argues with that one." She helped herself to a third portion of hash brown potatoes. "Daddy knows it too, so how do you explain that? More sausages?"

I did take three more breakfast sausage links. "He's upset about having spent so much money on me?"

"No, David. He's upset because you're apparently unwilling to see the nose on your own face."

I helped myself to more eggs Florentine. "What?"

"Okay. Let's play a little game. Say you have this friend who keeps complaining about some problem he's having in his life. Say he is seeing a therapist, is surrounded by a supportive family and friends. He has all the resources he needs to work through his problem. But he never seems to work out his problem, no matter how hard he is trying. What would you think is going on with him?"

I wasn't going to face this third-degree without downing another Mimosa. I slurped through the straw to emphasize my answer. "The poor guy doesn't see why things aren't changing."

"Wrong."

I removed the straw and took a long guzzle to buy some time. It hurt my throat to swallow so much at once. "What he thinks is his problem isn't really his problem."

"Getting closer there," Reynie said. "Will you stop drinking that so fast? You didn't get all the sugar off the rim."

"You're pregnant. You shouldn't be drinking coffee. If you know, then why don't you just tell me?"

"Because then you wouldn't learn anything, jackass. And I'm drinking herbal tea."

Mindful that Reynie was a hormonal woman I squelched my initial reaction to being called a jackass. "Let me tell you something, my dear Reynie." My voice sounded like a frosted beer mug. "Science can't explain everything I'm dealing with here. I've run into things I couldn't imagine before. And now that I've seen them I still can't explain them. How the hell am I supposed to invent some gizmo to do something when I don't even know how the things I've already *seen* work! In fact, I don't even know what's causing me to see them! So how can I—."

"I'm not talking about that part," Reynie said.

"So how can I create a viewing device to see something when I don't know what I'm seeing?"

"Well, I believe you're stalling—on some emotional level. I believe this because I know you're smart enough to have figured out those other things by now. If you really wanted to."

"What do my emotions have to do with anything?" I was so frustrated and angry that I knew Reynie must be right. "Did my *emotions* create this medicine man guy you've been looking at this morning?"

Reynie patted my arm like a mother pats her bad boy child. "In a way, yes. Your desire has led you all this way so far. And yet some strong desire seems to hold you back. Maybe it's guilt? Maybe it's the enjoyment of a fantasy and not the fantasy itself you need. Maybe if you realized your fantasy you would have nothing to strive for. Only a good friend would try to help you answer these things, you know."

"Maybe you've been taking Psych classes at CU," I said. I rubbed an itchy spot on my forehead with the heel of my hand. I knew Reynie had made a good point "Okay," I said. "You think I don't really want to find out why Lu and I broke up. You think I'm stalling because I'm afraid to find out?"

"I think that's closer to the truth. Have some more strawberries? Would you tell me what happened? I mean, how you remember it?"

"What else would have happened but what I remembered?"

"Oh, you might be surprised," Reynie said.

"I remember that we were making each other miserable and that neither of us had the guts to just say we should break up. In the Fall of 1966, after we'd spent a wretched few hours together, she broke up with me. I was stunned, even though, in a way, I'd been prepared for it all summer."

"You didn't have all the information you needed," Reynie said.

"But that's exactly why I'm going through all this!"

"Wrong."

"Tell me then, oh great Sibyl," I said.

"You needn't use that tone. It makes me doubt your friendship."

"I truly apologize. Sure I didn't have all the information I needed. I've wanted to find out those things I didn't know back then."

"Well, then why don't you just 'find' Lucille Muhr and ask her?"

I set my empty Mimosa glass down too hard. "Are you out of your mind? And risk my marriage? As I told your father, and as I promised Jeanie, I will not contact Lu! She probably wouldn't want to hear from me anyway."

"Aha!"

I just looked at Reynie.

"Now we're getting somewhere. Maybe she's forgotten you. Maybe you were her first but not her best love. Maybe you'll find that what you thought you and she had was just an illusion."

"You're rougher on me today than usual. And I'm just sure that's what getting holographic traces from her film would demonstrate."

"Maybe, yes. Maybe if you zeroed-in on a juicy frame in which she is reminiscing you'd see the image of some other man."

"That's it," I said bitterly. "That certainly must be it."

Reynie could see that she'd hammered me lower than whale shit one too many times. She said, "I'm sorry, David."

My eyes stung. Reynie was acting like some Tibetan swordsman, cutting away the crap that obviously lay between the truth and my view of it. But she was right. I couldn't risk meeting Lu at some airport or hotel lobby and have her see my little paunch, the wisps of gray hair that had appeared over the last two years. I couldn't risk finding out that Lu had easily forgotten the depth of our passion for each other. I couldn't tell Lu how she haunted my dreams, how I felt her presence so strongly that I was sure if I turned around she'd be standing right behind me. "We were so young" was all I could say to Reynie before I could no longer swallow.

"You both were. Love can't always overcome such great obstacles. Maybe if you accept that you'll forgive her for breaking up with you?"

"Hell. I forgave her for that years ago."

Compassion warmed Reynie's eyes. "And now forgive yourself for not being strong enough to stay with such a troubled young woman."

Court pulled up a swivel armchair and sat down beside me by the wonderful flatbed editor he'd bought for me. He looked with me at the backlit frame from Lucille Muhr's film. "You think this is a likely candidate for a hologram?" he asked. He looked through the loupe.

I told Court that, as we'd decided before, this scene would be ripe with holographic traces—and that I believed such magnification devices as that loupe weren't the answer. "Until I can decipher the most glamorous way to do this," I said, "I'll try for a sort of 3-D effect. You know: broadening the dimensions of the film medium."

Court held up his hand. "But wait. Wouldn't you have to start out with a film specially made for 3-D viewing?" If he felt impatient with my progress he didn't show it. He just sat there. He looked like he had all week to be with me. And he listened.

"3-D effects are designed to fool the *eyes*. I want to fool the viewing device I'll be creating."

True to his habit of asking exactly the right question, Court threw me the curve I needed: "How will you know you've got it? If you haven't created the viewing device, how can you know if this other part will work?"

I turned off the intense light. "I think if I tackle this problem using a logical progression, each step will set up the next. First I would bet that Lucille Muhr, perhaps unconsciously, projects *thought forms* of her past while she's acting in front of the camera. That means the material is inherently there. Secondly, I'm pretty sure that the Indian we see 'through' the crystal is really encoded inside the crystal. That tells me that through some optical phenomenon set up within the crystal, the laser was able to reconstruct the image into a three-dimensional one."

"But you work with such phenomena all the time, David. Where's the mystery?"

"The mystery's in how to do it *without* a laser. How to optically simulate what happens in that twin crystal."

Court looked sympathetic. "And that seems impossible."

"It *seemed* impossible. I called you to join me today because I think I know how to screen this release print of Lu's film for holographic traces. If I'm right, I want you to call Reynie right away, please."

Court looked like a diplomat taxed to the limit. "You're the older brother Reynie's always wished she had. And yet she's not sure just what to do with you. And so I'll bet she'll be glad to hear you're getting somewhere on this project."

I laughed. "It might save our friendship."

"And your work."

"And your investment," I added. "I must admit Reynie's my perfect foil, though why she takes such an interest in me I'll never know. It's like she feels responsible for me." The truth of this confused me because Reynie kept her cool, showed little affection for me.

"Well, don't forget that none of this would have happened had it not been for the appearance of 'Reynie Junior'."

"Yeah."

"Where do you plan to go from here?"

"Sort of *into* the crystal."

After Court left I set the cluster above me on the flatbed editor. Illuminated with only incandescent light, the crystal cluster shimmered with all the rainbow colors. I had never looked at it from this angle before. Suddenly on one of the planes ("faces") at the top of the matrix crystal I noticed a range of colors perpendicular to the main rainbow window. It formed what looked like the side of a pyramid. Testing a theory, I turned the cluster around to look at the plane opposite this new one. Sure enough, there was a spread of colors on this face as well. There was a bottom and two sides of the pyramid. Was there a top? I lifted the cluster and looked up through the topmost crystal. There *was* a point! It was the apex of a rainbow pyramid!

I felt sick, like I always do when I'm over-excited. I felt my heart rate double. My chest seemed about to collapse. I slid off my chair and lay on the floor. Heat flashed throughout my body. I thought, *How strange to have a heart attack while doing nothing.*

In semi-consciousness I opened my eyes. A white light so dazzled me that I could hardly see. "Ignorant human," a smooth female voice said. It was the Elemental of the crystal.

Now I saw I was again inside the twin crystal! "Hey!"

"Do not speak to me!" the Elemental said. "Your benefactor was right. Use the cluster as the viewing device or else you'll be at this for another hundred years!"

"What?"

"Forget the lenses. Forget the mirrors. Find a way to direct light through the double crystal and you'll be able to see what you want: everywhere. Just like you saw the Chief."

"But—."

"Get up and take your journey home. You'll find what you need."

Now I felt anxiety about something happening to my twin crystal, thereby cutting off future avenues of discovery. "I need to be able to duplicate this device or I won't be able to sell it."

"Is that all you're thinking of?" the Elemental said. "Most humans would give up everything for this revelation. Must you always crave what you *don't* have? The answers lie in your past. I gave you the means to pursue them. Do you want the woman to come here? She *will* come here. Just wait and see. She could open your eyes wide enough to pop them! But you haven't the courage to confront her, have you? Because you must save face at all costs."

"You don't act like a spirit. Or an angel. You act like you hate me. Why do you help me?"

"Because whether I like it or not, you're the only one who can help me evolve. And I'm the only one who can help you evolve. Do you believe that only an incarnate entity can feel passion? Anger? Do you imagine I *like* hearing the dissonance of your communication with me? I don't. But you are cacophony! You are atonality! You're a living violation of art, sense, and mathematics!"

"You sound a lot like my friend Reynie."

"If I sound like your friend it's because this is the only kind of tone you listen to. Someone who doesn't let you get by with things like lying to yourself about why you're so lazy. Someone who won't let you be any less than you can be. I left you on your own to discover the obvious. You failed because you're trying to avoid the truth as strongly as you're trying to find it. Now tell me what is true."

I swallowed about one hundred pounds of pride and said, "What you said is all true."

"Good, because this is your last chance. You know I can take this crystal right out of your life in the night. I can dematerialize it from you and make it appear to someone who is truly worthy. Take this crystal pair and direct light through them. Then see what turns up. It will be *you* looking at yourself in a mirror! Now leave me."

My queasy gut told me the Elemental had sent me back. When I came to, I lay sweltering on the floor. My body buzzed with the acceptance of what the Elemental had said. I admitted to myself that if Lucille Muhr walked in that door right then I would be more worried about losing my composure than be compelled to take her in my arms and kiss the breath out of her! But what did the Elemental mean by 'She *will* come here?' And looking at myself in the mirror? In my mind I heard the Elemental's voice softly intone: "Stop asking questions and take action."

"Right. Act." I resisted chastising myself because the Elemental had figured this out for me. I severed one 35mm frame from the rest of the filmstrip. I used the light table but not the laser. With tweezers I held this frame of Lu directly on the glass plate, right above the light. Above these I inserted the twin crystal. At first I saw only a wash of colors in the illuminated frame. I pulled the frame back toward me just a bit. Some shadows appeared within the scene, reflected by a green ray of light. No. It was an iridescent purplish green. Maybe if I used my film loupe to magnify the frame…

Sure enough, figures surrounded Luwhere she sat in the ballroom! The figure to her left was elevated above the floor about eight inches. Slim and feminine, the figure was turned away from Lu as though it were preoccupied with something far away. Another figure stood at Lu's right side like a barrier between her and a huge shadow looming just past and above her. This figure was also feminine, though heavier. It stood like a rock against the seeming undirected menace of the large figure, which was definitely male.

The slight figure at Lu's left side was Lu's mother Dora but in her early twenties. A pretty woman, even in her plain house dress, Dora looked unaccountably blurry. It was as if Lu couldn't remember her own mother distinctly. I thought this was odd because here *Lu* was creating her mother's image. Anyway, as I said earlier, Dora looked very spaced-out. Of the three images, Dora was the one toward whom Lu's body leaned within her chair.

The figure at Lu's right side was her grandmother, Lillian Muhr. Apparently Lu had been remembering her grandmother to be in her mid-fifties. A slightly heavy woman anyway, Lillian Muhr wore a full-length mink coat. The hand she extended protectively toward Lu showed a diamond bracelet and a white dress glove. Though gentle, her gesture seemed empty.

The shadowy figure behind Lu was her father Bern. During the shooting of that scene Lu had not even remembered him as a man. Rather, she had visualized him as an obese, terrifying *presence*. Even with his heaviness his cheeks were hollow, making his mouth recede the same way old people's mouths do when they take out their dentures. His eyes looked haunted. Witnessing this, I would also have expected to see pain and fear there. Instead I saw a vicious glee in them. This was the creature with hot coals for eyes. This was the monster I had seen months before in my nightmare about Lu.

Bern Muhr's malignant character struck me so deeply in that moment that I couldn't fathom how Lu ever stayed in the same house with him as a teenager, much less, as a child. Further, I realized for the first time what an achievement Lucille Muhr was, merely in having overcome the influence of this twisted man. Tenderness for Lu swept through me like an ocean wave. I knew I'd never get over the effect this woman had on my younger self. However, maybe I could learn from her how to be a hero. For hadn't it been cowardice that kept me from completing my work? Hadn't I been afraid of dealing with Lu's scary obstacles myself? Hadn't I wanted to remain safe within the normalcy of my own upbringing? To remain secure in my very identity as a holographer, not as a man?

I don't know if my arms ached because of examining the frame so long. I did know this time I had no way out of a new responsibility I felt about the knowledge I'd gained. I also knew that if I forged ahead with my journey, no one might be waiting for me when I returned.

CHAPTER NINETEEN

The chill of the past week with Jeanie clung like an odor to me. I stood by our bed and perused my empty suitcase. I hoped packing would help me keep my resolve. I thought, *If I'm going to be punished for following my dream, so be it.* I was a house divided. I was a man without a country. I was——. A ball of butterscotch colored fluff streaked across my field of vision and landed inside my suitcase. It was Swanky. He crouched and lowered his head as though if he couldn't see *me* I couldn't see *him*.

Amid this little chaos Eddie appeared at the doorway with an engraved envelope in his hand. "Hi, Dad. Aren't we going to R.S.V.P. this? Mom's had it for a month you know. Didn't want to disturb your work." He stuffed the invitation card in my hand.

I hooked Swanky around the middle and lowered him, growling, to the floor. "Court didn't mention it to me either. A fancy ball. At his mansion. A charity to raise money. To cure Multiple Sclerosis." I put

171

in three pairs of jeans, some slacks, and a pair of black dress shoes in my suitcase. Finally I stacked half a dozen shirts in the top.

Eddie tossed me pairs of balled socks, one at a time. "You'll need underwear too," he said.

"Are you and your Mom going to the ball?"

"Mom says a bunch of celebrities will be there. Laurie and I are invited too. I may go as Mom *and* Laurie's escort. What a blast." Eddie grabbed Swanky before the cat could leap into my suitcase again. "If you're not going, can I borrow your tux, Dad?"

I answered the phone. "Well, Karen. Yes I remember you. No. I'm going out of state for several weeks. Let me write down your phone number again." While Karen expounded upon everything she'd been doing since the past summer, I made a paradiddle beat with my pencil. It was obvious *she* wasn't going to stop talking. "Maybe I'll get in touch with you when I get back. Yeah. Okay. You too. Bye."

Eddie helped me close my suitcase. "Do you have to go to Ohio tomorrow?" he said. He pulled at a loose tuft of chenille bedspread. "Why not after the ball? After you see Mom and me all gussied up. After you see me in your tux."

I pulled Eddie off the bed so I could sit down. "It's tomorrow night. Why you wanna R.S.V.P. the day before such a big event? Oh, I get it. It was just a ploy to get me to go with you."

"You've always said I'm as transparent as Saran Wrap. No kidding, Pop. Mom wouldn't be half so mad at you if you'd go with us."

In my state of mind I couldn't imagine anything so hideous as attending a dress ball at the Raymond Mansion. While everyone else drank champagne with their pinky fingers raised, I'd want a can of Coors. And when I was through guzzling my beer I'd long to crush the can in my hand. The air would be filled with cigarette smoke and the sound of rhumbas played by a ten piece orchestra. Gross. Court would introduce me to some starlet who couldn't connect with me for more than a millisecond because she was looking for someone important. Jeanie would be going around with moon eyes trying to look like a somebody. And I would be crooking a finger under my collar to try to get some air under there while Reynie gave me one of those ridiculing glances from across the room. But I knew Eddie and Laurie would have a terrific time.

"I'll tell you what, Sport," I said to my son. "If I can change my flight I'll stay through tomorrow to watch you and your mother go through the ordeal. I'll even take photos of you in your formal clothes. You can take your Mom and Laurie down in your Mustang and I'll drive Woody to Denver later. I'll say goodbye to you and your Mom before I get my equipment out of the lab. But I won't go to the shindig itself. *Capiche?*" I rued my snippy answer even while giving it.

Eddie looked at me with the first genuine sadness I'd ever seen in his face. He clenched and opened his hands at his sides. "Can we take this to a higher court?"

I turned away from my son so he wouldn't see my eyes mist up. "Not this time," I said. After all, what difference could one more act of selfishness make now? I still couldn't compute why *I* should be seen as the villain here. I was tired of being routinely corrected, of being seen as such a jerk. Wasn't Jeanie being selfish too? Hadn't she made it clear that I should forego my dream because she was jealous of Lu? I needed the people I loved to see *David Leone's* emotions and thoughts as valid parts of his personality. It would have gratified me to know why I constantly failed them. All I wanted was to be myself. I was sure of one thing—I would let nothing keep me from my dream this time.

I looked at my flight to Circleville, Ohio, as a little vacation. Almost a vacation from myself. Backed with unlimited funds, motivation, and zest, I could take all the time I needed when I got there. Though I might not be able to keep myself from *thinking* while en route, I wouldn't be able to work. Once I launched my journey I would have no one else to justify myself to.

When I pulled up to the carriage house I saw Jeanie waiting for me. My son had driven his used midnight blue Mustang convertible up the long limousine lined driveway of Court's mansion. Patches of Spring snow still lay on the north acre of Court's property. Though no more snow was forecast for any time soon, the air felt unusually soft. This meant higher humidity for a change. The sounds of spirited conversations and laughter flowed out of the mansion. The music emanating from the mansion wasn't a rhumba. It was Mozart.

"I feel like a teenager jilted on the night of Senior Prom," Jeanie said. "Everyone's going to think it's screwy that you're not coming in." She grazed a clump of dried grass with the sole of one peach colored dress shoe. "And what about Court? Did you phone him to say you're not coming in?"

"Yeah. I did." Court promised he'd try to slip away from the party to say goodbye. I looked at my wife and decided she was merely pretty. Maybe my sour mood colored my impression. Anyway, as dressed up as she was in her peach taffeta poufy dress, as effective as the professional facial was, and as much makeup as she wore, she looked merely pretty. *This is the difference between a housewife and a movie star*, I thought. And I wasn't even comparing her to Lu. It had something to do with character, or the quality of *soul*, or something else. How a woman felt about herself. *Oh, yes*, I concluded. Women might say if a man *thought* of her as a movie star, she would feel and look like one. Because I was sick of being blamed for what my wife felt or didn't feel, I wasn't about to tote that barge or lift that bale for her again.

Jeanie looked scared. "Are you really leaving now? Oh David. This is no good. I'm going to miss you terribly."

I put my arms around her and kissed her. "I'll call you in the morning. Any messages for my folks? Well. You know where I'll be."

In my carriage house lab I felt blue. The light inside looked filmy and yellow. I turned on KOOL 105 full blast. The intro to "Never My Love" by The Association had just started. I flashed back to a country road outside of Circleville. With Lu beside me I was driving my cherry red Chevy convertible with the white top down on a country road at 55 mph. in a 40 mph zone. Lu and I held hands while the radio played "Never My Love" at top volume. As we were coming to a dangerous intersection Lu dared me to kiss her. Not just a peck but a full power, passionate kiss. Though I was scared shitless I did it. It was thrilling.

At times like that I knew the full depth of who Lucille Muhr was—not just Lucille, the volatile, headstrong, crossing the border of bitch-dom teenager but also the vulnerable, passionate, please love me angel of a young woman. Those glimpses of the Lucille Muhr that underlay the veneer of her survival tactics had often made my head swim. They kept me coming back to her after every shocking, hurtful fight she ever started. I learned that if I let her pick a fight with me, and if I stood up to her, she was a hundred times more passionate in our lovemaking. I learned that she needed to get her adrenalin up to kill her fear. That she needed to respect me to love me.

By the time Neil Diamond's "Solitary Man" came on the radio I had packed a brown leather equipment bag, my field kit. When I picked up my twin crystal it burned in my hand. It felt dangerous. And desirable. I was afraid the crystal's keeper had more secrets than I might ever learn from her. But I had taken up the Elemental's dare. I might even do something heroic despite myself. I thought: *You, my little Elemental bitch, are going to help deliver me from these travails of the heart. Together we're going to complete all our tasks. Together we may see things that will curdle your crystal blood. You demand growth? Well, you and I are going to get it in spades.* I carefully packed the crystal in square sheets of foam and went downstairs to my lab to fetch my helium-laser gun.

I turned off the carriage house porch light on my way out. I felt a pang of anxiety that was like something I could reach out and grab. Yeah. It was that old *chicken shit me* feeling. I figured that by now I had so many barriers to my core feelings that I'd be lucky if sometime before I died I could face them. Not dealing with those feelings in the past fooled me into believing I was content. Now that I could admit my cowardice I knew I would also have to deal with the memory of

Lucille Muhr. I realized that if I hadn't been such a candy-ass I would-n't have lost her.

Harlan appeared out of nowhere on the inside of the driveway in Court's gray limo. He opened the rear door and waited for me to step inside. "Court's orders," he said.

Something made me raise my eyes toward the mansion. A couple walked toward me. It looked like Court and a young woman who moved like Lu. Ha! I told myself that was a laugh. To the list of all Jeanie and Reynie had accused me of in past months I could now add hallucinations. Court and whoever was with him walked slowly. They bowed their heads the way people do when they're deep in conversa-tion. Though the woman walked very erect she also moved with a lovely fluidity. I sensed she was no ordinary guest. But I didn't feel like making small talk with a stranger. To pretend I didn't see them I ducked my head like an ostrich and plunged into the limo. Both Court and the woman he escorted stood still for a moment. Then Court waved at me and called out my name. "Hold up a minute!" he shouted.

When I leapt into the limo I knew I was being rude, bad, ungrateful, selfish, disgusting. But I told Harlan to step on it. To kick-start, grind gears, and otherwise get the hell out of there. I promised myself that I'd call Court the next morning to apologize. Like always I felt sure he would understand. I lay back against the soft leather seat and felt a deep sigh come up and go out of me. And as we approached the end of the long driveway I got the sudden feeling that if I moved my left hand on the seat beside me I would be touching Lucille Muhr.

CHAPTER TWENTY

"It's about time you rolled out of bed," Mom said. "How do you get jet lag from a three hour flight?" She poured me a cup of coffee.

"It's always worse going from West to East. It takes you one day to make up for each hour of time difference."

"Well, this is the third day. It's only a two hour difference, so I'm afraid your excuse time has run out."

I was used to Mom's manner, which to strangers often seemed abrupt. But if you watched her eyes you saw a twinkle of warmth. I suppose it's because of her German heritage. What I mean is, it seems everyone I know who has German ancestry has certain ticks. One is holding intense emotions tightly under feigned aloofness, the way my mother does. Another is obsessive neatness. Everything must be in its place, as though if it weren't you might go bats. For example, Mom's kitchen is like a garage mechanic's workshop. She has drawer dividers and cleaning supply holders and racks for knick-knacks…and brackets under the cabinet for her microwave oven. Every small appliance had its designated place. She folds laundry and bed sheets in perfectly aligned layers.

Mom saw me check out the brackets that supported her microwave. "Something I asked your Dad to do with his spare time, which is all the time now," she said. "Retirement had been hard on him. It's like every day he's trying to find himself."

"Where *is* Dad?"

"Oh your Dad's long gone! Went to the hardware store to get some do-dads. As I mentioned. Do-dads to fix things with. If nothing needs fixing he'll make up something that needs it. Or he'll insist on fixing the neighbors' stuff, though they're looking for things to do too." She laughed. "You know how he soaps down the driveway, then sweeps it and rinses it with the hose. We must have the cleanest driveway in the U.S.! Since Ed retired he's been a real pain to have hanging around the house. Says he's bored, so he's adopted the whole neighborhood."

I now revised my theory. I thought: *Germans and retired Italian males are obsessively neat.* "No wonder I'm messed up."

"What?"

"How'd a Teuton like you ever end up with a Leone?"

Mom gave me a *You're just being obnoxious look.* It was same one Reynie had given me dozens of times. Mom refused to play my game. "So we could have a messed up son," she said.

Smoked bacon sputtered on the griddle. In a glass bowl I could see Mom's scrambled egg mixture that I remembered as a taste sensation. Buttered English muffins with homemade strawberry jam. Fresh-squeezed orange juice. I felt like I was back in high school, when Mom took care of my every need.

"You know how tickled your Dad is to have you home?"

"He doesn't exactly show it." I had to admit that even *I* had heard the petulance in my voice. Even I had to acknowledge that it was Dad, looking perky and expectant, who met me at the airport at 1:00 a.m.

two nights ago. I did see that he was waiting for me to confide in him, though he didn't push it.

Mom sat down with me. "Here's your breakfast. Eddie reminds me so much of you when you were his age. My grandson's more outgoing than his father, though. You were always kind of oversensitive. I don't mean that in a bad way. And you were always looking for greener pastures, if you know what I mean."

I focused on my scrambled eggs.

"With you, something better was always just over the hill."

"God! This is the best breakfast I've had since last time I was here."

"And you've always been private about your feelings too. Ed and I have tried not to pry. In fact, some of the times when Dad was most worried about you he didn't say a word. He figured if you wanted to talk to him you would have."

Of course I had thought Dad just didn't care. At that moment I got that I had filtered out everything from my father's words and manner that didn't fit my beliefs about our relationship. And so I found the timing of this very personal information from my mother to be uncanny. I had a feeling this was just a taste of some expansive revelation, only part of which was about my past with Lu.

"I've learned we can't know these things until we have our own children," Mom said. "I'm sure Eddie asks you bunches of questions about a lot of things. I reckon he tries to make everything okay when the air at home's a bit chilly, if you know what I mean. Because you were an only child too, sometimes you must've felt it was up to you to make sure your Dad and I weren't upset with each other, and such. But things happen between a husband and wife that are, well, just part of life. You know? And just between them. It isn't good to make your child part of that because a child thinks everything centers around him. And so he thinks what's going on between his parents is his fault."

For now I glued my eyes to my buttery, milky scrambled eggs and how good they tasted fried in bacon grease. But seeing trenches of wrinkles on Mom's forehead told me she expected me to say something. "Sometimes I see that in Eddie's eyes," I said. My mouth was full of English muffin. It made me lisp my *s*'s. "In fact, right now I believe I can tell exactly how Eddie feels when Jeanie and I have a spat. He does take it personally, and he does tap dance sometimes to try and make up for that 'chill' in the house."

Mom stared at me cockeyed. Like she longed to ask me something.

"I pay our phone bills," I said.

Mom put another blueberry muffin on my plate. "And?"

"So I know how many hours you and Jeanie talk every month. And I know you wouldn't dream of bringing up the subject. But Ma. I just can't talk about it right now."

She nodded gravely and pushed the serving plate of bacon and eggs closer to me. "You want another English muffin?"

I looked into her little German-frau eyes and saw concern there. And I felt a love well up in me that hurt. I couldn't tell if the pain was because her love for me was so big or because I was so full of my own. It must have been both because it was the way I always feel when Eddie and I have father-son talks. When he looks so vulnerable and trusting. As though he would believe anything I said to him or walk off a cliff if I asked him to.

Evidently Mom couldn't take these intense feelings either. "Oh. I can't believe I almost forgot this. You got a FedEx overnight letter from Denver. Did you call your rich friend? I couldn't help noticing the return address."

The thick envelope puzzled me. I told Mom about my recent conversation with Court. That I had apologized for my awkward departure and that he said he wanted to tell me about the events of that night, but not over the phone. I told Mom it wasn't like Court to be mysterious. I went outside and sat on the back porch steps where I could be alone to read Court's letter. Not one to be neat about opening envelopes, I ripped the top of the packet into a jagged tear. On Court's business letterhead he had typed the following:

March 30, 1988

Dear David:

As I told you on the telephone, I decided it would be better to write you about the events of last Saturday night. Since then, I have been pondering whether your abrupt departure was a blessing or a tragedy. Only you can decide which it was, after you have read what I am about to tell you. I find it incredible that you did not see Lucille Muhr, who was walking with me when I tried to signal you. At the time, your wife's feelings notwithstanding, I took matters into my own hands by accompanying Miss Muhr from the party to the carriage house. However, I see that it would have upset you to encounter her.

The upshot of it is, Miss Muhr met Jeanie and Eddie in a most cordial way. Perhaps Eddie reminded her of you and she was drawn to him. (As I recall, you had been certain she didn't know you were in the Denver area.) Your wife quickly recognized Miss Muhr and introduced herself and Eddie on the spot. I have to say, Jeanie betrayed no jealousy whatsoever, and Miss Muhr was quite warm and seemed perfectly at ease. And I don't think her being such an accomplished actress had anything to do with her manner. Of course she wondered whether you were at the party too. Unsolicited, your wife offered that you were indeed on the grounds and that if Miss Muhr made haste she might see you before you left for the airport. I'm sure you will agree with me that Jeanie's offer was most gracious.

If you are wondering whether Miss Muhr saw you jump into my limo, the answer is Yes, and she did not conceal her disappointment. In fact, I saw on her exquisite face a wounded frustration and, for a moment, she rested her head on my shoulder with what felt like a tremendous sadness or weariness. Her gesture made me know she felt a daughterly trust in me. When she asked to see your lab, so that she could at least "touch something of yours," I decided you owed her that much after your rather cowardly exit.

While we walked arm in arm, down to the carriage house, she confided in me some very personal information, which she asked me not to divulge to *you or your family. Having earned her confidence, I will not betray it in this letter or in response to any question you may have of me relative to what she said, now or in the future. In reading this you may wonder why I have let this cat out of the bag with you, only to put it right back in. My purpose is to impress upon you a sense of responsibility for your actions of the other night and your feelings about Miss Muhr. You cannot deny that she is still very much alive in your own life! Let me say this directly: If you knew Lucille Muhr was with me, your only responsible action would have been to complete the destiny of that moment, because that moment was destined, David. Men make a mistake to think that their destiny is something <u>they</u> control merely through directing their will. Destiny is, rather, the result of your thoughts and your actions as much as it is the result of your talents. Your thoughts and actions <u>create the opportunities</u> for your destiny to unfold. You see, your thoughts (and apparently Miss Muhr's) created this chance for "kismet," if you will. However, you wantonly threw your mutual creation away.*

I do not mean to be overly stern with you, David. I just want you to develop some sense of how your behavior affects other people. If you think about Lucille Muhr not merely as a vehicle of your pain and remembrance but as a fellow human being, you will see that your denial of her last Saturday was not only dishonest but also reprehensible. This lovely, sensitive woman did nothing to deserve your treatment of her. Of you, on the other hand, she spoke with great kindness and love. She wanted to know whether you were happy, what you were doing in your work, whether you ever spoke of her, where you were going so hurriedly that night. Did I tell her? Yes, I did. Though I told her the ostensible purpose of your work there, I did not tell her the subject of your experiment.

When she and I entered your lab I showed her the Reynie Junior hologram and I let her see the parts of her film that you have been studying. I asked what she was thinking about in that scene and she said, "That's a very personal question. I don't usually give out my trade secrets, but I will tell <u>you</u>. I wanted to feel I was literally being haunted by people from my past. So, in my imagination I placed my mother, my Nana and my father close to my chair. During the filming of that scene I could feel them all so *strongly." Then I asked her what they made her feel. She said that from her father she felt envy and hatred. She said that she believes hatred is always based on fear but that she had no idea why her father should have feared her. From her mother she said she felt a passive, "almost apologetic" love. It apparently was a conditional, fair-weather kind of loyalty. She said that from her grandmother Nana she got intense pride and a feeling of <u>blood</u> relationship, unlike that which she had had with her parents. She told me that her Nana's love said, "You are mine and I am yours too. Forever."*

Upstairs she touched (no, caressed) your books, your plants, and your crystals. When she sat on your couch, though she did this ever so subtly, I could tell she was smelling the back of it where you rest your head. I tell you, it made me want to weep! She even opened your refrigerator to see what was inside. She laughed at your bucket of stale Kentucky fried chicken and the three Coors beers. Before we left the carriage house, she asked me if I thought you would be angry if she took one of your little crystals with her. Seeing that you had taken the important rainbow cluster with you, I gave her permission to take one of your little inexpensive amethyst clusters, which I know you can easily replace. "In trade," as she put it, she left her medallion for you because it has her "energy" in it. She said she was confident you would know what she meant by this. Feeling sure that having it in your possession might help you in your work, I will mail it to you by the end of this week.

Having talked with Miss Muhr at various times throughout the evening I believe she would not dream of following you back to Circleville. I also know she has no desire to disrupt your life or to upset Jeanie. But because she is strong, she is not a woman who denies reality, David. This is a difference between you that must change if you are ever to resolve your feelings for each other in a satisfactory way. She is aware, now, of the reality of your situation—your marriage, your son, your work, your geographical location. In a way, she has you at a disadvantage and, in your choosing to run away from her, you bear the responsibility for that. If you had given her the opportunity to tell you about who she is now, about the life she now lives, then you would have been liberated from your outdated perceptions of her as a person.

I have found that when we harbor memories of people from days gone by, we keep those people stuck in niches of the past. It is how we incarcerate them forever so we can continue to exert control over them. I want to tell you some things about Miss Muhr as she is now, because I believe it might be tremendously helpful to you to get some perspective about her place in the larger world, not just in your own.

Except for her occasional television and frequent film appearances, Miss Muhr is the quintessential recluse. She lives with her Golden Retriever in an artistic, comfortable home in Norwich, Connecticut. She has never married, though many eligible, wealthy men have courted her. Another female celebrity and friend of Miss Muhr who was at the party confided in me that it was "common knowledge" among her close friends that Miss Muhr never got over her high school sweetheart and the fact that he had married someone else. This actress described Miss Muhr as being like one of those characters in a 19th Century novel who loves only one man her entire life.

She is deeply spiritual. She takes her sustenance from, and is rejuvenated by, the woods and ponds near her home and from the wild creatures that inhabit that part of New England. She states that she has welcomed each new year more than the last because she has found a serenity within herself that continues to deepen. And she knows that she has chosen her way of life just as it is. You see, she believes that there are no accidents. That everything we experience is a direct result of those choices. She said it's not karma, exactly. Rather, she believes our thoughts and emotions are powerful, creative kinds of energy. She has an abiding interest in philosophy, art, and humanity, and she disdains politics, which she believes benefits' only those who are elected to office.

Having been with Miss Muhr and talked with her at length, I have changed the opinions I formerly expressed to you. Miss Muhr is not someone who should be feared. She is someone to be revered. Believe me when I say that I have deep compassion for your feelings. But you must not only face the reality of your feelings for her but also of hers for you. Don't you agree that this knowledge should make you deem it a whole new situation, especially *considering the work that you are about to undertake? I am certain that your having left prematurely the other night has merely postponed your inevitable meeting with her, and that because the strength of your mutual thoughts about each other created that opportunity at the party, you cannot avoid that destiny for long. Therefore, I urge you, with this inevitability in mind, to prepare yourself. I pray that the success of your work will help you accomplish this difficult task because, David, you both have set the wheels in motion. It <u>will</u> happen, perhaps sooner than you could possibly imagine, and not because Miss Muhr will have acted on her own to make it happen.*

I wish I could be with you when you read this letter. I wish I could be there to support you in hearing this news. On the other hand, I believe it is time for you to stand up to the truths I have imparted herein. You will agree, I am sure, that trying to deny your feelings has not dissolved them one whit. In fact, I have seen firsthand how your denying them has made them grow manifold. Therefore, I hope that when it comes time for you and this extraordinary woman to meet again, you will conduct yourself with integrity. In short, I hope you will tell her the truth about what you have been going through. Whether you act on that truth is a question of honor that only you can answer within the complex relationship you share with her from the past and with your family now.

In closing, let me assure you that what I have said does not mean my faith in you, or my respect and affection for you, have diminished in any way. I shall continue to bank on what I see as your tremendous success quotient. I will continue to back you with my funds and my confidence, and will I continue to have faith that, when all is said and done, you will finally emerge a complete, mature man.

Reynie sends her love and regards, "as usual," and you know you have mine too. I welcome your response, by phone or by letter.

My best to you always,

Court

I don't know how long I had my face buried in my knees until Dad's car pulled up next to the house. I do know that it was long enough to give me a stiff neck. Before Dad reached the steps I tried to shake this feeling that I was still a teenager living in my folks' home. He must have seen the damp places on my jeans anyway.

"You look like hell," Dad said. He nudged my shoulder with the palm of his hand. "Didn't think being with your Mom and me was going to be so hard on you. Well, now really. Want to talk about it? Want to shoot some baskets? I don't move around real fast, but I can still sink them from the foul line, even when it's windy."

"Would you mind driving me over to West 10th Street?" I watched parallel grooves form above the bridge of his nose.

He sat down next to me on the steps. "Like the rest of the houses in this town, Lucille Muhr's house ain't what it used to be. I've heard the people who live there are white trash." He glanced over at the letter on the step beside me.

"It's from Court," I said. I steepled my fingers and then observed my hands wringing back and forth like I was watching someone else. "I'm going to have to deal with those people sooner or later. So it might as well be now. I can take the car myself if you don't want to go there with me."

Dad surprised me by deliberating for the merest moment and then saying "Okay. Let's go."

"I'll tell you about the letter on the way over."

While driving down West 10th Street I was amazed at how narrow it looked, how much bigger the trees were, and how much smaller the houses seemed. I could see this phenomenon happening with a child-hood memory but not with one originally experienced by a young adult. It was like some optical illusion. No. It was like a distortion in the hologram of recalled *mind* pictures. *If memories are indeed holograms*, I thought, *then why is there such a difference in perception at the moment and the recollection of that moment?* Perhaps a memory is stored in our brains in more than one place. Maybe, like a hologram divided-down a few times, the perspective changes, even though the whole still includes all its dimensions.

When we turned into the Muhr driveway I could see the familiar sidewalk stretching up to the house. The sidewalk was in disrepair, showing big cracks which dandelions and other weeds had overtaken. Dad and I got out of the car and headed toward the house. Lu told me that from that gravel she used to pick out quartz stones that sparkled in the sun. She said she took them to her room and put them in a box like they were captive creatures. When she tired of them she tossed them back in the driveway so she could find them again later. The gravel was now so thin that you could see big patches of chalk dust and caked earth beneath them.

"You want me to wait outside?" Dad asked.

I needed to lean on him. "No. I hoped you'd come with me. I know it's kind of awkward, but I don't think these people will give us a hard time." I stared up at the familiar French chateau style red brick house with its hunter-green, wood shingled sloping roof. Directly in front of the leaded glass living room window grew the big blue spruce that used to be beautiful and stately. Now it was ratty and diseased. I prayed Lu would never see her old home like this.

A dowdy woman with bleach scorched hair answered the door. She wore a food stained house dress. She had a can of Miller's beer in one hand and a lit cigarette in the other. The beer smelled like horse piss. She held the cracked storm door open in the cold March air. "What can I do for you?"

"I wonder if you know who Lucille Muhr is."

She checked my Dad out like he was some guy in a bar. "Yeah. The movie star. Why did you come here asking that? You know her?"

"Well, she was my girlfriend back in the early Sixties. She grew up in your house and I was wondering if I could talk to you about some scientific experiments I want to do here."

"Do tell! Is that what brought you back here to her old stomping grounds? You want to come in and tell me about it? I know the place doesn't look like it did when the Muhrs lived here."

We stepped into the circular foyer. There were piles of newspapers, magazines, broken knick-knacks, and soda tab tops scattered all over the floor. I could see the back yard through the picture window of the master bedroom, which was behind the foyer. In back there was a worn picnic table, strewn with junk food bags and beer cans.

"By the way, we're the Barnetts. We do have plans to fix the place up," Mrs. Barnett said.

"How long have you lived here?"

"About ten years. The roof started leaking and what do you think? When the roofers tore off the old shingles they saw a tag under there left by the builders. It said '1939'. That's a good roof to last this long huh? We still haven't fixed all the leaks though. Got a big tarp up there in back with bricks holding it down."

Mrs. Barnet showed us into the living room.

"Now this here's the only room we have had a chance to redecorate. I don't let my sons or my husband set around in here. It's just for company." Mrs. Barnett was clearly proud of the lurid pink drapes and the tacky pastel furnishings she had selected for the space.

The living room looked like the parlor of a Wild West brothel. I last saw the room when I picked Lu up for Senior Prom. At that time a sort of frayed elegance still lingered there: ornate light sconces, built-in book shelves, gas logs with a recessed mantle above them. Now I saw only remnants of the refinement Lu's grandmother and grandfather had created within the space. Now the long room looked like an embalmed corpse painted up for guests at a funeral service. I could tell I noticed Dad was uncomfortable but I wanted to see a little more. To soak up a little more energy of the place, however awful. I needed to judge whether I could pick up something besides the somewhat primitive vibrations of these "Real McCoys."

"You probably remember this a lot different too," Mrs. Barnett said. "This here's the dining room. Pardon the mess. We *are* going to fix this up when we get the chance—and the money."

The dining room was in grubby chaos. Only the huge mirror at one side bore any resemblance to what I remembered. I felt my hands start to shake with anger. "I don't think we should take any more of your time. Thank you for letting us see the place."

"Well, all right then. But I thought you wanted to 'explore' the house for some reason."

One look at Dad told me to get us out of there. "Let's go outside and I'll try to explain what I have in mind," I said. "You can wait in the car if you want."

"I need to speak with the hubby of course," Mrs. Barnett said. "I don't think he'll mind as long as you're gone when he gets home."

What clinched the deal was my offering the woman money to let me set up my equipment and work there. I had heard about that gleam of greed that comes into people's eyes but I had never experienced firsthand how repellant it is. "What about at night? I can do some infrared work outside and you won't even know I'm around." I had to cover this other option, for I might be able to do my best work outside while the family slept.

"The neighbors will see you," the woman said. "If yor sneakin' around the house they'll call the cops."

From the car Dad asked hopefully: "You coming, Son? We got some errands to do. Remember?"

Feeling like a whore, I gave the woman my most charming smile. I handed her my phone number. I told her to let me know what her husband might think about getting paid even more if I wanted to work *inside* their house. From the money hunger still in Mrs. Barnett's eyes I could tell I'd be hearing an affirmative from her soon. I race-walked back to the car to join my Dad.

"Maybe you want to work in the room that was hers?" the woman shouted. She waved the paper with my phone number on it. "I can see my son clears it out for you."

"We'll talk about that when you call me," I shouted back. I got into Dad's car. "Let's get the hell out of here," I said. Dad had already started to pull away from the curb before I even shut my door. We continued back down West 10th Street and I recognized the houses of other high school friends. Like Lu's house, these homes were much humbler versions of their former selves.

Dad looked dazed. "How in blazes are you going to be able to work there? My God! If the filth doesn't get you, the owners will!" He clenched and unclenched his fingers on the steering wheel. He also accelerated and decelerated until it gave me a headache.

"Will you simmer down? You're giving me whiplash!"

"Sorry, Son, but I can't help it." Dad slowed down. "I just don't understand—."

"Because this is an all or nothing deal. This is why I'm here. Now I'd sooner be in Philadelphia, but I have to deal with this situation."

"Let's get a cool drink," Dad said. "We'll maybe even shoot some pool or go bowling or something, okay? I just want to spend some non-thinking, relaxed time with my son before he starts working in that looney bin of a place. Okay?"

"Lu always beat me at bowling," I said. "But I didn't mind a bit because for me the best part of the game was watching her hips move while she glided up to the line to release the ball! Half the time I didn't even know what the score was. *She* was so competitive she insisted on keeping score anyway. No matter how many gutter balls I threw, I knew that when it was Lu's turn again I'd get to experience the poetry in motion of her body again."

Dad laughed. "Yeah," he said. "I can't blame you there. And she was a kind girl too. We thought you would marry Lu of course. Did you know that we still hear from her every now and then?"

"You're kidding! Don't you think that's kind of pushy of her?"

"Why? Your Mom and I still love her. We didn't stop loving her just because you two aren't together." He put his hand on my knee. "You can't expect us to put her out of our lives. *We* didn't marry someone else. You did. Now you know how much Jeanie means to us. She's your wife, the mother of our grandchild. Of *course* your Mom and I wouldn't dream of hurting Jeanie with this. In a way it's kind of just our business. Understand? Whatever relationship we have with Lucille belongs to *us*. We only kept this back from you so it wouldn't interfere with your life. You're too private a man for us to know if you still have feelings for her, though it would be tough to imagine otherwise."

It bothered me that I couldn't even see Lu' films when my parents talked to her all they wanted.

Dad misinterpreted the look on my face. "Oh, don't be so upset about this, Son. You have been very private since you moved to Boulder. You rarely come home and so we rarely see Eddie. It's Jeanie who calls us to keep us up to date. It's Jeanie who keeps us all a family."

I let Dad go on because I knew I deserved it. I was at last understanding that I had caused my own perception that Dad didn't care about my life. That he didn't care about me. All these years he had been a grown man waiting for his son to grow up and reach out to him. He hadn't wanted to interfere or to complain, but now he was letting it all out. And how! I began to laugh, quietly at first. Soon I was bellowing, the tears rolling down my cheeks.

"I'm sorry, David," Dad said. "I guess I kind of got out of control, huh? Say something, okay? I do want to hear your side of the story. There's Kleenexes in the glove compartment."

For the second time that day I wiped tears off my face in front of Dad. I blew my nose too hard. "My side of the story is that everyone who really loves me has told me what an asshole I am." I laughed at my own elephant trumpeting. "Some have said it euphemistically and others have put it right out there. This morning I got a letter from Court saying the same thing but in words so careful that I could barely tell he was chewing me out. You know, when friends have called me a jerk it didn't hurt one tenth as much as when Court wrote that he hopes I will 'finally emerge a complete, mature man'. Somehow what you think of me and what he thinks of me carries more weight than what the women in my life do."

Dad kept silent until he turned into the A&W Root Beer parking lot and picked a sunny spot. "That's because you know women are more forgiving than we men are," he offered. "And because you know when a woman calls you a jerk she's telling you about *her* feelings. When a man calls you a jerk it hurts your ego." It was so chilly outside that the waitress wore a down jacket. Powder blue. Dad ordered two root beer floats, two chili dogs with cheese, and two giant fries. "Mmm. Mmm," he said. "If it don't make you sick, it ain't good!"

CHAPTER TWENTY-ONE

"Cash on the barrel head," Mrs. Barnett said. She fingered a strand of kinky hair that had apparently fled from a spongy pink curler. "You understand? We can't take checks from out of state. My husband don't wanna see you here. He leaves home every day at 8:30 and gets back at 5:30. You can work in that movie star's old room. That's all. The other rooms're off limits. Especially if I'm in 'em. Come upstairs and you can put your stuff in her old room. How long you figurin' on workin' here?"

I lugged my field kit up the worn carpeted stairs. "I don't know yet. Maybe a couple of weeks." We stopped on the landing, where I could see the same combinations of junk lying around everywhere. Newspapers, magazines, and sundry whatnots. "What about the hallways?"

"Huh?"

"What if I want to work in the hallway up here and downstairs?"

"You might be in the way while I clean," Mrs. Barnett said. A loose curler fell to the floor. She didn't fetch it.

I cast a doubtful eye all around me to make a point about her "cleaning." Then I opened my wallet. "Now if you let me work outside after dark, and if I can work in this hallway and the one downstairs, I'll give you twenty more dollars a day for your trouble."

Mrs. Barnett grabbed the twenty dollar bill right out of my hand. "I don't suppose Mr. Barnett would mind, as long as you are workin' outside and don't stir up my nosy next-door neighbors."

"Would you show me where Lucille Muhr's bedroom was?"

Mrs. Barnett emitted an ear splitting horse laugh. "You mean she was your girlfriend and you don't know where her bedroom was?"

"Well, how do *you* know where her bedroom was?!"

"'At's easy. It had to be the pink one. Hoo! Ha! Ha!"

I boasted that my equipment would show me anyway. "Which brings me to another subject. I need total privacy. I don't want you or your sons hanging around, asking questions. I'm paying you good money to let me work here, so I think it's fair to ask you to leave me alone when I'm working."

"But you never told me what you are planning on doing. How do we know you ain't the FBI or something? Spying on us."

I was impatient to begin. "I'm doing nothing illegal or investigative. I'm a scientist and I'm doing scientific research."

"In Lucille Muhr's old house?"

"Listen, Mrs. Barnett. I explained my work to you yesterday the best I could. I'm not even sure I'll get results. The benefit to you is that I'll pay you per day whether I'm finding what I need here for my research or not. But I need privacy."

"Okay, okay! Follow me."

On our right we passed the door to the tower that topped the circular entrance hall below. I thought it must be hollow inside. Maybe they used it as a storage room.

"I know this here's her room because the name 'Lu's on the back of her door. Pardon the mess in my eldest's room. See? She scratched her name on here with a ballpoint when she was a kid. We said, 'Leave it stay on there because it's kinda like having her autograph'."

After Mrs. Barnett had left me alone I wandered over to the west window. It faced out to the back yard. There a huge ancient maple towered above the house. Right now the tree shaded most of the back yard. Toward the back of the lot stood an even taller fir tree of some sort. Its branches flared out like antebellum crinolines all the way to the ground. Not much else looked familiar because I was only in the back yard once or twice, getting last-minute time with Lu after a date. I looked out the east window and saw only an extension of the Barnetts' driveway and the side of the next-door neighbors' garage. The east window overlooked the driveway. From this second story I had a clear view of the houses on the other side of West 10th Street.

Those delay tactics exhausted, I sat down on the only clear patch of floor in the room and wondered why I had been so anxious to begin. I hadn't the foggiest idea of how to start. I sat like that for maybe ten minutes. Then, from total boredom, I started fiddling with my rainbow crystal. I squinted one eye and peered through the cluster as though it were a monocle. Since the light wasn't good from where I sat I got up and put my back to the window at the front of the room. I looked through the crystal toward the other end of the room and saw what looked like cigarette smoke drifting upward from the Barnett boy's bed. But as I pivoted the crystal in either direction to try to see better I lost the image.

There was no wall space big enough for a bed anywhere else in the room, so I figured maybe Lu's bed was in that same spot. In case it was important I noted the time I saw the cigarette smoke. It was 9:50 a.m. I stood beside the bed and looked through my crystal cluster toward the front window. Though there was a heavy glare I could still see something small and green flying toward the bedroom door to my right. Of course it must be a parakeet. However, if I turned the crystal in the direction of the bedroom door the green bird disappeared. With the crystal in its original position, I tried to look sideways through the crystal's rainbow window. That didn't work. I only saw the inside of the cluster.

"No, Dummy!" I heard in my mind. Well, I was pretty sure I would never call myself 'Dummy', so I figured it had to be my friend who lived in the crystal. I admit I was awfully glad the Elemental had tuned in to my plight. Breathing deeply, I closed my eyes and placed the cluster to my forehead.

"That is the right idea," the Elemental said. Her words came to me more like a thought. "So here you are finally. At the hearth of your Love. As I foretold."

I resented the Elemental's tone, and so I shot a thought right back at her: *Would you mind if we were civil with each other? I would appreciate us showing some mutual respect here. I have put my money where my mouth is. I'm here and I'm deadly serious about doing this work. And I'm aware that your help is critical. I will treat you with the utmost regard, I promise. Just so we can be productive, would you please treat me the same way?*

I thought I heard the Elemental sniff and then say: "I only talked to you that way because that's what you are most comfortable with. Isn't that the way everyone talks to you? But of course I would rather our relationship be har-mo-ni-ous. That way our work will go much faster and easier."

"I thank you. And I respectfully ask that you help me see whatever that little green thing was again. It seemed to be moving in mid-air across the room toward the door."

"It's a bird," the Elemental said.

"Really?" If she had noticed my sarcasm she didn't show it.

"A little bird with green, and some yellow, feathers. A parakeet, I think. If you rotate the crystal toward the wall just past the door, you should be able to see its cage. I think you will continue to receive clearer traces in the areas of the room less 'lived in' during the past, like the corners. And your results would be more effective if you would meditate before you look for things. You cannot expect me or the cluster to fine-tune these vibrations for you."

Because I did see the Elemental's point I let myself get more and more excited. Just being able to use the cluster as a true viewing device in Lu's room was thrilling. Now I felt as though the hard part was over and I could really begin, unhampered.

"Just one caution," the Elemental said. "It is not that easy to filter out the, as it were, 'alien' frequencies. Some dark forces may hover in the spaces *within* the vibrations you wish to capture. In fact, to find your desired images you may have to live through some repugnant moments. This might require a great reaching of your spirit, as you are not used to being in this sort of state. If possible you must imagine that the woman Lucille is here—at whatever age she lived here. Whenever something *other* than your beloved's image interferes with your goal, you must think of the woman all the stronger. Do you like the way I am talking to you now?"

I was busy looking for the budgie that I'd momentarily spotted in my viewing device. I couldn't find its cage yet. "Uh, yes. You sound kind of formal but I like your tone of voice."

"Well, good then, though I don't really speak with a voice. Now I want you to look through the crystal again at the smoke you saw above the bed. And yes—you are correct that your beloved's bed used to be there too."

Her using the term 'beloved' caused me discomfort. "Okay, so what am I doing wrong?"

The Elemental continued. "You may find it hard to cut through the rather primal energies of the young male who now inhabits this room. To help you I will direct you from the cigarette smoke image down to the adolescent female who is inhaling the wretched weed."

"But Lu never smoked!"

"Show some compassion. She was only fifteen years old."

"How do you know that?"

"When you get a little further along you will learn of the Akashic Records," the Elemental said. "They are a sort of purely energetic library that contains non-physical records of all that has been said, thought, or done—and will be said and done—by every human being during every earthly incarnation. Unlike you and most of your kind I am free to go there at any time. To sip from past and future history as I have the interest, although I don't normally have the interest. If you could go within, pull out your highest Self, and let *it* look through your physical eyes, that Self would be able to see everything you desire. You could even sample probable future events."

"Since I can't do that yet, would you please help me find whatever within me can see Lu on the bed smoking a cigarette?" I interpreted the Elemental's silence as a nudge to go ahead and try to filter through these mucky vibrations. Facing the bed, I sat down on the floor again and leaned against the wall where I imagined the bird cage used to be. Now I was facing the side of the bed near a walk-in closet. Hot air blew from a floor vent to my left on the other side of the bedroom door. I closed my eyes and did the color spectrum stairstep meditation that Oceania and the Elemental had taught me. Then I meditated on the house size crystal. Red: the first step on the rainbow stairs. Then orange, yellow. I placed my foot on the green, then blue, then indigo step. By the time I got to the violet step I was already feeling pretty gassed. The physical room was now obscured and I seemed to be in a kind of waiting space.

I was so out of it that the Elemental spoke to me again: "When you see the white light I will come for you."

When I stepped off the violet step I saw the Elemental. I hadn't remembered how lovely she was. She seemed composed wholly of opalescent light with pastels of pink, blue, and yellow defining her features. When I say "light" I don't mean merely light. She seemed to also vibrate with sound. Her energy hummed like an electric wire, only I heard it more like music. As the Elemental moved, the pitch changed. It was like the sound of water shifting levels from ledge to ledge in some majestic rainbow waterfall of pure sound! When the Elemental took my hand I heard, and felt, crystalline tingling throughout my body. It felt much the same as that night when Jeanie struck the tuning fork above my solar plexus.

"Did you bring the cluster?" the Elemental asked.

I was surprised to find it in my hand, for wasn't I currently in my imagination? Wasn't the physical me sitting in a room totally removed from this crystal structure?

"Take my hand," the Elemental said. "Look through the viewing device. Look at the bed. See a young girl lying there?"

By now I had faith in the Elemental's words. But it still seemed to take forever to do what she had asked. Finally I was looking through the crystal viewing device at what should have been the big crystal structure. Instead I saw a young Lucille Muhr lying in her bed dressed in dungarees and a sweatshirt. She was smoking a cigarette, Greta Garbo-like. She coughed a little. She had a face full of freckles. A lot more freckles than I remembered. The image was so sharp that I could also see the auburn highlights in her hair. Her dark mane was short and unevenly cut, as though she had inflicted scissors on it with abandon. She wore a little spit curl in front of each ear.

The episode played like a movie. Here was the proverbial ugly duckling that would soon turn into a swan. I peered at the curves that Lu's newly forming breasts made in the soft sweatshirt. Her hips were still narrow and boyish. I watched her put out the half-smoked cigarette in an empty can of Sprite. She opened the back window of her bedroom full-wide and wafted the cigarette smoke out with the comic section of the Sunday paper.

To get my attention the Elemental squeezed my hand. She said to read the date on the newspaper. I tried, but I couldn't make out the date. From the strain I felt a headache coming on.

"Let go," the Elemental said. "Relax your forehead, your eyes."

Reading the words on the newspaper happened like going in with a zoom lens. "*Circleville Sunday Herald.* October 15, 1965." I could see the high school ring Lu wore on her left hand, with "19" on the left side of its ice blue stone and "67" on the right. Then my view zoomed out again. From a pack Lu took a stick of cinnamon gum and chewed with frenetic speed. She stuck the pack of cigarettes into the bottom of a sanitary napkin box at the back of her closet, grabbed a baseball bat and glove, and left the room!

"Now you will be able to see the bird cage," the Elemental said.

Still focused on the Elemental's crystal domain, I turned from her and looked through the viewing device. Where I really was didn't seem to matter. I merely had to *imagine* that I was looking in that corner of Lu's room. I followed the walls with my eye. Now I could see that the room was soft pink—not the off-white I had first seen that morning.

When I saw the green parakeet again it was perched atop its tall, round cage. "Is time sequential here?" I asked the Elemental. "What I mean is, is the bird now sitting on its cage *following* the flying that I saw it do earlier?"

"No. You have captured a random moment of the bird's life, determined by your wish to see its cage. You just learned how to 'tune in', and to control, the focus in time and space through your will and heart."

"With all due respect, I don't see what my heart has to do with it."

The Elemental's smile was appealing. "Your heart holds your intent. The greater and purer your intent is, the fewer obstacles there are to fulfilling your dreams. *Will* alone cannot create these miracles."

I knew I must remember that this entire conversation, which had its own logical reality and continuity, took place in my altered state. "Then how did I see the Chief in my lab? And how did I get the Reynie Junior image then?"

"You captured the image of your friend partly through good luck but also through the opportunity created by intense feelings and thoughts you generated during the months that preceded it. Indeed, *you* created the situation with your benefactor so you could do this work. He created this with you to enrich his existence in a way only you could give him."

"And what about the Chief?"

The Elemental's laugh was like tinkling glass wind chimes. "The Chief and I helped you with that. Though the Chief's line of work is more like magic, he could still help you. But you might not want to take the complicated steps required to connect with him."

I could feel my inner state morphing. In a panic that I wouldn't be able to get back to Lu's old room without the Elemental, I asked her if I could do these things without the viewing device. "What if someone stole it? Is this crystal the only place you will exist? Could you and the Chief evolve and go to another crystal? Or would you become a spirit out in the cosmos?"

"The Chief projects himself into the crystal," the Elemental said. "He does not 'live' here. He is a Shaman not from your century. In his time he uses the crystal to see the future. You saw him not only because of the laser but also because of your desire—and because he happened to be doing what you are doing now. If someone else were attuned to the crystal while you were using it, that person would see *you* in the same way."

"But that means the rainbow crystal exists both in the Chief's time and in mine! How can that be? I was at home, holding the twin crystal in my hand."

"The problem of time is only *perceptual*, not actual. Neither you nor the Chief really *owns* the rainbow crystal. It has its own reality apart from yours."

I was so amazed at this that I lost my concentration. The Barnett boy's room was coming back into focus. From far away I heard the Elemental say, "When the rainbow crystal and I reach our mutual destiny, we will no longer stay in physical earth reality."

When I came to, I was hunched over, right in the middle of the bedroom doorway. After what had just happened, the shock of seeing

Mrs. Barnett (who couldn't even be called "a looker" by a drunk) was too awful for words.

Like some gap-toothed Brogdinagian hag, she looked way down at tiny little Gulliver-me. "I want to know. Do you eat lunch? Do you plan to leave the house or did you bring your lunch? You are a strange one. Looks to me like you knocked yourself out. Maybe you should come back tomorrow when you're not so tired."

I got up on unsteady feet. "I was meditating,"

Mrs. B. laughed. "Yeah. I do that too. When I go to bed at night." She had that annoying insolence of a person who knows she is inferior. The kind of person who must attack you to keep from experiencing the dislike she really feels for herself.

I couldn't afford to alienate Mrs. B., so I stopped myself from saying what I really wanted to—that she was the most unattractive person I had ever laid eyes on. That she was the most unrefined and coarse woman I had ever had the misfortune to meet. That what I did up there was none of her goddamned business. That she had just interrupted one of the most lovely, satisfying experiences of my life. That if she didn't remove her gross cellulite-engulfed body from my sight I was going to send sadistic Dr. Liposuction after her fat ass.

I asked Mrs. Barnett for the time.

"It's after One. Why?"

"Boy, am I hungry! I guess I didn't think about bringing lunch but I sure will bring one tomorrow." I didn't know why I was so exhausted. That simple process turned out to have taken hours. I needed to go home, where I could go over this with care. "I have some research to do, so I don't think I'll be back 'til tomorrow morning, Mrs. Barnett." I reveled at the thought that in a few minutes I would be devouring a giant burger, fries, and a chocolate milkshake. It was a combo that I hoped would take my stomach, if not me, back to my teen years.

"I am sure you know best," Mrs. Barnett said. "You don't need me to show you the way out, do you?"

I wanted to punch her Pomeranian face in. Instead I returned her sarcasm: "Not unless there is something you know that I don't know."

"It's the strangest thing," I said to my dad. I was sailing toward the basketball hoop for a layup shot. "I sort of need my equipment and I sort of don't." I handed the ball out to him.

Dad stood well behind the faded black foul line painted in front of the garage. He shot and missed. "What do you mean?"

I gave Dad a break and shot from the foul line—his only, and therefore his favorite—shot. I made it easily. "Well, it's kind of hard to explain," I said. "You know how I told you about Lu and the cigarette? I don't think I was even conscious when I saw that. I was in some kind of altered state. For hours! I must be getting better at it."

Dad shot again and missed.

"G! Instead of 'PIG' let's play 'HIPPOPOTAMUS' like Lu and I used to do," I said. It makes a longer game. Did you know Lu's sister Carla called her 'Lucy'?" This time I missed a long shot from the corner. It bounced over the neighbor's fence. "I'll get it."

"All the way, Son!" Dad shouted, so I fired the basketball back to him. Being of the same opportunist stock from whose loins I sprang, Dad faded back into the yard, jumped off the ground amazingly high for a retiree, and sank it! "I used to watch you out the back window when you two shot baskets together. I've wondered something all these years. Did you ever let Lucille Muhr beat you in sports?"

My shot bounced off the rim just as Mom called us in. "Hell no!"

"H!" Dad said in triumph. "I'll show you some mercy so we can go in for dinner. You can tell your Mom and me all about this 'altered state' business. Oh, and David."

"Yeah, Dad?"

"After dinner I'm going to beat the basketball shorts off you."

"Dad?"

"Yes, Son?"

"You're sure free to try."

I thought my parents would never go to bed. I had managed to keep my eyes open through Johnny Carson but I kept falling asleep during "The David Letterman Show." After this breakthrough with my Dad, and the wonderful outpouring of love from Mom, I figured it wouldn't hurt me to go along with their wishes for a change.

I was eager to enjoy a delicious sleep for the next seven hours. I leapt up the stairs to my old attic bedroom and jumped into bed with my clothes on. With a sigh I lay back on my mushy pillow. Though my mouth felt like gauze, I was too tired to go back downstairs for a drink of water. First I couldn't get comfortable on my back. Then I tried sleeping on my left, then right side. Lying on my stomach didn't work either. I punched my pillow in irritation. *What should I do?* I asked myself. *Sleep sitting up?* I turned back over and stared up at the ceiling through the darkness. Maybe I heard my father snoring. *Why try to keep my eyes open?* I thought. *I can't see anything anyway.*

I heard high-pitched humming. *Must be the electrical box on the pole by the house*, I thought. The volume increased. Or maybe it only sounded louder because I began to focus intently on it. I tried to block out the noise by pushing the sides of the pillow up around my ears. Now I could hear both the buzzing and all these little rattles inside my head. The noises sounded like I was eating Rice Krispies while standing by a high-tension wire with someone playing tom-toms in the distance. You know how you get mad when you can't sleep? Your adrenalin starts to rise, and the more tired you are, the more awake you become.

I sat on the edge of my bed, that old bed I had slept in all through my teen years. The zinging got even louder. Now it seemed to come from the nightstand. "Zmmm-mmm-mmm-mmm." The buzzing drew my attention from my sleeplessness to the rainbow crystal on the nightstand. When I held my hand flat over it I felt slow vibrations. When I held it in my hand, the glow brightened. I stood up and walked toward the window at the other end of my bedroom. The glow faded. I walked toward the stairs and the cluster beamed brighter. With each step down I took, the light glowed still brighter and the humming amped up to an even higher pitch. In the living room the crystal was like a beacon. Now I could feel the sound vibrating in my teeth!

I walked downstairs to the hallway outside the bathroom. The light and sound faded from the crystal a little. I moved toward the front room. The crystal lit the area up like it was a movie set. What was it about this room? Barely used, it was situated at the front of the house. We usually came in the back door because that's where we parked the car. The family spent its time eating in the kitchen, watching TV in the living room, or sleeping in the bedrooms. This front room was a *nothing* room. *So what*, I asked myself, *does the crystal find so exciting about the front room? Let's just wake up the Elemental and see*, I thought.

I sat cross-legged on the floor and started my takedown. I said to myself: *Relax. Relax. Think of nothing but the colors. The colors will take you across.* With each step I could hear the sound intensify further. I had not seen such a fierce yellow, such a refreshing green, such a sublime blue. The violet looked alive. Its light particles whirled like sequins falling down from the ceiling. This time I saw the pure white light at the same moment I became aware that the Elemental was heading toward me. "You don't sleep, huh?" I said to her. "We have to stop meeting like this."

"I don't know what you mean."

Maybe I was in for a "biggie" this time. *It's nothing*, I said to myself. "Time to stop joking around? I sensed you calling me. I couldn't sleep, and I heard this humming. And then the crystal glowed."

"I did not call you," the Elemental said.

"What?"

"*You* did it."

"But that's impossible."

The Elemental smiled. "Not anymore. Not after this afternoon."

I crawled toward her like a child. "I don't follow you."

She sat down beside me. "Your feelings and your thoughts have started to make friends. Before, out of fearing your emotions, your thoughts controlled them. Your thoughts were like frontline infantry, shooting at any emotion that dared show itself. The reason you could not sleep is that another part of you has wakened. The part that has the power to bring your dreams alive. Your rainbow crystal is always humming with light. But now you are much more attuned to it, to us, so you perceive the crystal's energy more profoundly. We have developed a mutual sensitivity. Do you see?"

I felt extremely woozy. "But what about the light and sound intensifying in the front room? Did I do that too?"

"In a way," the Elemental said. "You have just met the mechanism of your inner guidance. This is not a voice, or a thought, or even quite a feeling. It is more like knowing—but not with your mind. You *knew* you must go to this room to experience something very important. Your thoughts didn't say: 'Go downstairs and walk into that room.' Your *Self* moved your body there with no conscious thought."

"Tell me why I have to see what's in that room."

The Elemental shook her head. "You no longer need me to tell you. It is time for you to take charge of your many untapped abilities. I will still be here, as always, though it is no longer necessary to invoke me every time you want to do these things."

I surprised myself by saying I enjoyed being with her. This was a new feeling that wasn't exactly vulnerability. It didn't feel threatening.

"Enjoy this total openness," the Elemental said, "for this is the space you must inhabit to be successful in your chosen journey."

"Are you part of me?"

"Yes, in the way that all Consciousness is connected."

I told her I didn't understand.

The Elemental stood up. "It is hopeless to try to interpret this with your mind. And it is useless to delay what you are to experience. When you need to find the truth, just remember to inhabit this open place within you. Focus there, and nothing can harm or elude you."

"You're going now aren't you?"

Without an answer, the Elemental left me completely alone in this luminous chamber of my imagination. Or was it a chamber in the physical rainbow crystal? Or was it both? "Stop thinking," I said to myself. I peered at where I last saw the Elemental. "Easy for you to say." She was no longer there. It was obvious that if I couldn't figure out where I was, I wouldn't know what to do next. Was I still in that open space? Again I told my mind again to stop thinking. I tried to still my mind chatter by closing my eyes and holding the rainbow crystal up to my forehead. Was I closing my eyes that were already closed as I sat in the front room?

"Trying *not* to think is useless," said the me in the Elemental's domain. *But wait a minute*, I thought. *I am still* in *that space. So all I have to do is let some truth drift up from what she called my "Self."* This me was as relaxed as Jell-O. This blanking out of the noisy mind was like falling asleep. Or like being stoned. Ever efficient, your brain stops alerting you because you can't respond anyway. In a squiffy haze, I lay down inside the crystal and soon conked out.

I held on to the last traces of dreaming by resisting a loud whisper and the sight of furniture in the front room. A streetlight down by the front walk weakly lit objects in the room, making them indistinct. The whisper became more insistent. It was a delighted, whispered laugh. "I can't get my sneakers off. They're double knotted!"

"Here. I'll help you," I whispered. I felt a kind of joyous impatience well up inside me. "No knot is a challenge for these nimble fingers."

Lucille Muhr and I sat intertwined on the floor of the front room. Her blouse was unbuttoned and her jeans unzipped all the way.

"God, I hope your parents don't come out to go to the bathroom," Lu whispered fiercely.

I had untied the first knot and had removed that sneaker and sock. "They never have," I whispered as I got the other knot untied. "Voila! In the hands of a master."

She lay back on the floor and pulled me on top of her. "Kiss me again, Davey. A long one this time." With one hand she loosened my undershirt from my pants. With the other she stroked my cheek, right by my mouth. "We are such great kissers." She panted a little, rhythmically moving her hips in a slow circle.

I thought I would burst out of my clothes. It was not quite pain, not quite burning. Rather it was an intense reaching, a tight straining outward from the center. Always careful with Lu, however, I let her control the pace of our lovemaking. I had learned that if I did this, she would take me into ecstasy beyond what I ever hoped for.

"Oh! Davey! I love you! I love you. I love you!"

"Ssh!" I whispered. "You know I love you too. But we must be quiet." Her body felt so fine, so strong. Every time felt like the first time. Her body grew more insistent, demanding. "Oh. What you do to me. Oh, Lu."

"Yes, Davey, yes. You feel so good. I hope you can keep this up for me. Yes. That's it." She pressed her hands on my buttocks now, pressed me into her harder, harder. We moved like the same violent heartbeat together. Her breath was in my mouth, my hair, my ear, my neck. Her hands were on the back of my head, my shoulders, now my stomach. God, now she was sliding her fingers between us so she could feel where we joined.

No matter how many times she had done this, it was always a surprise, like something she just happened to think of at that moment. I groaned. I was making love to her with every ounce of energy I had, and she was matching me ounce for ounce. I let her take my fingers one by one into her mouth as we moved passionately together. It was one of the most erotic things she ever did. To make it last longer I had to come out of her.

Feeling it, she gave a disappointed little "Oh." But she let me kiss her breasts, and then she let me move down her firm belly with my lips. I wanted to kiss her farther down, but she pulled me by the shoulders. She wanted me back up, inside her.

Now I knew I didn't have to hold back anymore. I knew she was ready for me to let it all go! Out of desire her tissues engorged to hold me in a tight delirium of sensation that now took me beyond my senses. Riding on wave after wave of each other's pleasure, we climaxed at the same time. Coming down now, coming reluctantly, slowly down. Coming down tired. Down relieved, down close and smiling. Still joined and pulsing quickly inside each other. Still.

"David?"

Still—.

"Are you all right?"

I found myself lying face down on the floor of the front room, my body on fire. A flash of light ripped across my closed eyeballs. My clothes were damp. Through squinched eyes I could see the high color in my hand, so I knew my face must be even redder. It was the most vulnerable moment of my life.

Mom had turned the lamp on in the living room. She looked frightened. She spotted the crystal in my hand. "Son? Are you ill?"

I thanked God Mom seemed not to know what was going on, though she didn't move. "Just the end of a successful experiment," I said. Every muscle of my body felt rheumatic. I prayed that Mom would not notice my condition. I got up on my feet and said, "Couldn't sleep, so I came downstairs to see if I could pick up anything with my crystal. Well, I did."

Mom remained stunned. "If you could have seen yourself the way I did when I came out here. I gotta tell you—you looked horrible." Finally she came over and stood in front of me.

Having no idea whether imaginary or real hormones might be bouncing off my body, I was afraid to let Mom touch me. So far my secret was safe. I looked into her concerned little German eyes and saw…complete innocence. I thought: *Thank God. Maybe the shock of light kept her from seeing me maybe undulating on the floor when she came into the living room.* "I'm okay, Mom. Go back to bed."

She patted my shoulder. "Need to talk? I'll make hot chocolate."

"No, Ma. Thanks. I got to get some sleep now too."
She indulgently patted my shoulder. "Good-night, Davie."
"Mom?"
She responded with a weary "Yes."
"Have I told you lately that I love you?"
"That old song was your dad's favorite when we were dating."

CHAPTER TWENTY-TWO

The next day I phoned Court. The urgency I felt left no room for sociable chit-chat. "Did you get that all down?" I asked him. "I really need the portable light table from my lab. I'm trying to get the volatile chemicals in Columbus so you don't have to ship them. I know what a hassle this is, Court, but I wouldn't be asking unless—."

Court chuckled on his end of the phone line. "I guess that means you're getting good results. It's lucky for you that I've taken time off to enjoy a couple of spring-like days outside. You know how it is in Colorado. 'If you don't like the weather, just wait a minute'. Did you receive my letter?"

"And how. I'm already not the same guy you wrote to. Lots going on inside me because of your letter. I'm learning as best I can. In fact, I want the portable light table from my basement. I didn't think I would need it when I left Denver. Now I'm trying to follow my instincts that say I must make holograms here. Mom's going to kill me when she finds all my stuff in the house. I'm not even sure where I can process my work yet. But I need to get a hologram of Lu and me. What she and I shared."

"You mean she's there?"

"No, not exactly. I've found that the past is as real as the present. What I've discovered is much more vivid than a memory should be. I'm finding dimensions of feeling that memory doesn't have. You know how when you remember something, your experience is from your own point of view? Well, I'm getting bleed-throughs of feeling from Lu. And I'm seeing that *where* an event takes place and the event itself are interdependent. I feel that's why it was so hard to get the traces from that movie frame of Lu, even though the film medium captured its location. I've just begun to learn what sensations you can feel through this process, I can't explain it yet. But the biggest thing I learned is that you can access future events as easily as past ones."

"Why, that is huge! I wish I could be there with you but I have some business in Dallas. So I'll be out of state for a couple of weeks. Maybe by that time you'll be back in Denver."

"I hope I deserve such good fortune and guidance."

"You are a rare bird. That more than makes up for the person you haven't become yet. Even beyond what you've accomplished. I see more and more that without your *heart* you won't find success."

"That's the second time in two days someone's told me that. Court, I had a—I don't know how to describe it—holographic memory experience with Lu that affected my entire body like it was really happening. You may have guessed it was erotic."

"Is that what you've been hinting at? I admit I envy you."

"But I'm worried I'll become addicted to these kinds of events with Lucille. What a temptation it would be to repeat those acts and relive those experiences over and over. I would get nothing else done for the rest of my life."

"You deserve to indulge yourself in this for a while—as long as you stay grounded in the reality of your life with your family. I don't believe you'll get stuck there because I've seen how deeply you want to know what forces created this woman."

"I'm guessing she created *herself*. How did she made it through without the kind of family support I have? I guess I was too young to be there for her in the ways she needed. But I did love all of her. Not just her beauty but her spunk and the ingenuity of her mind. I guess I'm rambling. You're right. I've come too far to become a holographic druggie now. I gave Court the phone number.

"What's Josh's surname?

"Peterson. Is everything okay with our mother-to-be? Is she pregnantly fat and sassy?"

"Reynie is as prickly as ever. Judging by the kicking inside her, Reynie the third is going to be, as you would put it, 'Hell on wheels'!"

"I've never heard you talk that way."

"The excitement of an almost grandfather. I'll phone your friend Josh and we'll get your light table back East in no time. Oh. One more thing. You should be getting Miss Muhr's medallion today. I sent it express mail. She was quite anxious that you have it."

Shivers scurried like battalions of ants across my shoulders. "I'll ask Mom if something came for me today. Thanks for all your help, Court. As I said when I first called, only a very good friend would have told me what you did."

Court's goodbye sounded hoarse.

Mrs. Barnett slipped out the back door so quietly I didn't hear her. Something made me go to the back window of Lu's bedroom just in time to see Mrs. B. head through a break in the scraggly hedge that lined the south side of the back yard. While she was gone I could check out the other rooms upstairs.

Just up the hall from Lu's bedroom on the right was a scummy bathroom. A small window with no curtains let light into the room. The tub and sink were a pinkish-salmon color with gross matching tiles layered with calcified hard water stains. The tiled floor's grouting was discolored from neglect. The room was altogether a gloomy little dungeon of a space. I was sure I would find nothing interesting there to look at through the crystal.

At the end of this part of the hall, forward of the bathroom, there was a huge bedroom painted yellow. Strangely enough, the linoleum tile hinted that this could have been a kitchen once. The room did have one alluring touch. French doors opening to a terrace that topped the kitchen below it on the ground floor. The terrace was bedecked with a black wrought iron rail. Though with the Barnetts it was hard to tell, this room seemed unused. It was littered with boxes. Most were filled with junk but some were empty. Used furniture was covered with moth eaten cotton quilts, and there was a vacuum sweeper and, yes, cleaning supplies. Unopened paint cans, packaged trays, and rollers stood in the far corner as if ready for action. The quarter inch of dust on them said otherwise. I could not say that this room, like the others, would ever even be on the *edge* of being clean. From what I could tell, the entire Barnett house was doomed to remain a turmoil of clutter until the end of its natural life.

I knew there'd be no time to look inside the tower, so I sneaked into a front bedroom at the top of the stairs. The room apparently belonged to the Barnetts' other son. It still bore its original paint and wallpaper. There was a charming alcove at the east end that enclosed a window seat beneath two leaded glass windows. Four panes set with deep yellow stained-glass fleur-de-lis decorated them. My instincts told me that this had been Carla Muhr's room. It would have suited the more reserved personality of Carla, Lu's sister.

The back door clicked so quietly that no one downstairs could have heard it. In a surge of nervous power I moved noiselessly back to Lu's bedroom like an eel through a dank lagoon. I cracked the door a hair'sbreadth so Mrs. B wouldn't hear it close. I also wanted privacy. I had escaped from Theodora Elphaba! (Just showing off here that I know the name of the Wicked Witch of the West.) Glee parted my lips from my teeth. I couldn't help it. From a kind of psychic recoil I reacted to all witchy looking women that way.

It was time to get down to business. Here was my chance to test the laser gun and the rainbow crystal. Here was my chance to prove that I could replicate my findings concretely. I had come back to Circleville to invent a device to pre-screen space for holographic traces from the past. As a scientist I knew that in the matter of inventions *psychic* results just wouldn't cut it.

With some of my father's tools and doo-dads I had found a way to attach my helium-neon laser gun to a nifty little tripod I got at K-Mart. I could set it up as a unit, move it around, or make it stationary. I stationed the laser gun on its tripod by the door and parked the crystal on its own platform. The stairs squeaked. Mrs. B. must be creeping up the stairs. On to her now, I moved the tripod about four feet from the door and waited. Mrs. B. took almost ten seconds to climb up each step. Every stair chirped under her weight. I began to sing to myself, "They're coming to take me away...to the Funny Farm, where life is beautiful all day long." When I sensed Mrs. B. standing outside the door I stood still. I didn't move for a full long minute.

Mrs. B. opened the door like Dracula emerging from his coffin.

I directed a short, harmless beam from the laser gun just past her head. "Look out!" I cried. "Oh, this could have hurt you! Lucky you weren't standing any closer."

Mrs. B. froze in the doorway. "What? What IS that thing?"

"It's a laser gun. Like in Star Trek."

She gasped. "You mean it could've killed me?"

I swiveled the tripod back into position and aimed the laser gun just above the bed. I scratched my head for effect. "Nah! Not unless it had actually hit you."

Mrs. B. tiptoed into the room. She gave the laser gun a wide berth. "You bust anything in here? You know you got to pay for anything you bust."

I thought: *How could she tell? Everything in her house is already wrecked.* "Dear Mrs. Barnett. You and your house are totally safe. But you promised to leave me alone while I work. And there you were, sneaking up to the door."

"I wasn't sneaking. I come up here to put some clean towels in the bathroom. Besides. You didn't sound like you was workin'. You was too quiet. I thought maybe you passed out again."

Somehow, without having to touch her, I indicated that I wanted her to leave. "Really. Don't worry, Mrs. B. I mean Mrs. Barnett. Your son's room is secure. I promise. Now I must get back to work. I'm getting a late start."

"Remember what I said about paying for anything you bust."

"I'll remember," I said. "But that won't happen."

Mrs. B. looked disappointed. She *galumphed* back downstairs.

Alone again, I set the rainbow crystal on a metal plate near the mouth of the laser gun. At each side of the plate I had inserted a piece from my old microscope—the double knobbed gizmo that lets you make the lens move up and down to bring a specimen into focus. The only difference was that I mounted it sideways with the platform so I could move the crystal back and forth. I prayed the simplicity of the design wouldn't derail my results.

I adjusted the setting on the laser gun from *pulse* to *beam* and aimed a shot through the crystal. The light worked like a film projector. It made the crystal's pyramid shaped rainbow spring out and overlay that end of the room. With the knob, I brought the crystal back in a little. The spectrum faded, creating an effect I'd never seen before. Instead of the colors looking holographic, or three-dimensional, they looked ghostly. What I mean is, they didn't seem to hover in the room. Rather, the colors looked like they haunted their own space. A sort of space-within-space. This was different than seeing the Chief. His image had clearly been caught *inside* the twin crystal itself. This array had a life of its own outside the crystal. My gut said it wasn't just a trick of the eye or the lens. What I saw existed as its own realm, separate from the third-dimensional space *I* lived in.

I was bent on solving how to optically enhance energy traces without meditating. I knew I'd have to attend to parallels between two processes. *There must be a way*, I thought, *to freeze this reality like splicing one frame of a film strip*. After about fifteen minutes of trying, I gave up. *I'm only fooling myself*, I thought. *There are no parallels.* I recalled what Dad had said about Thomas Edison and the light bulb. Edison had to experiment with a plethora of what he hoped would conduct electricity until he found the carbon filament. Edison's struggles—and eventual success—gave me courage to go on. After all, the main thing I had to do here was find the correct angle. I felt gratified to know that almost every invention is buggy at first.

I worked through lunch and spent the next three and a half hours fiddling with the crystal. I moved it one millimeter at a time in either direction and entered the specs and other details in my logbook. I turned the crystal from side to side in the finest gradations my fingers could accomplish. Then I recorded the results. I tilted the platform to increase and decrease the angle. Obviously something was missing. I did *not* want to believe what was missing was my meditation takedown. I did what scientists are supposed to do. I performed a reality check. I had light and I had degrees of position and, I thought, angle. At least I had tried to make the slight changes of angle that gave me results back in Denver.

Okay, I thought. *Maybe that angle doesn't work here. Maybe it's a time thing. Yeah. Maybe getting an image in the past calls for something different, like trying various tilts and angles of the platform from specific locations in the room. Moving the entire tripod in gradations of space, from different spots in the room. To get one image might take days. If so, I would have to narrow the prospects down to what I could manage, so the men in white coats would not take me to the Funny Farm. You are a brilliant scientist, David. Now think!*

This might sound crazy, but I felt *in my body* what I'm about to describe. I was not thinking. I heard no voice. Not even my own. Instead it was this revelation: "***Nothing material exists without Time. Duration of time.*** *Where time and space intersect, matter is created. Drawn from the energy of probable events which you create in your imagination, substance forms the event you most desire. Therefore it is the strength of your desire that magnetically attracts time to substance so that substance may materialize in space.* If I hadn't written these words in my log I might not have remembered what I heard. I had grasped a wondrous truth.

I knew I must make this knowledge functional. I sensed that creating reality involves not only how we reconstruct the past but also how we bring future events into the present. This must literally be what we do. We only perceive that time moves on a continuum. All events must have concurrent reality. What I accomplished with my equipment and the crystal, or with my imagination and the crystal, exactly parallels how we create our reality.

Somehow the crystal removed barriers to perceiving time as linear. But to activate the crystal's median properties I had to magnify my intentions. It was like I must build a bonfire inside me to produce a candle-power of light in physical reality. Thus the ingredient I had left out earlier an overwhelming desire to see.

It wouldn't thrill me to watch an adolescent Lu smoke half a cigarette again. I had come here knowing that whatever shaped her early years wasn't pretty. Wasn't that the rub? Maybe if I found what I sought, I wouldn't be able to handle it. Or maybe I would keep denying what I wanted most to achieve. Was I destined to remain a middle-aged Hamlet, forever wobbling? No. I would sally forth!

I followed my impulse to move the tripod by the bed. I wanted to view the room from the perspective of someone lying there. I pulled a chair over so I could sit lower down. Then I adjusted the height of the tripod. With the laser beam shining through the crystal I let my desire for the truth about Lu slowly build within me. I felt my resistance diminish as my craving increased. I let myself feel every painful, exhilarating peak of that craving. My head pounded. My arms vibrated. My shallow breathing quickened. I knew I must let it all go on no matter what might happen. My longing built unbearably until I thought I might keel over. Maybe I did go unconscious. I reached that center of experience without meditation.

The room grew dark and my head stopped hammering. I relaxed into peaceful, rhythmic breathing. I was in limbo. Nothing there, no one there. Maybe not even myself. I felt no emotions now. I had no thoughts. Just heightened kinesthesia and a slowly growing acuity of vision. It took a while for my brain to register that light had formed a strip of hazy yellow under the door of the bedroom. I saw a little girl's body stiffen in the bed. Fear churned in my stomach. The door opened. A blade of light cut a vicious slice into her small form. It was Lu! I knew it. A figure over six feet tall loomed in the doorway and stood immobile for a few moments. My heart beat. *Pretend you're asleep,* I felt Lu thinking. *Then he'll go away.* But the figure, whom I now recognized as Lu's father, Bern, just gawked at Lu. Her eyes were as tightly closed as her hands.

Bern Muhr looked glassy eyed drunk. This made his leer even more obscene. What happened next was indistinct—as though it might and might *not* have been happening. Bern weaved toward Lu and stopped at the end of her bed. Again he just stared. Suddenly he appeared back in the doorway again in the yellow light. The whole sequence replayed, as when you fast-reverse a video and replay it. Each time the weird sequence recurred, I felt Lu's terror. The tightening of her eyelids, muscles, and hands. Just to relieve my tension, I desperately wanted the event to finish, no matter how grueling.

I'm no psychologist, but I thought maybe this memory still existed so vividly, so compulsively, that Lu must be blocking it in her mind. Until she faced it, the sequence would keep repeating. But there might be another reason the memory kept playing—the late Bern Muhr. Maybe it was *his* old business that kept this sequence alive. My darkest conclusion was that this event repeated over a long time. This theory would certainly explain the instant terror Lu felt when the light came on under her door. Whether any of these theories was correct, I still deeply needed to help her.

Meanwhile, Bern Muhr stood in Lu's bedroom again, peering—no, leering—at her.

"If I just pretend I'm asleep—."

With all my will I tried to project my thoughts into hers. *Let him come in*, I felt. *He's going to do this thing whether you want him to or not.*

"No!" she shouted inside. "He won't. Not this time."

Lu's father stood at the end of her bed again. Now he reappeared in the doorway. It was like a horror film version of "Groundhog Day."

"You bastard!" my inner voice shouted. I know what you're gonna do. Go ahead. I'll watch every step you take. I'll memorize you doing this thing so I can spit on your grave, you sonofabitch!"

Bern Muhr stood at the foot of his daughter's bed and gaped at her. He untied the sash of his red plaid robe. Lu whimpered and I knew her father was going to go through with it now. He walked toward the side of her bed he put his goddamned hand on his goddamned genitals and started to jerk off. He stuck the fingers of his other hand inside Lu's panties."

Oh no! Stop! I felt Lu screaming inside.

But Bern sat on the side of her bed, sliding his hand up and down his sex organ. "You're not my blood daughter so it doesn't matter" he said. Lu pretended to be asleep. While he ogled his daughter in his alcoholic stupor, he continued to pump himself. "I said you're not mine." He groaned, then his neck twisted as he came all over himself.

Suddenly the room was pitch black again. Then the light shone under the door. Then the door opened again. The sequence was about to recur. But I couldn't take any more. I packed up my equipment and headed back to my folks' house.

I lay on the sofa in my parents' living room. Lu's pendant shimmered in my hand. It was a reflection hologram created in a circle of glass—an art piece made from laser illuminated shards. They fit together in such a way that the spectrum's seven colors shot out from its center. It was mounted in 14k gold and hung on a lightweight gold chain. Surely Lu suspected I had sent it to her. I pressed the stunning pendant to my heart. "Thank you, wherever you are," I said to Lucille Muhr.

"Oh. You found the express mail," Mom said when she saw the stiff mailer beside me on the floor. "What was in it? And what are you doing lying there in the middle of the afternoon? You want a snack? We got some thin sliced turkey and some old fashioned loaf in the fridge. How about some potato chips? I remember what a salt tooth you have."

I didn't know how to act.

Mom pulled a chair up beside me. "I know you. When you're not hungry it means you're sick." She saw the medallion. "That's so pretty. What is it?"

I held the pendant in my open palm. "Court sent it. It's Lu's."

Mom brushed the damp hair back from my forehead. "And Lucille gave it to Court when she was at his party?"

"Yes. She told him she wanted me to have it."

"You don't seem all right."

"It's lots of things, Mom."

"I don't mean to pry, but does one of those 'things' have to do with Jeanie? Have you called her since you got here?"

I didn't have the heart to tell Mom I hadn't thought about my wife. "Don't worry, Ma. These things have a way of working themselves out. Our problems are more about what I've been going through. So I guess being here, doing what I'm doing, is the best way to prevail."

Mom peered into my face. "You know, your Dad went through something like this when you were in high school. He was having all kinds of doubts about himself. He said he hadn't done anything with his life, and so forth. That's why he drank too much. Then there was a 'situation' beginning with another woman at work."

"You're kidding."

"I said 'beginning'. Well, I nipped that in the bud so fast your Dad didn't know what hit him."

"How?"

Mom brushed her hand across her thigh. "There'd been a lot of gossip in his office. I knew because whenever I went there to see him during that time, the rest of the workers were 'all eyes', if you know what I mean. Any woman sees the signals that people are 'talking'. I homed in on a secretary in the office who wouldn't look at me, and I figured she was the one. By everyone else's faces when I walked over to her, I knew I was right."

"What if you had been wrong?"

"I wasn't. But oh, I was careful not to say anything in front of any-one. I waited until your father came out of his office. That last time I waited 'til I could watch his face when he saw me standing next to that woman. And sure enough. When he saw me his eyes about skidded out of his head."

"Did you ever talk about it to him or her after that?"

"Didn't have to. My little visit brought them both up short."

"You were sure that it stopped?"

"Absolutely. Call it 'woman's intuition'," Mom said.

"Do you forgive him for what he did?"

"Yes, because I don't believe he was ever in love with her. And I didn't want to know what they did together. The important thing is that when I called him on it he stopped. He also stopped drinking. And he's treated me like a queen ever since. He says I'm psychic."

"Do you think Jeanie will forgive me?"

"Have you done something wrong?"

"I have done *nothing* wrong. Nothing real. I mean, nothing really with anybody."

"Just in your fantasies. With Lucille, right?"

Trying to hide, I scrunched down further into the couch cushions. "When I was still in Colorado," I said, "I found that my imagination spawns my work. It's a creative process. So that's the road I'm taking. The results are proof positive."

"I think I understand," my saintly mother said. "The sooner you get done with this, the sooner your family life will get back on track."

"I believe our marriage will be even stronger then."

"What are you planning to do next, Davie?"

"I'll go back to the Barnetts' tonight with my night vision scope."

"Why?"

"I want to find out if the kinds of things I've been seeing are like a film playback or if there's any real life to them."

"What?"

"It's hard to explain because you don't know enough about it."

"But you don't tell me anything."

I looked into her little blue-gray eyes and smiled. "Infrared picks up warm things. For instance if you stood far away from me at night, I could look through the scope and see you because of your body heat. Or on an evening such as tonight, when the ground and trees have cooled, I could choose a spot to lie down. I could lie there until my body warmed the grass. When I got up and aimed my night vision scope at the general area where I had been lying. Through the scope I could detect exactly *where* I was by the warm spot on the grass."

"Your father did tell me a little about your work. And I think I kind of follow. You can see things that happened in the past? So how can those things still have heat?"

"Good question. I was obviously not of an ignorant woman born." I closed my hand around the medallion. "I don't know if traces of the past can have heat. And that, my darling Mother, is what I intend to find out tonight."

"Want to share why you look like something the cat dragged in?"

I laughed. "Haven't heard that expression in a while! Do I really look that bad? Well, you said yourself that I've always been a private person. Don't get me wrong. I'm excited about sharing my work with you. It's just that what's turning up is intensely personal, and some of it is upsetting. Like today: I saw something from Lu's childhood that made me want to—."

"I hear your Dad's car. Need to make a getaway? Or do you want to stay here and explain it all again—to him?"

"Why don't *you* tell him all about it? I'm heading upstairs."

CHAPTER TWENTY-THREE

At 11:00 p.m. I parked in the subdivision behind Walnut Street. Things were going great until I plonked over a garbage can and woke up all the dogs in the neighborhood. Lights came on in the house up the driveway from my car, so I found a hiding place in the bushes bordering the Barnetts' lot. I sat on my haunches until the dogs calmed down. For kicks, I looked through my night vision scope to see what heat signatures would show up on this moonless night. Up in the Barnetts' huge maple tree I could see the zig-zag outlines of what must have been birds. I turned the scope in the direction of some voices and saw the forms of two people sitting in a backyard porch swing about three houses down.

Now I felt optimistic about using the rainbow crystal with the night vision scope to look for the same traces I got with the laser. For luck

I fingered Lu's laser medallion, which I now wore around my neck. In the darkness I could barely see my crystal, so in my first test run I refocused the infrared beam through the part of the crystal where I the rainbow plane should be. I could have predicted the results: energy vibrating inside the crystal. That was all. I kept fidgeting with the crystal, moving it around. I even turned it upside-down. But the crystal kept refracting the infrared light. I went back to using the scope. I aimed it toward the east side of the Barnetts' house. The bricks of the house still must have been warm from the daytime sun because the infrared caught their heat. I checked the crystal again. Why couldn't it conduct the infrared straight out? Without the visible spectrum of light, the crystal could amplify nothing my eyes couldn't already detect. I was obviously going to have to do my crystal cathedral takedown.

I had memorized the technique. I went to the red, the red, the red step. Now the orange, the orange, the orange step. Now the yellow, the yellow, the yellow step. Now the green, the green, the green…now the purple…step. Now the white light. Now the voice of the Elemental. The voice of the Elemental?

"This time what you're doing interests me," she said from around a corner of her crystal cathedral.

"I'm really glad you're here," I said.

The Elemental appeared by my side. "Hold it right there," she said. She looked even more shimmery than in our last encounter. "For this you will need your entire wits about you. *Where* you look will be more important than ever, because this time you will capture something you saw before in a dream. Even then, on a subtle level you were starting to see without using your eyes."

Since the Elemental was so sensitive about intrusion, I thought I should handle our meeting with care. "But I didn't want to cheat this time by coming here to *you*."

"That is because you want other *scientists* to accept these results? And other 'eggheads', as you say. Is what you have already achieved not enough for you?" She moved away.

"Don't go!" I pleaded. "I need your help."

The Elemental looked at me for a couple of long minutes. Finally she pointed east, past the house. "All you have to do is look east. If you keep looking east, you will surely find it."

"Find what?"

"You will surely find it." The confounding Elemental vanished.

Oh great, I thought. *How can I sense whatever I should be seeing if I don't know what it is?* I passed through the crystal wall as though it were air and found myself on the ground below Lu's old bedroom.

The sound of a window opening on the second floor above me brought me back around. I withdrew to the pitch darkness farther out from the Barnetts' back yard. I hunched down behind some thick shrubs and waited. Though I saw nothing, I could hear shoes on light metal. When I sighted through my night vision scope at the north side of the house, I saw a human form climbing down from the window! But I couldn't figure out what the figure was stepping down. The person was slight of build. It moved deliberately, gracefully, a step at a time. It was clearly a girl. I decided that though she was small, she moved more like a teenager than like a younger girl.

I thought maybe the Barnett boy had his girlfriend sneak up a fire ladder to his room and now she was sneaking back down again. But something about the line of movement signaled a directed kind of panic. The female figure looked like someone might be coming after her. And yet that wasn't quite it either. It was like the girl was trying to get away from *herself*. My heart pumped fast.

I heard the crunch of gravel under the girl's shoes. Through the scope, from fifteen yards away, I could see the figure heading zombie-like down the walk that skirted the front yard. I felt her emptiness, her deadly determination. Resting my eyes by looking away, I reflexively touched Lu's medallion with my free hand. It seemed on fire! Hearing more noises from the window above, I aimed my scope at the lower pane again. Another, taller form was climbing down! This figure appeared to be female too, and she was in a real hurry. This second girl came down fast, jumped to the ground from about two feet up, and went in the same direction as the first girl. I decided to follow them. I got up and felt my way along the house in the utter darkness. I hung out by the side of the house and looked out at the front yard. I could hear voices but with my naked eye I couldn't see anyone. However, from about twenty-five yards away, through the scope I could see the girls' outlines in the front yard. Their postures were rigid and intense. The taller girl aggressively yanked the arm of the other girl, who kept trying to pull away.

Feeling secure in the darkness, I moved around the front of the garage, across the front porch, and around to the cover of the diseased blue spruce. Now I was ten yards from the girls. I could hear better what they were saying.

"He's in there with some whore," the smaller one said. "I went downstairs to get some ice water and he was screwing her on the sofa bed in the living room."

The taller girl looked stiff with tension. "That's no reason to do something bad to yourself," she said to the other girl. "Where did you think you were going?"

The smaller girl's face looked like a Greek mask of tragedy. "I can't live in that house with him anymore. I don't want to live anymore."

From behind me I heard the front door *seethe* open. "I hear you…two out there. You…get the fuck…back in here!" a male voice bellowed. His eyes began to glow like orange Halloween string lights.

The two forms on the lawn crouched down and started creeping across the opposite side of the lawn. Then they made a beeline to the scraggly blue spruce and tried to hide on the street side of the spruce.

I rose to my knees to get a better look at the man. He was huge. Taller than six feet and weighing about two hundred fifty pounds. Even with the distortions of the scope I could see a lot of detail in his face. Especially heat coming from his eyes and his mouth. "When you…get back I'll…be waiting for…you. That will teach you to…spy…on me!"

Through the scope the man's eyes had looked like hot coals. *My God*, I thought. *What if he sees me?* Fear slammed my entire body. Lu's medallion felt like a cattle brand sizzling into my chest. My heart staggered, skipped a wobbly beat.

The girls moved faster now. Soon they were running past me toward the side of the house. I put my scope down and prayed they wouldn't see me. As it turned out, I didn't see them either. I looked through the scope again. I had lost the girls' outlines. All talking had stopped. All action had ceased. Bern no longer loomed outside the front door.

I sat on the cold ground for several minutes and wondered if any of this had happened. *Maybe I should be asking myself* when *all this happened*, I thought, for because of the total darkness there was no way to prove whether those figures appeared that night or a night years ago. I put on my deerskin driving gloves, the flexible ones, to warm my fingers and zipped my light down jacket all the way to the top. I crept along the driveway, retracing my steps to the back of the house. I was wide awake and hungry for answers about all these sounds and images I captured in such *out there* ways. I almost tripped over another garbage can by the back of the house. Luckily my gloved hands contacted the garbage can first, causing only a swishing noise.

I mulled over what I just saw and decided that none of these people had been the Barnetts. Though I couldn't prove the *when* factor, I could try something else—use the night vision scope to view that disgusting ordeal Lu's father put her through. If the infrared could pick up those traces, then I would have my answer.

I looked up at the now familiar bedroom window. One obvious problem occurred to me. I couldn't be inside Lu's old room tonight like I was earlier that day. If I somehow got up high enough, though, I could shoot an infrared beam through the Barnett boy's window and he would never know it. *Maybe*, I thought, *there's no way I can try this tonight.* I'd have to bring a ladder or set up a scaffold outside the next night. Discouraged, I leaned my back against the huge maple tree and continued to look up at the window. *Need a ladder*, I thought.

Even through my down jacket I could feel the rough bark of the maple tree behind me. I let the tree support me like a good friend.. Though I was sleepy I stood up to leave and looked up. There I saw a lovely big branch reaching across like a brawny arm toward me. Ready to help me. I could look through the bedroom window if I climbed high enough in the maple tree! Too bad the branch couldn't reach down. The branch was a good seven feet up. I tucked my twin crystal in a side pocket of my jacket and the night vision scope in the back pocket of my pants. I jumped only a foot off the ground. To reach that branch I would have to face reality. I was not in good shape. I would have to boldly go where no Leone has gone before. In short, I must jump another foot higher.

Desire propelled me upwards high enough to grab the big branch and swing Tarzan-like until I could scramble up the trunk. Up and over with one leg and then the other. Like mounting Reynie's quarter horse. Straddling the tree limb, I sat there, huffing and puffing. Cooking in my own sweat. Because at sea level you're getting two thirds more oxygen your heart slows way down. You just want to nap all the time. *Davey, Old Boy*, I thought. *You better shape up before you head back to Boulder.*

I needed to get an even higher vantage point. Hugging the maple trunk, I stood up on the branch and climbed four limbs higher. There I found a secure nesting place close-in and pulled out my night vision scope. I turned it on and sighted through the scope. The technique is just like shooting at any target: First you must know what you're shooting at. Then, if you are a skilled marksman, you find your chosen target, take aim, and hit it. Because of the angle I could see the Barnett boy's form only from the waist down as he lay in bed. Picked up by the infrared, his warm body registered clearly in the scope.

Seeing a currently living person with the infrared was one thing. I needed to re-create what I had seen that afternoon and then detect heat traces from the past if possible. When I began my meditation I felt warmth spreading from the crystal in one hand to the night vision scope in the other. It was like a circle of energy radiating between them. The yellow, yellow step. I no longer cared if this self-hypnosis was cheating. I no longer cared if this technique could be proven by pure science. The blue, blue step. After all, becoming famous would only steal my privacy. Obscene wealth wouldn't trouble me, though. White, white light. *Are you there, Elemental?* Nothing.

Through a transparent wall of the Elemental's crystal I could see into Lu's bedroom. Rather, in the darkness I *sensed* I was there in the room with her. The depth and peace of her sleeping affected me profoundly. The more absorbed in my own state I became, the more intimately I could feel Lu's state. She stirred. I knew she was dreaming. She whimpered. I dreaded seeing the light come on under her door.

But that didn't happen. Instead I fell into a kind of sleep *within my* meditation. First I was outside my body. I was no longer in the maple tree, inside the Elemental's crystal, or in Lu's room. I saw myself walking toward the fir tree in the Barnetts' back yard. Now back in my body, I went closer, to its base. On my knees I crawled under its long skirt-like branches until I felt my forehead touch the trunk. I began to climb. I used the very inside of the branches, where they attached directly to the trunk. I climbed straight up, as if the branches were steps on a ladder. About two thirds of the way, the top of the tree began to sway back and forth with my weight. The branches kept brushing against my jeans. I trusted the tree's flexibility. I pressed my weight against it to make the swinging more extreme. In the back of my throat I suppressed a yell: "Whee!" When I looked out I saw mostly fir branches. Despite the perilous swinging arcs the tree was already making with me aboard, I wanted to climb higher. Even in my altered state I knew this was dangerous.

I climbed higher anyway, but with much less gusto now, because the reasoning part of me wasn't keen on the tree's being the catcher in what might turn out to be my flying trapeze act. About three feet from the top, I held on tight to the tree and closed my eyes. I took long, slow breaths to make sure I remained *in state*. I did this so well that I almost got lost in it. The me in the maple tree, the me inside the crystal, inside Lu's room, and/or at the top of this fir tree "opened my eyes" and I saw Lu running toward me from the house and through the back yard. In terror Lu looked over her shoulder. Then she stopped. Now she waited at the base of the fir tree. I saw all this from way above her. Like Lu had done this dozens of times, she scrambled up the inside of the tree. She stopped in the middle, moved a fir branch aside with one hand, and peeped out. I also looked toward her house. His hands on his hips, Bern Muhr stood on the back porch, which was flush with the ground. Clearly he was looking for Lu.

Clinging more tightly to the trunk of the fir tree, Lu was breathing hard. Suddenly her father saw her! His long strides brought him quickly to the base of the tree. Lu climbed even higher until she was practically on top of me. But the fir tree barely swung. She was so close I tried to touch her but my hand passed right through her image.

Bern Muhr did not try to climb up after Lu. Instead he took out a book of matches and ignited the dead pine needles beneath the tree! The lower branches quickly caught fire. Neither wanting to climb back down where her father stood nor able to climb any higher in the fir tree, Lu was caught in a panic that made my own heart feel like it would shatter. It didn't matter if this was happening in the distant past or if Lu was having a nightmare. I was helpless too.

When the fire spread upward, Lu desperately pressed herself against the tree trunk. Now she was crying pitifully while her father bayed like some hellhound. A tiny presence of mind told me to take out my night vision scope. Through the scope I could see Lu's form closeup. The torrid scene below us lit the scope up like a 19th-Century photographic flash. Her father's hulking figure seemed to give off heat as intense as the flames, which had reached where Lu and I were balanced. Now I could smell smoke and feel the feverish fire energy closing in on us. Now I saw pure terror in Lu's face and in how tightly she clung to the fir tree's trunk.

"We have to climb down!" I shouted at Lu. "Down through the fire! It's the only way."

Lu didn't budge.

"Well, *I'm* not gonna burn up," I said. I tried to grab Lu around her waist but my arm gathered only sharp pine needles. Despite being aware I was inside several realities at once, my survival mechanisms stayed on red alert. This might sound dumb, but when I began to descend I tried to maneuver around Lu's form. At the time I was in a total confusion of realities. I lost my footing and grabbed air instead of branches on my way down. I slid down and then fell to the ground in slow-motion panic. The whole way down, my blood curdling primal scream followed my rude descent. In the moments of shock that immediately followed, I lay beneath the tree. I tried to think of my name, figure out my location, and determine my physical condition.

"What the hell was that!" someone shouted. Spotlights on the back of the Barnetts' house blasted my eyeballs. Shadows of three people moved toward me like men in spacesuits and hovered above me. There was no place to hide.

"Well, for cryin' out loud," bugled a woman I didn't recognize.

A man knelt beside me. "I think the fool's broke his leg."

I didn't care if he was right. When I looked up through the branches of the big pine tree I knew what I saw via the infrared light proved that the past is really still alive.

"We ain't payin' for no ambulance," Mrs. B. said.

"That's right," Mr. B. said. "Especially since you were trespassing. Climbing our tree at night."

I gasped in pain. "I am not crazy and I have medical insurance," I said. When I saw that the middle of my lower right leg was like an elbow, everything went black. But I could still hear the harpy.

"You're a wingnut," Mrs. B. said. "I should tell them to give you a psych test at the hospital."

"On *your* medical insurance," Mr. B. said, "I will call you an ambulance. "You're an ambulance. Ha! Ha!" He headed back into his loathsome house. He left me alone with his dental disaster of a wife in my hour of need.

CHAPTER TWENTY-FOUR

I lay on the couch in a stupor fueled by whopping pain killers. As I came-to, I felt I was treading in waters of events that happened that dreadful night. Me, on my back, helpless at the bottom of a tree. The hideous faces of the Barnetts sneering down at me. A wretched trip alone in an ambulance to the Emergency Room of Circleville Hospital, where they savaged my leg. My Dad in pants and pajama top, rubbing his eyes, waiting for my doc to release me. Here before me was the ugly truth—a plaster half-cast deforming my right leg from just below my knee to my ankle. This whitish eyesore showed through the untidy scissors cuts someone had made in my favorite pair of jeans. The more I woke up, the more pain I felt and the worse my mood. From the living room couch I could see into Mom's homey kitchen.

"Well, good afternoon, Son," Mom said. She was mixing walnut chocolate chip cookie batter in the kitchen. "Your Dad's out getting Kentucky Fried Chicken." she said.

"Ah! A bright spot!"

"*My* fried chicken's way better though," Mom said.

"Your fried chicken takes too long to cook. What time is it?"

Mom laid her spatula on a ceramic cabbage leaf spoon saver. "About four-thirty." I think I just heard your Dad's car."

I hoped my favorite junk food would keep my mind off my leg. My muscles throbbed and my ligaments and tendons were deadlocked in an unholy war with each other. *This must be how much it hurts women when they're in labor*, I thought. "When can I take more pain meds?"

"Not for another hour," Mom said. "I wish you didn't hurt so bad. It hurts *me* to see you this way!"

Someone knocked on the back door. "Package for Mr. Leone."

Mom wiped her hands on her green-leaf-patterned apron and went to answer the door. "May I help you?"

"I have a delivery for a Mr. David Leone. He has to sign for it. That box has been rattling all the way from the airport. I'll be glad to get it off my truck."

"Well," Mom said, "he's here but he can't come to the door right now. I'm his mother. Can I sign for it?"

The voice I heard sounded familiar. "You bet. I'll bring this on up and set 'er down wherever you like."

I winced when I sat up. "What kind of box is it?"

After some clanking of a handcart up the steps there was another short knock and the door opened. In walked my old buddy Josh. I covered up my blighted right leg so he wouldn't see the partial cast.

Josh wheeled the jumbo box in. On top of it he had set a bulging paper bag. He leaned on the bar of the hand cart and touched the heavy bag. "I thought I'd come and see what you're up to."

"You know each other?" Mom asked.

"Yeah. Josh and I go way back," I said.

Josh tipped the bag toward me and I saw a case of Coors! Josh's eyes said I didn't have to thank him. "Did Court send you?"

"Eee-yep!"

I had forgotten to tell Mom about the light table and my other holographic supplies—and about how much space the light table would take up in the front sitting room. I pointed at the sitting room behind me and Josh wheeled my equipment box in.

"My idea," Josh said. "Now that I see what you did to yourself—."

"So you *have* come to help me."

"I helped you with your work before, remember? We were all worried about you. I'll check in at the Holiday Inn so I won't be in your way. Gosh you look awful, Dave."

"You can make yourself at home in David's old room upstairs," Mom said. "He has to stay down here near the bathroom."

"Now that my leg is kaput I sure welcome your help, Josh. This is a big favor. I've been freaked out about how I can keep working and here you are!"

Josh's wary look made me laugh. "You mean you're not gonna lecture me about coming to Circleville? You're not gonna tell me to go back to Boulder?"

I pushed my leg painfully back across the length of the couch. "But that would be stupid. Especially since my Dad's coming back any minute with—wait for it—a bucket of Kentucky Fried!"

"Yes!" Josh shouted. He pulled up a chair.

"You want to know what really makes me glad to see you?"

Josh relaxed into his chair and popped a Coors. "I know, Dude."

The week I lived on the couch drove me nuts. I longed to shoot baskets with Josh. I longed to take off my own pants without help. I longed to go outside and feel the sun on my face! I don't mean to sound dramatic. It's just that when you're an *invalid* everything feels more intense. Doing the smallest things is a major challenge. The hardest part was the toll being an invalid took on my ego. The way I saw myself. Until my leg healed I would be an ungainly cripple, *stubbing* along like pirate Captain Long John Silver.

Josh somehow read my mood from *beyond*. He came in from shooting baskets the next afternoon and offered to chauffeur me around in his 4X4 rental truck. "I'll bet you haven't been to any of your old stomping grounds. Like your high school."

"I haven't even gone outside this house," I whined. I got up on my good foot and settled my underarms on my crutches. "You're right. It's weird lying around all day."

Josh stood up. "He lives!"

"Where's Mom?"

"Grocery shopping," Josh said. "With three big guys to feed now, meat runs out fast."

"*Two* big guys. You forgot about my little Italian papa." I hopped like Grampa McCoy over to the end of the kitchen counter. That's where Mom kept the most orderly supply of paper and writing tools east of the Mississippi.

Josh came up beside me. "You need help?"

I found a pad of large blank yellow sticky notes and a pencil with my Dad's old business logo on it. "I'm going to leave Mom a note." I balanced on my normal foot and wrote:

Dear Mom,

Got a hot date this afternoon after school.

Just kidding.

Will call if going to miss dinner.

Love you a lot,

Davie

With a plastic banana magnet I stuck the note to the refrigerator. There, in my youth, I used to leave anything I wanted my parents to see. In grade school it was untalented drawings I stuck to the fridge with my mother's odd magnets.

Josh read my note. A smile opened his face. "I just learned something about you, Dave. You can be one hell of a nice guy."

"Lu used to say, 'Nice is not enough.' Or she'd say, 'God save me from nice people'."

"I don't get it."

"Lu alleged that you can't tell what nice people are really thinking. Nice people just want to be liked—and they go 'wherever the wind blows'. I didn't agree then. Now I do. People should be up-front with you. If they're not, you can't trust them."

Josh looked serious. "What about your Mom?" he asked. "She's a *very* nice person. Don't you trust *her*?"

"I'm just repeating what *Lu* said."

I had the bucket seat in Josh's 4X4 rental truck all the way back. Still, I had to cram my crutches next to my bum leg beneath the dashboard. "I don't know why," I told Josh, "but I haven't gone back to Circleville High in years."

"I'm your driver. Leave everything to me. Which one will we get to first along the way? Your high school or the cemetery?"

"My high school. Keep going on this street until you get through the middle of town." We dead-ended at a closed mall in the center of town. "Oops. Forgot about this. Just follow the circle around to the right." We passed a 7-Eleven that was new to me and came to East Third. The street went one way by my old high school. "Here it is. There were two hundred in our class of '67. Look at it now."

Back in the day, our high school had two new buildings. The gymnasium and a classroom annex. Now *all* campus buildings were squalid remnants of their former selves. Josh walked slowly with me past the gym. "That gym cost over three million," I said. "We were so proud of the Olympic size swimming pool." Tiles from the mosaic decorating the West side of the old gymnasium had faded. Many tiles were missing. This made the huge tiger face look like it was riddled with the *mange*. "Dad told me classes are so small now that the city wants to tear the school down." We came to the main building. "See that annex over there? That's the band room."

"Think you can go up these steps?" Josh asked. "Here. Pretend you're a halfback who's just been injured in the big Homecoming game and I'm helping you off the field."

"But I've never been athletic," I said. I let Josh lift me around the waist and hoist me up each step. "It's so unfair that things don't stay the way you remember them. Look at those graffiti sprayed across the walls. Oh no—and across my school's name. When I was a kid, people felt the same way about vandalism as they did about murder. If anybody knew you drank or smoked they called you a 'hood'. It was the same if you cut class or cheated on exams. And if they found out you and your girlfriend had sex, they patted you on the back and branded *her* as a whore."

Josh helped me with the door. "You and Lucille never had sex?"

"Pretty close to it."

"Weren't you proud of yourself though?"

"Hell, yes! But I just let the guys wonder. They couldn't prove anything. I loved Lu too much to let them gossip. And I would never start that rumor myself."

"I won't tell a soul, being that Lucille Muhr is so famous and all."

We stopped inside the front door and stood on the neglected floorboards that led to the school's main offices. Most of the flooring was now dirty and heavily weathered. Quite a few boards had splintery chinks in them. "We better check in at the office."

An old biddy greeted this alumnus with a sour "Yea-us?" She said she wasn't supposed to let non-students or non-teachers or non-administrative personnel "wander around the halls just like nothing." She added that this rule "maintains security."

I inspected her name tag. "Miss Hogue, please tell me what is left of this school to keep secure?"

Miss Hogue remained unaffected by my sarcasm. "You haven't been back in a long time. You're a graduate and you can't believe how much *your* school has changed."

Her tone reminded me of someone. Here was an intelligent, perhaps still dedicated, educational administrator who had watched a high school slowly *devolve*. How does that woman cope? She shields herself from feeling the gloom that surrounds her every school day. She becomes an old lady smartass to protect her heart. I felt a sympathy for Miss Hogue that was unusual for me.

The veil lifted from Miss Hogue's eyes for a flicker. "Well, they've still got another half hour in class. Principal Taggart is out of town so I'm pretty much in charge here. I guess it wouldn't hurt to show you some empty classrooms. Maybe that'll bring back good memories." For Miss Hogue this must have been an impassioned speech. A stark sense of our mutual humanity had passed between us. This enchantment felt painful. Now Miss Hogue treated Josh and me like visiting dignitaries. "You remember the cafeteria? That's been closed for ten years. Here's the chemistry lab. Want to go in?" She opened the door.

I was nervous. "No. I'll just take a look from here." The classroom was painted the same institutional green as before and there were big gashes in the rubber lab tabletops. Here was where my love of science had blossomed during my junior year. "My Chem teacher, Mr. Martin, told me that someone so good in science shouldn't be that good in English too." The truth was that Lu was in my sophomore English class and made straight A's. I made it my mission to do likewise.

Josh said to me: "It must be your talking. You've had so much practice." But an immediate apology showed on his face.

Miss Hogue had laughed. "Here's the auditorium," she said. She peered into my face. "I saw Lucille Muhr perform as 'Kate' here in 'Taming of the Shrew'. She was a good actress even then."

I was thinking, *Little does Miss Hogue know how apropos that role was.* Sometimes Lu showed her artistic temperament with anger, her eyes blazing. But I said to Miss Hogue, "If you worked here when Lucille Muhr performed, why don't I remember *you*, Miss Hogue?"

"Because then I was an administrator at the middle school across the street," Miss Hogue said. "But I came to high school plays and sports events here. About two years later I got this job. Were you in the same graduating class as Lucille Muhr?"

"She was Dave's heartthrob," Josh said.

Miss Hogue looked like she wanted my autograph. "*Now* I remember you! Imagine that!"

I started to get emotional. My feelings must have had a meeting and decided to rush down to my right leg to have a party because a giant pang collapsed my knee. "I think we'd better get back to the car," I said. "I need to sit down."

"Come to the office with me," Miss Hogue said, "and you can sit and tell me all about Lucille. I mean, Miss Muhr! I'll make some fresh coffee and—."

"That's nice of you but my doctor told me to take it easy on this leg or they might have to amputate."

"Oh, my goodness," Miss Hogue said sincerely. "Well, you're welcome back any time, Mr.—."

"David Leone. This is my best buddy Josh Peterson."

Miss Hogue walked us to the door. "You ever see her?"

I pivoted painfully around. "Who?"

"Lucille Muhr."

"I married someone else," I said.

Josh drove us between two granite towers at the entrance of Forest Cemetery. I remembered the cemetery, with its precisely groomed lawns and carefully kept graves. It looked more like a park. Like everything else in town, the cemetery was now timeworn. Along the borders, weeds had won a battle with once-tender grass. Now Forest looked more like some rural graveyard. I told Josh to take the left fork in the road. "Somewhere over there's where my mother's people are buried. The Obermeiers. Stop. I think this is it. *Großvati* died when I was too young to go to his funeral, but I remember *Großmutti* as clear as day. She still spoke with a thick accent, though she'd lived in the States for decades. Yes, here it is. She was a baker. She used to say, 'You cannot be taught to bake. You must be born a baker.' And she was that. She made angel food cakes from scratch that were so light they dissolved on your tongue. She didn't ice them because she thought no cake so light and sweet needed icing."

Josh pointed at *Großmutti's* gravestone. "Your grandmother died in 1953 so you were what? Only seven years old? Did you have to go to her funeral?"

"Yeah. It was the first time I ever saw a dead person. I looked at my grandmother and said to myself: 'That's not her anymore. She didn't look like that'. It felt kind of like today at Circleville High. You're in this weird space where most of you wants things to stay the way they were. And yet here is the reality that something you loved has changed, and death is the biggest of those changes. Your high school can be torn down, and your memories can keep playing on, but once it's torn down it's gone forever. You finally accept that you won't see your grandmother again. You know you can't create new memories with her because she's gone forever."

Josh hesitated before saying: "And what about other memories?"

I braced myself on Josh's fit shoulder. "You don't have to mince words with me. You're referring to Lu and me. Because she's still alive, this memory thing is different with her. I want to rest here for a while and think about what you just said. Okay?"

Josh clearly read my need to be alone. "All right if I kind of look around? Don't worry. I know not to walk on the graves." He left me on a bench near my grandmother's headstone.

Across the years I had often fantasized about what it would be like to bump into Lu somewhere. She would have changed since I saw her so long ago. I figured she'd find *me* changed too and wondered how we would meet. Perhaps in a hotel lobby or airport. Would she like me the way I am now? Would I like *her* the way she is now? Most of all I wondered if we both had found meaning in our lives and about how the paths each of us chose might change the way we saw each other. I knew one thing for sure. If I met Lu I'd have trouble keeping my head. And yet I felt I *could* handle seeing her. In the past, even a month ago, I would rather die than let her see me lose my cool. I saw Josh coming toward me.

"I want to show you something across the road," Josh said. "Let me give you a lift. Oh. You won't budge until I tell you why? Have you ever just walked around and looked at headstones? Not even out of curiosity? It gives you a big dose of reality. Probably none of these people believed *they* would die. You know? You don't even think about it happening to you."

"I got that bigtime on my birthday," I said. "But why can't I just look around on *this* side?"

"Because there's a big headstone over there that says 'Muhr' on it, and I thought you might know a name or two. Maybe it's the same Muhrs as Lucille Muhr?"

I relented. "Take me for a ride then." That reality shook me. The one thing I spent all my adult life resisting kept jolting me in all these obvious ways. A voice inside me said: "You are hopelessly tangled up with Lucille Muhr. I was sure that this life is *it*. That you have only one shot at it, however unfair. If I had believed in reincarnation the last time I saw Lu, I would have asked myself what I had done to her, or she to me, that kept us in this endless circle that started in...Circleville.

There it was. I had declared it to myself: "Lu still loves me." Not admitting this fact had kept my more tender feelings at bay. Not facing that she shared my obsession made it easier *for me* to handle the truth. When I first read in Court's letter how Lu touched my books and my plants, and how she had left with one of my crystals, I denied that Lu still loved me too. After all these years, even with the major differences between us, we still had a close bond. My denial of this intensified our connection. Now I saw that the truth doesn't go somewhere else just because it disturbs you. In the dark little cave you design to hide the truth away, it waits. It gathers energy and expands its force. The light of truth filters through the one or two little openings your growing self-knowledge creates. Then KA-BLAM! Truth levels you.

From far away I heard Josh speak: "Who's *Lillian* Muhr? I don't see a date of death."

I hopped over to the Muhr plot of graves. "That's Lu's grandmother. There's Bern Senior's grave. That was Lu's grandfather. And there's Bern Junior's grave."

"Her father died in 1973? He was young."

"At age forty-eight. A violent death. Cerebral hemorrhage. I didn't find out 'til years later. It came up during a chat my mother was having with a neighbor."

"Would you have gone to the funeral?"

"I don't think so. Jeanie and I had been married long enough to have Eddie. Jeanie was going through postpartum depression. So even if I *had* known about Bern Muhr's death I couldn't have come back for the funeral anyway."

"You don't even think of Lucille Muhr as a *friend* now?"

"How could we be just friends?"

"That's a shame."

"Yeah. Usually being so close to someone makes you remain friends. Like Reynie. I care about Reynie a lot, as I do you. But she's more like a sister. I'm not saying Reynie's unattractive. You know how it is. You toe the line. You kind of shut off certain senses."

"Yeah, I know," Josh said. He pointed at Lillian Muhr's gravestone. "According to this, the old lady was born ninety years ago. So she's still kicking. Do you remember her?"

I certainly did remember Lillian Muhr. "Lu and I used to go to her grandparents' house in Columbus. Lillian and Bern Senior built the house here in Circleville that Lu grew up in, but Lu's grandfather died when she was a toddler. Lillian later remarried. Lu calls her 'Nana'."

Josh helped me walk to his rented 4X4. "Here we go." He helped me in. "Let's stop and get a couple of meat lovers' pizzas to take back."

"Sounds good to me. But Dad can't eat cheesy pizza because of the cholesterol."

"Have you started checking *yours* yet?"

"You really know how to make a guy feel old."

CHAPTER TWENTY-FIVE

The next day I felt good enough to set up my portable light table. I elevated the lenses, mirrors, and laser higher than usual. I hoped doing that would help me capture a holographic image of Lu and me together. Mom was so happy to see me perk up that she didn't complain about my gear. I wanted a sexy hologram, and I didn't want to embarrass myself again in front of her. I needed Josh to run the laser while I zoned out at the other end of the light table.

"Aren't you standing too close to the table?" Josh asked.

"Mom? You got a measuring tape?" To Josh I said, "I should actually be sitting *on* the table."

Delighted to be included in my experiment, Mom brought me a mustard-yellow measuring tape from her sewing basket. "Can't I please watch? I'll stand back here in the kitchen doorway so I won't bother you."

I measured the distance from the laser to where I had stood.

Josh's forehead wrinkled. "Let your mom help too. In the name of all romantics?"

I reviewed the situation. Once I got into a torrid scene like I had reexperienced with Lu in the front room a while back, could I stop myself short of kissing her in my mind and have Josh make the shot? I would have to stay in control anyway. That way, at least I wouldn't be caught smooching the air in front of my mother. If I couldn't hold the re-creation there, I might slip out of the laser's range, passionately bumping and grinding the carpet with a partner visible only to me. "Josh, make sure I snap out of it after you've shot the hologram."

But Josh teased me: "How can I promise ahead of time? I remember how weird you were acting last time."

"Listen, Josh. I don't feel so great, so I'm only going to say this once. This isn't a game to me. If I can't depend on you to do this exactly as I say, then you'll blow the whole experiment. And Mom, you don't know what you're asking. Letting you watch me work makes me feel like you're still changing my diapers. If both of you can promise you know how serious this is, then we can go on. If not, I won't be able to work here anymore."

Josh's eyes looked huge. "I was just kidding. Honest."

"I know," I answered. "But this *is* serious. Time might be running out for me to do what I came back here for. Let's set it up. Now I have to meditate, so please don't stare at me. If you make me self-conscious, I'll lose my concentration. So Josh, when I say 'Now', shoot the image, okay? I may not say it loudly or clearly, so be a friend and pay attention. Mom, could you keep busy somewhere else? If you hear something weird, please don't come in here to see if I'm all right."

The phone rang.

"*Damn* it!"

Mom spoke quietly into the phone and hung up. "It was Mrs. Barnett. She wants to know if you're going over there to work anytime soon. Isn't that nice? She was checking on how you're doing. Is she someone I might like?"

I refrained from telling my mother that Mrs. Barnett was probably more interested in the money she was losing in my absence. "The Barnetts aren't 'our kind of people'," I said. "Could you kindly unplug the phone while I'm working?"

Mom retreated to the back end of the kitchen when I began to breathe *in* deeply, and rather noisily, for a count of seven. I held my breath for seven. *Out* for eleven. Again. Again. Again. I pictured myself lying on a white sandy beach, feeling warm sand sift through my fingers. I felt sunshine caress my body, felt the breeze, and smelled the salt air. I heard the seagulls calling and watched them shift above me in the wind. Relaxed. Relaxed. Relaxed. Then the color sequence. I breathed deeply, saw the rainbow stairway, and stood on the red step, the red, the red…the orange…the yellow…the green…blue…indigo…violet. Would I see the Elemental today? "No need," my inner voice said. "Don't be afraid. You are in the crystal. Do you see the white light now?" My own voice urged me on. Though it was my voice, I sounded different than normal. My voice was gentle, even detached. My voice also sounded tender. It implied no judgment, inflicted no sarcasm. My usual mind chatter was gone. There was just my own, now loving voice. I couldn't remember hearing myself sound like that before. The stillness around me was almost fragrant.

A voice whispered, "I don't know how long this takes him."

I stood inside the Elemental's crystal. I felt euphoric. I thought of nothing but this sensation, this stillness, this ecstasy of oneness with my Self. I wanted to stay there forever. More like a feeling than a thought, my own voice conveyed there was something specific I should remember. Something I should do now. It felt like "image of love," though I didn't get it at first. I stood inert in the Elemental's crystal, feeling *image of love* like that earlier sea wind on my body. *Your work*, the sensations told me. *Image of love.*

"David. I'm here, my David." She stroked my hair, my lips. "Kiss me. Don't be afraid."

I tried to open my eyes but I could only see glimmers of light. I couldn't see who the woman was. Because of the resonating effect of the crystal I didn't know her voice either. It scared me that my eyes wouldn't open. "Who are you?" I felt her fingers pressing on the medallion, caressing, clasping it.

"Kiss me. This will be more than a kiss. Kiss Lu now."

"Now," I murmured. I thought: *Kiss her* and I felt her full lips on mine. We kissed. And we kissed…until a door slammed somewhere.

"Hey! What's going on!" a voice shouted.

Lu and I were jerked apart. I zoomed out of the Elemental's crystal so fast that the walls scraped me when I passed through them.

Mom panicked. "Ssh! Edoardo! Be quiet!"

In the distance I heard "Sorry."

I dropped out of the sky and landed with a thud on the floor of my parents' front room.

"Did you get it, Josh?" Mom asked.

"Eee-yes!"

Mom came to me and passed the palm of her hand over my eyes, my forehead. "Are you okay, Son? You fell."

I felt the carpet under my fingers. My right leg throbbed."

"I got it," Josh said. "I got the hologram."

"What the—." Dad said.

Mom stuck her hand up. "Just hang on a minute," she said to Dad.

Josh helped me to the couch. "Here. Easy does it with the leg. You are really something, buddy."

I didn't know whether to be embarrassed or ecstatic that my experiment had worked. I wasn't even sure what had happened. I decided to put my neck on the line. "What did you see?" I asked Josh.

Dad had come to the end of the couch. He looked like a man visiting a loved one in Intensive Care.

Mom knelt on the floor beside me. "You looked like an angel."

"No. Come on, Mom. Tell me the truth."

"She's not kidding," Josh said. "I had no idea you go into your meditation so deep. I almost didn't hear your cue to take the shot."

Looking at me now, Mom had the eyes of a rock star groupie. "Your face was, well, innocent as a baby's."

"Or a saint's," Josh said sincerely.

I sat myself up. "Where's my pain pills? You guys are putting me on. Okay. Have your fun. I don't care."

"When you feel better," Josh said, "I'll tell you what I think you've really pulled off here. You might not be able to see the forest for the trees. I wouldn't normally be caught dead saying what I'm going to tell you, but you made a believer out of me today. Your parents as witnesses, and stone cold sober, I'll say it: You have reached something spiritual inside you that I'm sure *I* never will."

Josh's face was so open and earnest that I trusted him. At least I saw he believed what he just told me. "Well, they say the greatest saints were once the greatest sinners," I noted.

"No, I mean it." Josh said. "Is there anything I can get for you?"

I sank back into the couch. "A beer would be sublime."

The Next Night

Josh parked his rental truck in a cul-de-sac behind the Barnetts' property. An ambient glow from streetlights and from the windows of night owl neighbors seemed to drift across lawns like a light fog. The shadows of varying hues of gray would not fully hide Josh or me. And so we needed to be wary of detection.

Josh opened his rental truck door for me. "So this is where you were the night you fell out of the tree?"

I extracted myself from the passenger seat and pulled out one crutch so I could free up my left arm. "Yeah. Except that I didn't have a camera with infrared film in it then. Here. You'll be using the scope and the camera, so you carry them. But don't get your hopes up. I have no idea if it'll work with someone else using the scope. You remember the plan, right? You have to pay attention. You'll probably be able to tell when it's time by my rapid eye movement. REM happens when a person's dreaming. You'll be looking for two figures. One's a big male and the other's a petite female," We hunkered down behind some hedges in front of the house, closest to the street. Let me note here that squatting down with a cast on your leg ain't that easy.

"How will I know I'm not seeing the Barnetts?" Josh whispered.

I told him that Mrs. Barnett was a big woman. "A big ugly woman," I added.

Josh walked, and I limped, between two darkened houses. A dog barked in the distance. We stopped just beyond some hedges at the edge of the Barnett's property.

"So if I think I've got Bern and Dora Muhr in the viewfinder, I should also be able to take infrared photos of them too. Right?"

"*Seeing* these things is the tricky part," I whispered. "Yesterday you saw my process of getting to that point. But you did see Lu? Did you hear her voice too?"

"I heard you say 'Now'. Some part of you made you say 'Now'?"

"That part was an accident. It was something Lu said to me when we were together in that moment."

"Then *she* told you when it was the right time!" Josh said too loudly. "Shh!"

Josh jiggled his legs like he had ants in his pants. "But don't you see what that means?" he whispered fiercely.

"What happened with Lu when I heard the word 'Now' means that your *souls* must be connected!" Josh said.

"You've been in Boulder too long," I purred. "No matter what happens with me, the Barnetts must not wake up. That is the 'Prime Directive'. Capiche?"

"Yes, oh Captain, my captain."

I responded, "Who *didn't* read Walt Whitman in high school? Follow me," I said. But I struggled to advance to a position behind the maple tree centered in the Barnetts' back yard. I put a hand up to quiet Josh again. "Go around to the other side of the tree," I said. "The master bedroom will be straight in front of you." I thanked God that the Barnetts' drapes were open. "Look through that picture window. Okay. While I'm doing my takedown, you can practice finding the Barnetts in the scope. By now they should be asleep. You might need to leave this spot and spy from an oblique angle. Get closer if you need to. Do whatever you must to find them while I'm getting ready. That way you'll know if it's the Barnetts now or the Muhrs from the past."

That night I got *in-state* fast. From the red step I seemed to whiz right up and into the Elemental's crystal.

The Elemental was waiting for me. "You have come far. Far enough to help *me* now."

Astonished, I replied: "Me? Help *you*? How?"

"By finishing your work," the Elemental said.

"You mean tonight I'll succeed? I'll get what I came here for?

The Elemental's smile held mystery. "You will get more than you ever imagined. Auspicious events are converging. Even your mending bones play a role. Are you ready to send us to the stars?"

I told her I had my seatbelt fastened. "I'm ready."

The Elemental told me to put the rainbow crystal cluster down.

"Don't I have to be holding it?"

"Trust me," the Elemental said. "Tonight you should lay it down."

I set my crystal on the top rainbow stair.

"No," the Elemental said. "Over here by me. You will need the stairs free."

Because I couldn't recall going back down the rainbow staircase I felt bewildered. But I did what the Elemental asked. Then I waited.

"I have one last thing to tell you before you finish your work," the Elemental said. "No matter what happens, know all is as it should be. The coming events are predestined. Flow gracefully with each moment and you will enjoy a peace of mind you have never known. Try to fight what's going on, or regret it in any way, and you will make a hell for yourself."

I asked the Elemental how Josh was doing.

The Elemental stepped back. "He is a most noble and loyal friend."

When I told the Elemental I was glad she had come, she smiled. Then she vanished. Poof!

It seemed a long time before I could act. Through the mirror-like wall of the Elemental's crystal I looked for the Muhrs' bedroom but saw, instead, a thick white fog. The harder I looked, the thicker the haze grew. I guessed I would have to leave the crystal sanctuary as the Elemental had said.

Going back down the rainbow stairs was new to me. With each step I felt less attached to my bliss, less attached to the Elemental. I felt I was waking from a deep sleep. I walked away from the big crystal structure toward the old Muhr house. The farther I went, the thinner the haze became. Finally the fog cleared.

I saw myself standing beside Josh! As though outside my body, I watched myself point at the big picture window of the master bedroom. I looked over at the me who was watching the me who was standing with Josh. I could see that my clothes were the same as those the other me wore. I heard a woman crying. The other me said to Josh, "Don't you hear a woman crying?"

Josh was looking through the night vision scope. He said: "I hear *nada.* But I see a big guy standing in the bedroom. He's staggering around to the end of the bed. Now he's going over to…I can't make it out. Maybe a dresser. He's reaching his hand into something. I can just make out the edge of what's in his other hand."

I don't remember how, but I projected the observer-me into that bedroom. Though it was dark I could see every object in the room. Dora Muhr was sitting up in bed. Her mouth quivered with terror, as if she were trying not to scream. Bern Muhr stood by a chest of drawers near a doorway to the dining room, which was straight past the end of the Muhrs' bed. He grasped a revolver in one hand and held a box of bullets in the other.

Bern sneered at his wife. "There's no reason to live. You know that. It will be easy to end your pain first. With *this*. Then I'll join you."

"I'm afraid!" Dora said. "I don't want to die. Bern, put that gun away and come back to bed. You'll feel better in the morning."

"I never feel better in the morning," Bern said. "This is a .22 Colt Courier six-shot revolver. But I tell you what. I will put only three bullets in. Every other slot. That way there'll be some sport in it. You know I got to spin if for you first so if you die, I can still shoot myself after." Bern Muhr twirled the cylinder and cocked the trigger.

Dora crept out of bed and moved toward the back bedroom door. The door opened to the circular foyer just inside the front door.

Fear and rage made me try to wrestle the gun from Bern's hand. Maybe not such a good idea. As if he did feel something, with the back of his hand Bern scratched his hand that held the revolver. Then he started after his wife.

By this time Dora was whimpering louder. "What if the girls come downstairs? You'll scare them."

"They'll stay asleep," Bern said, "until it's too late. Now don't make it hard for me." Towering over Dora at the front door, Bern rubbed the cold gun barrel against her neck and pointed it at her ear. "Feel this?" he asked. "That's all there is to dying. You feel cold. That's all."

Dora squirmed, showing mostly the whites of her eyes. "That is not all of it." She cried softly. "There's the girls. And you'll go to hell."

Bern continued to stroke Dora's neck with the gun barrel. "Mother will take care of the girls. You know that. And as for 'hell', there isn't any. And there's no heaven either. There's only a big fat nothing. Wouldn't a big fat nothing be better than what you feel every day?" Bern pointed his revolver at Dora's temple. "Wouldn't it?"

I heard a child's voice. "Mommy?" A little girl was coming down the stairs at the other side of the foyer. About three years old, she clutched to her chest a white toy dog with black spots. "Mommy?"

"Let her see it!" Bern said. "She's not mine anyway."

"Lucy. Go back upstairs, honey. Daddy and I are just playing a little game. I'll come up in a minute and tuck you in. Bern. Please stop."

Still half-asleep, the child Lu stood in the middle of the stairs.

"Get back upstairs, kid!" Bern yelled.

Lu looked at her father. Her eyes were incredibly, unjustifiably loving. "Okay Daddy. I go bed now."

Every cell in my body wanted to reach out and hold the child Lu. To carry her back up the stairs and be the father she deserved.

But now Bern held Dora's arm behind her back and forced her back into their bedroom. "Maybe I'm not ready for you to go yet. Maybe I want you to do something for me first. Something you never do. I'm tired of begging for it. I'm tired of you turning me down. You are my wife. You're supposed to do whatever I want, whenever I want it." He shoved Dora onto the bed.

"Please, Bern. Don't. It hurts me too much."

I yelled: "You goddamned gorilla sonofabitch bastard! Get away from her or I'll kill you with your own gun. Before I do that, maybe I'll shoot your hellhound penis right off!"

I came up behind Bern too late. As I dove on top of him, a tremendous explosion shook the room. I fell *through* Bern and landed face down on the ground outside. The light and sound from the explosion went on and on, forming rings of golden white and sounds of shattering glass in the darkness. Groaning, I turned over and saw the huge cloud of golden white turn into an impressive aurora borealis. The intense colors swirled, then blended, incredibly in the sky. The cloud of colors grew bigger and bigger. Then, sparkling with beautiful shimmering light, they lifted higher and higher above me. I lay on my back and watched the patterns fade out. When the last polychromes disappeared I opened my eyes.

Josh stood over me. "Thank God," he whispered fiercely. "I thought it had killed you."

"What?"

"It exploded."

"I know. Is Dora all right."

"Bern didn't kill her if that's what you mean. You jumped on him, right? You meant to jump on him?"

Something else preoccupied me. Blood dripping on my arm from a cut on my forehead. "What the—."

"That's the only wound I found on you,"

I stared at the Barnetts' house.

Josh said, "Must be heavy drinkers. Haven't even stirred. But I saw everything through this scope."

"I can't believe you saw me jump on him. Did you capture it with the infrared?"

Josh helped me up. "I tried. Though I couldn't see it well, I figured Bern had a gun. Being a sportsman, I could tell by the curve of his hand. Through the scope I could even see you in the front hall."

I was still groggy. "That sonofabitch was going to shoot Dora and then take himself out. You know, I think I may have stopped him."

"Well, obviously something stopped him. Dora's still alive, right?."

"But didn't the gun go off?"

"No," Josh said, "or I would have seen a burst from the muzzle through the scope. I do know what caused the explosion."

"Yeah. I jumped on him. Then his gun went off and I started coming back to reality. I had myself a bright, colorful trip back."

Josh looked more serious than I had ever seen him. "That's not what happened The *crystal* kind of *detonated*."

"That's impossible!" I shouted. I whispered: "I have it right—."

Josh pointed. "You laid it on the ground over there. Right at the beginning you put it on the ground. Remember?"

"Show me," I whispered through clenched teeth.

Josh helped me over to where he claimed I had put the crystal. He aimed his key chain penlight on the spot on the ground. "See? There's some slivers left. That's all."

I scooped up what was left of my crystal—a few fragments—and put them in the little watch pocket of my jeans. "Help me to the car," I said. "Get me a six pack of Coors and drive me someplace where there's no one around. Find me some goddamned things that I can beat up on. Then leave me alone. I don't want to see one fucking person until tomorrow morning!"

"Maybe you did make a difference. Maybe you saved Dora's life."

I told Josh that as far as I was concerned, *my* life might as well be over. "That crystal was my whole future. It was key to why I came back home to Circleville."

"No, Dude. You came back to help the love of your life."

CHAPTER TWENTY-SIX

My digital watch read 9:30. I was sprawled face-down over a pile of rubber tires near the edge of the city dump. Along with rancid fast food wrappers and empty unwashed cat food cans, halves of rotted cabbage heads odorized the air. *How did I get here?* With my good foot I kicked away an empty, throttled can of Coors. "Hey! Where's the rest of my beers? Peterson!" But Josh was nowhere in sight and yelling hurt my head. "Are you out there?" In the distance I could hear dump trucks chugging and rattling into the dumpsite.

I looked around. I must have made some night of it. My clothes were a stinking mess. Both legs of my jeans were torn. Putrid stains and smudges decorated my once pristine walking cast. "Peterson?" I vainly called out to Josh. "Please come and get me," I wailed. "I don't like it down here."

"You liked it well enough to crash there overnight," Josh said from above me.

"But now I can see it. And smell it. Where've you been?"

Josh came striding toward me down a hill of landfill. He wore olive-green rubber boots. "Waiting for you to get it out of your system. Remember? I followed you around most of the night. Oh you didn't *start* with the rubber tires. You started with the high-tech trash. You threw shredded documents around like confetti. You stomped on dead parts of word processors." He pointed at a dented blue aluminum bat on a pulverized heap of refuse behind me. "It sounded like a bell ringing every time the bat made contact. You smashed up a hefty number of burnt out video boxes. You said you liked hearing them hiss. Then you bashed a bunch of those tires."

"How did I get this crap all over me?

"That happened after you fell down in the residential garbage. Hey. I got some handy wipes and a McDonald's breakfast in the truck for you. Here. Grab my arm. I'll help you up. Look at your down jacket. Pathetic. And your left sneaker! PU!"

"I can't look any worse than I feel. Ow! Not so rough on the leg! Ouch! My head."

Josh said he called my parents from the liquor store the previous night. "I tried to sleep in the truck off and on. It was hard, though, with you down there clobbering and throwing things around all night. And it was cold outside!"

"Oh come on. "Not *all* night."

"You didn't pass out from drinking until six this morning. You crawled back to the rubber tires and made yourself a bed in them. That's when I came down and put the blanket over you."

"You're a pal."

Josh hoisted me up and practically carried me up the hill through land mines of rusted and encrusted tin cans, broken glass, food-rotted

Styrofoam takeout boxes, a couple of dead lamps, and a half-dozen open greenish black garbage bags. I found Josh's haste callous. "I'm hyperventilating," I complained.

"You should try lifting dead weight uphill," Josh replied. "Right now I'm trying to remember why I offered my help." He slid me onto the passenger seat of his truck.

"Take it easy! You're killing me!"

"You know what, Dave?"

After stars stopped whizzing around in my head I said, "What, Josh?" I held my breath.

"You used to be a lot more fun."

I just glowered at him.

"Oh. And I talked to your Mom a while ago. She said she has some news for you when you get home. Someone you haven't seen for a while is coming to town. I'll give you a hint. It ain't Santy Claus. In fact, it isn't even a man."

I figured Jeanie must be on her way there. "That's all I need," I said. I took a sip of coffee. "This is tepid. I hate tepid coffee."

"Yeah? Well, when I bought it half an hour ago it was hot. I've been waiting for you to wake up. And you're welcome for making me sleep in my cold truck all night. What an ingrate! You're lucky I didn't leave you down there for that nice warm bed in your parents' house."

"I am thankful," I said. But I felt compelled to add: "For you I should act like Mary Poppins?"

"Here's the point. While you were throwing trash all over yourself, did you figure out what you're going to do, now that the crystal is gone?" Josh waited. It was the first time I'd seen him so ticked off.

To stall for time I bit into an Egg McMuffin. Ordinarily it would have tasted great. But the English muffin felt rubbery between my teeth and the egg had no flavor whatsoever. I took another swig of tepid coffee. "No. Maybe you should go back to Boulder. I'll stay a few more days with my folks before I fly back."

"I mean it, Dave. Your mind is in worse shape than your leg. You need a new goal. Something to keep you going."

"There *is* something," I answered. "My whole body feels like shit. And I'm not talking about what happened to my leg. Maybe I'll swear off junk food or even become a vegan when I get back to Boulder."

"Right," Josh said. "Can't see that happening."

"It could happen," I said. I tried to curl up against the inside of the truck door to sleep but my stupid right leg wouldn't let me.

Mom was out by Josh's truck before I could climb out. "Are you all right, Honey? We're so sorry about your crystal. Oh. You're a mess. Let me take your equipment bag. I'll cook some sausages and make your favorite blueberry pancakes. Your Dad's taking a shower. Do you need help up the steps?"

I clenched my mother's hand. "Stop doting, Mom. Okay? My head hurts and I feel like raw meat."

Mom looked at Josh. "You told him."

Josh changed the subject. "I saved your crutches from the wrath of a Godzilla sized bulldozer," he said to me. "You left your sticks far, far away." He hustled me to the kitchen and pushed me into the booth behind the kitchen table. "Uh no," he said to Mom. "I didn't exactly tell him." He braced his shoulder against the kitchen doorframe.

I rubbed my eyes. "Whatever it is, could you break it to me gently?"

Mom sat down with me. She held a note in her hand. "Lucille called this morning. She's coming back to town."

I could feel the blood drain from my face ."What?"

"You look like a dried up soda cracker," Josh said to me. "You know. Like E.T. when he was dying in that creek."

Mom kept on: "Lucille's grandmother died a couple days ago. Lu's flying into Columbus from Connecticut today and will take a puddle jumper to Bolton. She sounded like she's taking it hard. I remember how close she was to her grandmother. Your Dad and I would love to pick her up at the airport but—."

"You *know* Jeanie would kill me if I saw Lu. Lu's not just some grieving *friend* to me."

Mom grasped my arm. "Lucille said she'll rent a car and drive down from Bolton field."

I still had a thumping headache. This news landed on me in funky *whirls* of dread and hope. "I feel bad for Lu," I finally said.

Josh plucked at the corner of the door frame. "Yeah. She's only a gorgeous, rich movie star."

"But she's got no close family here. Her mother and sister live in different states out West. Did Lu say if Carla's coming? Or Dora?"

"She did mention they're *not* coming for the funeral," Mom said.

I felt protective of Lu. "She's coming home for the first time in years to bury her closest relative. She'll walk off the plane and go to the gate. No one will be there to meet her. She'll be just little lonely nobody Lu again."

"Davie," Mom said, "if you feel that strongly about it, then just go pick her up at the airport yourself."

"I tell you what!" Josh said. "*I* will gladly make the sacrifice."

"Not in *that* truck. And Court said she is a recluse. This means she avoids strangers, which you are."

"What about sending a limo?" Josh asked. "You have the money."

At first I thought it was a great idea. "Yes. And we can keep it anonymous. Lu won't know I hired it, and that will give me time to sleep and spruce up."

"But Mr. Raymond told her you're here, right?" Mom said. "She'll know you sent the limo. Besides, as I said, she's renting a car."

"She'll want to be independent while she's here," I said. "So if she's glad to see me—."

Josh soon burst the bubble of my imagination. "Are you sure she'll be glad to see you?" Josh asked my mother. "When did she say the funeral is?"

"Tomorrow. Because of the shooting schedule for her next film."

"How awful," Josh said. "She'll probably be awake for the next two days straight, finalizing things."

Lu's being busy hadn't occurred to me. Naturally I figured I'd be the first person she would want to see. For a moment my own selfishness troubled me. "Did she say where she's staying, Mom?"

By the phone at the end of the kitchen counter, my mother found a piece of paper. "Here it is, right here. The Holiday Inn. She'll be in Executive Suite Four. She said she warned all hotel personnel not to tell anyone she's here. Especially the press. But she wanted *us* to know. I've got to tidy up. We might be having famous company."

"If she *is* coming here, don't tell the neighbors."

"Of course we'll need to move your light table out to the garage, David," Mom said.

"Ma! Lu's seen the place a hundred times, just the way it is."

Dad came into the kitchen. He towel dried his hair. "What's going on out here?"

I suddenly realized where I had gotten my lousy sense of timing.

I took a sponge bath and slept until lunchtime. Thank God Mom and Dad had plans to go to a neighborhood barbecue. Thank God Josh was bored enough to go with them. I found Mom's note under a fluorescent green broccoli magnet on the refrigerator.

David Dear,
Chicken salad and deviled eggs in fridge.
Cherry Garcia in frezer.
Eat some carrot sticks too. Be back by 6.
Your loving Mom

Alone at last, I devoured my lunch. With no "Couth Squad" on the premises, I ravaged my meal. No napkin touched my lips. After downing six deviled eggs, two chicken salad sandwiches, two carrot sticks and a scoop of ice cream in fifteen minutes, I checked the Yellow

Pages for florists near the Circleville Holiday Inn. I was still chewing when I ordered a dozen yellow roses from FTD and had them sent to Suite Four. "No name," I said into the phone receiver. "Don't worry. The right person will get them if you deliver them by 5:00 p.m. today. The card? Oh, yeah. Say: 'These yellow roses are *not* for jealousy'. Love from you know who."

I only had a few hours left to develop the latest hologram. I ran— I should say, "hobbled"—around my parents' front room while I gathered the chemicals and trays I needed. I placed them in order on the kitchen countertops by the double sink. Then I took my exposed holographic plate out of its protectives sleeve and went to work. The chemicals had to stay at room temperature. I forgot that I could turn on the stove's ventilator fan, so the fumes got bad toward the end of the process. But I finished around five o'clock and clipped the hologram up to dry.

I went outside to clear my lungs and gave in to a sudden urge to shoot some baskets. With my usual overconfidence, I thought I would easily make my shots. The basketball would drop straight through— no net—and bounce back to me. Like a human pogo stick I chased the ball down the driveway and into the street. I came back up the drive, shot from the corner, and missed. I was already putting my basketball away when I heard the phone ring inside the house. I knew it must be Lu!

The phone rang seven times before I could get to it. "Hell…hellooh?" I panted. "Huh. Huh. Huh. Who? Huh. Huh. Huh. Yes? Lu! I was just out back shooting baskets. No, that's okay. You're in town already? You're calling from your limo. That's great. How did you know? Yeah? Who else could it be? You're welcome. Yes, I do want to see you. Maybe after the funeral? No, I don't have other plans. Hmm. I was just catching my breath. I'm sorry I missed you in Denver too. Yeah. I guess I always *was* in a hurry to leave. Uh, can I come to the viewing? Tomorrow, right? Yes, I remember your grandmother well. You think she would? Which funeral home? Okay. An afternoon service: 1:30 p.m. for family viewing. I'll be there if I can get into my suit pants. I am *not* fat! I broke my leg in the line of duty. That's okay. Not much. Yes. It's a lot better. Really, it won't be a problem. Well, I'm kind of taking a vacation from my day job. Yeah. It feels good. Okay. I'll hear from you tomorrow. Yes. All right. Bye, Lu."

When I hung up the phone I could feel my arm shaking. My knees felt like Silly Putty. My skin smelled chalky and dank. "Lucille Muhr doesn't affect me at all," I lied to myself. "No. I'm cool with seeing her. She's just a girlfriend from long ago." I sat down with a thud. "This doesn't bode well for my date with destiny," I said out loud.

Mom, Dad, Josh, and I sat around most of the evening watching TV. I ate from my own bowl of popcorn. I hoped Lu would call me again. During irksome commercials Mom tended to the loads of laundry we three men had built up. Dad untangled wads of fishing line.

"You're a sportsman," Dad said to Josh. "Ever notice when you put two fishing rods side by side, even a foot apart, and turn your back on them, when you turn back around, the lines are tangled?"

Except for Mom, we all laughed.

"Why is that funny?" Mom asked. She handed each of us a folded pile of laundry. "Because of just that," she said to Dad, "you now have a mess of knotted cat gut in your lap."

"I guess you had to be there," Dad said.

"Thanks, Ma. These clothes smell great." I wiped my buttery fingers on my tee-shirt and felt special glee to think how Jeanie would hate that. I set the empty popcorn bowl below me on the floor.

Together we endured another stream of stupid commercials like the Oscar Meyer hot dog "that keeps going and going, all the way to the end" and astrologer Jeanne Dixon's taped offer to interpret your chart by touchtone phone "at 95 cents a minute." When at last Channel 9 News came on the air I leaned on the heavy pile of clothes in my lap. Suddenly my stomach lurched. "You washed my jeans!" I shouted. "What was left of my crystal was in the little watch pocket!"

Mom looked like she would cry. "But you didn't tell me!" Then, as if this redeemed her, she said, "I mended the pants legs."

Josh clasped my shoulder and sat down with me. "Think of it this way, Dave: Those little slivers washed down the drain and are travelling through the sewer pipes on a journey to——."

"The sewage processing plant!" I felt miserable. "My crystal. What chance have the pieces of surviving there? They'll be pulverized."

"Maybe slivers of crystal *like* being pulverized. You said you are about to reach your destiny."

"My destiny depended on that crystal."

"That's what you *believe*," Josh offered. "Why, it's like Dumbo and the feather."

I felt my blood begin to simmer. "What the hell does Dumbo have to do with my dead crystal?"

"Remember? Dumbo thought the feather was magic. That he could only fly when he held his feather by the tip of his little trunk. Waiting high up on that platform in the circus, he held that feather and got ready to flap his ears."

I sniffed.

"...but then he accidentally dropped the feather! It floated down in slow-motion, out of his reach."

I told Josh I had gotten the point.

"Yes," Mom said. "And though Dumbo was scared, he still jumped off the platform. That's when he knew he could fly without the feather. His ears were so big!"

Mom had been completely earnest. Dad and Josh were laughing behind their hands.

"Knock it off, you guys," I whined. "The point is, I've lost key proof of——."

"I know, Dude," Josh said.

Dad looked up from his tangled fishing line. "It's gone, Son. You'll just have to accept it."

I checked my watch. Lu hadn't called. "I'm not very good at 'accepting'," I said. "I'm going upstairs to sleep in my own bed. Hope you don't mind the couch, Josh. Could you wake me up before you head back to Boulder tomorrow morning?"

Lu put her arms around me, caressed me, and pulled me down on the bed. Like a kitten she snoozled my neck. She lay on top of me and held me tight. It was more of a deep maternal embrace, as though I were her child, whom she adored. It was like she was filled with such absolute love that it was painful for her not to be this close to me. In laying her body against mine, she released all the feeling she had stored up for so long. Released it in the most endearing, most fulsome and non-erotic way. She fluffed up my hair. She kissed my forehead, my eyes, my chin, the palms of my hands. She then pressed my hands together and caressed them. She turned us over on our sides, put her arm across my collarbone, and fell asleep.

Sad to say, I woke from my dream. I closed my eyes again, hoping I could hold on to it. Though I fought to return to the dream, I was now fully awake. I ached everywhere, but this pain was not in my body. It was in the spaces between my cells, in my nerve synapses, the air in my lungs, the bioelectricity of my thoughts and feelings. These were sensations of my spirit. Expansive, so fragrant that they were beyond endurance. I was afraid if I didn't get up and move around now I might leave my body and never come back.

Because of my sore leg it was hard to get down the stairs without making noise. I carried the developed hologram in its protective sleeve under my arm. I continued through the tight hall outside the only bathroom in the house and came to the living room. Josh was asleep on the couch. I made it to the front room and was relieved to see my light table. The lasers, mirrors, and lenses were positioned exactly the way I left them. I set up the hologram display apparatus and held my breath. This had been a one-shot deal. I was about to see if Josh's instincts had come through for me. "He is a capable and loyal friend," the Elemental had said. My chest tightened because I knew I would never see the Elemental again. I had destroyed her "home." But a quiet voice inside me said, "She has given you this hologram." I turned on the reconstruction beam. As if in slow motion my transmission hologram took form. Mom had been right. I looked like one of God's angels. Lu looked like the Queen of Heaven. We stood in profile, eyes connected with beams of light, lips slightly parted, inches from a kiss. In real life we could never glow with this much radiance. Large ovals of pure white light expanded from our bodies and extended our fingers. In the Elemental's crystal we had met as if in Paradise.

"It's magnificent," Josh whispered.

I whipped my head around.

"I heard you on the stairs," he said.

"Look at us! It's like in the dream of Lu that woke me. It's like the way God must look at us. It says so in the Bible. With pure love."

"Yeah," Josh answered. "That *is* how He would look."

The hologram was riveting. I asked Josh to go to the fridge and see if there was any beer. My laser hummed in the background.

Josh didn't even mention how early in the day it was. He quietly cracked a Coors tab for me. "Here you go," he said. "That hologram looks supernatural. I don't mean you look like you're ghosts. It's more like in 'Star Wars'. Like when Obi Wan Kenobi appears to Luke after Obi Wan has joined the other dead Jedi knights."

"Josh, thank you for giving this to me."

"Giving it to you?"

"For taking the hologram. This means I can prove my experiment worked, even without the crystal."

"Are you sure you want the public to see something this personal?"

"And Jeanie?" I *took in* the holographic miracle. "But how can I shut this away? I honestly don't care about the scientific part anymore. I only care about sharing what made this creation possible." I liked using the word "creation" to describe my hologram. The hologram was clearly a gift from loving entities. To Josh I said, "You, the

Elemental, Lu, and I rendered this." I closed my eyes. "I'm dead on my feet but I can't stop looking at it. Our hologram seems to have a life of its own."

"It sure does, Michelangelo," Josh said.

I bumped down the back steps to see Josh off. He leaned against his rented 4X4 like he was just going down to the local convenience store. He handed me my camera. The exposed infrared film was still loaded from the other night. He said: "I found this with my stuff when I was packing. If these pictures turn out, they'll just be icing on the cake. They'll make you famous for sure."

"Even if they do turn out great, how will I prove it shows the Muhrs and not the Barnetts?"

"I'm your witness."

"And then what?"

"Then we'll try the same routine, say, in the Hotel Boulderado. Remember the story about the rocking chair that moves by itself? And the lady in yellow who appears on the mezzanine by the rail?"

I reminded Josh that I'm the one who told him those stories.

"Well, think of the *traces* that must be floating around in that place!"

"And me without my crystal," I said.

CHAPTER TWENTY-SEVEN

Dad dropped me off at the entrance of Wellman Mortuary, just inside the front gate of Forest Cemetery. "Call me if you need a ride," he said. "And tell that pretty Lucille we'd love to see her if she has time."

The air had that damp, bone chilling, fifty humid degrees in Ohio. Used to the high-altitude passive solar effect of March in Colorado, I shivered in the dress wool overcoat I had bought for Lillian Muhr's funeral. I should have added a wool neck scarf. Like a foolish boy I had waited all morning for Lu to call. Maybe she hadn't called me the previous night either because she chickened out—or maybe she was just too busy. A hundred times during the night, and all morning, I had rehearsed my pending reunion with Lu. Some of those scenarios were painful. Others were provocative episodes in which my comforting arms aroused in her an abandon of sexual desire. Every time I ran another version through my mind I felt guilty for picturing only my gratification, not her grief. Finally I decided to swear off guilt. I felt so burned out that I gave it all up. I finally told myself Lu had a lot more to handle than seeing *me* again. I lurched up the steps and entered the mortuary. The reception area was shallow from back to front. However to the left it formed a long rectangle with a doorway to a make-shift viewing room. That's where relatives and others bereaved of the departed could see their dearly departed.

Lu stood in profile just a few people up the line from me. I couldn't recall her looking so *slight*. Though she was almost five feet six inches tall, her delicate structure created an illusion of her being more petite.

In the gauzy fluorescent light I blinked until I could see her face better. Unlike me, Lu had barely aged. Her hair was still the same lus-trous dark auburn with no apparent gray. Her face was a bit fuller, and I could see tiny hints of laugh lines. Except for little streaks of mascara from her crying, Lu looked as glamorous as she did in "Journeys Home." She had filled out. She was still trim but more rounded in the hips. Her loveliness had remained soft. I almost broke down.

Lu talked to a decrepit old lady, who said: "Lillian was my oldest friend." Then the woman sobbed. While Lu embraced the lady she looked right at me like she had seen me as soon as I came in. She turned back to the aged matron, said a few more words to her, and handed her off to an usher. Several other people stopped to talk to Lu before she could break away. Among them was a Rev. Henderson. "I remember you from Nana's church," Lu said.

"Yes," the kindly pastor said. "Trinity Lutheran."

I stayed just inside the entrance. Like everyone else I couldn't take my eyes off Lu. In the past I had seen how her poise and beauty turned heads when we walked downtown or went out dancing. It was obvious these visitors had seen her on the big screen. Her presence was larger than life. I was surprised I felt no discomfort. I couldn't wait to hold Lu's hand. Renewing our "friendship" would not be enough for me.

Finally Lu came up to me and grasped my hand. "At last." She looked deeply into my eyes—pierced through all the barriers I had built against her power over me. "Thank you for the lovely roses," she said. "I'm touched that you remembered they're my favorite."

"Of course," I said.

An elderly lady across the room held up her white gloved hand to get Lu's attention, and Lu acknowledged her with a nod. "I'm sorry I didn't call you yesterday, David. Nana made her own funeral arrangements years ago. That's so like her. But there were still a lot of details to take care of in Columbus. I had to see her attorney, go to her house, talk to her nurse and her housekeeper. As it turned out, I got here late and——. But I'm so glad to see you."

"How are you holding up?"

Lu looked down for the first time. "It's hard to tell. I swing back and forth between my business head and feeling deep sadness. I'm going along thinking I'm doing okay." She peered into the interior of the funeral parlor, where her grandmother lay in an open mahogany casket. "I don't know why Nana's people needed this barbaric ritual of lying in state. I only remember *Nana's* mother the way she looked in her casket. I don't want to remember Nana the way she looks in her casket." Tears welled up in Lu's eyes. "Her mouth. It's frowning. Her hands don't even look human. I wonder how much pain she suffered in the end. It breaks my heart."

"You'll be fine," I said, because *I* was so pained by Lu's grief.

"Of *course* you would know that," Lu said.

"You've always been resilient. Once you told me that's the way your Nana was at funerals."

"That's right," Lu whispered. "I used to judge Nana for behaving like a socialite at funerals. Always flitting about, greeting people with smiles, and showing people to their seats. Today I found myself doing the same thing! It's because I want everyone to feel comfortable. It's because I'm so grateful they came to pay their respects. I hope maybe they see something in me that reminds them of Nana. Then it won't hurt them so much that she's gone."

I stared shamelessly at Lu. "You also told me that when your Nana died you would lose your whole world."

"Yes," Lu said, "but you want to know something? Because you're here I feel happy, not sad. At least the way we are right now makes me happy. I feel a little guilty about that."

The organist began to play the intro to "Fairest Lord Jesus."

"Nana loved this hymn," Lu said. "Time to take our seats." She took my arm and we walked together to the front pew. She asked me to sit with her.

"People might think that's weird," I said.

"Well, then sit behind me."

I smiled inside, remembering how easily Lu took command. She never meant such statements to come out like orders. She was just definite about everything she did or said. Because she trusted her own values, she rarely hesitated when she made decisions. And because she had such good instincts, she reacted flawlessly to every situation. First and foremost I felt deep respect for Lucille Muhr.

A middle-aged soprano in a slick blue choir robe with a gold hood parked herself at the end of Lillian Muhr's coffin. She began to sing "Fairest Lord Jesus."

While I listened to the beautiful melody of this hymn I thought about the reality of the senior Mrs. Muhr's death—and of the life that preceded it. I made myself look at Nana's face. Lu's grandmother did not look like a ninety year old woman. Her face was smooth, almost without wrinkles, except for her deep, crisscrossed laugh lines. I remember Lu once quoting Nana saying: "In youth, beauty is a gift from God. In old age, beauty comes from within." Lu turned around to study me. I marveled at her gleaming hair, her smooth face. I knew she would age as gracefully as her Nana had.

The soloist sang:

Fair is the sunshine

Fairer still the moonlight
And all the twinkling starry host."

I felt unmoved that Jesus shines brighter and purer "than all the angels heaven can boast." I was sitting behind the love of my life, feeling the force of her presence, smelling her light floral cologne, and recalling she hadn't once looked down at my walking cast. Knowing Lu missed *nothing*, I got that she meant to spare me from humiliation.

When my limo pulled up near Lillian Muhr's gravesite I thought my own intense emotions would thwart my being Lu's White Knight in her time of need. My concern for Lu merged with passionate expectation. I also felt a bleak foreboding about losing my crystal and the Elemental. I was proud Lu showed she welcomed seeing me. I also regretted that I didn't reveal how much I wanted her. To be discreet I had ridden in the third limo behind Lu's. When Lu's limo stopped I jumped out so fast to help her that I almost fell down. She clung to my arm and we literally supported each other all the way over to Nana's gravesite. Into the headstone I had seen only a week before were now freshly cut the words: "Died March 30, 1988."

By the time the Rev. Henderson read the part about "dust to dust," Lu was slouching from the pressure of her repressed grief. Her hands formed fists at her sides. Her face contorted with grief. I'd seen it in Mom's face at *Großmutti's* funeral. It was like her face muscles pulled down while her *will* tried to push them back up. Lu's visage showed this battle. It was like clay setting. In the bright sunshine the dark amber lenses of her sunglasses hid her eyes, even from me.

At the end of the graveside service Lu added a single red rose to the huge blanket of roses on her Nana's casket. I had to keep Lu from collapsing from grief when the grave diggers began to lower her Nana's casket into the earth. We turned away from Nana's grave. We walked to the winding cemetery drive where the limos waited. It wasn't easy—walking while also trying to hold Lu up.

Lu surveyed her grandmother's gravesite. "When I think of Nana," she said, "I still feel like I'm a child. She has always been, and always will be, my Nana. Last night when I was so tired I just soaked in a hot bath. Suddenly I realized I was crying. The way children cry when they're hurting deep inside. No noise. Just streams of water shooting out from their eyes. You know, David? Some of my grief is for *us*."

I put my arm around her waist. "Us?" *That was stupid*, I thought.

Lu caressed my hand. "We were too young and too proud to talk things over instead of breaking up."

I ached when her fingers brushed mine. "*You* broke up with *me*."

"Because I knew I would keep making you unhappy if we stayed together. But Davie I feel I could make you happy now. Because of how much I've changed. Knowing this makes it harder to live without you. On your birthday and Christmas every year I imagine what I would buy you if we were together. An exquisite silk tie from Bergdorf Goodman. A dress shirt from Armani Emporium."

I hadn't imagined buying gifts for Lu. Like a slug I crawled away from what Lu just said, leaving a slimy residue. I couldn't think of a noble transition so I said, "You might not like how *I* have changed."

Lu did not hide her disappointment.

I persisted: "Until today I've felt like some New Age Walter Mitty, muffing every challenge but moving forward anyway."

"A new age Walter Mitty?"

"Well, sort of. Are you headed to your hotel now? Do you have to go back to New York tomorrow?"

Lu must have known I changed the subject on purpose. She paused before climbing into her limo. She rolled down her window. "Yes. Sadly I start production on my new film. But I hope you'll come to the hotel later." She peered at me through oversized amber sunglasses. "I feel myself sliding. I'm not doing well. Maybe it's a delayed reaction."

"Why don't you go back and freshen up? I'll take the limo back to the funeral home and call Dad to pick me up. I'll meet you at the Holiday Inn in about an hour. Dad will bring me by. I'll have them ring you from the front desk when I get to your hotel. I don't know about you, but I could use a drink. There's a lounge there, right? That way, if you get too tired you won't be far from your room."

Lucille looked past me, out the window. "There is a lounge. But I rarely drink. And only wine and occasional champagne. What about you? I remember you love beer."

"You're right. I don't usually drink hard liquor. But this might be one of those times. I'd love to take you out to dinner if you feel up to it. There's a little Italian restaurant near your hotel where we can talk."

"That would be a blessing," Lu said. She reached out the open limousine window and took my hand. "Thank you for being here for me."

The limo driver started up the vehicle.

"I'm sorry I'm such a mess," Lu said.

I looked into her boundless eyes. " I *am* here for you," I said.

"I am David Leone," I announced at the Holiday Inn reception desk. "Could you ring Suite Four?"

"You're to take the private elevator up to the fourth level," the clerk answered. "With the bell captain."

The elevator ride was smooth as hot-waxed skis on a Bunny slope. The bell captain ushered me to what I thought was going to be Lu's suite. Instead he opened the door of a secluded lounge at the other end of the hall. In the lounge there was a bar, a bartender, and a black Yamaha baby grand piano being played by a young male in a tuxedo. He looked Italian. He was in the middle of his number: theme from "The Godfather." Three tables were set for two. On each was a crystal vase in which stood a single long stemmed yellow rose.

The bartender looked suspicious. Like maybe I shouldn't be there.

"What do you advise for a guy not used to drinking hard liquor?"

"Depends on the occasion," he said. He looked Italian too.

"A rendezvous with my hometown sweetheart, whom I haven't seen in twenty-one years."

"A Tequila Sunrise," the bartender said. He inspected my clothing.

"—who's a very famous and beautiful actress."

"Ah," the bartender said. "Cognac."

"—whose favorite relative's funeral was today."

"Champagne," he said.

"You're kidding."

"May I ask your name, sir?"

"David Leone."

"Leóne. All right!"

"I am half-Italian and *she's* a WASP," I said.

The bartender smoothed back his thick wavy hair with the palms of his hands. "I am Gio. This filly has class. Gets us up here in no-time-flat. Pays us big bucks to stick those roses in vases and hires my cousin Nicky to play the piano. Yo, Nicky! Anyway you must be some special guy for a movie star to do all this for you." Gio's wide gesture took in the entire room. "Okay. Whatta you drink most of the time?"

"Coors. Exclusively," I answered. I felt like a medieval peasant.

"That will not do for this night," Gio said. "Nicky! Play 'Da God-fatha' again, will ya?" To me Gio said: "It is a good idea for you to be primed before she gets here. With a lady like that, you want to be cool. Do *not* take off your coat and tie!"

My tie choked me and my shoes pinched.

"Why do you think we have three tables set?" A rhetorical question.

"So you can choose which one you want," Lu said from the door of the lounge. She had changed to a soft black pleated skirt and white blouse with gold buttons.

"Let's take this one in the corner," I said. I tried not to stare at Lu but I did admire her blouse. In this light, its semi-transparency made up for the restrained rest of her outfit.

The bartender served us champagne and left the bottle in an ice bucket on a stand next to our table.

"Grazie," I said.

The bartender smiled. Leaving us he said, *"Prego, Signore Leóne."*

Lu lifted her champagne glass. "*Salute*," she said in Italian.

"*Alla vita*," I responded.

Just where our champagne glasses touched I thought I saw a burst of light. I jounced it off when Lu seemed not to notice. Then I asked her if she was hungry. "We can send for something," I said.

"Not yet," Lu said. She drained her first flute of champagne. "You know how it feels to be dead on your feet and still be unable to sleep?"

I refilled Lu's glass. "I've heard it's like that when you go overseas."

"You've never been abroad? You would love it," Lu said. "Just listen to me. I sound like those people I can't stand to be around."

I couldn't tell if she was stroking her glass suggestively or nervously. "Your cologne—. What did you used to wear?"

"Desert Flower. But now I find it cloying. You: English Leather."

"True," I said. "What are you wearing now?"

Lu held my hand. "Creed Fleurissimo. Grace Kelly's favorite."

"Yes. It would be. I can't quite describe it."

She held my gaze and murmured, "…notes of bergamot, tuberose, Florentine iris, and Bulgarian rose. But you're not wearing cologne."

Truth is, there was no reason to pack my spicy Calvin Klein "Obsession" men's cologne. Jeanie had given it to me on our anniversary in 1980. Some of its "notes" could grace a cappuccino. Nutmeg & clove. I hated the cologne and was glad its shelf life had expired. I figured Lu would have hated "Obsession" too.

"I don't suppose there's a way to make this easier," Lu finally said. "Aren't you drinking?" She hadn't noticed that I was on my second glass of champagne too.

"We could just forget about all the years and talk to each other the way we used to. You know. Pretend we're out on a college date."

Nicky magically heard us from across the room and began to play the love song from "Romeo and Juliet."

Gio brought over a tray of *antipasti* and a tray of *hors d'oeuvre*. "So. How's it going you two?" To Lu he said, "May I presume to tell you,

Signorina Muhr, that I am your *numero uno* fan? I know I'm not s'posed to bug you, so just whistle if you need something, okay?"

"She *can*, too!" I said.

Gio's eyes widened. "Whistle? Go on. Through your fingers?"

"I can!" Lu said. She demonstrated by emitting a shrill, ear popping whistle, using her thumb and middle finger. "That's how I hail cabs in New York, though I don't let cabbies see me doing it. My image you know." Clearly she enjoyed shocking Gio.

Gio waited by our table. "Do tell. You are a lady of many talents."

Lu's eyes held mine for the extra second it took to convey impatience. When I didn't get *why* right away, she leaned forward and intensified her stare.

I dismissed the nosy bartender. "Thank you, Gio."

This time Gio did not say "Prego." Instead he parked himself back at his station behind the bar and avoided eye contact.

Lu touched my arm. "Do you mind if I ask what happened? I mean, to your leg?"

"Kind of hard to miss, huh?"

Lu blushed. "I didn't want you to embarrass you."

"And I thank you. Maybe after more champagne my story about breaking my leg will sound more believable." I stifled a burp. "It's like this. I was up in the fir tree in your old back yard looking through my night vision scope. It was night, of course, and I actually fell out of the big maple tree and broke my leg."

Lu lifted one eyebrow. In that one expression I could read paragraphs. Without looking at Gio Lu asked him for more champagne.

"Lu, please slow down so I can keep up with you."

"You are referring to the champagne?"

"Here, Lu. Have an *hors…hors…d'oeuvre.* Anyway I'm paying the Barnetts, the family who lives there, to let me work in your bedroom."

Lu looked surprised but said nothing.

"I haven't tried the living room yet." I forgot to explain why I was in Lu's bedroom. "That's the only room Mrs. B.—Mrs. Barnett—let me use. Court told you all about my work. Right?"

Lu smiled. "That's okay. I'm not used to drinking so much champagne either. Court is wonderful by the way. He did tell me *some* things about your work. It sounds complex. I don't think I understand it well. But Court also spoke of your, um, *growth*."

I was floored. "You mean as in 'growing up'?"

Lu's stolid look flattened me.

Nevertheless I deflected. "Say. Aren't you curious about your old house and the Barnetts?"

"Actually I'm curious about how you think of my films," she said.

I must have looked stricken because Lu looked down at the tabletop. But when her eyes met mine again I saw angry sparks sizzle briefly in them. She did not look away this time, so I got that she would only accept the truth. "My wife won't let me," I said.

Now Lu showed abject disappointment. "Your *wife*," she drawled. Then she shook off her visible pique and said: "I hope to stop by my old home in the morning. Before I head for Columbus International."

I felt like I was stewing in a steam bath from Lu's incinerating gaze. I loosened my tie and waited for Gio to object. He didn't. "Maybe you shouldn't see your old house," I said. "It might be better to remember it the way your grandparents left it."

"But it wasn't the way my grandparents left it when *we* lived there!" Lu said. "Honestly, why do people treat me like I'm so breakable? If I were, I wouldn't have survived my childhood. Now you're doing it too. I'd rather we get totally smashed and forget about anyone or any thing outside this lounge."

"Right-o!" Nicky chirped as he began to sing and play "Volare."

I blinked at Lu in the artificial glow of the track light above our table. "I'm trying. This ain't a piece of cake for me either. As beautiful as you look and as alone as we are here together, I still feel the terrible gulf of the past decades since I last saw you."

Lu covered my wedding band with both hands. "I do see you have grown up *some*, David."

"Oh," I answered. "I thought I was just being somber."

Lu saw me stare at the antique sapphire ring on her right hand. Old fashioned mine cut diamonds surrounded the oval uncut sapphire. I had seen the ring before. After Lu graduated from high school. It was a gift from her beloved Nana.

"I assume you know I never married," she said.

"Yes, but why not?"

Gio appeared as if by magic and left as quickly when Lu told him we'd had enough champagne. "*Molto bene*," he said. His words trailed off into the distance.

Then Lu blurted: "I don't know if I'm still in love with you or if I'm just in love with the way you felt about me."

Heat engulfed my body again. "Have you changed so much that I wouldn't love you now?"

"Excuse me?"

"I'm sorry," I said. "I didn't mean it to come out that way."

"I'd better eat something." Lu briefly covered her mouth. "I really didn't hear you."

I repeated my question while helping myself to three *hors d'oeuvre*. I thanked God these had some kind of meat on them.

Lu looked surprised at my question. "Well, yes and no. I am basically the person you knew, but I think I'm more evolved. Do you know what I mean? The way I imagine you change when you reach a new level in your work."

"Yes! Exactly." I stripped off my tie and unbuttoned my top two shirt buttons.

Lu encouraged me to take off my coat.

"You don't mind? Great!" I stood up to remove my coat and draped it around the back of my chair. When I sat down again I saw Lu staring at my chest. "Oh, yeah. I finally did get hair on my chest."

Lu blushed again. "I noticed when I was looking at the medallion."

"I wear it for luck and I see you finally did develop bigger—." Every capillary in my face must have opened. "I mean, you look beautiful all over. *Not* that you weren't beautiful before, but—."

"You are the only man I would thank for saying that," Lu said. "They just sort of happened later, along with my hips. When you and I were together I was pretty thin. At home I never had enough to eat. School lunch was my best meal of the day. Only our senior year I was taking theater as an elective. Theater class was held during my lunch hour that semester and so I didn't get to eat lunch."

I remembered being shocked when Lu walked down the stairs of the old Muhr house in her golden yellow gown on the night of Senior Prom. Of course he looked beautiful but she was also emaciated. Even in the photograph of us published in the newspaper, the camera had not added the customary five pounds of weight. I cleared my throat of excess emotion and asked Lu if she wanted more champagne.

Lu was deep in thought. "Not just yet," she finally said. "David? You didn't finish telling how you broke your leg."

I stopped drinking. I didn't want to get so drunk that I couldn't track what was going on between us. "May I ask you something? Did that big fir tree in your back yard ever catch on fire?"

Lu's eyes widened.

"I guess that was a stupid question. If it *had* caught on fire I would have seen scarring. You know: damage to the tree."

"What did you see? How did you—?

"I have this…I *had* this crystal that helped me detect things that human eyes can't see." I believed Lu would think I was bats and end our rendezvous. But she stayed, looking interested and serious. "Then I went into kind of a meditation and I saw things in that house. That's what I was doing up in the tree." Almost unconsciously I moved my chair so it touched hers. "I was trying to see you in your bedroom. And I had to go there at night to try to record that on infrared film.'"

Lu's expression now landed between confusion and fear.

Gio brought me a coke and offered Lu coffee.

I told Lu that Gio and Nicky didn't think I was Italian enough. "But if they knew what is going on inside me they would be proud."

"*I* am proud that you're Italian," Lu said.

"You are?"

There was a sheen on Lu's upturned face like that of a young girl tilting her face up to the hot sun. "A couple of my actress friends brag about their Italian lovers and their self-avowed amorous skills. What they stereotype as 'lips and hips'." She laughed. Then she looked longingly at my mouth. "What I can personally vouch for are Italian lips." Then she leaned so close to me that I could feel her breast on my arm.

"Yeah!" Gio affirmed. "Lips and hips." Thereupon he gyrated his stocky pelvis.

I felt miffed. "Really, Gio?"

Gio frowned. Nicky the piano player flicked his bushy black eyebrows and started playing the introduction to "Al di là."

La la la la la

La la la la la

"Rome Adventure," I said. "With Suzanne Pleshette."

La la la la la

Lu pretended to swoon and said, "Mmm. Troy Donahue." Mischief jived in her eyes.

Non credevo possibile, se potessero dire queste parole.

"I didn't believe it was possible these words could be said," I translated as I pulled Lu up, into a slow dance embrace. We held each other and barely moved to the music.

"Yes. Beyond," Lu said.

I couldn't help myself. I kissed Lu and I kept kissing her. And boy did she kiss me back! I felt the old fire whipping up from my thighs and into my chest. The heart palpitations of a young man in love. We prolonged our kiss for rapturous minutes.

Al di là means you are
far above me, very far.

....

You're my life,

you're my love,

you're my own. Al di là

I felt pressure on the back of my neck. I became Lu's leading man in a movie. We kissed deeply. *People in the audience ate popcorn and watched us with greasy voyeurism.*

La la la la la

La la la la la

La la la la

Al di là

Under the grubby gaze of Gio and Nicky, Lu whispered close to my ear: "Come back to my suite with me."

I grabbed our half-empty champagne bottle and glasses. "You don't know how many times I dreamed of this. I've never felt more Italian than I do right now."

Lu smiled. "David Leone," she responded. "*My* lion. *Mine.*"

"*Buonanotte, fortunato Signor Leóne,*" Gio said with a scrap of mockery. To Lu he said, "*Buononotte, Donna Meravigliosa.*" Then he clasped his hands over his heart.

Lu smiled and said, "*Ringraziamenti speciali,* Gio. Ciao."

In that moment I knew that Lu was much more proficient in Italian than I was. My ego crawled into a corner behind the Yamaha piano.

Nicky broke into a new chorus of *Al di là.* We decamped from the lounge and the pristine hallway met us. We both stumbled a little during our approach to Lu's suite. Especially me. She gave me her keycard.

I tried to sound confident when I said, "Allow me." But I didn't feel suave. I wanted to be the Casanova of lips and hips when saying "Allow me." The truth was that seeing the inside of Lu's awesome suite disarmed me. "I didn't know there were rooms like this at the Holiday Inn," I said. I poured champagne for us and we interlinked arms to drink like lovers in a 1950s film noir.

Lucille dabbed her mouth once with a tissue. "I still dream about you. The dreams intensified about five years ago. At first, in the dreams, you were supposed to meet me somewhere. And I'd go there but you wouldn't show up. I would wake up crying in frustration. Then in one dream I caught a glimpse of you standing in the exit by some grandstand in a football stadium. You were wearing a sky blue cap. Then you disappeared."

"I don't own a sky blue cap," I said. *Why couldn't I have said something more scintillating?*

Lu sipped more champagne. "In another dream I waited for you again. Just when I was about to give up I saw you in the open back of a station wagon that was driving away. You were with some friends. You laughed at me. In the dream I sat down and sobbed in my hands."

I took Lu's half-full champagne glass from her hand. "Didn't I ever come to you like this in your dreams? Didn't I ever take you in my arms like this and——."

Lu broke from my arms. "I don't care about your wife. I mean, I care that you're married to her, not me. And I even liked her when I met her at Court's mansion. But my time with you is borrowed and I don't feel one bit of it should belong to *her*."

"Where did that come from?" I held my arms open again and she walked into them.

"I don't need comforting. I've done without yours all these years."

"You broke up with *me*, Lu."

Lu pressed her face into my unbuttoned shirt. "I told you why. I remember what I said: 'We fight all the time. Maybe we both want to break up but neither of us has the guts to say it.' And you agreed. So I raised my courage and said, 'Okay, then. *I'll* say it: Maybe we should break up.' After you left I paced back and forth in my bedroom like a crazed animal, crying over and over: 'I hurt! I hurt.' I even threw things against the wall. But nothing broke."

We held each other. She leaned into me and caressed my neck.

I softened my voice. "I don't recall it that way. I was in an identity crisis. I couldn't express my feelings. Maybe all you saw was that I always acted like a wimp. Maybe you stopped respecting me because of that. And here I am now, a newer living version of self-doubt."

"I just thought you were miserable with me."

I turned her face up and kissed her. "I was miserable with *me*."

Then Lu unbuttoned her blouse and kissed me again with an urgent strain of her lips and body. She held my face with both hands. "But only a few months after the last time I saw you," she said, "I heard you got married. I couldn't believe you did that so fast. With someone you couldn't have known very long."

I didn't tell Lu that I was already dating Jeanie—mostly just for sex—when Lu broke up with me. I unbuttoned the rest of Lu's blouse and pulled my shirt open all the way down. "And you thought I married Jeanie on the rebound," I said, feeling like a rat. *Tell the truth. Then hedge a bit*, I thought.

Lu kissed the hollow of my neck. "I thought you were crazy not to talk to me about it first. To ask me if I still cared enough about you to stop you."

I had my hands behind her, trying to undo her brassiere. I wanted to share that I had to marry Jeanie but I was afraid it would ruin what was about to happen. I was being a cad but I didn't care. "And did you still have feelings for me then?"

She held me by the small of my back and pressed harder against me. "*I* never married. *I* have lived alone all these years. After you, I could never fall in love with another man. Because I don't trust easily, but you earned my trust."

I peeled myself off her. "But surely you could have found somebody else."

She tried to get back her cool by moving away from me.

"Don't," I begged. I went to her again and held her. "Feel me," I continued. "Feel what you still do to me. I dream about you. I make love to you in my fantasies. My work is filled with you. I'm here in Circleville *because* of you. Lu, please don't turn off to me. I've never been closer to my real feelings about you than I am right now."

Lu looked up at me with those huge doe-like eyes. "You still love me. I have felt it all these years. I knew that what we had could never fade away, no matter where you or I lived. Or who we shared our lives with. Kiss me again, will you? Kiss the breath out of me!"

I kissed Lu like an Olympian. Exhausted, she still matched my passion. We moved as one, into the bedroom and stood beside her bed. The pink satin sheets that she had turned back so neatly promised I would soon be wrapped in a lovely ardor that made her body arch toward me. We were both bare to the waist. I unbuttoned her skirt. It slid down her hips to the floor. Then Lu helped me remove her slip and stockings. I took off my socks and she helped me with my pants.

Lu lay back on the bed, tugging me forward and on top of her. She didn't even seem to notice the cast on my leg. Anyway, I had artfully positioned my leg so the cast wouldn't distract us. She eagerly moved her hips in a way that I hadn't imagined a woman could do. She was so strong! The fact that we still had on our underwear made it even more exciting, for I could feel myself enlarge as I pressed against the front of her panties. I could feel that she was already wet with pleasure. It was something like those many nights at the drive-in movies, except that then we had held back because we feared she'd get pregnant. Now we held back because it had been so long. Neither of us wanted to rush our lovemaking. To have it end.

We kissed deeply now, as if we needed to literally drink each other in. Drenched in moisture, we pushed harder. Lu slid the sheet off my back and we moved together, totally uncovered, until I could no longer bear *not* to be naked. "I have never wanted anyone so much in my life."

"I have never wanted anyone but you my whole life," Lu said.

"May I come inside you?"

"Oh yes, Davie!"

The phone sounded like Big Ben.

"No," Lu groaned. "Ignore it!"

The phone rang and rang. The part of me that had been a virtual lightning rod started to fizzle like a burnt out sparkler on the fourth of

July. The jangling had reminded me of Catholic school. I felt myself continue to shrivel. "I'm sorry, Lu. Maybe after you answer the phone we can unplug it."

"But I told them not to bother us," Lu said. She started to cry. "Don't answer it," she said.

The phone's knell persisted. Finally Lu answered it. "Yes. He's here. Just a minute." She thrust the receiver toward me. "It's your mother. How did she know you were here?"

I told Lu it must be important. "Hello?" I felt like a flounder gasping for air in the bottom of a fishing boat. "Mom! What's wrong. An emergency? You can yell at me later."

As if my mother had just walked into the room, Lu wrapped the pink satin sheet around herself.

"I *am* sitting down. What is it, Ma? Is it Jeanie? Eddie? Reynie's been what?! My God! Court wants me back right away? Is Court still in Texas? He's at the mansion. There'll be a private jet waiting for me at Bolton Field. It'll be a long flight from here, even on a private jet. Of *course* I understand why he's so desperate. But I don't see how *I* can help. Okay. I'll get to Bolton as soon as I can." I hung up and told Lu that Reynie Raymond LaSalle had been kidnapped.

"Oh no."

"And she's pregnant. *Well* along. Court wants me to find the crooks but I don't have my crystal anymore. How the hell am I gonna help Reynie without it?" By this time my recent thrilling potency had 'shuffled off its mortal coil'. Given the news about Reynie, and given the painful interruption with Lu, I feared God would undermine my sex life until the end of time. I hadn't felt this much self-reproach since Lu and I parted those long years before. I stroked Lu's cheek. "I'm sorry, Lu. Mom says you can call them anytime. You know they still love you. And I know you still love them."

Dejected, Lu plucked at the pink sheets. "I know you must help."

In my past with Lu I had never been a grownup. Nor had I felt an adult man's passion for this woman. Now I had to deal with going back to Boulder, back to my wife. This deep emotion still bound my body as I sat at the edge of Lu's hotel suite bed. I asked myself what difference another hour would make. I might book it back to Colorado and then fail to help Reynie. Totally let Court down. Spend futile months and years without my crystal.

I unclasped Lu's pendant from around my neck and slipped it into her hand. "I want you to keep this because I'm the one who sent it to you. And because it belongs to you."

"Not very romantic that you merely handed this back to me," Lu said. But she wrapped her arms around my neck. "You'd better go now. You still have to pack. Please give your parents my love." She looked at me with the same angelic, unadulterated, all-accepting, satisfying love that I saw in that hologram I had so recently developed. "I love you more fiercely every year that goes by."

"I still love you too, Lucille Muhr. If things were different—."

"That 'if' is as big as forever."

I slid my rumpled dress shirt on. "Why didn't we just keep talking about it that day? Just keep hashing it out until we could let go of the bad parts of our relationship?"

"Because we were young and foolish," Lu said. She looked away while I pushed my right pant leg into my pants. Then she dressed in brand new jeans and a white cable-knit sweater. "Before you go," she said, "I want to tell you something about the fire you saw in the pine tree. It didn't happen in real life. It happened in a dream."

"I saw it! The infrared picked up the heat from the fire. Your dream *was* still alive. It was as real as we are now. But I also saw other things in your house. Unspeakable things. Your father—."

"—was a very sick and unhappy man," Lu said. "Over the years, and in therapy, I've worked it out. First I was enraged, then sad. Then I forgave him. Pretty much."

"It's a real shame he thought you weren't his," I said just before the elevator doors opened. We entered the elevator. I stood with Lu in the back corner to ensure our privacy.

"How in the world—? We must finish this talk someday," she said *sotto voce*. We must meet again and finish this."

"I don't know if my heart could take it."

The door opened to the front lobby on floor one.

Lu laughed. "Well, yes. There's that."

"I can't even get a handle on how I'm going to help Reynie."

The desk clerk watched us with seething interest. I glared at him. I felt invaded by the eyes of every person in the lobby.

Lu lowered her voice. "What I really meant was that I want to hear *all* about your work. I pray you don't go underground again."

"Who knows?" I said. "Maybe you'll read about me in the papers someday." In the shadows outside the hotel I gently leaned Lu against the side of the building. In seclusion of that darkness I kissed her. Because I thought it *should* be the last time we were together, I believed I had to make this kiss convey a lifetime of feeling. I had never left myself so open to another human being. The heat flashed on again between us. When Lu pressed her lower body against mine, pressed into me with urgency, I thought I was going to come, right there in front of the Holiday Inn.

Lu asked me if she would ever see me again.

"I want to very much but I don't know when or how."

It was Lu who moved away. Her face looked ashy and moist. "It's not fair. I just don't feel finished with you. Maybe we'll never be finished. And maybe we can't do this again."

"No. We can't." I was a breath away from picking Lu up in my arms and taking her back to her suite.

Lu brushed her damp bangs back from her forehead and suddenly became all-business. "May I call you in a few days? At your lab in the carriage house of course."

I wasn't ready to say goodbye to her. Yet I hadn't prepared myself to stay in touch with her either. But how could I not? I took an old OPTIKS business card out of my wallet and scrawled my carriage house phone number on the back of it. "How can I reach *you*?"

"Don't worry about that right now. Remember? I start filming to-morrow. I won't even have time to go home to Connecticut first."

"You mean you stayed over just for me?"

Lu straightened my collar. "Of course, my precious fool. I hope all those things I said won't—."

"I was already thinking about you every minute," I answered.

"You look so handsome in that navy blue sweater," Lu said. She cried. "At least we had tonight. I don't think I'll walk you to your dad's car. That would make it harder to say goodbye."

I wanted to ask Lu's forgiveness. I wanted to confess that I had to marry Jeanie because I got her pregnant. I wanted to say how much my parents loved *her*—not Jeanie.

But Lu put her arms around me and kissed me again.

A camera flash ambushed us. When I could focus I saw a dishev-eled reporter. He pulled out a little flip top notebook and began to write in it. The goddamned desk clerk must have called the local press.

Lu squeezed my hand. "Don't worry," she said. "You can blame it on me. You can tell them I 'assaulted' you." She made a beeline back to the hotel lobby without looking back.

Dad opened his car door for me and called out to Lu. But she was gone. Dad looked dejected.

I dove into the front seat of Dad's car and banged my bum leg. Wow! That hurt! It was like a fisherman's knife had gutted my leg from ankle to knee.

CHAPTER TWENTY-EIGHT

The pilot started his approach to Jefferson County Airport, where Jeanie waited for me. The last three days had been rough. Being with Lu again was far different than what I had imagined when I turned forty. I hardly recognized myself anymore. Reynie and Court had become so important to me that Reynie's kidnapping eclipsed all my other woes. More harrowing than trying to reach mega success with my experiments was seeing my rainbow crystal take a trip to the outer Pleiades at warp eight. Even more traumatic than losing Lu when I had her right in my hands was having my emotional life die just when it was coming alive again. I had reacted to a ringing phone like Pavlov's dogs when I heard my sidekick was kidnapped. After that phone call my life might forever be summed up in the words *coitus interruptus*. I would gladly have sold my soul for some happy continuity instead of these dire intrusions. But my "family troubles," obstacles in my work, and longing for Lucille Muhr felt dinky compared to Reynie's current plight. The bottom line was that could not let Reynie and Court down.

I paid a porter at Jeffco Airport to push my equipment boxes along on a dolly. Under my arm I held the sleeve that contained the hologram of Lu and me. I also had my carry-on bag. It contained the usual stuff like toiletries plus my night-vision scope and the exposed film from my infrared camera. When I reached the terminal I saw Jeanie. Now I'd be stuck in my continuing role of scoundrel and lothario.

Jeanie hadn't spotted me yet. She kept bouncing up on her toes to see above the crowd. Her arms flew up in welcome. When she noticed my limp she gawked at the cast on my leg and stifled a laugh. "My conquering hero returns," she said. "I can carry your bag."

I longed for Jeanie to take me as seriously as Lu had. I declared I could carry the bag myself.

"I'm so glad you're back," Jeanie said. When I said nothing she added, "I know you're upset about Reynie, but I thought there might be a little room for missing me too." Jeanie put her head on my shoulder. "Nice cologne. Really light. Did you try something new? Ooh! You smell so…sexy."

Uh oh, I thought. I had no time to shower after being with Lu. I could see the headlines now: "Woman Kills Husband for 'Technical Infidelity'." "Must be Mom's perfume," I lied. "I had no time to shower after she said goodbye." I looked at Jeanie's shining face and felt meager compassion. I did love her—but not like I loved Lu. Jeanie had not earned this coolness I felt toward her through fault or karma. As my wife, Jeanie had a right to expect me to honor our marriage vows. My faithfulness of body and heart, my warm and loving companionship, my interest in her feelings and activities.

On the other hand, I believed I had rights too. The right to be true to who I am, the right to explore my own growth and to achieve excellence, even if that meant growing away from my wife. Trying to stifle my emotions only made them grow stronger. Still, I knew it would serve no purpose to be honest with Jeanie about Lu. I had changed, and so I steeled myself against feeling remorse. I committed anew to being true to myself, even if I had to lie.

Intense pain throbbed in my right leg from my labored walk across the terminal. Worse, I was out of breath from having one-third less oxygen at high altitude. When I stopped to rest, the porter halted beside me. "Jeanie, have you talked to Josh? To Court?" I worried that Josh had told her I saw Lu at her Nana's funeral. "Give me a minute. It's been grueling. Especially these past few days."

When we, and the porter, got to the mouth of airport parking, Jeanie pushed her hand against my chest. "Wait here and I'll bring your SUV up."

While I waited I realized how bone tired I was. Thunderous *toms* pounding in my head signaled I was also hung over. Or was my heart beating extra loud? How could I help find Reynie before morning?

Jeanie pulled up and opened Woody's back gate for the porter to load my equipment. Then I *galumped* into in the passenger seat. We pulled out of terminal parking and headed to Denver. "When Court talked to your Mom, he said Josh was back in Boulder already. Court asked Josh if your work succeeded."

"What did Josh tell him?"

"He told Court about your broken leg and about your crystal exploding. And about one of your holograms that showed something that didn't happen in real time."

"You got that from Court?"

"No. Paul LaSalle. He and Court are waiting for us at the mansion."

I can't do this, I thought. But then I got a whiff of Lu's alluring cologne on my shirt collar and felt my body spring back to life.

Squad cars lined the curved front drive of the Raymond mansion. A wall of Denver metropolitan police packed the long wraparound porch. We had to get clearance before the police would even let us get out of my SUV. A friendly Lieutenant escorted us to Court's library.

There Court and Paul LaSalle sat with Bill Waters, Denver Metro Police Chief.

Court looked awful. "David! Thank God. Sit with me."

Seeing Court lose his cool like that really upset me. I plunked down next to him on his burgundy leather couch and looked around the library of this very cultured man.

Pale and exhausted, Paul LaSalle paced nervously behind us.

Court got right down to business. "David, I know you just got in but I need you to get started at once. Whoever did this is capitalizing on the fact that Reynie is eight months pregnant. They're holding her for a ransom of two million. And they know I will pay it. I don't care about the money. I only care about getting my daughter back. But even with the police working on it we might not find her in time. They threatened to kill her! Please help me find my Reynie."

I didn't want the police chief to think I was a weirdo. And so I whispered to Court, "Josh told you what happened to my crystal?"

Court acted like he hadn't heard me. "Now Bill Waters is an old friend of mine and—."

"We're doing everything earthly possible," Chief Waters said. "We've dusted the LaSalle house thoroughly for fingerprints. And we questioned a witness who saw the getaway car."

I asked what time the kidnappers took Reynie.

Paul LaSalle loosened his necktie and kept squeezing the bulb of it between his fingers. "It must have happened early this afternoon when I was at the office. I always call Reynie at four o'clock to see if I can pick up anything for her on the way home. Today she didn't answer, so of course I was alarmed. I drove right home and found some things knocked over in the living room. And then this note." He handed me a lined page from a yellow legal pad.

The ransom note said: "Get your wife's Poppy to pay 2 million dollar. Or kiss her and bambino goodbye. You better be waiting for are next call."

"Did you catch the word 'are' here?" I asked Chief Waters.

"Yes. It clues us into our kidnappers' socioeconomic status."

Not giving a shit now about insulting anyone I said to Chief Waters: "Plenty of middle-class people don't speak standard English. TV anchors on news broadcasts say stuff wrong all the time. Where's my wife anyway?"

"She said she would head home and wait up for your call."

A female servant I had never seen at the mansion before brought in a silver coffee service and set it down on the glass top coffee table in front of us.

I stood up to stretch my legs. "What about the witness?" I asked no one in particular. I couldn't understand why there were so many officers here if the kidnapping took place at Reynie's house. "Are they threatening *you*, Court?"

"No," Chief Waters said. "We just set up base camp here."

Court's hand shook when he lifted his coffee cup. "That will be all for now, Lupe." To me he said, "The witness saw a rusted gold Pontiac leaving Reynie's driveway about 3:00 p.m."

"And the witness's best clue," the Chief added, "is that the car looked like it got hit pretty hard by that hailstorm that went through Denver last week."

"But if the hail was that bad," I said, "it must have pitted hundreds of cars."

"Not in this part of town," the Chief answered. "That storm was selective. Because of the size and extent of the damage seen by our witness we can narrow the owner of that Pontiac down to within eight city blocks. It's an area just west of I-25 off Federal, somewhere between 2nd and 10th Avenue. Some of my men already drove around the target area tonight. They report heavy enough hail damage that some houses have boarded up windows from busted glass. The whole neighborhood's a mess. That hail must have been the size of golf balls."

I wolfed down a cup of tepid coffee to keep myself going. "What kind of neighborhood is it, Chief Waters? In general."

"On the West side. Mostly Mexican. There are a lot of industrial buildings and other sorts of nondescript businesses close to the expressway. You know. Printers, shippers, packaging plants."

Something felt *off* to me. "What makes you think the owner of that Pontiac wasn't visiting some relative during the hailstorm?"

Court tried to smile at me. "We talked about that just before you came. All the police can do is keep the area under surveillance to see if that Pontiac shows up. We assume they're smart enough not to use their own phone when they call."

"So that close to Federal they could use a pay phone."

Chief Waters looked at me sternly. "We *have* thought of that. Even if they laid in supplies there's bound to be *some*thing they forgot. Something they must drive in their car to buy. We've seen these types before. They get antsy when they're cooped up. That's something they don't figure on when they plan their crime."

I saw I was wringing my hands. "But if they do get antsy won't they be even more of a danger to their hostage?"

Court turned to Chief Waters. "I told you David is brilliant, Bill." But Court's smile looked *wan*.

I felt my eyes stretch with the effort it took not to let them film over from fatigue—and a hangover. "Okay," I said to Court. "You've decided I can help the police find Reynie. I do have some ideas, but I need to set some parameters first so we don't get in each other's way."

Chief Waters looked offended. "Be clear, Mr. Leone. It was Court's idea that you help us, not mine. If we let you 'help' us, it is you who needs to play by *our* rules. After all, you'll be in danger too."

I was both exhausted and enervated. "Like hell I will obey your rules!" I ripped my cardigan off over my head. "I didn't drop everything back in Ohio and race out here to have some Pinko-Bozo like you limit me when I'm trying to save my friend!"

"David," Court said.

"Josh was with me and he saw what I can do." I was high on adrenaline and I let it all go: "Hell!" I shouted. "I've got a camera here full of infrared pictures of some guy who died in 1973! You think I can't get a picture of someone who was at Reynie's house this afternoon?!"

Court's chest sank with relief.

"Yeah," Chief Waters said, "but we're not talking about ghosts."

Court put his hand up to stop Chief Waters' objection.

"I'm talking about real people," I said. On this film I got people doing things in the past. I broke my leg after being in someone's *dream* about in the past. In my car I have a hologram of something I merely fantasized about. What none of you realize is that it's all the same! Whether it happened a minute ago, a year ago, or before we were born. It doesn't matter if we did it, imagined it, or dreamed it. Or if we forgot all about something that happened to us. It's all the same. There are no *time* restrictions. Time is the grandest illusion of all."

Chief Waters looked taken aback. "But if the film is still in the camera, how do you know what's on it?" he asked.

I guessed he thought he had me there. "Because someone *else* saw these images through the viewfinder of an infra-red camera at the same time I saw them. And because that other person is who snapped the infrared photos."

Chief Waters steepled his fingers together. "All right. All right."

"You're referring to Josh Peterson," Court said. "We should phone him to help you."

"Absolutely. He's my right hand man."

"It *will* be risky," Chief Waters added. "That's why I talked about police boundaries. If we don't abide by some basic rules you could put yourselves *and* Mrs. LaSalle in worse danger. You could also blow our cover. Then they might move her. Or get rough with her."

Court stood, grasped my forearm. "You can see that, can't you?"

I told Court I could. "I need to go down to my lab and process this film as soon as possible. What shows up could settle exactly what methods I should use to catch these guys."

Court looked most anxious. "You can get clear images of the kidnappers on infrared film?"

"I want to see what turns up in those photos. Then I'll know if just looking through the night-vision scope while using my other techniques will be enough. Once I have the goons' traces in the scope I'll know what they look like. Their height, build, gender. Some funky way one of them walks. Even if one wears a hat. Those kinds of things. When the Chief's surveillance team narrows down the location more, I can use the scope to investigate the houses for those same guys."

Court's downcast eyes looked drawn. Chief Waters looked skeptical but also hopeful.

"I know this sounds paranoid," I said, "but I want officers posted around my lab twenty-four-seven. No one must disturb my equipment." I decided not to discourage Court by mentioning I might not succeed without the Elemental's crystal. I could still do my hypnotic takedown to enhance my vision. At least I could try.

"Full-time security," Chief Waters said. "You got it."

The phone in my lab rang. It was the Lieutenant. "There's a guy outside who says he's your best friend.

"Yeah. Josh."

"Lieutenant, why didn't you ask Mr. Raymond to identify Josh?"

"Mr. Raymond and Chief Waters aren't here anymore."

"Bring Josh on down, please." I was just about to develop the negatives of the infrared photos Josh took back in Circleville. If the Lieutenant had called me just a few minutes later I wouldn't have answered the phone. Josh had been instrumental in taking that incredible hologram of Lu and me, and I was glad to have his help now. I had faith that the infrared photos he took would be just as useful.

"Hey, buddy!" Josh shouted from the doorway. "I brought you a cane. Figured it would help you get around better."

"Just prop it against that counter. I'm about to print the infrareds."

Josh opened the fridge. "Do my eyes deceive me or is that full of brew? And a bucket of Kentucky fried chicken. You want a beer?"

"Fuck yes."

"Yech! This fried chicken's got green fuzzies all over it."

"Never mind the Kentucky Fried. Close the light safe door behind you. If I'm right we'll find a gold mine here. Like maybe it'll launch a new, even stellar, career for me."

"As long as I'm your partner," Josh said. "So did you tell Jeanie?"

"About what?"

"By the way, you smell like sex," Josh said.

"Great. So if I don't tell you anything you won't *know* anything."

"That's bullshit. It's written all over you. Jeanie may know you had someone, but she may not know *who*. If you need an alibi—."

"I have enough to handle without dealing with my wife."

"Buddy, I wouldn't be in your shoes for a million bucks."

"Even re: Lucille Muhr?"

"I might have to rethink that," Josh said.

Into the developer I placed what I hoped would become a revealing first print. "Don't get your hopes up, Josh. From the negatives it was hard to tell what showed up. You only got six infrared photos."

"But it took so long to figure out what you wanted me to shoot."

"Well, if even one of them shows Bern and Dora Muhr we'll be sitting in the catbird seat."

In the first print, ghostly, jagged white lines began to appear on a dark background. Then an L-shaped blob came into the foreground.

Josh looked over my shoulder. "Whew! That stuff really stinks!"

I held the print by its corner with smooth bamboo tongs. Then I rinsed the developer off the print and viewed it under the red light. "Yeah? This picture stinks too."

"Let me see that."

"It shows a big arm," I said.

"But it *must* be Bern Muhr's arm, when he was getting the box of bullets out of the dresser drawer."

"We have five more to go. I hope they'll give us what we need."

The next print showed a woman's torso and a big arm reaching toward her.

"Didn't you get them both in one frame?" I asked. "I can't use *pieces* of people!" I couldn't shake off my stress.

"You got no right to yell at me yet. I was warming up. Remember? After that they moved to the back of the bedroom. It means they went farther away from the camera, which means they——."

"Fit better in the frame. Okay. We'll see if you got both of their whole bodies in this next one." I sloshed the print paper gently back and forth in the developer, and a light-colored outline of two people with some extra arms began to take form. "What the hell is that?"

Josh studied the print. He looked dejected. "Maybe one of the Barnetts got up to take a whiz."

"The bathroom's just to the left of the picture window. The figures in this photo are standing by the door to the foyer. That's a room's width away from the picture window. What is going on here?" I pointed. "This one's obviously Dora. And this big tubby figure must be Bern. But Bern looks like the hunchback of Notre Dame. Like he has a Siamese twin connected to his back. See? It's like he has four arms. And then there's this other head on the back of his neck!"

"Beats the hell out of me," Josh said.

"Did you see what I was doing when you were snapping these?"

"Yeah. You were laying on the ground, totally *out*."

"Okay. Let's just put these two up with the first one and see what the fourth one shows." With clothespins I clipped the prints side by side on the thin nylon rope hanging above the table of chemical trays. The fourth print began to develop. Finally the print showed a clear outline of two people. One tall, one short. "That's Bern and Dora! See how his index finger and thumb look like he's pointing at her jaw? Josh. That's when he was holding the revolver to Dora's neck."

Josh thought for a moment. "You saw the whole thing like you were there with them, right?" He peered at the other print again. "This one with the arms—Dora headed for the foyer fast. So what's happening in this photo must have been going on just after what we saw in the other photo."

"Hand me that magnifier. On the shelf to your left." I held the "Siamese twin" photo under the magnifying glass and grinned like a Jack-o'-lantern.

"What is it?"

"It's me."

"You're kidding!"

"No. It's me. This proves it was all real. It proves I was there."

"Let me see it again," Josh said. "It looks like half an octopus. How can you be so sure you're part of this? I can't even tell if the head belongs to a man or a woman."

"But I remember now! I saw Lu's father load his gun and go toward the bed. Then I heard Dora cry out. That's when she got up and split from the bedroom. In the doorway I was standing behind Bern. So I had to reach around him to try and get the gun out of his hand! He was so big bellied that I could hardly get to the damned gun."

"And you're sure these people aren't the Barnetts?"

"If it were the B's, the woman would be as tall as the man. I got a good look at Mrs. B's husband the night I fell out of the tree. He's about five-foot-eight. Bern Muhr was six-foot-three."

"What about the Barnetts' oldest boy?"

"He's about five-foot-ten," I said.

Josh started doing a little dance in the cramped space beside me. He clutched his can of Coors so none of it would spill. "I did it!" he shouted. "I did it! I did it! I did it!"

"*We* did it. With the help of the crystal." My stomach ached from hunger or from too much champagne. Or maybe because I was scared for Reynie. I put the paper into the developer for print number five and said to Josh: "Bern followed Dora into the foyer. Remember? Then they stood by the front door and Bern held that fucking gun to Dora's neck again. Could you see them from your angle? Then Lu appeared in the middle of the stairs across from the foyer. She had a little stuffed animal. Dora told Lu to go back to bed and Lu did go back upstairs. Then Bern pushed Dora back into the bedroom. Were Dora and Bern both in the bedroom when you took the last two infrareds?"

"I can't remember. But I don't think I would've shot the photo if nobody was in the viewfinder."

The photos already printed were more than I had hoped for. "Well, here goes nothing," I said. I slid the fifth negative into the developer pan and swished it back and forth. The developed print showed Dora Muhr standing against her husband's looming frame. He was more than a foot taller than she. "That must be when Bern had Dora in that death grip. I thought he was going to rape her. That's when I lost it."

"This is awesome!"

"You did great. One negative to go." I felt deep fear that the photo would be empty. Or maybe I was afraid because this was the last infrared Josh shot. "Please, God," I said. Immediately I saw that this photograph was totally unlike the others. No clear outlines formed. In fact, the image was almost completely filled with shades of gray and white. Most infrareds have a lot of black in them because only heat sources show up white. "This image is teeming with heat," I said.

The print was nearly developed. Josh and I continued to examine the results. He pointed at a blob of kinky light that took up almost the whole photograph. "What *is* that?"

"One thing's for sure. It took a humongous amount of heat to overexpose that film."

Josh looked crushed. "I blew it."

"No. You did not. See how the rays emanate from the center of this ball of light? I also see shades of gray in the background. Note how the center bands are darker and gradually get lighter towards the outside?"

"But what does that mean?"

"It means each ring of light is a different color, starting with red. See how the red is darker and how the next band is a little lighter? Then the others are gradually lighter shades."

"The different hues of gray are colors?"

"Yes. That's what happens when you use a monochromatic medium to photograph colors. Just like black and white photos."

"What did I capture then?"

"I think this shows the crystal blowing up."

"Holy shit! But wait a minute. How can that be? Your crystal was out in the back yard with *me*. Not in the house. I was snapping infrareds of what was going on inside the house. Remember?"

"The crystal cluster must have co-existed in some *past* dimension, where the Muhrs were. Don't you see, Josh? It wasn't just a physical crystal or I could not have placed it by top of the rainbow stairway inside the crystal *and* be in that room with Lu's parents at the same time. The crystal also had to exist in other dimensions too."

Josh stared at me.

"See, when I was inside the crystal, the—."

Josh paled "You were *inside* the crystal?"

"Well, that's part of my takedown meditation. When I was in the crystal, before I was in the bedroom, the Elemental told me not to leave my own crystal in *her* crystal."

"I'm confused. The elemental? Your crystal in her crystal?"

"Yes. The Elemental told me to lay my crystal down to the side of the rainbow stairs."

Josh's frustration showed. "What stairs?"

"The *rainbow* stairs inside the crystal!"

"Please bear with me, Dave. I had no idea you had so many other things going on while you were in that bedroom."

"The Elemental knew my crystal was going to blow up."

"Which crystal?"

"Both crystals—hers and mine. The Elemental was like the soul of my crystal, which was the form her own *energetic* crystal took on the physical plane. The Elemental's crystal—the one I went inside, the one at the top of the rainbow stairs—was like her astral body."

"I need to sit down," Josh said.

"That's okay. Everything is cool now. Don't you see? It was all part of a plan. After I jumped on Bern Muhr to get the gun away from him, I thought the explosion was the gun firing. I thought he had shot her."

"Who?"

"Lu's mother. But it was the crystal shattering. You were right."

"About what?!"

"Somehow I must have kept Lu's father from killing her mother. These prints prove I was there. See? With the crystal I time travelled. When I stopped that bastard I fulfilled the Elemental's destiny too. Then the Elemental was free to leave."

"Leave what?"

"*My* crystal."

"Now I get it," Josh said. "You know I was being sarcastic, right?"

"It's all clear now. I thought my fate was to invent some outrageous holographic device. Maybe it was to save Dora Muhr's life."

"And maybe to save Reynie's now." Josh scratched his head. "Mind if I ask you one more question?"

"Ask away."

"If *your* crystal burst, where's the Elemental's crystal?"

"That *is* a question. I don't know."

"I don't understand half of what you said in the past ten minutes. But I do get one thing. You don't need your crystal to find Reynie's kidnappers."

"You got that right!"

CHAPTER TWENTY-NINE

"You fell asleep," Josh said. "Take a shower. Change your clothes. It's time to find Reynie Raymond LaSalle."

It was almost 1:00 a.m. I hadn't heard from Court. "Josh, don't you have a job to go to?"

"I work straight commissions now. I outsell the other guys by a hundred and eighty percent. And I don't have to work eight-to-five to do it. Are we going to rescue Reynie now or not? Mr. Raymond has been pacing his portico for the last hour, waiting to talk to you."

"Oh no!"

"He said to let you sleep. He and I had a nice little talk while you took your power nap."

"You did *not* tell Court about Lucille Muhr."

"Didn't have to," Josh said.

"Oh, come on."

"Really? All kinds of things go on behind the scenes when you're taking naps. You know what Mr. Raymond told me? He went into this little spiel about how when people are in love they kind of look like each other. He said when you first came in tonight you had traces of Lucille Muhr on you."

"I can't believe he told *you* that," I said. I was flattered in a way. But I also felt panic clog my throat. "Court's too damned perceptive." *I shouldn't have told Josh that*, I thought.

"Why shouldn't he trust your best friend? Me. Court also said he was afraid you seeing Lu was his fault. Something about a letter where he 'condoned' your behavior."

"That's crazy. Court's letter about Lu made no difference. Once I found out she was coming home to Circleville that was it. I've dreamed about this for years. Nothing's gonna stop me from seeing her again."

The phone rang. It was Court. "David, I could wait no longer. I haven't wanted to hound you, but surely you understand. When can you find my Reynie?"

"Court, name me Reynie's favorite song."

"What? Well, she likes the oldies. You know. Songs her mother liked. Why on earth—."

"Because I want to know her *tone*. It just hit me. Remember how I played with tuning forks early-on?"

"Wait a minute. Reynie asked your wife to figure out her tone. It was, um, 'G'. Yes. That's what she said: 'G'. David, surely this isn't the time to experiment with—."

"Excellent!" I shouted. "Josh and I will get right to work. Let Chief Waters know we're coming over to Federal and Second with some light equipment."

"But I thought you were going over to Reynie's and Paul's to try to pick up something on your infrared."

"Don't need to now. Trust me, Court. I got this knocked."

It was nearly 2:30 a.m. by the time Harlan dropped Josh and me off on Federal Boulevard. Four police cars waited in a parking lot under bright streetlights.

I headed up to an unmarked patrol car that had tinted windows. I tapped on the driver's window while I leaned on my cane. "Aren't you guys being too obvious?"

The cops scowled. Josh elbowed me in the ribs.

Chief Waters climbed out of his own patrol car. "Look who's talking, 'Gimpy'."

Josh clenched his fists.

I *slitted* my eyes on purpose. "Have your boys found the target area?" I waited to see if Chief Waters got my hint that the cops' failed to narrow the target area. Then I punctuated my point. "*You* know. So I won't have to 'gimp' around an entire eight blocks."

Josh rushed in to defend me: "He's really tense because he and Mrs. LaSalle are close friends."

"Yeah," Chief Waters said. "Okay. Here's the scoop. We found the gold Pontiac abandoned on Eighth Avenue on this side of I-25. The car's body was in real bad shape, plus it looks like it shot a rod. We ran down the plate but got bad news: It's stolen."

"So you don't know the address," Josh said.

"But we got an anonymous tip about the Pontiac," Chief Waters said. "That witness said he heard the sound of metal dragging on the street. When he looked out his window he saw three Mexicans get out of the Pontiac. I assume they're Mexican. Should I say 'Latino'?"

"I think 'Latino' means from Latin America. We don't know— ."

I shifted my field kit to my other shoulder. "And?"

"We don't have the paperwork to do a house to house search yet. We can only do surveillance until a judge signs our blanket warrant."

Josh looked antsy. He said to me, "Dude— ."

"Chief Waters, can you let me and my friend get to work?"

Chief Waters just couldn't drop it. "Aren't *you* the primadonna? You want our help or not?"

"Just tell me where you think we should start," I said. "Within a four block radius."

"We'll take you down to Fifth Avenue," Chief Waters said.

"Nothing doing. Drop us off a little farther out, and Josh and I will walk to Fifth alone. No police cars. No lights. Especially no lights. You'll screw up my infrared scanner and the film too. We'll go alone. *Capiche?* You promised to leave me alone." Though I loved it that the word "capiche" had slipped into my speech, it kind of made me sound like a "gangstah."

"They're armed. And that's why you need our protection."

I tried negotiating. "How about this: If you hear shooting, you'll know we found them. But that might make it even more dangerous for Reynie. My plan is just to quietly find her. Then you guys can send in your SWAT team or whoever can guaranteee she gets out safely. So just let Josh and me 'gimp' around the neighborhood for a while, and you guys stay out here in your cop cars. For sure the kidnappers aren't gonna show their faces *here*."

"He's right," Josh said over his shoulder. We headed East on Second Avenue. Josh carried the camera, and I had the night vision scope plus the "G" tuning fork.

"I'm positive we'll find her," I said.

"But how the hell are we going to do it?" Josh whispered.

I told Josh I didn't know. "To tell the truth," I whispered back, "I can barely remember my own name right now. It's just been too much at once. You know?" I glanced aimlessly through the night vision scope. "There's a squirrel nesting in that tree." I panned across the area. "This is not the right neighborhood."

"How do you know?" Josh asked.

"It doesn't feel right. We need to go north. Which way is north?"

"Hey! You're the one who said to go north!" Josh said. "We have to go left. Am I going too fast for you?"

I resented having to stump along like this. "We're going the right way but it's farther over."

"Where are you getting that?"

"I just know."

Josh suggested I do my "trance thing."

I told him I'd never tried it without the crystal.

"What've you got to lose?"

"True," I said. I did my crystal meditation takedown before we headed toward a dark area between two houses and dead-ended at a chain link fence. When I closed my eyes, fear warped my perceptions. *You're a fraud*, a voice in my head buzzed. *You'll never find her without your crystal. You're not pure enough to find the Holy Grail.* I made myself breathe deeply. In my mind I reached the rainbow steps. But the colors of the steps looked faded and spider webs had draped across them. In a panic, with my cane I whipped through the spider webs on the faded red step. To my right a mirror projected the image of a tottering old geezer. "That's NOT me!" I shouted. When I put my hand to my face, the geezer did too. When I reached up to feel my hair, so did the geezer, and I could *feel* the baldness I saw in his mirror reflection. *This ain't gonna work*, I said to myself.

"Don't believe what you see," a different voice said. "It's an illusion. Bring yourself back to your heart."

"Are you my old friend? Did you come back to help me?"

"I am you," the voice said. "I have always been you."

"I need your help. If you *are* me, then please help me. Why can't you just help me?"

"You didn't ask before," the voice said. "Your fear blocks you from finding the truth. You only need to remember how you got into the crystal before because remembering will be the same as living this moment. You can do this."

"Yes," I said. "I can do this."

"Focus on the heat in your chest," my inner voice said. "Focus on the heat in your stomach. And below your stomach. See the rainbow stairs glow at their peak brightness. That's it. Now take the steps, one by one. Yes. That's it. You're on the yellow step. See how clearly the yellow shines. The green, soothing you and balancing your emotions. The beautiful aquamarine blue, like looking through polar ice. The majestic indigo, like a deep uncut sapphire. Now the violet. Violet is the color of the highest vibration. Now do you see the *white* light at the top of the stairs? It is opalescent white. You might see gold too."

I felt intoxicated, elated. "Yes. I see the white light."

"Now think only of your dear friend. See her face in every detail. See her whole body. Feel who Reynie is. You're sitting across a table from her on a beautiful Spring day. She's laughing at something you said. Hear her laughter. Remember the *sound* of her laughter. The Reynie sound. She leans closer to pat your hand. Feel your friend's touch. Her very touch *feels* like Reynie to you. When she leans toward you, her scent reaches you. Breathe in her scent. Reynie's essence. You remember her scent now and you breathe it in. It becomes part of you. She feels you're close by. She's trying to reach you. She's telling you she's not far away. Just another two blocks. She says to keep going north. Pick up your scope!"

I began to prance along like an antelope and leap like a gazelle across streets, through yards, and around corners. I had no idea if Josh was keeping up with me. It was like a dream. As if I was sprinting in broad daylight I could see the neighborhoods clearly. Without losing my breath, and with no limp, I kept jogging. Then I stopped. I stood in the back yard of a cute little bungalow. Even in the relapsing darkness I could see that everything around the house was trim and maintained. Nothing about the residence signaled it concealed kidnappers. I felt compelled to go behind the house. As though outside of my body I watched myself stand up on a picnic table and lift the night vision scope to my eye. Now *I* was looking through the scope, into what I knew was a bedroom window.

Think of Reynie's essence, my own voice repeated. *Think of the sound of her laughter.* I could see a form on the bed sit up with effort. That scared me the shit out of me! When the figure rose off the bed I ducked down behind the picnic table. *Make the tuning fork sound*, my inner voice said.

Quietly. Ever so softly I tapped the tuning fork tines against the heel of my hand. *Now look through the scope.* I saw the figure come to the window. The form pulled the curtains back and peered this way and that. I could see it was Reynie!

When Josh caught up with me he saw I was focused on something. He lifted the infrared camera but I waved him back. "Not yet," I said. I wanted Reynie to know for sure it was me so I tapped the tuning fork again a little harder. Somehow she knew me, even in the dark. I held up one hand, palm facing her, to warn her to be quiet. Then I pushed both hands toward her to tell her to back away.

Reynie nodded. Then she clasped her hands over her heart and smiled. In that moment she looked like the Blessed Mother Mary pouring her love over me.

"Take the shot, Josh," I whispered. "Take it now!" I had no reason to believe he was ready but I heard the camera shutter click.

"Did you find the kidnappers?"

"Shhh! Did you get the shot?"

"How should I know? I couldn't see a thing."

I motioned for Josh to follow me away from the house. When we got about six houses up from the bungalow I asked Josh again if he had taken an infrared photo.

"Yes I got it." Then he grinned. "What did I get?"

"That was Reynie."

"You're kidding!"

"Josh, I don't know where we were. Do you?"

"Not where we were supposed to be," he said.

"Where's that?"

"A better neighborhood. Still Hispanic, though. About a mile from where you took off running. I honestly don't know how I found you. You ran like the wind. You didn't even limp."

I was amazed myself but I couldn't savor my victory just yet. "Reynie came to the window. That means no one's guarding her."

"Oh, yeah. We can just slip in and rescue her," Josh said.

I saw a vehicle heading our way with just its parking lights on. It was a patrol car. "They'll wake up the whole freaking neighborhood," I whispered. "Let's head through here and lure them to a different street. Until I'm sure they won't screw things up I don't want them knowing what *we* know."

"Oh. You mean keep them away from that little house?"

"Yes. 'Give 'em the slip.' Then we'll go back to Reynie."

We ambled over to the next street. A patrol car speeded up and followed us.

Josh panted. "We're leaving her alone?"

"I don't think she's in danger for now," I said.

The patrol car's search light came on.

I felt like a young buck. "Those peckerheads will ruin everything. Let's give them a chase."

"On foot? Dave. No. They might turn on their siren."

"Yeah. You're right. We'll just let them pick us up now. But don't say *anything* about finding Reynie."

"You boys having fun?" the patrolman asked through his open window. "You are way out of the target area. That was quite a sprint you performed back there, Mr. Leone. If I hadn't grazed a drunk when I ran a stoplight, I would've picked you up sooner. Get in. Chief Waters wants to know if you two have have found out anything useful," the officer said.

Now my leg vibrated. "Oh please, Mister Policeman. Let us stay outside and play a little longer."

"Wait 'til Chief Waters hears about your little adventure. You should leave the hunt up to us experts."

"I'm not doing this for Chief Waters," I answered. "We just need some more time."

"Okay, but I'm telling you: You're working the wrong zone."

"Nevertheless, we are heading back now," I said. "See you later."

The patrolman tapped his window frame and eased away like a black snake moving along a water line.

Now I was limping badly. "Maybe we can sneak Reynie out through the window."

Josh reminded me that Reynie was eight months pregnant. "You just sent the patrol car away. How fast do you think we can travel with her on foot?"

"I guess I wasn't thinking. But somehow we *will* rescue her."

This time we stood at the front corner of the little abode. I looked through the scope into what appeared to be the living room. Four people stood in darkness.

"Look," I whispered. "I think that's Lupe."

"You know her?"

"Get down here with me." I said. We were behind thick shrubs next door. "She's Court's new housekeeper. Wait a minute! There's three guys with Lupe."

"Why are they all still awake?" Josh asked.

A man's voice said: "I tol' you wan ohf us shood stayed weeth her." The man opened the front door. He wore no coat.

"Juan," Lupe said. "Don't hurt her."

Juan went over to comfort Lupe.

"That must be Lupe's husband," I whispered to Josh.

Josh's white face glowed like a ghost in the night. "Reynie must have climbed out the window by herself," he said.

I felt my stomach do a double back flip when I saw a different man put on his coat. "Why didn't she wait there for us to come back? We have to find her before *they* do."

Josh and I squatted down again. Two men came bounding out the front door. Each held a gun. They headed south, which I would have done if I had been Reynie. That's because the neighborhood north of there was shabby.

"I tol' you theese wahs *loco*," Lupe's husband said.

"*Ir más rápido!*" the other man said. They disappeared around a corner in the darkness.

I memorized the house number and told Josh to follow me to the back. I knew we could talk there. "What street are we on, Josh?"

"Sixteenth Avenue."

"If you're Reynie, and you know I'm out here, and you want to hide from kidnappers with guns, where do you go?"

Josh said he didn't know.

"Okay. If you're Reynie, where would you think the kidnappers would go to look for her?"

"Away from the house."

"Yes, and that would mean—."

"She's around *here* some place," Josh and I whispered in unison.

I got my scope out.

One of the Hispanic men yelled "*Stupido!*" He was back in the front yard but he wasn't talking to us. He was talking to the other Hispanic male. The one who spoke bettter English. Apparently he had gotten the same idea as I. He cocked the hammer on his gun. "She will be hiding *here*."

"They're *armed*," Josh whispered.

I whispered back, "No kidding. Let's get behind that car in the back alley." We knelt down behind an old Buick sedan parked by Lupe's one-car garage. The Hispanic males reached the back yard. Then I thought: *This is dumb. This is the first place they'll look for her.* I motioned for Josh to follow me and we inched along the ground to the back of the garage. "Listen, Josh. They're going to be looking here any second. We have to leave. Somehow with Reynie. We can't talk anymore, so I want you to follow me."

"You have a new plan, right.?"

Josh followed me around the garage and down the alley until we reached a street corner. *If Lu could only see me now*, I thought. Staying out from under the street lights wasn't easy but we managed to end up a few houses down and a few houses behind where Reynie had been held. I got my scope out again and checked the neighborhood.

"What if *they* find her while we're dillying around here?" Josh asked. "I think it's better if they don't find us so we can get to the police. Those men probably stopped looking behind the house. Maybe we should go back there now."

"We better stop talking, Josh. Use sign language or something." Creeping low to the ground, we stopped at the house next door. I looked through the scope and saw a shape huddled behind the garage. "Go get the cops," I said to Josh.

"But—."

"Go!" I whispered fiercely. "And don't look back."

Josh took off like a bat out of hell.

I sighted through my scope and moved toward the huddled shape. By the time I got close enough to see if it was Reynie, I could hear her breathing in the darkness. Short, shallow breaths. I threw the scope to the ground and clapped my hand over her mouth.

"Stop it, David!" she hissed. She shivered and tightened a thick blanket around her body.

"I'm glad to see you too," I said quietly. "Are you all right?"

"I heard the tuning fork so I knew it was you. I was so happy to see you I almost cried. But right now I've got this problem. My water broke. And labor pains started right after you and your friend took off. That's why I didn't wait for you to come back. I didn't want to have Baby Reynie in that place."

"Josh went for the cops. They're about five blocks away. In the meantime we'd better wait right here."

Reynie clutched her lower abdomen. "I don't think I can travel with you anywhere."

I asked Reynie if she was afraid the men would come back.

"Well, if they do, they'll find us both."

"Say. I thought you'd be a basket case. But here you are—this serene madonna who might give birth outside a cold garage." I was proud of her. "I'll do everything I can to help you."

"If I'm serene it must be the hormones."

In our faces a flashlight cranked on. "Lookee what we got here," a male voice said. I was hoping it was the police.

"Oh, crap," Reynie said.

To avoid being blinded by the flashlight I looked down—right at the barrel of a gun. "I'm a doctor," I said, feebly. "And this woman is in labor." It seemed like a good idea at the time.

CHAPTER THIRTY

The desperate kidappers dragged me inside Lupe's house. "Honest-to-God," I said to them. "I've never seen this woman before in my life!" Before I saw it I felt it. One of the men slammed the butt of his revolver against my jaw. He had held his gun in the flat of his palm. After spinning sparkles vanished from inside my head, I gave Reynie an *I'm okay* look. I could feel my jaw swelling up like a fairy mushroom in the spring.

Lupe and Juan shrank in the corner. "Felipe. You said you would not hurt him," Lupe said.

"I said I would not hurt *her*," Felipe said. "*Tu marido* owes me *mucho dinero*. This is the only way he is gonna get it. Right? So *silencio!*"

"*Si*," the other Hispanic male said. "*Silencio.*"

"I say you are working with the cops," Felipe said. "Are you working with the cops?"

To stop the gory blood dripping down my neck I pressed my hand, hard, on a gash in my cheek. When I saw blood all over the front on my sweater, and I almost puked. "If I *was* working with the police," I puffed, "they'd be here by now, right?"

"That depends," Felipe said. "Roberto! You saw *policía* down on Second and Federal this night? You think they know where we are?"

"No. I don't theenk so," Roberto said.

"They're never there when you need them," Reynie said. She huffed and puffed. "Listen fellas. I'm trying not to scream. *You* know. From the pain. But I'm possibly going to start yelling any minute because I can't take the pain much longer."

"Lupe!" Felipe shouted. "You said not for another month!"

"You scare her *mucho*," Lupe said. "Sometime *puede traer bebé*."

"Why don't you call a taxi?" I said. "Let her go."

Felipe sneered. "Then the money goes too."

"No." I said. "Mr. Raymond will pay just as much for me as for her." I hoped they would believe me.

"I don't theenk so," Roberto said. He pointed his gun at my now wide open third eye.

"It's true. I'm like a son to him. You've got to call a cab to take her to the hospital."

Reyie let out a sharp cry. "They won't, David. By the way, this is hurting me more than it's hurting you."

"Right," Felipe said. "Besides, *Señor* Raymon will get money to us *con la primera luz*." After Lupe goes to work for rich man, Juan drives *Señora* LaSalle to Market Street Bus Station, and calls *Señor* Raymon in his car to bring money to drop spot. When *Señor* Raymon brings money to drop spot, Juan waits by pay phone in bus station. *Señor* Raymon calls pay phone number in bus station (only he does not know it is bus station) and *so hija* answers. When *Señor* Raymon sees *Señora*

LaSalle is okay, driver drops money at spot. There Roberto hides. If *policía* are there at spot, Roberto calls Juan at bus pay phone and tells Juan to take *Señora* LaSalle away."

I had a terrible thought. With Lupe at the mansion the next morning, what would keep Reynie from telling Court about Lupe and her husband? Surely the kidnappers had thought of that too. What would keep Lupe and Juan from turning the kidnappers in? Unless Felipe didn't intend to let any of us go. "And where will Juan go after he leaves Mrs. LaSalle at the bus station?" I asked Felipe.

Felipe tilted his head buzzard-like. "I see you are *un hombre pensante*. But you are not so smart like you think."

"I know this," I said. "Juan stays alive just long enough to keep your ass out of the sling."

Felipe cocked his head again. "Sling?"

I hoped that Juan and Lupe had gotten the message that these cockroaches would not spare them. Their faces betrayed nothing, so I couldn't tell. Clearly they were too afraid of their keepers to do anything but comply.

Unfortunately Reynie had tuned in to my meaning too. So far she had managed to stifle the sounds of her moaning. Now her face glistened. Clearly she hadn't realized how lethal these kidnappers were until I opened my big mouth. I wondered where the police were. "Let Lupe help Mrs. LaSalle. Please," I begged.

"She *is* going to have her baby here," Lupe said to Felipe. "If you want your money, you better let me help her. Now."

"Okay," Felipe said. "She does not get away." He jerked his chin in Reynie's direction. "Put her back in the bed."

I rose to help Reynie. Felipe swung his arm around in the air to show he'd take another swipe at me.

Reynie's eyes filled. "I'm so sorry, David." She wailed. Lupe and Juan helped her back into the bedroom.

"Yeah," Felipe said to me. "You never saw her before."

"Lupe told you anyway," I said.

Like a UFO tractor beam, a search light invaded the living room. Then a voice yelled through a bullhorn: "This is the Denver Metro Police. You're surrounded. Come out with your hands on your heads. This is our final warning." Then another voice repeated the commands over the megaphone in Spanish.

I felt relief expand my chest. It was over. Reynie would get a police escort to the nearest hospital, I could go to my penthouse and take a shower, get some sleep and—."

But Felipe and Roberto leapt to the front windows and began firing their weapons. I hurled myself to the floor and lay there heaving. Return fire from the police ripped through the curtains. It was like Buffalo Bill Cody's Wild West Show, only Annie Oakley was giving birth to a baby behind the main circus tent and I was eating sawdust.

Felipe and Roberto were so busy shooting that they didn't check where I was. And so I crawled on my belly like a reptile to the back bedroom. I opened the door and dragged myself in. I asked how Reynie was doing. No one answered. I lay on the floor, my shirt sticking to my body. "Reynie!" I shouted. "Reynie?" I rose to my knees to try to find her but the bedroom was empty. A bullet whizzed through the half-open bedroom door and ricocheted off the closet doorknob. It finally landed under the window, just beside me.

"Psst! David! Out here!" It was Josh. He whispered, "Get the hell out of there! Go to the alley. We'll be safe there."

"Where's Reynie?"

"On her way to Denver General—by helicopter."

"Thanks a lot for letting me take fire," I countered. I tried to move commando-like over the sill, my bum leg dragging. Then I wriggled down to the ground.

"That's how the cops kept the gunmen out of that bedroom," Josh said. We huddled behind the garage with two police officers. "Perfectly executed plan."

Farther down the alley, almost unseen, unmarked police cars idled.

"I can't take anymore, Josh. Where do we go from here?"

"To the hospital."

By the time we pulled out of the alley the gunfire had stopped. Muffled voices issued from the front yard of Lupe's house. My head *tromped* and I felt a bloody split in the flesh of my cheek where Felipe had struck me with his gun. I said to Josh: "Thanks for finally calling in the cavalry."

Josh and I ducked into the back seat of the police car. Josh told me the story of his part in the rescue. "The police crept around the back yard while you were in the living room. I was sitting in this squad car and one of the cops had his own night-vision scope. He asked me how it works, whereupon I grabbed the scope and jumped out of the squad car. I stooped low to the ground and inched along to the back of Lupe's house to see if Reynie was still in the bedroom. She wasn't. Through the scope I saw three forms in the bedroom, and so I signalled the cops to go in. Lupe and Juan gave up without a fight, and the police got Reynie out through the bedroom window. The cops in back signaled the SWAT team in front to storm Lupe's house, which made it very noisy. Seems that Juan and Lupe are illegals. The bad guys in there are in the business of forging green cards, work visas, and other stuff illegals need. When people can't pay them on time they keep jacking up the fee. They're real knee cap busters when people can't pay. Apparently Lupe's husband thought he could pay after he'd worked in Denver for a while. It's a shame. I don't think Lupe and her husband are bad people. They just made some bad choices."

It seemed we'd been driving on the turnpike only a few minutes before we arrived at the emergency entrance of Denver General.

"Here we are," the patrolman shouted. "Just in time for the birth of another Raymond child."

"You wouldn't be so cheery if you'd been in that house with live ammo parting your hair. I was in there with those…those vigilantes!"

"Hey, guy!" the patrolman said. "You're the man of the hour."

"What?"

"Man! You're a hero. Channel 7 News wants to interview you."

"Get me out of here!" I shouted. "Take me around back. Find some way to help me up to Maternity without the Press seeing me."

Josh smirked. "Too late."

The press swarmed the police car. I got out before I saw Channel 7 News cameras rolling and an aggressive anchorwoman blocking my path. She rudely seized my arm and dragged me in front of a TV camera. I was too tired and weak to resist. The news reporter read some cue cards, which I'm sure was the only way she could have chirpy-talked one of the longest sentences I had ever heard: "I'm speaking with Mr. David Leone, whose bravery made it possible for the Denver City police to rescue Mrs. Paul LaSalle, wife of the prominent Denver attorney and daughter of Denver's own Harcourt Raymond, III, from kidnappers just minutes ago. Mr. Leone? We've been told that you used a unique invention to end this near tragic event we've been covering for twenty four hours now."

"Uh?"

"And that you used some novel device to scour the West side of I-25 to locate Mrs. LaSalle when police couldn't find her."

"Well—."

"And that now you're going up to Maternity to wait for the birth of Mrs. LaSalle's first child, heir to the Raymond fortune."

"Yeah," I said. Then something knocked my feet out from under me. In a brain cloud of murky fog I dropped down. I felt my knees hit the pavement.

"Why, the strain of all this seems to have overcome Mr. Leone," the anchorwoman said. I heard her voice echo…echo…echo, like she was in a big underwater tunnel.

Next, two seven foot tall white angels zoomed me along a narrow hallway. Whizzed me past fluffy white walls and white tables. White sheets. White *everything*. I finally landed in a white bed.

There are times when no man can escape his fate. I knew this was one of those times. But I also realized that my having passed out at this turning point in my holographic career was somehow moot. I sensed that whatever was dripping into my vein through an IV tube was more sedative than nourishment. And so I remained dozing just below the delicious stage of alpha, aware of my mind's incessant *busy*-ness only because of the images flickering inside my eyelids. There, in those little drive-in movie screens, I saw particles of light. I also felt trembling sensations. The capillaries in my brain hummed with the frantic flow of blood that was trying to answer the adrenaline peaks that had hours ago been urging me to "Flee! Flee! Flee!"

Now my thoughts were pretty general. I could recall outcomes, but few of the in-process details of the escapades that had landed me here. I remembered breaking my leg and being with Lu. I was aware I had returned to Denver and Reynie was safe. A few minutes before, my face had smacked the frosted concrete sidewalk outside Denver General Hospital. I had collapsed. I had pitched forward into a clump of weakened flesh. Just one man who had tried to take on too…

"Hey, hotshot!"

A hero, unsung and underappreciated, who could no longer…

"David?"

Just one scientist who went over the…

Someone sat on the edge of my bed. "David."

"Lemme sleep."

I felt someone stroking my forehead. It was the most loving, gentle, maternal touch I ever felt. I lay there smiling like a newborn, while my body sank into a deep and peaceful languor. I didn't care if it was a dream or if it was really happening. By not opening my eyes I could remain suspended in this blissful, womblike state.

"You are my hero," some woman cooed. "One side of your face got mauled by that creep. You scraped the other side even more when you fainted. And your bum leg."

When I opened my eyes I saw Reynie. My leg was propped up on a pillow. The pain felt *screechy*. "What are *you* doing here?" I tried to pull myself up. "I thought you were Jeanie."

"Um, you just missed her. I had a scarey helicoopter ride here while you cavorted around with my kidnappers."

The little parentheses around Reynie's mouth irked me.

"I thought you were having your baby any minute!"

"That was two days ago. I've brought someone to visit you." In her arms she held a little pink bundle. "Mr. David Leone, may I present Alicia Reynelda LaSalle." Reynie held her baby out to me with a trust I doubted I had earned.

My left arm ached from the pressure of the IV tube but I didn't care. When I was growing up I had always wanted a sister. When I married Jeanie I wanted a daughter to spoil and to be a hero for. I cradled baby Alicia in the crook of my right arm. "What a beautiful, new little friend. But I'm afraid she looks like *you*, Reynie. I mean, she'll probably be as hard on me as you are."

"Just wait 'til Daddy gets here," Reynie said.

"What?"

"He's outside. I got in first because I'm a new mother. I hope the novelty of this event never wears off for you." Reynie's laughter was musical, jolly. Then she looked serious. "I don't know how…what I'm trying to say is that the way I've teased you. I mean I'm afraid you'll think I'm making fun of you if I try to say how grateful I am for what you did. I'm afraid you won't believe me."

I looked into the new mother's eyes of my dear friend. The one who believed in me enough not to let me bullshit myself. The friend who had been a magnificent teacher. Suddenly I realized Reynie had just tried to tell me that I had somehow graduated from her school of self-realization. I saw I had *earned*, and kept, her friendship the hard way. She had praised me for coming through for her. She had conceded that I was worthy of the faith she had placed in me. Now I could see how tired Reynie was. "I'll believe you if you're honest with me about something."

"What is that?"

"Were you stroking my head just now?"

Reynie retrieved her baby from my arm. "I've always wanted a brother. But I'd be crazy to admit I was stroking your forehead. That might ruin the power position I hold in our friendship." Then she winked at me. Though she didn't say it in words, the lights in her eyes said, *Yes. I admit it. I was stroking your head, you turkey.* "And now the exquisite Alicia and I are going back to my room, so that my delicious husband will find us there when he returns."

I tried to keep Reynie from seeing I had "caught" her being vulnerable. Actually I didn't want her to see how delighted I was. Then I thought: *What the hell. I can't hide anything from my friend anyway.* So I looked back at her, into her, and let her eyes look as deeply into mine as they dared. I marvelled at that. Reynie showed me she could look into my eyes unguarded—and that, for a little while longer, I might turn away first because I couldn't accept her candor yet. "Maybe someday I will," I said.

As if she had read my heart she said, "Oh, you're closer than you think." And, just to make a point, and with her usual brilliant timing, Reynie brushed the hair back from my forehead just as I was thinking about how lucky I was to have so many women vying with each other to civilize me. That was just before I saw Harcourt Raymond, III.

Court looked both pumped up and pale. "Anything you want, my boy. Just name it. I've had the greatest idea for your work. You're going to love it!"

I drew the IV from my arm and winced.

This alarmed my loyal benefactor. "Why did you do that?"

I pressed my thumb into the small wound to stop the blood dripping down my forearm. "You're going too fast for me, Court. I think we all must be a little nutso right now. I know *I* am confused as hell. I'm going to try to find my clothes. Pull up that chair. You look like *you* should be in this bed, not me." I limped over to the closet door and opened it. Except for a few padded hangers the closet was empty. "Where did they put my street clothes?"

"Sorry. I forgot to tell you: Jeanie came by to see you yesterday and brought a change of clothes."

"Where are they?"

"Well, let's see. It's about two p.m. now. Jeanie got here about two hours after they checked you in. That would have been about quarter-to-four two mornings ago."

I panicked. "Did she go back to Boulder?"

"Your wife and I took turns sitting with you. I went back and forth between the maternity wing and here. Let's see. Jeanie left clothing for you in a shopping bag on the back of the bathroom door. She hung it on the doorknob."

"How about that Reynie? Having a little girl, easy as you please, after being kidnapped and all. I don't feel tired. Can we go out to a sit-down restaurant? I'm so famished I could eat a whole buffalo. Wait a minute. I might not eat meat again. Maybe an omelette. Here we go. Blue jeans and a plaid flannel shirt. Perfect! Does my wife know me or not?! And my most comfy sneakers. I'll just check myself out and we can go eat. You have no idea what happened to me in Ohio. There aren't enough hours left today to tell you all about it."

Something in Court's face stopped me in the middle of my tucking in my shirt. He pulled a folded newspaper out from under his arm.

"I guess we made the front page? Reynie getting saved from the kidnappers and all." I tied the lace of one sneaker and pulled a sock over my other foot. "Are you laughing? You look weird, Court."

"*You* made the front page of the *Denver Post*. Entire top-half. The rest of us made the bottom half." The way Court shook his head expressed both amusement and anxiety. "And there's an entire spread in *Variety*."

"I don't get it. Why *Variety?*"

"Show business. And your life will never be private again."

"Let me see that."

Court handed me the *Denver Post*. "It's going to be a shock," he said.

I held the front page out in front of me with hopeful enthusiasm. There, across three columns, was a clear AP Laserphoto of Lucille Muhr and me in a passionate embrace! It sizzled with the realism of *cinema verité*. The headline turned my stomach topsy-turvy: "Local 'Knight-Errant' Has Busy Day." The article identified the location as a Holiday Inn in Circleville, Ohio.

Just hours before returning to rescue Denver socialite Reynelda LaSalle, scientist/Don Juan, David Leone, says farewell to actress Lucille Muhr. Acording to informed sources, the pair met in a certain executive suite at the Holiday Inn, ending a 22-year separation. It seems Ms. Muhr and Mr. Leone were highschool sweethearts.

"Oh no! Has Jeanie seen this?"

Court came to me and put his arm around my shoulder. "Who *hasn't* seen it, my boy? I'm afraid that in the public's eye this photo eclipses your rescue of my daughter. I won't lie to you. This scandal won't fade from people's memory any time soon. In fact I expect it to bring a good deal of notoriety to your work. You know—enhance its artistic value as well as scientific" Court led me out of my hospital room. "Of course I can't predict how this will affect your marriage. All I can say is that I wouldn't want to be in your shoes. I'm afraid this time you're on your own."

We passed the head nurse's station. A pretty young nurse looked at me like I was the star of some popular TV soap opera like "A Different World." "Here's a FedEx 'overnight' for you, Mr. Leone. It's from New York."

I felt embarrassed *and* paranoid. So I checked the packet to see if anyone had steamed it open, either by teakettle or by moist curiosity. "Uh, I think I'll open this later," I said to Court.

"Oh. By the way," Court said. "Jeanie asked if Harlan could bring you home with me."

"So I can stay in the carriage house," I said.

Court did look sympathetic. But he said: "I believe I may have been guilty in the past of taking you too seriously. Now I can see why my daughter gets such a kick out of you."

CHAPTER THIRTY-ONE

I dropped my field kit in my lab and went upstairs to my penthouse. In the West, orange and magenta streaked the sky above the back range of the Rockies. Behind me my sound system quietly played Gordon Lightfoot's "If You Could Read My Mind." The events of the past several days so compounded their effect on me that I couldn't sleep. Yet I was soul weary too. I had drunk half a beer before remembering the FedEx letter from New York.

I figured it was from Lu—and that it was a "Dear John" letter because of the photographer outside the Circleville Holiday Inn. Yet that didn't seem like Lu. I knew she had risked a lot emotionally to see me but so had I in going to her hotel with her. I was the most grateful that Lu took me seriously. She was the only female in my life who didn't shoot me down left and right. And Lu *wanted* me. She had made me feel like a hot Italian *man*. But then I remembered I didn't ask her to share her grief about her Nana. I had thought only of *my* yearning and of the magnificent way she had seduced me, slowly, in the bar. "*Al di la…*" *I didn't deserve her before*, I thought, *and I don't deserve her now.*

Lu hand wrote her two page letter on pale blue stationery. A faint scent of *Creed Fleurissimo* made me long for her again and made what she wrote even more personal. Her cursive had matured since she and I were in college. The letters of each word were more regularly spaced, and the lines straighter across the page. In the old days the letters in her words slanted all different directions and the lines across the pages were as up and down as her moods. And her writing was now larger and more expressive—not compressed, as in the past, with tight margins on both sides. I could easily hear her *mezzo* voice when I read:

The morning _after_…

My Poor David,

I am so sorry for all the "exposure" my meeting you in Circleville caused. Can you forgive me? I had no right. But how could I not be with you?! For the rest of our lives, when else could we have been brought together like that? I want you to know that when you and I shared those lovely hours, you helped me forget the pain I felt about Nana. I want you to see how important you will always be to me. I remember the scent of your skin, the sound of your voice. Now I know these must hold me for the rest of my life.

It is clear that we have both changed in such different ways that we can never _be_ together. I saw that you miss who I was in the past and who _we_ were in the past—not that you would want to share your life with me now.

I am afraid the news coverage of us will ruin your marriage. I don't believe you want that. I know you have a teenage son, and I'm sure he needs you as much as your wife does. You must tell her that the newspaper photo shows us saying goodbye for good. And you must tell her you didn't sleep with me, because you didn't really. Almost doesn't count, though making love is what we both intended.

I read in the Times how you saved Mrs. LaSalle, and I'm beyond proud of you for your loyalty and your courage. The article says you have deep

*facial contusions and are suffering from exhaustion. It's no wonder! I am
keeping you in my thoughts every day, and I hope your life returns to
normal with your family soon.*

*Even if we never meet again, you know we will always be connected.
That must be enough. Sometimes what is most beautiful is almost too
painful to enjoy. And so <u>help</u> your wife and your son get over this
"calamity." Help yourself, too, by taking time to rest. You will resolve this
later. Finally, and I mean this from my very soul, I understand what's
probably ahead for you. Blazing fame for your holography—not the
fleeting, glitzy kind I'll continue to enjoy until I start "showing my age."
Yours Always,*

Lu

Lu's letter distressed me. I felt so sorry about my *shotgun wedding* to
Jeanie that I couldn't sleep. Joan Rivers once said: "Guilt—the gift that
keeps on giving." Boy, is that the truth! For a long time I had enjoyed
my guilt-free fantasies about making love to Lu. Now I hated myself
for not fessing up. Lu didn't trap me like that. And if Jeanie had been
taking "the pill," I might have tired of her and gone back to Lu. But it
was way too late now.

Now I only had enough energy to wonder if my trials had been
worth the time, energy, and passion I'd spent. I no longer gave two
cents for something I only knew in my head. I could no longer be a
guy who never says, "I believe" or "I feel." I had learned that when
you know something in your gut, it really is a feeling. And that feeling
usually turns out to be true. That's why I could finally admit that I
wasn't proud of how I behaved. In fact, I felt guilty, guilty, guilty. And
yet I still had to endure that distraction because I still wanted Lu. Again
and always.

When I woke up I found Lu's letter lying on the floor beside my couch.
It was late in the day. By the big clock on the kitchenette wall of my
penthouse I saw that I had slept thirteen hours. I made my way to the

bathroom downstairs. Seeing my image in the mirror I thought, *No woman in the world would want* that. My face was a composite of unattractive patches of stubble, deep purplish brown eyebags, stitches crusted with dried blood on one cheek and reddish swelling on the other. Matted cowlicks stood up on the crown of my head. I could shower but I had no clean clothes. They were either back in Circleville or in Boulder. Maybe I could order-out clothes the way one orders Chinese takeout. The lab phone rang. It was Court.

"Well, good day, my boy. My groundskeeper saw your bathroom light on, so it seemed a good time to call you." He paused long enough for me to wonder if we'd been disconnected.

"Court?"

"Your wife has been here since nine. She wants to come down and talk with you."

My brain surged with panic. "No! She *can't.*"

Court's voice was fatherly: "I'll send Harlan down with a breakfast tray and a change of clothing for you. And I'll keep Jeanie occupied while you clean up. Just ring the house when you're ready."

I knew in my core that I had finally grown up. Before Circleville I wore my holographic triumphs like medals. How could I see Jeanie? I'd be crazy to face her harpie's wrath—her Medusa peepers turning me to stone. Why would I welcome the emotional blackmail Jeanie would wield against me for the rest of my life? After showering I toweled my hair dry and combed it straight back instead of parting it on one side. I looked like an Italian mob boss. My teeth *itched.* When I finished brushing them I heard Harlan's knock on the door.

Harlan did not come inside. Instead he handed me a breakfast tray through the open door. He also handed me hangers holding navy slacks, a casual light blue shirt, a plastic ziplock bag with underwear and socks, and my Nike Air Epic sneakers.

I needed more time to rest, to space out. I needed more time to think. At that moment multitasking was my nemesis! Too much had happened. I was still on overload. I would have been happy to hole up in Court's carriage house for a month. Why couldn't Jeanie leave me alone? I was so pissed, tired, and emotionally spent that I sank into my couch and began to sob. As a man I had let this happen three times— once in front of Reynie and her horse and twice with my Dad on my parents' back step. Now I just let it rip. The sounds I made were haunting. And oddly comforting. I didn't care how long my catharsis would take because *not* feeling had gotten me nowhere for too many years. *Let Jeanie wait*, I thought. *Let me take more time off from my life in Boulder. Screw my holography! I'll go back to work when* I *am ready.*

I switched on my stereo boombox and found my favorite Oldies radio station: KOOL-105. The refrain from "You Can't Always Get What You Want" drifted into my brain. Cruel joke. Perfect timing.

The phone rang again. This time it was Jeanie, and I thought the next sound I'd hear would be psycho banshee screeching. Instead Jeanie was calm and suprisingly warm.

"I just want to make sure you're okay. I won't know until I *see* you." She paused as if waiting for me to say something. Her response to my silence was, "We don't have to talk if you don't want to." After another long pause she said, "Is that the Rolling Stones on the radio?"

Oh great! I thought. *She's gonna grind me into the ground about* "You can't always get what you want." It wasn't just the Stones' song that made me feel whipped. I was also reliving the scene in "The Big Chill"—at the funeral of the former classmates' friend. The "Chloe" character plays the tune like a dirge on a small church organ and it takes the theater audience a while to catch on. Then the audience's laughter moves through the theater like a crowd wave across an NFL stadium. Humiliating. I could only manage to say to Jeanie: "I'm here."

"*I* have had enough time to think," she said, "and I want you to take all the time *you* need." Again Jeanie waited.

Again I offered no answer because I felt myself balanced on a precipice of a critical *soul* breakthrough. Something about the Greeks having so many words for love. Different kinds of love—each profound in its own way. And about whether I could earn the love so many people in my life showed me every day.

"I'm sure you're shell shocked," Jeanie said. "Like you have PTSD."

This made sense to me.

"If you weren't, you'd be talking up a blue streak," she continued.

I caught that she had just used 'THE VOICE" on me.

"Could you please just answer one question though?"

Get ready, I thought. *Here comes Thor's hammer.* "Okay," I said.

Jeanie's voice was gentle: "Are you going back to her?"

I was stunned. "Of course not."

Now Jeanie was quiet. But I could hear her shallow breathing. She sounded like she'd just been rescued from a sheer cliff. "I'm glad, because I want to share your glorious future. I want people to know I'm the wife of a man who might win the Nobel Prize someday. And I want us to be happy again."

"I don't need a Nobel Prize."

"I'm afraid you have no choice. Three scientific journals, including *Scientific American*, called to ask for interviews with you.

"They can wait."

In the most relaxed tone I'd ever heard from Jeanie, she said, "In that case, then so can I."

About the Author

Jo Deniau was born northeast of Indianapolis and raised in the house her paternal grandfather built. Her debut novel, *Stiff Hearts*, earned a 5-star rating from Chanticleer Book Awards in 2023, First Place in the 2022 Somerset division of the Chanticleer International Book Awards, and an International Impact Award for Women's Fiction in 2021.

Jo's studies of English Literature and Language complemented her rich Liberal Arts education from middle school through undergraduate studies at Butler University, where she began as a Journalism major. Jo served on the editorial staffs of three National magazines and earned an M.A. from Ohio University's Graduate Writing Program. After teaching Literature and Composition part-time at Temple University in Philadelphia, Jo moved to Boulder, Colorado, where she lived for twenty-eight years. There she not only explored "all things metaphysical" but also became a Traditional Usui Reiki Master and learned many other "high-tech" healing techniques. She says that, like her novels, her life has been "steeped with magic realism."

Jo now lives in Central Gulf Coast Florida with her "little feline family" fifteen minutes from the nearest beach. She is working on a fictional memoir titled *The Autobiography of Lucille Muhr*, which she describes as a "bookend" to *Hologram*.

Contact Jo at **noesisimprints@gmail.com**

About the Cover Artist

Roksolana Tkatschuk McFadden is a proud first generation American-Ukrainian. Her Ukrainian parents and sister Alya emigrated to America as World War II ended. While they worked in factories they also attended school to learn English. They imbued their creativity with their culture as multi-talented artists in theater and opera after settling in Buffalo, New York, where Lana was born. Both Lana and her sister graduated from universities with honors.

After earning her B.S. and MFA in Art Education and Design, Lana taught art in upstate New York and in Washington, D.C., while sharing her expertise as a Cultural Specialist with the Boys Clubs of Western New York State. She began to paint at age ten while studying with the revered Ukrainian artist Leon Kosciushko, Illustrator and oil painter for the space projects initiated by President John F. Kennedy. Later, in Colorado, Lana enhanced her career by working as an Illustrator for the Solar Energy Research Institute, as Technical Illustrator at Johnson Engineering, and as Art Director/Owner at Sage Creek Illustration & Design.

Following many years of living in the mountains above Boulder, Lana moved with her husband Brian to the Western Slope. There, they live the mountain life, *sans* two grown daughters, with their two wonderful canines and two working equines—and "any other wildlife that wish to join" them.

Contact Lana at **mylabriver@gmail.com**

Stiff Hearts – Reviews ★★★★★

"Stiff Hearts is a tale of resilience in the face of fear, and the courage to leap into new opportunities even if one might falter. All the characters are well-hewn, creating a rich and complex narrative with important lessons to teach.

Deniau is an author whose concept of life is exceptionally alluring, and whose strong convictions and regard for current subjects weave throughout her writing. This story will fill myriad readers with empathy, adoration, and understanding, as Gillian's struggles relate to the social conflicts of the modern day. Highly recommended!"

— Chanticleer Book Reviews, by L. Amanda

"I love reading debut novels and I loved Stiff Hearts! Gillian Rysert's heart is set on starting a new life in Greenwich Village, leaving the isolation of Missouri and the emotional torment of an abusive relationship behind. Ms. Deniau's writing captures the atmosphere of time and place beautifully. Gillian's journey of self-discovery is a complex adventure as she encounters romance, mystery & intrigue and even the supernatural while she finds her sense of belonging. Overall this book is a love story, one of lack of love, love and loss, the family we were born into and the family of our hearts. Once you begin reading you will not want to put the book down. I highly recommend this novel!"

— Amazon.com Book Reviews, by Susan R. Leutheuser, Certified Hypnotherapist focusing on trauma release

"Stiff Hearts is an in-depth examination of how pain can be transformed, cracked open, with the slightest touch or word from another living thing. The protagonist, Gillian Rysert, explores the reckoning of parent-child relations, the bonds of friendship, and the stirrings of first love. Through Harry, the owner of the bar where she works, and Dolores, the friend who shares her apartment and helps ground Gillian in unfamiliar surroundings, and Janis, the Latvian refugee, Gillian starts to hope for a better tomorrow. She slowly learns to trust the people she meets in her new city of New York City, and as she does, she skirts danger without knowing it until she faces it head on. Jo Deniau's novel is a sobering reminder that

sometimes taking a hard look at the past can help uncover a future that once felt impossible. Enjoy this twisting, page-turning, redemptive tale!"
**— Amazon.com Book Reviews, by Tessa Floreano,
author of *Slain Over Spumoni***

"…[A] brilliant, incredibly well-written, evocative, moving story, so strong in its descriptive genius that I was wholly transported into the time, the genre, into the plot, into everything.

A strong subplot involves a group of Latvian expatriates who have escaped their warring country with only their lives and with a bitterness and political anger that our heroine, Gillian, only very dimly understands. And yet she is drawn in to their world, and I won't say how for fear of spoiling the plot.

Each amazingly strong character, from the beautiful Latina Dolores, who becomes Gillian's best friend, to the eccentric owner of an antiques store, to the owner of a neighborhood bar, is so strongly rendered that I absolutely felt I knew them.

I highly recommend this book. In fact, I BEG you to read this book. It deserves recognition, it deserves to be noticed and talked about. . . Wow. Just...Wow. I am so impressed."
— Amazon.com Book Reviews, by Wendy Kaplan

"What is it we all search for in a book of fiction? I think it is that rare find that completely transports the reader to another place and time. That quality is becoming harder to find these days. 'Stiff Hearts' draws you into that other place and time and keeps you there. The book is a joy to read. It is skillfully crafted and a delight to the mind and heart."
— Amazon.com Book Reviews, by JBtoo

"Stiff Hearts is an absorbing, fascinating read. From the Midwest to Greenwich Village, I was rooting for the compelling, young protagonist Gillian. Part coming-of-age story and part historical fiction, the novel surprises with its complexity, depth, and compassion. Stiff Hearts is an intelligent page-turner that doesn't disappoint."
— Amazon.com Book Reviews, by Lynda Boyer

"Stiff Hearts" is beautiful, sensitively written literature in which Jo Deniau masterfully portrays a period of her troubled mother's life with compelling descriptions of life in the postwar era. The author's fascinating characters are spellbinding. This is a wonderful, must-read piece of art."
— Barnes & Noble Book Reviews, by Murali

(Greenwich Village: Late May 1949)

The bright light outside Harry's Bar dazed Gillian. If she hadn't felt the unlit cigarette in her hand she would have thought she had hallucinated her encounter with Jānis. She wanted to open the green door behind her to see if that classy man, textured in light from the stained glass window, was still there. But Dolores gripped Gillian's arm the way men do when they aim women where they want them to walk.

Gillian shook off Dolores' grasp. "What's wrong with you?!"

"I get grouchy when I'm hungry," Dolores said.

This lame excuse did not fool Gillian, who was both vexed with her friend and excited about the young man. *Gillian believed Dolores was jealous of* Jānis. Yet she admitted to herself that she did need the love of this smart, passionate woman. Dolores had rescued her from loneliness—and from an alien city that threatened to turn Gillian back out in the cold. For the time being, Gillian couldn't see that her friend was just being protective. She said nothing.

They now headed for MacDougal Alley. Dolores clutched her shopping bag close to her side and Gillian looked up between the buildings at the sky. They passed the IRT station near the corner of Christopher Street and waited to cross in front of a shop called Village Cigars. One story high, vertical signs along either side of the doorway advertised: CANDY & SODA and CIGARS & CIGARETTES.

The door opened inward and a lanky, repugnant man darted out. To Gillian at this moment, the man's skin and clothing seemed all of one piece. His hands, neck and face were a sort of transparent yellow. Beige stripes ran vertically down his brown shirt like wires. His cream-colored pants wrinkled heavily at the knees. He moved lizard-like. He spoke in another language and leaped into a Yellow Cab.

"What a creep," Dolores said. "Looks like he's been too long on the oolong."

"What?"

"That means he smokes marijuana," Dolores retorted.

Gillian *had* felt an unpleasant prickle on her forearms, where danger always registered like little electric shocks. Of course, it was absurd in this case. That man had nothing to do with her. Normally, one-on-one, Gillian could tolerate those she thought of as the un-beautiful: unshaven derelicts who reached their hands up for coins, maybe for something else. The ungraceful mentally challenged, whose half-perceived realities bounced and flickered on their faces. The insane, whose slights and failings etched terror in, or took life from, their gaze. The repulsive man Gillian had just seen made her think of all these unfortunates at once. She also sensed that his ugliness ran deep. She decided that what could be seen of him on the surface was a projection of his entire being—that the *source* of his pock-marked skin, and his reptilian movements, was some grotesque spirituality.

Tune in to Julia Brewer Daily's **"Authors Over 50" podcast interview with Jo Deniau** about her award-winning novel, *Stiff Hearts*

on <u>Amazon Music</u>, <u>Spotify</u>, <u>Apple Podcasts</u>, <u>Google Podcasts - authors over 50</u>, or anywhere else you listen to podcasts.

YouTube link: <u>https://youtu.be/9-SzA7zhwnk</u>